MAKE ME
DISAPPEAR

MAKE ME DISAPPEAR

JESSICA PAYNE

bookouture

Published by Bookouture in 2022

An imprint of Storyfire Ltd.
Carmelite House
50 Victoria Embankment
London EC4Y 0DZ

www.bookouture.com

ISBN: 978-1-80314-263-0
eBook ISBN: 978-1-80314-262-3

To my mother, Diana, and my daughter, Emma, both of whom remind me our time here is precious, and we must do what we are meant to with this one life we have.

PROLOGUE

NOELLE

Now

There are rules to survival:

Always agree with him.

Never stop smiling.

Don't mention anyone you care about—*anyone*—because they might become his next victim.

But soon, I'll be able to forget these rules. Soon, I'll have my life back.

I'll be free.

I hold tight to this fact, wrap it around myself like a shawl against the blast of wind off the Puget Sound, bringing razor-sharp rain with it. My phone buzzes as I pace down the wet Seattle street, shoes soaked, rain trickling cold down my spine. I ignore it all. I'm late, and he doesn't like that. But as long as I show up—I force myself to inhale, exhale—he won't do anything rash.

The sight of his Porsche yanks my attention from my inner demons. He's parallel parked it in front of the restaurant, because while he's of the societal class to demand valet parking, he wouldn't dream of trusting the twenty-year-old who parks for the restaurant with his Porsche. It gleams in the light of the streetlamp, rain beading along its red exterior. Like me, it is a prized possession.

But not for long.

My body flushes with adrenaline, the confidence this will be the last date at "our" restaurant making me surer of myself than I've been since I met him. Since I began this downward spiral I've been unable to escape.

My hands clench around my keys. Suddenly, they are out of my bag, and I'm leaning close, pretending to admire the car in which I've suffered his company for far too long. The steel teeth of the key digs into the paint job as I take another step, a smile curving at my lips—is that *joy* rushing through me?

Yes, yes, it is.

I take a moment to savor it, to examine my love note etched into his carmine-red special upgrade paint.

Dear Daniel, consider this a parting gift for all the pain and suffering.

I pause. Swallow.

And death. Don't forget the death.

ONE

NOELLE

Now

The front door of the restaurant stands open under the doorman's hand, daring me to enter. I hesitate—Daniel waits within the French-themed bistro, probably impatiently drumming his fingers over the table. I can't see him, but I know him well enough to know he's not happy to be kept waiting.

The doorman greets me with a kind smile and calls, "Welcome, Ms. Thomas."

Usually I reply with something like, "You can call me Noelle," but I skip our usual song and dance, because as much as George, the doorman, is a welcome friendly face, what lies within—the man who waits for me within *our* restaurant at *our* booth—is anything but.

I steel myself against what I hope is our last night together. Walk past George with a nod. Pull my jacket off, hand it to the waiting attendant. But before I step beyond the foyer, into the dining room of the restaurant Daniel adores and I abhor, I check my phone, just in case.

My cousin Kari's baby bump stares back at me—33 *weeks!*,

she exclaims via text. Which means there are seven weeks left before she is at her most vulnerable.

I swipe away from the image and open my e-mail. My heart goes double-time as I scroll to the real reason I pulled out my phone.

An e-mail. *The* e-mail, the one I've been waiting for since I met with the private investigator. My jaw sets when there is nothing but junk in the inbox—but it's only Friday. She promised a deadline of Saturday. I refresh it again, just in case, but nothing changes, and I deflate a little, tucking the phone away, trying not to think of the reason I hired her in the first place—my aunt's death, or more accurately, her murder.

"Ms. Thomas? Are you waiting for Dr. Ashcroft? I believe he's already here." A hostess in a long black apron offers me a warm smile and extends her arm, as though she'll usher me back to the booth Daniel and I share every Friday night.

"Thank you." I turn to make the trek through the restaurant to where Daniel waits. Mahogany tables make up the main dining area, crystal chandeliers sparkle overhead, and staff bustle back and forth in the open kitchen behind the bar. There is no denying it's a nice restaurant. But it's also the sort of place that judges you if you don't know how to order wine properly or can't pronounce coq au vin with the right accent. In other words, it's Daniel's idea of heaven and my idea of hell.

A residual chill tingles through me as I catch sight of him across the way. Short blond hair, flawless tanned skin, wide shoulders encased in a button-up collared shirt. He turns my way, eyes skimming me. Blue eyes so bright they catch people off guard. But I know those eyes shine as much when he hurts me as when he makes a patient laugh or flirts with another woman. My heart quickens as I approach, and his lips twist in distaste as he takes in my outfit—boots, jeans, a flowy tank top, a black cotton zip-up sweater. Technically, I meet the restaurant's dress code; apparently, not his.

I start to sit across from him, but he makes a sharp sound in his throat, the sort people use to correct a misbehaving dog.

"Sit here." Daniel taps his finger on the booth beside him. It's not a suggestion.

Our eyes meet, and I almost say no. A lot has changed in the past week, but he isn't privy to that. Not yet.

I slide in beside him.

"You're late." He wraps a long arm over my shoulder, letting his fingers run through my hair. When he snags a tangle I didn't bother to brush out—these dates get less prep than a shift at the hospital where I work as a nurse—he yanks on it until I flinch.

The confidence I felt as I keyed his car melts away, in its stead, anxiety. The pressure in my chest that has become the norm in the last month swells and all but spills over. Tears prick my eyes. I take a long slow breath.

This will all be over soon. Just one more date.

"Traffic," I manage after a moment and feign a smile. "You know how it is."

Daniel gives me a squeeze, the good boyfriend type, and plants a gentle kiss on my forehead. My stomach turns, and I can't help but think of that quote—something about hate being the flip side of love. Whoever said that knew what they were talking about. The only thing worse than his touch is the yearning beneath my skin for the touch that once was, which makes me hate him all the more.

"You should leave earlier next time." He opens his mouth to continue his lecture, but the server bounces up, all smiles and high ponytail. She peeks through thick-rimmed black glasses and holds up a notepad and pen.

"*Bienvenue!* What can I get you to drink?"

"A bottle of the chardonnay," I say. "Just one glass." I'll need the whole bottle to get me through our date.

"The eighteen-year Macallan," Daniel says and winks at the waitress. She blinks, likely as mesmerized by his square jaw and defined dark eyebrows as I'd been when I first met him over a year ago. Mere months later, in the throes of new love, he saved my life, cementing an infatuation that has become anything but healthy. Sometimes, I wish he'd left me for dead.

I relax my fist as his hand drops to mine, intertwining our fingers in what surely looks loving to the server, who now peers at us from behind the bar.

"Any movement on the lawsuit?" Daniel sounds distracted, still watching the waitress as she wanders off.

My whole body tenses, and for once it doesn't have to do with Daniel. Instead, it's because I'm replaying the moment one of my patients slipped away a while back, and there was nothing I could do to prevent it. The husband filed a wrongful death suit, claiming that I incorrectly administered her medication, though it's going nowhere. "No," I say. "They don't have a case. He thinks that—"

"Ridiculous," Daniel interrupts, apparently done listening to me. "People die all the time. Her husband needs to accept that."

A break of silence stretches between us. *People die all the time.*

It isn't the first time he's said that to me.

I exhale to keep from trembling with rage at his cavalier attitude toward life. Doctors are supposed to keep people *alive*.

"How was your week?" he continues, rubbing his thumb over my knuckles. I fight the urge to pull sanitizer from my purse and douse my hand with it.

"It was okay." I look up to see if the waitress is coming with the wine yet—I need it. But my phone vibrates where I've set it on the table, and Daniel glances down to see Kari's name flash across the screen.

"Kari?" He purrs. "How's her pregnancy going?"

I stiffen and fight the urge to wrench my hand from his.

"Is something the matter? I'm merely asking after the welfare of your cousin."

But he's not, and we both know it. Despite being impressed by him in the early days—a doctor, a *rich* doctor, a *generous* rich doctor—Kari has grown to dislike Daniel and doesn't mind being obvious about it. Daniel doesn't abide anyone who thinks he's less than perfect. They barely tolerate one another, Kari not willing to risk our bond over a man, Daniel not considering her disgust at his general existence worth acknowledging.

When Kari announced her pregnancy via social media, he jumped at the opportunity to remind me pregnant women are particularly vulnerable; that he knew where she lived, where she worked; that, hell, he might even be the anesthesiologist assigned to her case, as she is high risk and will deliver at the hospital where we work.

One more way of keeping me under his thumb.

I'd almost said something to her, almost warned her to leave town, to find a way for her insurance to switch her to another hospital. I'd gone so far as to open my mouth and say, "I want to tell you something about Daniel." But she'd pinned me with a look, nodded at the baseball bat she keeps behind her front door, and asked, "Did he hurt you?"

I knew then I'd only put her in more danger by telling her, because she wouldn't run. She'd go after him, baby bump and all. And after what he did to my aunt, I know how that would end.

No, I had to find a different way to keep her safe. So, I kept my mouth shut and tried to figure something out. My aunt's death shouldn't have been an opportunity, but that's what it has become.

"Your week," Daniel prompts.

The waitress arrives with my wine, and we sit in silence while she pours and makes eyes at him. I grab the glass as soon as she sets it down, the buttery flavor hitting my tongue and numbing the anxiety clawing through my chest.

"It was fine," I say. "I worked an extra shift. Did my long run for the marathon. I went to painting class." I don't mention the best part—meeting with the private investigator—or how I'm practically trembling to check my e-mail again.

"And how was your painting class?"

"Great. I'm painting a vase of flowers." I can't force real emotion into my voice, but he doesn't seem to notice. Nothing new there.

"I'd love to see it. Did you take a photo?"

He's not asking about the painting, not really. He's checking to make sure I went *and* participated. A proper future wife of a leading physician has creative interests, he's informed me, like playing a musical instrument or painting. Something to help her pass the time when she's no longer working. Something to entertain his co-workers, to be a discussion point at dinners and lunches with the other wives. Like a dog who can do a fancy trick for others' amusement.

I grab for my phone and swipe until I find the photo.

He gives it a cursory glance. "Lovely. Maybe they should look a little more alive, though?" He tilts his head. "They're so... wilted."

Like me.

I set my phone down and top off my wineglass.

But not for long.

TWO

NOELLE

Fourteen Months Ago

Dr. Ashcroft is perfect. Too perfect for me. But he doesn't seem to think so, and that leaves me hopeful in a way I haven't been in a long time.

He says hello as we pass in the hospital hallway, a gentle smile curving at his mouth.

He's brought me coffee four times—inexplicably, just the way I like it.

Twice now, he's joined me in the middle of the night when I take "lunch" at midnight, a night shifter's noon. He sat across from me and peppered me with gentle, teasing questions on both occasions.

And last night, he asked, "Do you like French food?" and I said yes, even though I'd never *had* French food, but I liked him, and if he were asking me to share it with him, I suspected I'd like it in his company.

It's our first date. We're in his car, streaking down a Seattle highway. It's a Porsche, and it's like him—sleek. Expensive looking. Unapologetically itself, flashy, showy, but able to back up that promise. For the car, that means a growling engine. For Dr. Ashcroft, it means precise words, opinions he states out loud rather than keeping to himself, money he spends easily—coffee at the hospital; flowers upon picking me up; a French restaurant I wouldn't dare step inside on my own; talk of a vacation he's planning with his mother, a surprise for her sixtieth birthday.

"She's sick," he murmurs, but does not expound, and I cling to those words, turn them over in my mind. It could mean many things.

"I'm so sorry," I say. "I hope she gets better." It's not enough. Apologizing for someone's illness never is—but sometimes that's all there is to offer. I peer at him, trying to understand how he can be kind and cheerful in the face of an ill parent and decide it's something I admire about him. Which reminds me of how in this moment, no matter how kind he has been, how generous, we have different lives—I, a tiny apartment I can barely afford; he, a popular anesthesiologist who doesn't hesitate to introduce himself to a woman, who doesn't blink an eye at spending five bucks on a coffee.

I pick at my hastily applied nail polish, tug at the jacket I'd purchased this very morning—adornments that aren't common-place in my world of nursing scrubs and running shorts. But men like Dr. Ashcroft aren't commonplace in my world, either, and I want to show him I can exist in his. I can keep up.

"What do you think?"

My stomach bottoms out, and I clutch my jacket tighter. His vivid blue gaze is on me.

"Excuse me?" I smile, try to hide the fact I completely missed something.

"Would you like to meet her?" he says. We're at a stoplight. The rain on the car window keeps the temporary silence from being uncomfortable. He's asking me if I want to meet his mother. His *mother*.

I clear my throat and search for the correct answer.

"Dr. Ashcroft—"

"Daniel," he corrects me. His brows draw together, dark accentuating lines over blazing blue eyes. The definition of his cheekbones grows as his mouth curves into a frown. "We're not at work. For you, it's just—Daniel." His face shifts again, as if something occurs to him. "I'd like you to meet my mother one of these days. We always have dinner together on Sunday evenings."

I have to work Sundays. But I know I'll be there, whenever he asks.

Meanwhile, I'm still dealing with the fact Dr. Daniel Ashcroft asked me to call him Daniel. Suggested he might want me to meet his mother. I'm not the best at relationships, but I know what that means. When he extends his hand across the seat, I take it, relish the smooth warmth of my palm in his.

A single parking spot waits empty before the restaurant, as though no one else would dare park in Daniel's place.

A doorman gets the door for us, nodding at me with a respect I'm not used to. A doorman whose entire job is to open that door. To hold an umbrella as women tuck themselves into vehicles. A doorman who doesn't know who I am, or that I moved here from Boise to escape my ex. He doesn't know that I'm not quite up to Daniel's speed.

I resolve to keep it that way.

Daniel motions for me to sit in a corner booth at the back of the restaurant. He murmurs something to the server, who returns two minutes later with a bottle of pale wine. She pours. He nods approval. A glass is set in front of me.

"An unoaked chardonnay," he says. "You mentioned it's your favorite. They didn't have one on the list, but I wanted to bring you here, so I contacted the sommelier—"

As he talks, I'm caught up on the fact one can talk to a—what had he called it?—*sommelier* and request a specific wine. Daniel watches me, and I raise the glass to my lips. My bottles of wine range from actual boxes to bottom shelf. Kari and I swear we can't tell the difference.

But we were wrong. There is a difference. A smoothness, a texture I can't quite define. It runs over my tongue. The wine is cold, and as Daniel's hand stretches across the table, he is hot, and I sink into the moment, so different than the last several years of my life, struggling to get by, struggling to get free. I like the wine. I like Daniel.

Is he the answer to a question I didn't know to ask? He makes trusting him easy. People adore him. Doctors, nurses, patients.

And he seems to adore me.

"Tell me about your family." His hand squeezes mine gently. "I want to know about you."

"Well, there's my aunt. She's lovely. She teaches art—" I give him the abbreviated version of my family history. The safe version, leaving out details of my troubled relationship with my mother, who all but disowned me when I broke it off with my ex-boyfriend, Michael. I don't mention my father, who I haven't seen since I was a child. These are details Daniel might find less savory.

But then he asks, "What about your parents? I couldn't help but notice you didn't mention them."

I almost make something up—tell him they're dead, or living far away, or—anything but the truth. But I can't lie to him because that's not how you start a relationship. I don't want something built on lies.

So, I tell him every detail, and it's as though I'm digging my own grave. My father who left us, my mother who shunned me for leaving Michael, who I thought loved me, but only loved hitting me. How I escaped that life, first securing a job elsewhere, then leaving in the middle of the night. I bare my soul in a way I'm sure will lead to rejection because that's how it works. You share yourself, who you really are, and that's when people realize you're as complicated as they are. As messed up. And that's scary. What they want is perfection—that first date look, shiny and polished. That first date feel—all the positives, none of the negatives, none of what's real. They want the illusion, at least at first. This is too much, too soon, I know this, but I continue.

When I stop, Daniel stands. He's finished his drink. The food hasn't come yet. This is the moment he leaves. The moment he realizes I'm not worth the trouble.

He steps away from the booth. My heart seizes. I should have lied. Now I will have to leave here alone. The waitstaff will eye me as I walk out the door, wondering, *What did she say to him?* And then I'll have to find a way back to my apartment somehow. Jesus, I'll have to get a new job, because I can't go back to the hospital where I'll walk by Daniel shame-faced, knowing that he knows how messed up my past is.

I'll be alone again. Which was better than being with Michael, but not by much.

At least I have my aunt Beatrice and cousin Kari. With them, I'll never be truly alone, even if it so often feels that way.

"Do you mind?"

I look up, because I'm sure he's asking if I mind paying the bill, but that's not what his body language says—he's close, leaning over me. He gestures to the booth. He smiles. Relief floods me, and I make room.

Daniel comes in beside me, the scent of a spicy aftershave bewildering my senses, and his arm encircles me, and he says, "This seemed better. Heavy conversation for a first date." His lips press to my hair. "I'm sorry you've been through that. Things won't be like that with us."

And just like that, he is mine. I am his.

He is almost too good to be true.

THREE

NOELLE

Now

After dinner, we go our separate ways.

Usually, Friday nights don't end until Saturday afternoons, when I have to prepare for my night shift at the hospital. But I told him I had my period, that I wasn't feeling well, and for being a medical doctor, he's squeamish about blood. Maybe that's why he decided to stay on the other side of the sterile drape as an anesthesiologist.

I stop in at a convenience store and buy tampons on the way home to keep up appearances, and when I walk in the door of my first-floor apartment, make sure to pull them from the paper bag and set them in plain view on the kitchen table.

Daniel is always watching.

I purposely don't look toward the camera he nestled inside a painting he "gifted" me. A painting similar to the one in his own living room, and almost identical to the one he gifted my aunt and Kari. I discovered the cameras around the time I tried to end our relationship six months ago. I'd walked into his home office after he rushed to an emergency C-section and realized the half-dozen monitors weren't displaying his own home's security feeds—they were displaying my apartment. And my aunt and cousin's house forty-five minutes away in Renton. The house is gone now—foreclosed on, after her death. But Daniel has found other ways of keeping tabs on me and Kari.

I settle onto the armchair that was my aunt's, a mystery novel at the ready. My phone vibrates over and over, Kari trying to get my attention. I've been avoiding her. I have some notion that if I hold her at a distance, Daniel won't use her to manipulate me. Or maybe knowing I got her mother killed makes it difficult to face her. I shouldn't have moved here. Shouldn't have involved them. Kari's been right all along. "He's bad news, Noelle," and "Why would a man like him be interested in a woman like you?" She hadn't meant it to be mean. She'd been honest. And she knows men better than I do, knows that a woman once a victim is twice as easy to victimize again. But my aunt had adored Daniel, and I adored him, and he was so perfect in the beginning—

The book drops from my hand back to the table, and I stare at my phone, pressing back the memories.

Was out with Daniel, I finally type, then add, *On my period. Not feeling well.* Further carrying my story along for Daniel's sake.

In addition to the cameras, I found the spyware on my phone months ago, thanks to a YouTube video that showed me how to check for it, when I realized Daniel knew where I was a little too often. Thankfully, my location is all it shows him, according to the internet—but I err on the side of caution, because I have to imagine Daniel would love to know who I'm texting and calling, too. I have no doubt he'll find a way to do that soon if he hasn't already. My world, slowly growing smaller.

I get it. Morning sickness should be called all-day sickness, she answers. *Can't believe you're still with him.*

I stare, wishing I could say the truth. *I need to get out before he kills someone else—probably you. Maybe me.* Then again, his mother likes me too much for that. He doesn't dare disappoint her by offing her future daughter-in-law. At least, I hope not. His last girlfriend isn't around to ask, so maybe I'm wrong about that, too.

Kari keeps typing away, the dot-dot-dot holding my attention.

We still on for tomorrow?

I hesitate, then type back.

Sure.

Good. I miss you.

Her message sends a stab of regret through me.

Why had I agreed to date a doctor in the first place? Most doctors I've worked with are kind, good people. But others got into the business for the wrong reasons—the attention, the money. A few are borderline sociopaths, but smart enough to hide it. Like Daniel.

Miss you, too. What are you up to tonight?

Just hanging.

It's code for "I have a guy over," but I don't press for details, knowing she'd give them if she wanted to share.

I pick up my book, then set it back down and flick to my e-mail, just in case.

I almost gasp when I see the e-mail from Allison Montgomery, PI. Daniel knows where I am at all times thanks to the

GPS spyware on my phone, so she met me at work during my "extra shift," somewhere he wouldn't notice as an abnormality, and we'd shared coffee and scones in the hospital cafeteria at midnight.

"If there's something to be found, I'll find it," she'd promised, then reached out and touched my hand. "I lost a parent to malpractice. It's different, but I get it." I rested easier, knowing she understood.

The book practically falls from my lap as I scramble to open the e-mail.

Subject: Investigation

Dear Noelle,

I'm sorry to inform you that the second autopsy results are in line with the initial autopsy. A consulting pathologist confirmed all information is similar enough to not raise any red flags. He also double-checked the toxicology reports, and all remain negative.

In addition, the security cameras in the cardiothoracic unit your aunt was assigned to were active the day of her surgery. However, all records are deleted after thirty days, so we missed the chance to review them.

I know this is not the news we were expecting, and again, I am sorry.

I stop reading, my gut twisting in a knot. This wasn't at all what this e-mail was supposed to contain. It was supposed to be *evidence*. The evidence I needed to put him in prison. To prove he'd killed my aunt. I squeeze my eyes shut, take a slow deep breath, and continue reading. Maybe she found *something*. *Anything*. I need to be free of him.

*Please rest assured I will continue searching for evidence in
this case. I've spoken to the hospital liaison and will follow up
with her early next week regarding any visitor records. We can
also consider consulting with a cardiothoracic surgeon to look
for any evidence of malpractice in the operating room. Expect
to hear back from me by Wednesday at the latest.*

Sincerely,

Allison Montgomery
Private Investigator

I reread the e-mail, then look it over a third time, as though
the words will magically reconfigure to something along the
lines of *You were right—she had a lethal dose of a drug in her
system* or *The security footage proves Daniel Ashcroft was in
your aunt's room prior to her death.*

But it doesn't change.

I sit back in the chair and try to remember how to breathe.

Daniel had been there to play perfect boyfriend in the aftermath, the last person I wanted at the funeral.

The last person I wanted in my life, but he gave me no
choice in the matter. I read the e-mail one last time, then delete
the message in case Daniel finds a way to hack into my e-mail.
Allison has more to investigate, but I feel as though I've lost
what little hope I had.

I press my hands against my eyes, racking my brain. I don't
know what else I can do.

This means tonight wasn't the last of our dates. It means
Kari and her baby won't be safe. It means I'm still pinned
beneath Dr. Daniel Ashcroft's thumb.

FOUR

NOELLE

Twelve Months Ago

Daniel's home is an extension of him the same way his Porsche is.

As he leads me up the steps to the front door, I can't tear my gaze away from the modern floor-to-ceiling windows, the view of the Puget Sound the balconies must provide him. *Balconies.* Plural, as in more than one. My heart squeezes in my chest—that inner voice reminding me this home costs more than I would make in a decade. In two decades.

You're out of your league, the voice says.

My hands go cold, clammy. I wait for the jangle of Daniel's keys, but it never comes. Instead, he raises a sure hand, taps in a code, there is a low buzz, and then the door—steel and glass, like the rest of the house—swings open in a slow smooth motion.

My heart drops into my stomach.

Jesus.

I must have been staring. Hesitating. Preparing myself to flee.

"Noelle." Daniel's voice breaks through to me. I look up to his eyebrows raised in question. "What's wrong?"

"Nothing."

He closes the distance between us, wraps his arms around me tightly, pressing me to his chest. He works sixty hours a week in the hospital—at least—but somehow, he finds the time to work out. Usually, feeling his strong body against mine steadies me. Reminds me there's someone in my life now who cares. Who wants to hug me and spend time with me, and call, just to say hello.

But tonight, it's a reminder that while he's a ten out of ten—an attractive doctor with his life figured out—I'm maybe a what? A seven? A pretty face but living paycheck to paycheck. A car that won't last another year. A rent payment, that if it goes up again, which it will, since it's Seattle, I won't be able to afford. I'll have to find roommates. Move in with my aunt. Pick up overtime to make ends meet.

"You look like you're about to be sick," he murmurs. "Was it the sushi?"

"The sushi was great." And it was. So was the miso soup, the sake, the after-dinner cocktails. Even better was that after two months of dating, after gaining my trust and respecting my desire to go slow, Daniel had invited me back to his house for the first time.

"I want to show you my home," he'd said, a swell of pride in his voice. Then he'd held up his hands. "No strings attached." He winked, gave me a teasing smile—and I'd laughed.

We've kissed. We've held hands. And we've otherwise kept a physical relationship on the back-burner, his patience exactly what I needed in the aftermath of my ex.

I'd said, "Yes, I'd like that," no hesitation. I knew I had nothing to fear from him.

I hadn't considered seeing his house would be the problem.

That I would realize he wasn't just a doctor with a nice car—he had it *all*. And I couldn't imagine how I could fit into that picture.

Daniel grasps my hand, his eyes narrowing, face turning serious. "Stop being defined by your past. You belong with me now." His voice is gentle, yet firm, but that's not the problem— the problem is his words. *Belong*. Michael had said something similar, but he'd said *belong* to *me*. Not *belong* with *me*.

I take a breath, trying to puzzle out the difference, but Daniel is already taking my index finger in his hand.

"And this is my home. Which means"—he uses my finger to enter a six-digit code—"this is your home now, too."

He lets my hand go and it drops to my side. I can't look away.

"What?" I barely manage to get the word out.

"If I used a key, I'd make you one." His hands skim from my shoulders to my forearms. He pulls me close, and for a second, it's just the two of us. "But the best I can do is give you the code to my home. You're welcome to come and go, whenever you want."

Tears well up hot in my eyes. That's what he meant—not that I'm his, but that we belong together. That he's inviting me into his home whenever I want to be here.

Daniel leads me inside, and the house is even more overwhelming. High ceilings, natural light flooding through those full-length windows, modern minimal furniture. The open-concept foyer merges to an ultra-modern stainless steel galley kitchen, which overlooks a dining area and living room. A staircase leads up along one wall to the second floor. Daniel takes me room by room, telling me where he procured each piece of furniture, how he chose one wallpaper over another, what country he was visiting when he purchased this rug or that lamp—

It's unreal.

And apparently, I get to share it with him.

It's too much. But there is power in feeling as though you belong with someone. And I settle into that. If he belongs here, I belong here with him. In fact, I can't imagine wanting to be anywhere else, ever again.

FIVE

NOELLE

Now

I sit frozen, staring at my phone for too long. When I jolt back to life, I go to my bedroom and grab my running shoes.

I lace them up. A run won't fix this situation, but it might make me feel better, let me think with clarity. It's also my one respite from Daniel, one of the few things he doesn't try to put a stop to—after all, a prominent physician's future wife needs to be slim and fit nicely into a gown for the countless galas and dinners he will be invited to. I also leave my phone in my apartment when I run, leaving the miles I pound on pavement the only moments I'm free from his scrutiny.

Outside, the drizzle has become a light sprinkle of sleet and snow. I hesitate—it's cold, and the trees blow sideways in the wind. But I have to get out. Have to escape. Even if it's just an illusion as I sprint through the streets, racing toward something —I don't know what, but anything is better than reality.

The driving wind slices through my running tights like tiny razor blades. It lets me forget for a moment what I've just read and that my plan is defunct. I'm still trapped, and Kari and I are still in danger. Not to mention, my aunt Beatrice is dead, and I have no way of finding justice for her.

Beatrice's face pulses through my mind. When my parents abandoned me, she made it clear she would never do the same—and when I left my boyfriend, exhausted from fights that lasted all night and sometimes turned physical, my emotional life in shambles, she invited me to stay with her. I soon got my own apartment, but then she got sick and had to take leave from her job teaching art at a local high school.

In the months leading up to what was supposed to be a life-saving surgery, I'd spent more and more time in Renton with them. Daniel was supportive at first—as a physician, he knew how draining it could be to care for a sick person. My aunt's ankles swelled. It became hard for her to breathe as she sank into heart failure. But the cause of her heart failure was fixable—blocked arteries. She needed a double bypass. The surgeon said she was a good candidate, and the surgery went off flawlessly.

But then, she died. The surgeon, who I work with, shook her head, pressed a gentle hand to my shoulder, and said, "I'm so sorry, Noelle. I don't know what happened."

She meant it to be comforting. But it wasn't. Because I knew what happened. In the weeks before the surgery, Daniel grew tired of my days and nights spent away, expressing his displeasure to me more than once. "You're always gone, Noelle. What about me? What about us? Is this going to get worse *after* the surgery?" He knew her operation involved months of recovery, time I would be away from him. And then, after she died, well—it was obvious. The timing. That he already *knew* when she had only just passed. That he swooped in, ready to come to the rescue, yet again. That he did so gleefully.

I lope toward Pike Place Market, the wind lashing my face as I come around a corner, but that doesn't bother me—if anything, it distracts me from what I can't escape: Daniel.

Screw him. Screw my utter lack of privacy. My inability to have a life. To speak my mind without threat to the people I love.

I'm sprinting before I know it, dodging pedestrians and nearly smacking into a cyclist covered head to toe in winter cycling gear who runs a red light. For a second, I think they're going to hit me or I'm going to smash into them and lay them out on the pavement—panic makes my pulse go wild, adrenaline dumping through my body—but they swerve and zoom through the intersection just in time. I stumble backward until I trip and fall on my butt on the sidewalk, the drizzle instantly soaking my tights.

I'm too caught up in my head. Too focused on fixing what is unfixable. I can't escape him. He's going to force me to marry him. Force me to have his children.

His children.

I lean over, retching, trying to keep dinner down.

I sit like that too long, until I realize people are staring—probably thinking I'm out of my mind. I climb to my feet, but I'm fighting through the rage just to breathe, sucking in sharp gasps of ice-cold air. I step back against the nearest building as the world spins around me.

This is a panic attack, I realize, heart thudding against my ribs.

"You all right?" A young woman's voice, to my left. I jerk my head up. She has purple hair, sparkly mascara, and wears overalls with a purple shirt that matches her hair. "You want to come in for a minute? Warm up?"

It takes me a second to put together what's right in front of me: a woman in her early twenties, inviting me into her shop. The distraction from my inner turmoil lets me take a second to inhale, exhale. I force myself to focus on her.

"I have coffee, too." She holds the glass door open wider.

I hesitate, but it's the first time in a long time a stranger has offered me kindness. I follow her.

"I'm Miranda. Mira for short." She has a paper cup of coffee in her hands already. "Cream? Sugar?"

"Both, please." I look around—it's eerily similar to a hospital waiting room. Bare walls, cheap chairs, plain white tables, blue-gray carpeting. The only difference is there are computers at half the desks. The others are empty, power supplies at the ready. She hands me the coffee.

"Thanks. Is this an internet café?" I ask.

"It's a twenty-four-hour co-working space. I'm usually gone by now, but"—she beckons at the door—"thought I'd wait for the snow to stop to walk home. It'll be a while, so feel free to stay until the weather lets up."

I want to ask her if she actually gets any business, but she's been kind, and I don't want to be rude.

"Did you get caught out in the snow?" she asks.

"Kind of. I'm on a run." I shift my gaze back outside. The snow has picked up and with the wind looks more like a blizzard. My pulse slows in the warmth, and I almost feel normal. As normal as I ever feel these days.

She gestures. "Feel free to grab a computer."

"Thank you."

Mira goes back to her desk, and I look over the dozen computers. It occurs to me I could do this regularly—come here and use the internet without worrying that Daniel will record my keystrokes, check my search history. If I do it mid-run, he won't even know I've stopped in.

I grab the nearest computer and pull up the internet to check the weather. The door jingles, a man ducking in. He waves at Mira like he knows her and takes up position at the other end of the room, sliding a laptop from his bag. I glance back to the computer; the homepage is the local news, and in Seattle that means the Seahawks and a smattering of other headlines—protests downtown, a train derailing, and the human-interest stories.

I blink, my eyes stopping on one headline in particular.

How to get yourself kidnapped

"Oh, fun."

I whip around to see Mira peering over my shoulder.

Maybe this isn't the place for privacy after all.

"Fun?" I stammer.

"Yeah, I did that for my girlfriend for her twenty-first birthday."

I look at the headline, then back at her. "What do you mean?"

"They call it extreme kidnapping. You've never heard of it?" The blank look on my face must answer her question because she continues. "It was so much fun. They have like two or three guys fake an actual kidnapping. And it's run by a real-life ex-criminal, so you know it's legit. They wore masks and everything. I told her boss about it ahead of time, of course, so he wouldn't call the cops, but they were *so* believable."

"A fake kidnapping?" I murmur, more to myself than her. My mind whirrs, imagining such a thing.

"Yeah." She bobs her head, purple hair swaying back and forth. The phone rings up front, and Mira excuses herself to answer it.

I turn back to the computer. If I can't remove Daniel from the equation, maybe I can remove myself. With these people, it would be easy—a *fake* kidnapping. Mira said they'd made it look real. Real enough Daniel would believe it?

And Daniel already has cameras set up in my apartment.

Daniel would never know it was pretend. I could disappear, and he'd think I was taken against my will. He couldn't be mad at me for that. He wouldn't hurt Kari if I didn't *choose* to leave him like I did Michael. And there's no reason to hurt her if I'm not around to control. If anything, this is my ticket out and the best way to keep her safe. Especially since plan A, to get him arrested for killing my aunt, isn't panning out.

No one else dead. I'd never have to marry him. There would be no children.

I could be free.

I click around the article until I find the website for the actual business, Ultimate Kidnapping. Their phone number is prominent on their website, right next to a guarantee that the victim-to-be will be so caught up in the moment they'll forget entirely it's pretend—"for a birthday, a bachelor party, or to prank a best friend!"

I take a deep breath and give myself a moment to think it through. Disappearing would mean leaving this life behind. It would mean never seeing Kari again. Never working as a nurse again. Starting over, with nothing, yet again. But I would be free. And it would also mean Kari gets to have a life, that neither she nor her child will be in danger. And I'll give up just about anything for that.

I don't stop to think it through further because certainty hits hard—this is the only way.

I swing around to face Mira. "Can I use your phone?"

SIX

NOELLE

Ten Months Ago

Daniel is not perfect. I've learned this a little bit at a time.

He can be reckless when he drives and gets a case of road rage; he can be jealous when he sees me talking to another man; he dislikes it when I'm away for very long, with friends or visiting my aunt and Kari. And sometimes, I'm sure he misremembers something on purpose—in such a way that he's right, and I'm wrong. But he always stops; he always apologizes. We end arguments with hugs and evenings out and promises to try harder next time.

Besides, these are not red flags. If anything, they are *yellow flags*, but we all have yellow flags, including myself. Things a therapist would suggest we work on, but not things that make or break a relationship. Not like with Michael. Daniel has never hit me. Never shoved me against a wall and held me there until I acquiesced.

He, too, had a hard childhood. His father's death, which he witnessed, years during which his mother worried where a car payment or rent would come from, failing to get into medical school on the first try, but then going on to specialize in a highly competitive field. And now, he serves on two boards and volunteers time with a charity—the same charity whose gala we are at tonight.

Somehow, I love him more for his imperfections. For knowing that while we both polish up fine, our own pasts still haunt us. That together, we're stronger. We're on an even playing field, as opposed to his perfection highlighting my shortcomings. Together, we have a future to look forward to.

Across the ballroom, Daniel catches my gaze as I accept a champagne flute. He winks, lets me know he's there, even if he's busy—talking to donors, showing kindness to the women who hang on his every word.

I'm almost used to this life—on the top floor of a fancy hotel in downtown Seattle, an entire wall made of glass, looking down at Pike Place Market, the Ferris wheel, the lights of West Seattle across Elliott Bay. Daniel's peers acknowledge me with nods, and careful, respectful handshakes, while their spouses eye my empty ring finger, and I wonder if that will change once we are married.

Marriage. It's too soon, but we talk about it in that roundabout way couples do, using words like *someday,* and *if we ever,* when in reality, we mean *when,* not *if.* His mother, Eve, is far less shy about the word. Also, about the word *children,* never asking if I even want to be a mother, just presuming.

Every now and then, I can see the cracks in Daniel's façade —not that I think he dons one often, but occasionally, same as I do, as we all do in certain situations. I sip my champagne and watch him, and see it now—the big smile, the booming laughter. He's putting on a show, creating a more outgoing version of himself for these people whose money will help save the lives of children. Certainly, a worthy cause for a little extra charm that costs him nothing but his time. And I like that I can help him with that.

Spouses huddle on one side of the room—about two-thirds women, but a few men, too. Daniel's informed me there are more women graduating medical school than men now, though I couldn't quite read his tone as he said it, and it's not reflected in this crowd. I smooth my gown and ease closer to the spouses. I'm in heels, which I despise, but Daniel asked me to wear them for him, and I'd agreed. I shouldn't have—his gaze slips my way again, drops to my feet as I walk, and my face colors red—he, too, knows I shouldn't have worn them. Anyone can see I can't walk in the damn things.

Another smile, just for me, but I know he'll suggest I wear them more often—learn to walk in them, so I'm not awkward at events like this, when eyes are on me.

I turn away and find a place to perch against the wall, pretending to be absorbed in the string quartet playing a vaguely familiar tune. But the music isn't what catches my attention—it's the voices of three women I've seen before at other events.

"That's *him*," a woman about my age whispers. She points with a pinky, then turns her back, sips her champagne, gives the other two women a look. They wear almost matching gowns—soft, long shimmery things. They wear heels not unlike my own, except they know how to walk in them. I go unnoticed.

"Who?"

"Dr. Ashcroft. The one I was telling you about," the first one hisses.

I freeze. Turn my back, in case they might recognize me. More whispering behind me. The women drop their voices, and I can only hear snippets.

"The one whose girlfriend disappeared," is the next snatch of conversation I catch, and I take that moment to walk away, heart pounding, suddenly sweating through my gown, to find my bag stashed beneath our designated table.

I've never googled Daniel before—it felt like a betrayal to

think I needed to. His unflinching loyalty to me, not caring about my past, meant I, too, accepted him as he was. And I didn't need the internet telling me who that might be.

But I'm two glasses of champagne in, and I do it now, not because I suspect him of anything, but because I want to know more. He'd said on our first date he'd had two serious relationships before me—it felt strange, after all we'd been through, I'd never heard so much as a word about either of them. He knew plenty about Michael.

What pops up leaves my mouth agape. I quickly shut it and wave to let him know I'm running to the ladies' room, then scurry to hide in a stall.

The first three articles are society pages from recent charity events. But below that, what the women were talking about.

SARAH MACCLEARY, LOCAL SEATTLE WOMAN, GOES MISSING

SEATTLE NATIVE STILL MISSING, PRESUMED DEAD

LOCAL ANESTHESIOLOGIST PLEADS FOR GIRLFRIEND'S RETURN

The articles don't stop there. I blink down at my phone, wondering how the hell I've never known about this—but then I see a date. It happened two years before I moved to Seattle. Two years before I met Daniel. Long enough ago that no one's talking about this case anymore. Just another woman, disappeared.

I click on the third article, because it is about Daniel as much as it is about his missing girlfriend. I skim the words, coming to a stop on a quote from him: "I just want Sarah to come home. Please, if you know anything." The reporter went on to detail the tears streaming down his face. The way he'd offered a cash reward, no questions asked, for her return. The way his mother stood beside him and comforted him.

Daniel is sensitive, but I can't imagine him crying.

Though she is kind, I've not once seen Eve so much as hug Daniel.

And in that moment, tears come to my eyes. My heart breaks for them. No wonder I've never heard of Sarah. No wonder Daniel was so open to me, so kind in those early days. He hadn't just lost his father—he'd lost a woman he loved. Of course he would want to keep me close after that. Of course, he'd be protective. He didn't want to lose me.

And that, I can understand.

SEVEN

DANIEL

Now

I ease into my office chair, glass of ice-cold bourbon between my fingertips, and turn on two of the half-dozen monitors propped on my office desk. I bring up the video feed, but you're not home yet. Did you have a stop to make? Where? Why didn't you mention it? It's Friday night; you should be going straight home if you're not with me. I'm concerned, but I'll give you another minute before I check your location.

It's not that I don't trust you, Noelle. It's that I expect you to behave a certain way, like a proper girlfriend should, so that when the time comes, you can be a perfect wife. Having the right encouragement is all you've needed. Like any human, you're trainable.

This is my favorite part of the day. Since I made my expectations clear, you've been less apt to spend the night in my bed, but that's okay. We'll get married soon—the sooner the better—and it won't be my bed, it will be *our* bed. And then, you'll never be out of my sight.

Not that you often are.

I raise the glass, the smooth velvet of my favorite bourbon skimming my lips. The cameras were worth the money, worth the risk. I had them installed when you first attempted to break up with me, first forgot we are meant for one another. Like I would ever let that happen. Fate brought us together, made us fall in love, allowed me to find *you*. And then you nearly died. I nearly lost you, nearly lost my chance to prove to my mother I could give her what she so desperately desires. Had we not been on a date that rainy day, had I not been mere steps away, you would have died when that car struck you. But I was there. I saved you. And now nothing will tear us apart.

I refill my glass, check the news, and just as I become truly worried, you arrive home with a frown on your face. I sit forward, analyzing the camera feed, analyzing you. You set tampons on the table and go to the stove to brew tea. You move slowly, like you're unhappy, and I can't for the life of me understand why. You have *me*. We dined at our favorite restaurant, as we do every Friday, and I dropped two-hundred dollars on dinner. Why can't you appreciate that? Be grateful that you've snagged not just a doctor, but an *anesthesiologist*, as your boyfriend. And soon, fiancé. Our marriage is a foregone conclusion—it won't be a proposal so much as presenting you with a ring others will ooh and ah over, making it official. Maybe I'll give it to you on Valentine's Day. The anniversary of the day I saved your life. Mother would approve.

You retrieve your phone from your bag and yank your long hair from the bun that sits atop your head. I can all but feel the smooth tendrils running through my fingertips. I wanted to fuck you tonight. I run my hand over my cock, thinking of it, thinking of you. I grit my teeth.

You told me you're on your period, but I know it's a lie. I won't tolerate lies between us, Noelle. You'll have to learn that, too.

I clasp my glass once more, observing as you sit in that damn chair you insisted on keeping, stare at your phone, type some-thing, and stare at it some more. I can trace who you call, check your location. But I can't see your texts or e-mails without looking up your passwords on the keystroke recorder I installed. Maybe there's an app to make that easy to track, too?

You sit up, a quick movement that catches my attention. I release myself, watching, waiting to see what you do. You set your book down, raise an open hand to your mouth, and go utterly still.

I go still, too. What has upset you so, Noelle? Once, you would have called. Would have shared with me what it was. I could help, you know. If you'd just tell me.

I drain my glass, one eye on the camera feed, one eye on another monitor as I search for the new app I have in mind, another way I can monitor you, anticipate your needs. It's avail-able, but I'll need your phone to install it, which means I'll need you to spend the night. You've been avoiding that this last month. Avoiding me.

It's almost like you don't want to get married, Noelle. And you are getting older—closer to thirty than twenty. Almost too old for me, at thirty-three, but my mother adores you.

My mother adores no one.

Besides me, of course. And now, you. I don't know why; maybe because you feign enjoying the godawful port she drinks, but regardless, it's perfect. We will be the perfect family, despite our little... issue. But I think I've found a way around that. It's just a matter of time, you'll see. A matter of reminding you that we're meant for one another.

I sigh and relax back again. We're spending the evening together, but you don't know it. It's the compromise I decided upon when you began to withdraw, so long ago. I need you, Noelle. This way, I have you, even when you're not here.

You continue gazing down at your phone. Irritation stirs in

my gut, and I wish to god I knew why you can't look away from it. It's not like you.

The plan is in place. It's just a matter of time.

I mentally count down the days until our anniversary of you surviving the accident that nearly tore us apart. My mother has already given me my grandmother's ring. I have a plan to keep you close.

Soon, Noelle, you'll be mine.

EIGHT

NOELLE

Now

When I wake, the sun is high in the sky, and someone's knocking on my door, a crisp *rap-rap-rap* of impatience. Night shift, even on my nights off, doesn't lend itself to a normal sleep schedule. I blink at the fuzzy numbers on my phone. Nearly noon. The previous night comes back to me in a jumble of memories: my date with Daniel, the e-mail and consequent snowy run, ending up at the co-working space where I—

"Noelle!" Kari's distant voice shouts from outside my front door.

I scramble from my bed before I have neighbors calling the landlord to complain.

"What took so long?" Kari snaps as I open the door.

"I'm so sorry," I manage, and stare at her, dressed in maternity jeans and a V-neck shirt beneath her coat, which no longer zips up over her belly. "I was out late."

Kari steps inside without an invitation and takes a long look around, one eyebrow quirked. "Is there a man here?"

"A man?"

"Is *he* here?"

Kari prefers to not say his name aloud.

"No, he's not. Like I said, I'm on my period."

She makes a *hmph* sound and seats herself at my little square dining table.

"Coffee?" I manage through a yawn.

"Do you even have to ask?"

"Decaf?"

"Girl." Her tone carries warning, and I pour regular beans into the grinder.

I steal a glance at her, legs spread to make room for her belly as she perches on the chair. Her phone is in her hand, and she's busy texting someone, and I pause, taking in the moment—my cousin just a couple months before she's due to give birth. A birth I will not be there for, thanks to what I just set in motion. She will have no one to turn to—her mother gone, and soon, me. But she'll be alive. That will have to be enough.

The rest of last night returns to me in a skin-crawling rush.

"A kidnapping is a thousand bucks, cash only." The man's voice was like gravel, icy wet gravel sliding down my back, as I clutched the phone and hoped Mira wouldn't come back to listen in.

"Other things cost more," he'd continued. "It's extra if you want interrogation or the victim beaten or—"

Every word was a jolt to my body, shock after shock. Realizing what I was about to initiate, I'd shivered, even though between the heat and coffee, I'd actually warmed up. Was I really going to agree to it?

I was. I knew it without a doubt. What other option did I have? Letting my life continue this way, risking Daniel killing Kari and her baby, not to mention a future trapped with him.

"Will it look real?" I asked, my hand shaking as I gripped the phone tighter.

"We're criminals keeping our noses clean. We've done this before. For real."

For real. The words hung between us for a long moment.

"Still there? I'm not getting paid to listen to your breathing."

Which was an unfair statement because I'm pretty sure I'd stopped breathing altogether. *Criminals. Real kidnappers. But a fake kidnapping.*

"Can you do it this week?" I asked.

"You need a specific day?"

"No. I want her to be surprised. Off guard. I want it to look as real as possible."

A low dark chuckle. "That won't be a problem. Send me her name. Her photo. Don't want to grab the wrong girl."

I breathed in, out. And set it in motion: "You have her name already. I'll send you a photo."

A pause.

"I have her name?"

"Yes." I swallowed, cleared my throat. "I gave it to you when you answered the phone. It's me. The victim is me."

And just like that, I'd hired a criminal to kidnap me.

Kari taps her foot at the table, impatient for caffeine. My hands shake as I reach for the coffee pot.

It had occurred to me it might not work. Would Daniel, catching it on his cameras, volunteer those videos to the police as evidence? Wouldn't any reasonable business come forward if the individual they had fake-kidnapped was reported missing *for real*? Or, as Mira had said, the business was run by a felon. Maybe said felon would keep his mouth shut, for fear of being shut down. The website assured privacy. It gave the impression this was at least partially to protect the reputations of people who got off on the kidnapping experience.

I spare a thought for where I'll go, maybe California. It's warm there, and there are plenty of New Age communities where people go by a name they make up. One of my nursing school friends lived in one for a couple years before he decided to go back to "real life" as he'd called it. He still went by his old name though—Diem, as in *carpe diem*. He described the community as welcoming, and no one asked where you were from. Maybe I could disappear somewhere like that. It sounds like a good enough life, even if I will miss being a nurse. Helping people.

"Noelle? Did you hear me?" I jerk my head up to find Kari watching me. "You going to bring the coffee over or what?"

"Yeah, of course." I pull mugs from my cabinet and pour. Last night's phone conversation fades away as I return to reality —a reality that will end the moment my extreme kidnapper fulfills the job I've hired him for.

"Did you find a crib yet?" I ask to make conversation.

"Nope. Figured we'd do that today."

We're going shopping for the baby items she didn't get at her baby shower. Kari doesn't know who the father is—or rather, she won't acknowledge who he is and for whatever reason, hasn't shared his name with me. So, she's doing this on her own, now that her mother has died. She's confident because she's strong like that, sure of herself, but also because she thinks I'll be on standby should she need help.

The tightness in my chest increases. I force a breath out and pull the cream from the refrigerator. *I have to do this.* Not only for me, but for her, too.

"We'll find the perfect one," I say, trying to stay in the here and now. "And I'll pay for it."

"Noelle, you're not paying for—"

"Yes, I am. I haven't gotten you a gift yet."

"You threw me a baby shower, that *was* your gift."

I summon a smile and stare at her belly. "With that slowing you down, you won't be able to stop me."

Kari mutters something but lets it go, and I bring the coffee over.

"How's stuff with the man?" she asks, stirring in cream.

She doesn't usually ask about him, so I sneak a look to see if this is the beginning of one of her many tirades about how we'd have more fun if I were single, though this argument has abated since she became pregnant. She's careful to never insult him directly, just suggest I'm better off on my own.

"The usual."

She snorts. "Let me guess. French restaurant. Booze. You finished off an entire bottle of wine, which is why you slept in so late." Once upon a time, her words held envy—she'd always been impressed by the idea of money, having grown up solid middle class. But these days, the words held venom, as though she somehow knew how much Daniel had changed over the year-plus we'd been together. We are cousins, but also best friends—maybe somehow, she can sense it.

"It's a nice restaurant," I say. He doesn't need any more reason than controlling me to prey on Kari. "We should go. I'll get dressed."

As I stride back into my bedroom, I remind myself to act normal. This may be the last time I ever see Kari—if all goes as planned, it almost certainly will be. I need to stay in the moment, treasure the memory of shopping for Kari's daughter's crib, of having this last day with her. I need to be totally normal, so she—and Daniel—don't suspect anything.

I've pulled last night's jeans on with a long-sleeved shirt when my phone lights up, and it rings. *That ring.* His ring. It's one of the dozen preprogrammed jingles, but I've come to associate it with his voice, his demands, and the bolt of nerves that shoots through me leaves my heart pounding in my chest.

But it's just a phone call.

"Hello?" I manage and force a smile into my voice.

I jump when Kari leans in the door, as familiar with the ring tone as I am. Her eyes narrow, and she shoots daggers at me. "Why did you answer?" she mouths.

Out of habit. To keep her safe.

"Noelle." Daniel's voice is snappy, efficient. The *beep-beep-beep* of a patient monitor is in the background. He's at work, on a case.

"Yes?"

"My mother called."

"Okay." I stare down at my bedspread and wait for him to go on. For reasons beyond me, his mother seems to like me and demands my presence at her home nearly every week. She'll thrust a glass of port in my hand, the only alcohol she ever drinks, and point to a stool where I'm to sit and chat with her while she cooks a roast and mashed potatoes or spaghetti and meatballs. If she were anyone else's mother, I suspect I'd have come around to liking her by now.

"Mother's busy Sunday night, so we'll do Monday night. I'll pick you up at six. I'd like to take her flowers, so pick up a bouquet."

"I have to work." The sudden reminder of my Monday night shift zings through me like a "get out of jail free" card, but the silence on the other end of the line tells me it's not working.

"I understand," he says. "Would you like me to speak to your manager about getting you the night off?" He's reasonable. Controlled. The way he appears to the outside world. The underlying threat: *I can get you fired.*

I open my mouth. Shut it.

"No, it's okay. I'll—I'll call in sick."

"Sounds perfect." There's a purr to his voice, a warmth the nearby circulating nurse no doubt assumes is the sign of a man satisfied, in love. It's easier to believe than reality—that Daniel's threats don't have to be spoken out loud. I hear them loud and clear, regardless.

The line clicks as he hangs up. I stare at the phone, then silence it on a whim. If he calls back it can go to voicemail.

"Girl." Kari scoots onto the bed beside me. "What'd he say?" She touches my back. "You okay?"

I fight the flush creeping up my neck and cheeks. "It was nothing. Just a dinner with his mom he needs me to go to." It's not a lie.

"You sure?"

"Yeah, it's fine." I pull away and sort through my closet for a jacket.

Hopefully, they make me disappear soon.

NINE

NOELLE

Nine Months Ago

I wake alone.

No, that's not right. I wake in the company of *pain*. Searing, ripping pain over my abdomen. A dampness, but my left hand won't rise, won't seek it out—I can't quite conceptualize why. I try for my other hand, and it moves, and my eyes blink open, and I recognize where I am in a flash of reality that must be a nightmare—the hospital. My hospital. But I'm not working. I'm in a bed, and my right hand comes up, but it's not my hand—it's a gauzy mess, tape and a clear catheter tube of an IV. I try to adjust, to sit up, but that pain comes back worse, stabbing now.

An alarm blares overhead, and just before I lose consciousness, Daniel comes to the door, eyes wide, hands tense over the doorframe, not staring at me, but at the monitor above me. He's terrified, I think. Absolutely terrified. I wish I knew why.

"She's crashing," he calls, and the world fades to black.

When I wake again, I am not alone.

This time, I don't move, because everything is numb. Bliss-fully numb.

A man's voice I don't recognize. "Dr. Ashcroft, you saved her. If you hadn't gotten to her when you did—the artery was nearly sliced through where the car struck her. She would have bled out in another couple of minutes. This sort of injury is rare." Murmured words I can't quite make out. The whisper of a door opening, closing.

I want to know what happened, but the thought is transient, disappearing as soon as I think it, as I start to fade back into darkness. But then a voice I do recognize.

"You do like playing the hero, Daniel." A pause. "The poor dear. She could have died. Just like your father. You could have lost her, just like—"

"I know, Mother. I know." *Daniel.* I try to move my hand. Try to flutter my fingers, to show him I'm right here, I'm listen-ing. But Eve keeps talking, and I go still, listening, hoping maybe their words will tell me what happened.

"Why weren't you beside her? Why weren't you—"

"Mother, I can't watch her every second of the day. Don't you think—" His breath hisses out. "Don't you think I *know*? Don't you think I've relived seeing her get hit by that car a hundred times? It came right at her. They didn't even hit the brakes. It was like they were *trying* to hit her—" A hiccupped sob, words bitten back. "And I know what happened to Dad. I was there for that accident, too."

A car. A car hit me.

Daniel and I were downtown, buying flowers at the market. A typical Saturday morning for us. I'd convinced him to go on a run with me, and he'd complained about how short my running shorts were. I'd rolled my eyes and his gaze had darkened, so I'd walked away to grab coffee, to give him time to rationalize his own thoughts, and then—

Then, nothing.

"I'm sorry, Daniel. It's just—your father. Then Sarah. And now, Noelle." But she doesn't sound sorry. She *blames* him. Blames Daniel. *Sarah* echoes in my head, and thoughts of the newspaper articles I'd all but forgotten in the haze of our growing relationship, but consciousness fades before I can focus on them.

A long silence follows, or maybe that's me falling back asleep. My brain is a fog of drugs and pain. I try to think of what they've given me—Versed probably. Maybe fentanyl. Possibly propofol... Complex drug names stream in and out of my consciousness. Pain medications. Sedatives.

I wonder how bad the damage is.

If I'll ever work again. If I'll ever run again. Thank god, Daniel was there. Thank god, he saved me.

When I come to again, Daniel's there. I can hear his breathing, close to me. Quiet crying punctuates the silence. His hand curls around mine, and relief floods me that I can feel it, feel anything besides this numbness. Things have not been easy this past month between him and me—a growing need on Daniel's part to know where I am at all times. To have a copy of my work schedule, to ask repeatedly if I'm ready to move in full-time with him yet. He goes with me to visit my aunt and Kari once a week, but he's grown distant with them—asking if instead, we can stay in Seattle. It chafes. It leaves me uneasy.

But in this moment, all of that is left in the past.

In this moment, he saved my life. He's here now. His mother blames him. And I feel sorry for him, even though I'm the one in the hospital bed.

I push my muscles to move, to curl my fingers in his.

A hitch in his breath. "I'm here, Noelle," he murmurs. "I'm so sorry I let this happen. I won't let anything bad ever happen to you again. I'll make sure we're together always. I won't let anything keep us apart. No matter what."

TEN

NOELLE

Now

I reserve the Sundays I don't work at the hospital for myself. But today, I don't sleep in like a typical night shifter. I don't meet Kari for brunch. I don't read a book on my couch until I fall back asleep.

I get up. I dress. I strike out on an eight-mile run, and along the way, I say goodbye to Seattle. To the coffee shop I frequent enough they know my order by heart. The bookstore that preorders my favorite authors for me. The aquarium, where I've spent many Sunday afternoons pretending I'm someone else—someone with a regular family, a loving boyfriend, someone who's happy. I don't bother with the Space Needle, or the Chihuly glass museum—these are places Daniel has taken me. Places with good memories that soured as he changed, as we changed, and I won't miss either of them. Mostly, I'll miss the Puget Sound and the sighting of orcas and seals through the waves.

My goal is California, but I can't make definite plans. These moments when I'm out running, sans phone, are my only moments of true privacy. No cameras. No spyware. All I can do is withdraw small sums of cash from any ATM I pass, ask for money back when I use my debit card, and save. It's become my habit since my aunt died—once a week, sometimes twice, I hoard cash. It gives me control, because I've known someday I might need it, but until two nights ago, I didn't know exactly what I'd spend it on. Now, I know. I'm paying to be kidnapped. When I'm gone and the police or Daniel check my bank records, no red flags will be raised.

There's an ATM on the corner, and I slide my card from my sports bra.

"Noelle?" The voice grates on my nerves even before my brain processes who it belongs to. We're in downtown Seattle, not far from Pike Place Market, near the fancy stores—Nordstrom, Anthropologie, Sephora. The older woman gazing at me from ten feet away is tall for her generation at five-foot-eight, though she's told me she was once five-foot-ten. She has silvery-blonde hair blown out and laid over one shoulder, always so perfect I've more than once suspected it might be a wig. A deep blue cashmere wrap is thrown across her body despite the relatively warm winter day—it's in the sixties, whiplash after the chilly nights—and she smiles with a dark lipstick that gives her the sophisticated look Daniel is always telling me I should try to emulate.

Daniel's mother.

"Eve, hi." I step back, away from the ATM. Thwarted.

"What are you doing, dear? Daniel has today off, didn't you know?"

It takes me a moment to respond. She presumes I have no life outside of her son. Since her own husband passed away, and according to her, he hadn't been that great of a husband or father to begin with, I can't be certain where this sense of duty comes from, but it chafes. I rub my arms and step in place.

"I'm out for a run," I say. "My physical therapist finally cleared me to train for another marathon."

She tilts her head and even on the cloudy day, her hair shines in what little light the sky offers. I'm suddenly very aware of the messy windswept ponytail that sits atop my head. And the fact that she's literally covered from head to toe, maintaining a level of conservatism that I am not in my running shorts and T-shirt.

"Oh?" She steps closer, summoning a smile. "I suppose it's important to stay in shape, you working as a nurse and all."

I freeze for a moment. Had she emphasized the word *working* as though it were a bad thing?

"Were you needing cash?" she asks kindly and nods to where there's now a line of three people.

It had to be my imagination, surely.

"I was, but it's not important. I think I'm seeing you tomorrow night for dinner, is that right? Is there anything I can bring? A dessert, maybe?" It occurs to me that, besides in old photos, I've never seen Eve outside of her own home. I've been under the impression she keeps mostly to herself, the majority of her outside contact being with her son.

"No, thank you, dear. I've got it covered."

Her eyes trace me, and fresh discomfort awakens inside me. I need to end this conversation and get away from her. She's always kind, considerate. If she were anyone else's mother, I suspect we'd be good friends by now.

"Are you meeting friends for lunch? Shopping?" I ask, hopefully prompting her to go about her day.

"Meeting a friend, yes." Eve's smile returns, and I can't help but think of a patient who swears they're not an alcoholic even in the midst of liver failure. I don't know Eve well enough to know if she's lying to me. And it really doesn't matter. Soon, I'll be gone. Besides, it's not her fault her son is a sociopath.

"I need to be off," she says. "But I look forward to seeing you tomorrow evening. I just bought a tawny port I was thinking we could crack open."

"Oh, that would be great." I say it with a tight smile. I'd suffered through a glass of it on our first meeting, to be polite, and now she's decided it's *our* beverage.

Eve is one part of Seattle I will not regret leaving behind.

ELEVEN

NOELLE

Nine Months Ago

Aunt Beatrice sits in the chair beside my bed when I wake. Her eyes are shut, her breathing deep and even, and her head tilts back against the wall behind the chair. She clutches a beaded purse in her hands, and though she's fast asleep, her brows furrow and her mouth pinches. She looks tense. She's visited twice before, but always with Kari. When I fight through the fog of pain medicine, I look around—but my cousin isn't here. The room is otherwise empty, save the latest bouquet of flowers Daniel has left on the table opposite.

Time loses meaning in the hospital. Nurses and doctors come and go twenty-four hours a day, and I'm woken every four hours for vitals and an exam. All I really want is one night of deep uninterrupted sleep. I blink and squint at the clock, but it's too dark to see. Which must mean night has fallen. I've been asleep awhile, at least. That's good. The surgeon said I needed rest.

A fractured femur.

Internal bleeding.

It's been a week.

The surgeries are over and done with. A physical therapist comes in twice a day, and even with screws holding my femur in place, I'm already up and walking, albeit slowly, painfully.

A cup of mostly melted ice sits on a tray table to my right, and I grab it, take a long drink. It tastes like plastic, and I wipe my mouth on the sleeve of my hospital gown. My phone was destroyed in the accident—Daniel promised me a new one, but he hasn't made good on that promise yet. Which means no texts, no calls, and I never know when anyone is coming or going; it's disorienting.

"Bea?" I murmur.

My aunt twitches, and I wonder how long she's been here, waiting for me to wake up. It can't have been more than an hour or two—I'm never left alone longer than that.

I repeat her name, then reach out and touch her shoulder. She snaps awake, as disoriented as I was. Hospitals have that effect on people.

"Oh, Noelle, dear." Her lips tremble into a half smile. Her eye shadow is smeared, and she leans in, presses a warm firm hand in mine. "How are you? I spoke to Daniel. He says you're going to be all right."

I nod. Close my eyes. Let a rush of warmth fill me. I would have died without him. Would now, even surviving, be lost without his twice daily visits, the long lunches where he holds my hands and tells me how I'll be running again in no time, he'll make sure of it. "I'll get you the best physical therapy, Noelle. And they'll come to the house to work with you. I already called to set it up. You'll stay with me," he'd promised.

"Is it true he saved your life?" she asks, and a romantic twinkle comes to her eye. "Playing the handsome hero?"

"I don't remember anything, but yes." I nod at the flowers. "Those are from him.

"Oh, Noelle. I really think he's the one."

Our eyes meet, and there's a silent communication—she's telling me it's okay. She's giving me her approval, which she never gave with my ex. Not that I asked for it. But I could tell she hadn't liked him, and she'd been right. But then her lips curve down, and she shifts, and I can tell she's holding something back.

"What's wrong?" I ask.

"I—" She scrubs a hand over her face.

"Is it Kari?" I ask.

"What? Oh, no. Kari's fine. I just—" She gives a dismissive wave. "She was so rude to Daniel last time, I thought it was better I came alone."

A vision of Kari flits through my mind—she'd once all but worshiped Daniel, asking with a wink, "Does he have a brother?" Entranced by his ability to float through life effortlessly. To pay the bill without hesitating. To have nice things.

But the last time she visited had been disturbingly different.

"Noelle should be with family." Her hands were on hips, glaring across the room in response to him suggesting I temporarily move in with him as I recovered once I left the hospital.

A stunned silence filled the room. She was forgetting that both she and my aunt worked full-time and neither would be around during the day, whereas Daniel also worked full-time, but had varied hours, and could take night shifts as long as needed, could be around when I was home. He could also afford to hire someone to help me on the occasions he couldn't be there. Besides, he had multiple spare bedrooms, one of which was on the first floor. His home also put me a mere ten minutes from my frequent follow-up appointments instead of nearly an hour.

I tried to explain this to her—that it wasn't a slight against her or my aunt—but she left in a huff, only calling on the landline later to apologize, but holding firm against Daniel.

"What do you have against Daniel?" I had asked.

She'd taken a long time to respond but finally said, "I don't know. I just... I don't trust him." I'd resolved to figure out why she felt that way all of a sudden. Daniel didn't know, either. But in the midst of narcotics and interrupted sleep, it was just too much to deal with at the moment.

"What's wrong, then?" I ask Beatrice. I'll talk to Kari when I get out of the hospital. She doesn't have to love Daniel. But if she could at least be kind, it would make the situation better.

My aunt hesitates, and I look over at her, and she's twisting her purse in her hands. *Scared.* My aunt is scared. Above me, the monitor beeps faster—keeping time with my heart rate. Annoyance flits through me, and I almost reach up and turn the damn thing off—except I can't reach it, and with a broken femur, I'd only hurt myself.

"Well, I am having some trouble with my heart, that's all. And the heart doctor said it's no big deal, but I might need this bypass thing."

"Bypass," I repeat.

She's lying to me. The doctor did not say it's no big deal if she also said she might need a bypass.

She nods, lips pressed together. "It sounds scary, Noelle. It wouldn't be for a little while. They're trying me on a different medication, but—" Her gaze comes to rest on my leg. "I'm sorry, dear. You of course have been through something awful, and here I am—"

I reach out and touch her hand. "It's okay. A bypass is scary."

My aunt holds my hand and gives me a brave smile. "So, let's talk more about your beau. I always liked him, but I've been so impressed with how he's cared for you these past days. He's called and updated me and—" She continues singing Daniel's praises, but I'm calculating how fast I can get well, get moving again. If my aunt has a cardiac bypass, she will need a caregiver,

too. And as a cardiac nurse, I can do that. I *want* to do that—
after she took me in last year, it's the least I can do.

TWELVE

DANIEL

Nine Months Ago

You nearly died, Noelle.

If I'd gotten to you even thirty seconds later, you'd have bled out of your femoral artery, would have had your life force drained into the gritty asphalt of the rainy Seattle streets, while onlookers filmed with their damn phones and murmured between themselves about how they were *traumatized* by your death. No doubt, their therapists would assure them it was post-traumatic stress disorder. Never once would a single one of them consider it was your death, not theirs.

My death, too, in a less literal way.

How could you do that to us? To me?

Mother blames me, but you're the one who walked away. That said, she's right that it's my fault, too—I should have kept a better eye on you.

I swallow. Grip your hand in mine. Ignore the whisper of a nurse who insists I leave the room for your procedure, because I am Dr. Daniel fucking Ashcroft, and no, I will not leave my girl-friend's bedside. Even if I am mad at you.

Your blood still cakes my hands, is imbedded beneath my nails. Pink and gritty on my pale flesh. I hate blood, Noelle. But for you, I didn't think twice.

That's love. You're welcome.

I lean closer, watch your eyelashes flutter, feel my stomach curl at the flecks of blood that litter your face alongside your freckles. I let my gaze stray to the monitor above your head where your heart rate blips along, a little too fast, a result of your blood loss. A bag of blood hangs crimson on your IV pole, next to the normal saline. It's the third transfusion you've had in five hours.

I'm glad you will survive this. I screwed up, too. But Noelle, this was your fault.

If you hadn't run off in Pike Place Market like a child unable to do as told.

If you had stayed beside me where you belong.

If you hadn't insisted on going to grab coffee.

If you'd stopped to look both ways.

I'll have to watch you more closely from now on.

This isn't the way I planned to bind you to me. I never would have wanted it to come to the point you'd get hurt. In all honesty, I merely wanted to put a ring on your finger. To hear you utter from your lips, "In sickness and health, to love, cherish, and to obey…"

Obey.

If only you'd obeyed, Noelle.

Then we wouldn't be here now, would we?

THIRTEEN

NOELLE

Six Months Ago

I missed the warnings signs. I know that now.

Daniel jumped at the chance to be my exclusive caregiver. And maybe it is because he loves me, but it is also because having me in his home, under his constant watch, fulfills his need to control every aspect of my life.

The first week out of the hospital wasn't so bad—I couldn't do much for myself, regardless.

But now, three months out, I've been back at work for two weeks. I've suggested moving back into my own apartment and I've been there to visit twice. Against his wishes, I've started driving again, and have been out to visit my aunt and Kari—my aunt, whose surgery is scheduled for a month from now. Who I intend to go live with part-time, both to help her, but also as an excuse to leave Daniel's house, where he's decided I should take up permanent residence.

Life is getting back to normal, one basic task a time, tasks that for too long have felt beyond my reach. But I can't fight the gnawing realization that Daniel's goal is to keep me from achieving them.

For a while, I've allowed it—he's a doctor, after all, and I nearly died.

But I can't anymore. I wait at the front window, fingers tapping over the windowsill, watching for his arrival. I need to go home. I need to finish recovering on my own and regain my independence. We will see each other constantly—at work and going on dates.

I bite my lip. I cross and uncross my arms. I pace the room.

I shouldn't be this nervous to talk to him. It stirs up an old feeling, the sort that reminds me of the huge amount of mental energy it took to be around my ex—to monitor his emotions and to watch his body language for tells that things were about to get bad.

I push back the thought. I turn back to the window. This is Daniel. Kind caring Daniel. He will understand.

Daniel does not understand.

"You're leaving me?" he asks.

"No." I sit back on the couch. He's still in scrubs, his hair a wreck from the surgical cap he wears in the OR. But now, he's at the bar in one corner of his living room, pouring himself an amber liquid, tossing it back, pouring another. "This was never permanent. I have my apartment. I want to go home. For a while, at least. And my aunt is going to need my help recovering, so it makes sense—"

"So, you're leaving me," he says, quieter now. I can only see his back. He drinks more.

I sit up, perch on the edge of the couch, squeeze my hands together. I wish he would just *listen*.

"Daniel, I am not leaving you. We are not breaking up."

But as soon as I say the words, I imagine a world without

him. A world where I can come and go as I please. Where I can hike with Kari and visit my aunt, and never have to text or call as though I'm a child asking permission.

That world appeals to me.

Daniel turns on his heel and paces back to the couch where I am. His movements are quick, almost jerky. The hair on my skin rises, and were this Michael—he's *not*, I know that, yet he reminds me of him in this moment—I'd expect a backhand next.

But Daniel is too smart for that.

Instead, he turns to face me. His bright charismatic eyes are anything but kind, loving, charming—no, they are filled with anger and hurt.

And something inside me snaps.

"I think we need to take a break," I say.

I hadn't planned on breaking up with him. Not even close. But sitting beside him is bringing back every bad memory I've ever had about my ex, and I've ignored the warning signs for long enough.

Daniel goes still. A halting laugh escapes his lips. I had planned on bringing up Sarah today, too—gently probing, because maybe that's part of why he's become so overprotective in the aftermath of me being hit by the car.

But then he says, "I'm sorry, Noelle. But we are not breaking up." He shifts closer, and I flinch—but he only takes my hand in his. My heart palpates in my chest, sweat breaking out along my collarbone. Inside me, panic rises, but I press it back, because despite his words, he's gentle. His lips curve into a smile.

Something inside me screams this is *wrong*, something is *off*, but I can't identify what, and so I sit, deer in the headlights, waiting.

"Let me get this right. I've spent months catering to your every desire trying to make you happy. I saved your life for god's sake, and you—"

His words fade as my hand is crushed in his—as bones grind together, as nausea sweeps over me from the pain.

"Daniel—" I gasp and wrench back. But he doesn't let go.

Silence. Our eyes meet, my hand still squeezed in his grip. My whole body shakes, with pain, with fearful anticipation of what comes next.

"I understand you need a little alone time." He nods to himself. "Not a problem. You can move home. I'll give you a few days, and I'll see you Sunday to go to my mother's. That should be long enough." He releases my hand, and that hurts worse, the bones shifting back into their proper position. "But we are not breaking up."

"Daniel, I'm not—" My voice shakes, and I hate myself for that.

"I covered for you this morning," he says.

"What?" I blink up at him, confusion and pain swirling together in a kaleidoscope of disbelief.

"You gave morphine to your patient. You didn't properly catalog disposing of the leftover amount. It just... disappeared." His lips curve into a bland smile. "One can only assume you stole it. Stole a controlled substance. It makes sense—you were taking narcotics after your surgery, it's likely you'd form an addiction. Stealing, though, that could cost you your job. Your nursing license. But I took care of it for you."

Words escape me. It's only half true. I *had* given half a vial of morphine to my patient this morning. But I had cataloged dumping the rest in the bin specifically designed for disposal of leftover controlled substances. Usually, a nurse would sign off on it with me—verifying one another, confirming no one was stealing drugs. I hadn't this morning because I'd verified it with Daniel, instead. As an anesthesiologist, he could do that.

I stare at him, wondering if he's lying, or if he truly didn't sign off the verification of disposing of the morphine.

I can't afford to lose my job—to lose not only the income,

but the health insurance that comes with it. My medical bills before insurance were in the hundreds of thousands, and even with it, they have totaled over ten thousand dollars.

Daniel pats my knee as though we've had a good conversation. His message is all too clear.

He leans in and kisses my temple. "I'll pick you up Sunday at six."

Words die on my lips.

There is no escape. And for the first time, I wonder if Sarah didn't randomly disappear—I wonder if she found a way to escape him.

FOURTEEN

NOELLE

Now

Though none of it will be real, I can't help but question each and every person I pass by. The man on the phone hadn't said who would come for me—a man or a woman, one or two people or, shoot, a whole group. Will the man in the coffee line kidnap me? Or the woman walking the dog? Who will be my savior? Are they following me right this moment to learn my habits, when to best nab me as I enter or exit my apartment?

These are the tensest moments—every time when I unlock my front door, and wonder, *Will this be my last moment of captivity under Daniel's watchful eye?*

The irony does not escape me; being stolen from my life is the only way for me to be free.

I stop at a coffee stand on a street corner to purchase a drip coffee, add cream and sugar, and continue down First Avenue in the direction of Pike Place Market. There are lots of places to buy flowers in Seattle, but Pike Place is the cheapest I've found, and besides, Eve likes the arrangements a specific gentleman puts together. Making her happy has become a means of survival. Her happiness equals Daniel's happiness. Daniel's happiness keeps me—and Kari—safe.

On a Monday morning, Pike Place isn't busy, and I ease through pedestrians, coffee in hand. The open-air market leads to rows of bouquets, the thick, sweet scent of flowers, business owners steadily making more arrangements as they wait for customers.

I purchase two: a small one with yellow daisies for my apartment because a bit of cheer will do me good, and one for Eve, in purples and pinks, her favorites. I finish my coffee and search for the nearest trash can, only to nearly lose both bouquets when a man bumps into me.

"Pardon," he says, but his tone is harsh, inconsistent with the word of apology. The fabric of his leather jacket scrapes over my cheek as his shoulder brushes me. I manage to stay upright, dropping the empty coffee cup but keeping the flowers from falling. Adrenaline spikes through me; this isn't right, I'm not supposed to be kidnapped in public. But just as fast, I realize it's an accident, his form fading fast as he rushes from the market.

I whip around to study him as he escapes, wondering if he might be my future kidnapper—tall, slim, dark jacket, jeans, short dark hair—but that's all I can make out before he turns a corner.

"Are you okay, ma'am?" a freckled sandy-haired man asks from behind a booth advertising five flavors of honey.

"I'm okay," I murmur, glancing back toward where the man disappeared.

"Do you need another coffee?"

"No, I was—" I rearrange the flowers and grab the empty cup. "It's empty. Thanks." I offer him a smile, chuck the cup in the trash, and turn on my heel, going back the way I came, following the man.

He ducked out of the marketplace proper, into the open-air

space where cars can drive, albeit at a crawl. On one side of the street is the backside of the flower shops I emerge from. On the other, coffee shops, a French bakery, and a man at an outdoor piano, banging away on keys. I recognize the song from a movie. My gaze sweeps left and right along the road, and the pianist's song goes faster and faster, reaching a crescendo, and a sudden horn blares close to me—too close.

I leap backward, barely keeping my legs from being swept out from beneath me by a sleek blue Ford Mustang.

Memories crash over me from a year before, almost to the day, when I hadn't moved fast enough. I exhale harshly, the moment relived in the half second it takes me to pull away and back to the sidewalk, to safety.

"Ma'am?" A hand closes over my elbow.

I yank away, still scanning for the man with black hair who'd brushed by me. It was an accident, surely, but—

"Whoa." It's the sandy-haired man from the honey shop, hands raised as if to show he means no harm. "Are you okay? You nearly—" His eyes follow the Mustang's path up the road away from the Sound.

"I'm okay," I say.

But I'm not. And I haven't been in a long time.

FIFTEEN

NOELLE

Now

I wake from a late afternoon nap with the awareness Daniel will be at my apartment door in less than an hour. The knowledge sits heavy in my chest, and I linger in bed longer than usual, staring at the ceiling. Now that I have a plan, each moment waiting for it to happen is arduous, like slogging uphill through mud.

I want this part of my life to be over.

Three texts wait for me on my phone. Two are from Kari, asking if I have time to go to baby classes with her, and one from Daniel.

Don't forget the flowers.

No greeting, no farewell, just his orders. Another thing that changed after I tried to break up with him—niceties gone. Straight to the point. As though being his girlfriend is a job I'm obligated to fulfill.

I get to my feet and shove the necessities—phone, wad of

money—in my pocket in case tonight is the night my kidnapper comes, and go to make coffee. There's Baileys Irish Cream on the counter, left over from a holiday party the year prior, and I don't hesitate to add a heavy dollop. Pregaming is not in my repertoire, but tonight, in anticipation of both Daniel's and Eve's company, it's necessary.

The coffee comes with me as I return to my bedroom, opening my closet door and sorting through hangers to the left, where I keep my small collection of outfits Daniel has deemed appropriate to wear in Eve's presence—longer dresses, shirts with sleeves and higher collars, things I wouldn't be caught dead in at any other time, merely for comfort reasons. Likely, I'll hear about the running shorts and T-shirt sighting from when I ran into her yesterday—but, from Daniel; it's his job to keep me in line, not his mother's.

A distant knock at my front door makes me pause.

"Come in," I call, because it's Daniel. The clock reads five forty-five—he's early.

The door squeaks as it opens, but he doesn't say anything. That's fine. I don't particularly want to talk to him, either. I shut the closet door and throw the outfit on the bed, taking my anger out on the clothing instead of the man who will be sure to remind me of what he can do to keep me in line—hurt me. Hurt someone close to me. Plant drugs in my work locker to get me arrested and fired. The list goes on.

I pull my shirt over my head right as he comes through the bedroom door behind me.

"Almost ready," I say, softening my voice like I always do with him.

"Good." That one word, spoken in a voice lower than Daniel's, freezes me.

I turn.

It's not Daniel.

SIXTEEN

NOELLE

Five Months Ago

I'm desperate to escape him. I may be living in my own apartment, but I found the cameras—I know he's watching me. And I know he's watching my aunt and Kari, too, maybe because of how much time I spend there, avoiding him.

I can't shake that I'm not the only one in danger.

And now that Kari's announced she's pregnant via social media, he's dropping hints that suggest as much.

It's a Friday night. Another date at "our" restaurant, another bottle of wine, another forced conversation to keep him happy. Summer is here, and the front windows are open, a breeze coming up from the Puget Sound, soft to my skin. If I were anywhere else, with anyone else, I'd say it's the perfect night.

"Does Kari know maternal morbidity is at an all-time high?" Daniel asks, and I tense.

"No," I say. "I've tried to help her have a healthy pregnancy. There's no need to scare her."

Daniel shifts in his booth. He reaches for my hand, and I let him take it.

"I would just hate to see something bad happen to her," he says. "You know?" I look at him. He stares back at me. There is a moment, a brief moment, where I believe he is threatening her life, and, therefore, the life of her baby.

But the moment breaks, and he says, "Noelle"—in a voice that I haven't heard in weeks, the kind tone of the Daniel I fell in love with—"you're a good friend to her. A good cousin," and I wonder if I imagined it all.

I change the subject. "How was your week? How was the board meeting?"

"Not bad," he murmurs. His hand squeezes mine, and some tension drains out of me. "We raised half a million dollars for the children's charity."

"That's good." I offer a smile.

"I've been thinking," he begins. "What if I hire a private nurse for your aunt? I know you're so busy taking care of her."

There it is—the other shoe drops. He's not asking out of the kindness of his heart. He's telling me what he wants. Indicating there is a problem.

"It would have the added benefit that they could also help Kari. Did you know that Kari is high risk? I was talking to her obstetrician, and apparently Kari has gestational diabetes. Higher risk of mortality for the child, too."

Silence.

Now, I'm sure I'm not imagining it. A threat, carefully cloaked in the veneer of concern. And not just a threat—a reminder of rates of mortality. Of *death*. Which reminds me of someone *presumed* to be dead.

Sarah.

A sudden clarity leaves me cold and all too aware of what our relationship has been reduced to. Daniel is a gaslighting manipulative asshole who's trapped me in a relationship—that's a far cry from a murderer. And yet... and *yet*. It's always the husband, always the boyfriend. He's hidden *cameras* in my apartment. None of this is normal, no matter how I've tried to rationalize it in the past. Daniel might not strike me hard enough to knock me out like Michael did, but what he's doing to me isn't any better. If Daniel treated Sarah the way he does me and she pushed him hard enough, it's possible it turned physical —that he killed her by accident and then made it look like a disappearance.

A cavern of dread builds in my gut.

I go home and check the internet for news on Sarah MacCleary—there is nothing. Still missing. Still presumed dead. The Facebook group created to keep her disappearance at the forefront of Seattle's minds has no updates. And I still haven't found so much as a name to help me identify who Daniel's other girlfriend was—he had mentioned two prior to me, after all. With Sarah, there is a plethora of information, unhelpful though it might be—but with the other, a woman whose name I don't even know, there is the opposite.

No photos in the society pages.

No social media ties to Daniel.

That could mean nothing. Or it could mean *something*. People don't disappear into thin air.

The following Sunday, at Daniel's mother's house, I flip through Eve's photo albums looking for her, but neither of his previous girlfriends grace their pages. Only Daniel and myself, always dressed conservatively, always posing, always smiling.

Always pretending perfection.

But that Sunday, I get lucky for the first time in a long time.

It's Eve who gives me the tidbit of information. Three glasses of port at eighteen percent alcohol, the belief I'm outside grabbing the dessert I forgot in Daniel's Porsche, and just as I step through the front door, I hear it.

"Her complexion is similar to Justine's. Remember how she

looked in that emerald-green dress for prom? Make sure Noelle wears something like that for the Christmas gala."

Justine.

Prom.

It's a start.

SEVENTEEN

DANIEL

Now

You're late. As usual.

I press my palms into the doorframe of your apartment, shoulders bunching as I squeeze my frustration into the wood and consider my options. I know I can get inside—through charm or kicking in the door. I can manage it. There's always suggesting to you that I'll call Kari to let me in. She, of course, has the spare key. A mention of Kari is all it takes where you are concerned. Most nurses I know are deeply loyal to their friends and family, and you are no exception. Especially after your aunt died, leaving Kari without her mother in the face of having a child. It's your greatest weakness, and, therefore, my best tool.

Then again, I could be reasonable. My therapist says to take a deep breath, or several, if that first one doesn't help. Of course she says that, she's a shrink. Not a *real* doctor. I don't believe in psychology, but there is one person in my life I'll listen to, and she told me to go. So, I am.

I straighten, force myself to take two breaths, and remind

myself I'm in charge of this particular situation, not you. I am the man, and it's my job to take care of you, of our relationship.

"Noelle, let's go. My mother's waiting." I temper my voice, so I don't attract attention. The last thing I need is a video of me yelling at my girlfriend uploaded on the internet for the whole world to see.

Still, nothing. A silent apartment behind a locked door.

Where are you, Noelle?

I dial your number for the third time. It rings until it switches to voicemail.

"Goddammit." I smack the door, unable to restrain the burst of anger slamming through me. My head pounds as the tension rises. What had the therapist said to do now?

I don't remember. I don't care. Everything I do is for you, Noelle, and you can't even take a single night off work to make my mother happy. My dying mother.

I stalk down the hallway toward the parking lot, shoving away memories of the oncologist—another fuck of a doctor— giving us the diagnosis. Screw him. Screw his diagnosis. My Porsche 911 waits for me, double-parked in the future resident parking, and I swing in before the blonde in the other car can get out and give me a piece of her mind. Screw her, too.

The drive is fast, because when you donate enough money to the city of Seattle, you can get out of just about any offense a cop would pull you over for. I pull off the West Seattle Bridge and coast along through the neighborhoods until I reach older, respectable homes, high on a hill cresting over the Puget Sound. The sun is a fiery red over the Olympics, and it seems perfect for a night where I'm all but seeing red from your refusal to do as you're told.

You will pay for this.

You could have at least called. Texted. My mother will blame *me* for this. Another girlfriend I couldn't keep in line. Another failure on my part.

Yes, you were supposed to work, but this is far more important. Besides, you won't be working much longer. I'll propose, and you'll say yes, and then you'll understand how capable I am of taking care of you. You won't have to work anymore, won't have to worry about money or having your own place or doing anything other than being my wife. It will be exactly what I need. And what you need, too, though you clearly haven't figured that out yet.

Work. You must have gone to work. Of course, you did. You're obsessed with that place, those people.

"Call Seattle General," I say. My phone beeps, making the call, and seconds later, it rings.

"Seattle General," a woman says. "How may I direct your call?"

"Cardiac intensive care," I say. The line switches to shitty music, and then clicks as your department answers.

"CVICU," mumbles a man.

"What?" I say, though I heard him perfectly well.

"CVICU," he repeats, enunciating each letter.

"This is Dr. Ashcroft," I snap. "Who is this?"

A moment of silence.

"Sorry, sir." He stumbles over his words. "This is Matthew, the secretary. How may I help you?"

"I'd like to speak to Noelle."

"Noelle?"

"The nurse? My girlfriend?"

Another pause.

"She called in sick, sir," he stammers. "Said she had a migraine."

This time I'm the one who doesn't speak. I disconnect.

If you're not at work, then where the fuck are you?

EIGHTEEN

NOELLE

Now

I almost drowned when I was eight years old.

It was one of the last trips my family took, before everything unraveled, to camp in the mountains of Montana. It was one year before my father would leave my alcoholic mother. Two years before my mother would clean up her act, and we'd move to start a new life elsewhere. We didn't have much money then, so we camped down a dirt road, pulled off through the brush, and walked a quarter mile toward the river. In other words, there were no other people. Just my father, my mother, and myself.

My father warned me to stay near camp, but my mother, free thinker she was, encouraged me to wander—just to stay within hollering distance and watch out for the river. Like any child, I was drawn to the single thing I was warned away from.

Pine trees hung around me, their sharp, sweet scent brushing against my clothes along with their scratchy needles. I plowed through them, stepping over rocks, stumbling now and again over a fallen log, caught up in the freedom of the moment, so unlike my world in urban Boise, Idaho, where concrete and deciduous trees reigned.

The low roar of an immense body of water pulled at my attention. I ducked through the brush, catching sight of it, and squatted at the water's edge, staring into its silver and gold depths—actual flecks of gold glittering in the sunlight, traveling through the water so fast I couldn't catch them if I tried.

But of course, being eight, I had to try. My parents would never know because I would be careful.

I took my shoes and socks off, rolled up my jeans, and reaching to balance myself on a huge boulder, waded in. Cold water rushed over my toes, numbing them instantly. After a hot car ride, it felt wonderful. One step, then another, up to my knees. My feet wobbled over the rocks, and my breath caught as I nearly fell, but the boulder steadied me. The river was icy cold, and yet, I felt like I could breathe for the first time in my life. Wind whooshed over the water, the river the one clear path among the trees down which it could travel, and I looked up, laughed as joy rushed through me. It was amazing.

And then I slipped, the rock beneath my foot slick as, well, river rock. The sky became all that I could see as I tipped backward, until I could see nothing, because I was underwater.

When I surfaced, my head snapped against the boulder and the rush of the water pinned me against the rock. I couldn't think—could only act—trying desperately to save myself, aware even then that if I failed, I would die. My arms flailed, my legs kicked, and I tried to find ground beneath my feet, but they only slid on another rock, then another, and somewhere in there, my body sunk deeper in the water.

I kicked up, gasped a breath of air, but the current pulled me under, and cold water filled my lungs. My chest screamed for air, and I came up again, only to be yanked down, my vision going fuzzy as my whole body thrashed in the ice-cold water.

And then, somehow, I was on the shore. Even today, I don't

know how it happened—maybe the river current caught me just right and thrust me back to the clay embankment. Maybe an angel from heaven snapped me up and deposited me on the bank because it wasn't my time. I would have believed either, I was so relieved to take in a lungful of crisp clean air. What I do know is I nearly died that day, and the memory of nearly drowning, of gasping for air and there being none, has never left me.

Which is why, almost twenty years later, when I wake in a small cramped space, duct tape forcing my lips together, obscuring my ability to breathe, I panic.

NINETEEN

DANIEL

Now

"Oh, Daniel, come in, come in." Mother's tone has that crinkly edge to it all grandmothers' voices do, though she is not yet a grandmother. She will likely remind me of this fact at some point before tonight ends. "Where's Noelle?" She peers around me, looking for you.

My fist clenches around my phone as I realize your absence means I don't have flowers to give her. I should have thought of that.

"I tried to get you flowers, but they weren't fresh." I step around her and take in the living room I pay someone to clean twice a week. The carpet is filthy, and the windows haven't been washed since the last time I was here. I'll have to fire them and find someone new. Again. It's their job, why can't they do it right? Why can't anyone do anything right? You'd likely tell me I should lower my expectations, but you're wrong—keeping my expectations high is how I've come to have such a perfect life, a perfect life I intend to share with you.

"I don't know why you bother," she says. "They all die

anyway. Such a waste. Just like this house." She mumbles some-thing and wanders through the living room to the hallway leading to the kitchen.

The house was a gift after my first-year post-residency and fellowship—a way to say thank you, for not abandoning me the way my father had, for acting as mother and father to me. I owe her everything I have, and all I'd given her was a new car and a 2,500-square-foot house with a nice view of the Puget Sound. It was barely anything compared to my own home or what I've invested in real estate, and yet in her eyes, it's too much. And here I am without you, her beloved future daughter-in-law, screwing up again. It seems I can't do anything right, either.

"So, where is she?" her voice rails through the hall.

I swallow hard and follow Mother into the kitchen, taking one, two, three deep breaths. When she holds a glass of port in my direction, I hold up a hand. "I'm on call," I say, but she shoves it in my hand anyway. If you were here, I'd pour it in your glass when she wasn't looking.

"It's one glass, Daniel." She coughs hard and sips at her own glass of the dark red stuff, sickly sweet, in my opinion.

"Noelle had to work." Now you have me lying to my own mother.

"Work?" Her eyes raise to mine. "A woman shouldn't work unless she must. I had to. Marry her already. You're not getting any younger. Neither am I. Where are my grandchildren?"

I open my mouth to explain I intend to, but her sharp eyes jab my way, and I shut it fast, the tension through my arms leaving them almost trembling. I set the wineglass down. She's always wanted grandchildren, but when she got sick, it became an urgent matter. I'm about to tell her my plans to propose, but she cuts me off.

"I hope this doesn't go like it did last time." Mother's voice is her usual no-nonsense, but I hear the undercurrent of concern in it—concern that I'll end up alone, that she won't get her grandchildren in time to ever know them. "You told me Sarah was the one, but then—"

Mother continues talking, and I work on controlling my breathing. *Sarah. Last time. But what happened with Sarah wasn't my fault.* Not that Mother doesn't hold me accountable, regardless. *See, Noelle? It would be better for both of us if you stepped into line. I won't let what happened with Sarah happen to you.*

When I tune back in, Mother's shifted direction, going on about a woman she met at the cancer center where she went for her treatment and now for follow-up appointments, who at seventy-two is still working because she *likes* it. Mother explains this last part with air quotes. I swallow, looking anywhere but her. I grab my phone and text the only friend I've let you keep.

Is Noelle with you? I hit send.

"Daniel, can you please put the phone away?" Mother's forehead crinkles in a frown, hands on her hips, wooden spoon stained red with sauce in one hand.

"I'm on call, Mother. I told you that." But I shove it in my pocket—she's done so much for me and all she asks for is one night a week of uninterrupted time. *If you were here, she and I wouldn't be arguing. She'd ask you about what book you were reading, or hint at a family vacation we might all take together once we're married.*

"You know the rules," she says and goes back to the sauce. "You tell Noelle she owes me lunch. We need to discuss this work situation. She's a good girl. The right girl for you. She should know better." A pause as she stirs. "How's therapy?"

"Fine," I answer, but my attention is back on my phone as she focuses on dinner. I've turned my ringer off for my mother's sake, but the screen lights up with a simple *No* from Kari.

There are plenty of explanations. You could be on one of your ridiculous runs. I've urged you time and time again to go to the country club like the wives of my colleagues, to play tennis or swim, something safe, but you prefer to run. That's something else that will have to change. I'll need to know where you are at all times, and the country club allows for that. Your damn runs don't, since you refuse to carry your phone with you. You claim it's because you'll drop it—and indeed, when I insisted, you *did* drop your phone, and it *did* shatter the screen, and I swear to god you did it on purpose. But even I know when to pick and choose my battles; soon, you'll learn you can't win.

I still as another thought occurs to me. You could be with another man. It's preposterous. You don't know other men; I make sure of that. The only one I've even heard you mention was your ex-boyfriend, but that was when we first met, and I know for a fact you haven't spoken to him since you arrived in Seattle. But you do work with men at the hospital. I'm not the only male doctor by any means, and there are male nurses in the ICU where you work. Hell, you run with a group once a week, and I'm sure there are men in it. I've seen you all out running in big packs, clogging up the streets and sidewalks, a complete nuisance to Seattle.

How did I never realize how many other men you spend time with?

"Daniel!" Mother's spoon smacks the counter next to my hand. "Are you listening to me?"

I jump, put the phone away once more, distracted. I take a long slow sip of the port, even though I hate it, and keep breathing.

"What?" I manage, finally. "What is it, Mother?" I try to lighten my tone, to keep from sounding rude, but I'm on edge, wondering where you are.

"Can you set the table, please?"

"Sure."

I wait until she's stepped away to move again. I take out plates, silverware, and the cloth napkins she insists on using.

They go neatly on the formal table in the room adjoining the kitchen, and I position them as I learned to decades ago, the knife facing the plate, beside the spoon, the two forks on the opposite side. I do this mindlessly because my mind is elsewhere.

If I ever discover you're cheating on me, there will be consequences. I want to marry you, more than anything else. But the thought of you touching another man leaves my teeth clenched, and I try again for the *Zen breaths* my therapist recommended. I am feeling anything but Zen.

"Daniel? Are you all right?"

Mother touches my arm.

"Fine, Mother." I straighten, smile. "Do we need soup spoons?"

"No, of course not. Soup with roast?" She shakes her head and goes back to the kitchen.

We have a lot to look forward to, Noelle. I can provide an exchange of an easy life and financial security for the simple services a woman provides her husband. But first, the real question—the one I'm still trying to figure out—where the fuck are you?

TWENTY

NOELLE

Now

A person can only panic for so long. If it were a disease, we might call it "self-limiting"—at some point, you pass out from hyperventilating, and in a state of unconsciousness, your respiratory rate slows, your heart rate returns to normal.

When I wake again, I'm still in the confined space. The tape still keeps me from taking a proper breath. But I force myself to breathe slowly, carefully, through my nose, in and out. Passing out won't help. The panic stays at bay, and in its wake, realization.

I've been kidnapped.

I'm likely the only woman who's ever lain in a trunk, bound and gagged, realizing she's been taken forcefully from her home, and grinned like a madwoman.

Noelle Thomas has been taken from her home against her will. My kidnapper did it perfectly. Should I tip him? I can't remember every detail—and my head aches—had he hit me? That seems rather unprofessional, but I had said I wanted it to look real. I can envision him before I lost consciousness, medium-height, broad shoulders, brown eyes, and a ski mask. He'd stepped toward me slowly, and then—I woke up here.

The world sways around me, the grumble of the engine resonating to where I'm stuffed in the trunk as the car accelerates. It's cold in here, dark, and the fabric scratches at my face. Yet these discomforts seem meaningless in light of the bigger picture—that I've left Daniel far, far behind. The ultimate discomfort is in the past.

Something vibrates nearby. My phone, in my back pocket. I curse. It's an oversight on my kidnapper's part. He was supposed to leave it behind at my apartment per the instructions I gave him—or his boss? Whoever I'd spoken to. But it's a small problem, easily fixed once we stop.

I asked to be left somewhere quiet, deserted, to avoid witnesses, but with easy access to a motel, a clothing store, a place to get food. A place to stay, a way to disguise myself, and a meal in peace with no camera watching me before I buy a bus ticket the hell out of Washington State.

I figure I have twenty-four hours before Daniel calls the police. I know him. He won't want to ask for help. But at some point, he'll realize he has to or look suspicious himself. Especially after Sarah's disappearance. It's always the boyfriend or husband, right? And, if he doesn't call, Kari will.

In other words, I have twenty-four hours to get as far from Seattle—from Daniel—as I can. I have the locations of two communities in California memorized, both in the foothills of the mountains, just outside of small towns. I have a couple thousand dollars in hundreds rolled up in my back pocket opposite my phone, and half of that is to go to my kidnapper. The other half is what I have to live off until I find my way to California.

I'm on my own.

Part of me relishes the sudden freedom—no more Friday night dates, Sundays drinking port with his mother, or awareness that even in my own home, I'm being watched.

Part of me is scared.

But it's done. I have no option but to move forward. If Daniel discovers the truth of what I've done, he'll find me. My heart races, picturing it—him storming into a shitty motel room, all Nordic handsome, his looks and confidence and status as a doctor assuring all nearby that he is in the right, dragging me back to Seattle. The words he'd whisper when no one else could hear, the bruises left behind when he held my arm too tightly. The drugs he'd make sure were found in my work locker, to get me fired, losing my stream of income so I'd have to depend on him, or the physician friend he'd call up to diagnose me with god knows what, something, anything, to declare me lacking mental capacity to make my own decisions. Or Kari. He'd go after Kari.

Have you seen the statistics on maternal morbidity?

Overnight, he'd all but become an OB-GYN.

I blow out a breath, halting my frantic worries. I have to disappear. Completely.

The car stops with a suddenness that rocks me. The engine shuts off. One door slams, then another. Footsteps, first near the front of the car, then coming around to the rear.

I'm about to meet the man who effectively saved me, even if he is just doing his job as part of an extreme entertainment business. He has no idea, of course, nor will I tell him. As far as he needs to know, this was all a game. I'll just have to hope he doesn't see my picture on the evening news tomorrow. And if he does, that he'll keep his mouth shut, concerned for the reputation of his business, the fact the owner has a criminal history.

A clatter, keys hit the pavement. Muttering, one man to another. I can't make out their words.

Why aren't they opening the trunk?

I was cold before, but now, with no heat radiating from the interior of the car to the trunk, I'm shivering, wishing I could free my hands from behind me and wrap them tightly around myself.

"Stop talking. Get the job done. I'll be back for her when we're ready to hand her off—later tonight, maybe, but probably tomorrow." A man's voice, deep, in charge, pissed. The first one fades away as though he's turned his back.

The voices grow louder, closer, and I can make out the occasional words—"Girl" and "Keep it quiet" and "Scare her a little," followed by, "But don't hurt her. Strict orders."

I hold my breath, trying desperately to hear over my rapidly beating heart. They should be letting me out, not telling someone to scare me. And why does he have to specify to *not hurt me*? I didn't ask for any of this with my kidnapping.

More muttering back and forth.

"You want me to what?" a man's voice growls, suddenly right above me. Right outside the closed trunk.

"Just do what you do best, asshole. We'll get her from you when the client's ready to retrieve her."

Do what? And what do they mean, when the client's ready to retrieve me? I'm the client!

The website flashes through my mind: *We do it all. Make up any story that excites you—you're a mafia don, a money launderer, a spy for the CIA, or you're just an average Joe mistaken for some asshole who pissed us off. We'll make the perfect counterpart, and we offer a variety of services to make it so real you might even piss your pants (hey, it's happened!). Choose from being held at (fake, rubber) gunpoint, slapped by a sexy female kidnapper, waterboarded by a masked villain, even beaten with a sausage (you can eat it afterward!).*

That's it! Everything I'm hearing now is part of a storyline. Someone *else's* storyline. It has to be. I breathe a sigh of relief—as much as I can around the duct tape. They've gotten me confused with someone who wanted more than a simple kidnapping. All I have to do is explain the situation and—

The trunk opens.

It's night, but a streetlamp illuminates enough that I can see two black masks, the whites of eyes, and a gun pointed at my head. Light shines off the sleek smooth black exterior of the gun, not the blue rubber like the one on the website. I can think only one thing.

The gun is real.

TWENTY-ONE

DANIEL

Now

You're not home.

I sit behind my desk, an array of monitors before me. My desk serves many purposes. It's where I finish patient notes after a long shift, where I teach online courses for the University of Washington, where I earned my medical degree, and it, of course, serves as headquarters for where you and I spend the majority of our time together.

There are three cameras in your apartment—your living room, your kitchen, your bedroom. Out of concern for your privacy, I didn't put one in your bathroom.

All the rooms are empty. All the rooms are normal.

Your living room is its usual barebones couch, your aunt's chair, and side table, all secondhand, evidence you don't make enough money as a nurse to make your job worthwhile. Your bedroom is its usual mess of clothes and running shoes, and it occurs to me this is another behavior you'll need to change when we're married. Or, maybe, I'll hire a live-in maid. I'm happy to pay that cost, because in addition to cleaning up, she can be an extra set of eyes on you.

I check each room again, but they remain empty. My eyes catch on the purse that sits on the kitchen table. You nearly always have it on you. The only time you don't is when you're on a run.

You wouldn't have been running this whole time, though. Perhaps you are with another runner, and you're out and about enjoying one another. Perhaps he is footing the bill, and you didn't need your wallet, which you keep in said purse.

Again, just my imagination, toying with possibilities.

My phone lights up—my mother calling. I ignore her. Guilt stabs through me, but it's for the best. I'm in no mood to gossip about her neighbor or plan our next meal together.

I sip my bourbon, savoring the rich, sharp flavor, considering our most recent date. You were distracted, but not unusually so. It's no surprise to either of us that I'm the focused, controlled one in the relationship. I am a doctor, after all.

I've been considering ways to bring myself back into sharp focus in your mind. What do you think, Noelle? Would that help us?

I click out of the security camera app and open an internet browser, navigating to cSpy, my favorite spyware company.

You should at least have your phone on you.

The phones I track materialize on the screen, and I click on yours. The website loads, and in seconds, I can see you, my beloved girlfriend, are headed east on I-90, out toward the mountains. Now, why on earth are you going that way? Who could convince you to take off on an adventure to the one place I specifically forbade you from visiting?

My lips curl up, but not in a smile.

I imagine it is a man from your running group. Probably one with a goddamn beard, who drinks IPA and fancy lattes instead of real coffee. Runners tend to enjoy other athletic pursuits, like hiking. But why go so late at night? Are you camping? Doing an overnight trip to a romantic lake? Did you watch a sunset with a fellow runner while my mother asked me repeatedly where the hell you were? Did you kiss him, enjoy his touch, as I defended you?

Am I making this all up, in the hopes that coming to find you, to drag you home, will be entertaining? Proving to you yet again, that I'm the one in charge?

Bad things do happen in the mountains. Cougar attacks have been numerous this year. Recently, a serial killer took hikers hostage, killing two before the cops came in. Occasionally, backpackers get lost. And on rare occasions, a storm rolls in, dumping snow and killing the adventurer from exposure. Many dangers, dangers I will not have you exposed to. Plus, there's the danger of an unknown man. Just because he's a runner doesn't mean you can trust him.

For someone who's lost so much, you forget how bad the world can be, how quickly death can come. Someday, you'll learn to appreciate the way I watch out for you.

Maybe, tonight.

I refill my glass, mute yet another phone call from my mother, as well as a follow-up text asking me to call when I have a second, and begin watching the moments of your life in fast-forward. The sense of control this gives me overtakes me, and I relax back. I start with footage from two weeks ago. Mostly, you're asleep, preparing for work, or in the kitchen making coffee. Sometimes, you read.

But have you ever had a man over? Screwed him in the bathroom, where I might not notice? Have I missed some detail of your life?

Doubtful. I'm very good at keeping an eye on you. But let's check, just in case. I pull up the list of camera recordings and go back several days. What have you been up to, Noelle?

As far as I can tell, your life is boring when I'm not around.

I knew this but watching your life for the sake of watching it is about to put me to sleep.

After an hour, I switch to coffee—real coffee, not a fucking latte—and sip it, staring at the screen through bleary eyes. Finally, here you are—home. You wander around your apartment until you go to your bedroom. You start to get dressed. You—

I sit up straight.

There. A man, in your apartment. He walks right in. I pause the video, rewind it, and play it again in normal speed, analyzing every moment, every detail. You call to him on one monitor, and he doesn't stop, but walks right into your bedroom.

My ears pound. My fingers twitch over the mouse, as I imagine my hands around his throat. Around *your* throat.

The monitor in your bedroom gives me a direct view of his face, and he's wearing a ski mask. What kind of fifty shades of bullshit are you into? If you want a man to whip you, all you have to do is ask. I'll gladly show you who's—

My breath stills.

His arm is around your throat. Your eyes are wide, and you smack at him, but it's over in seconds. You're unconscious, limp, head dipped and extremities flaccid. He holds on a moment longer, as though to make sure you're really out.

Another man comes in, grabs your feet, and seconds later, the two of them have carried you off screen. You're gone.

My monitors are empty of life.

I wait a beat, as though you'll magically reappear—I hit Fast-Forward, and indeed, a third man does come in, a different one than before, but he's gone just as fast. Maybe one of the first two forgot something. I stare at his form as it disappears from your front door, heart galloping in my chest as I form a plan.

It's like Sarah all over again—my girlfriend disappearing without a trace—except this time, I can do something about it.

Maybe it will be good for me—therapeutic, in a way. What do you think, Noelle? Would my therapist approve?

I switch back to cSpy.

You're near the highway, right before the mountain pass.

I grab my keys, slam the rest of the coffee, and head for my Porsche.

Don't worry, Noelle. As my mother said, I do like playing the hero.

TWENTY-TWO

NOELLE

Now

I'm blindfolded and yanked from the car. A hand on my back forces me forward, and I stumble, unable to see my surroundings, aware I'm shaking—from the cold. Or maybe from the gun shoved in my face.

Something is wrong. Very wrong. This isn't what I asked for. All I wanted was to be taken from my home. Dropped off somewhere. No ride in the trunk, no blindfold, no gun, none of whatever this is.

I hold still as they pat me down with rough brisk hands, somehow missing the phone tucked into my back pocket—likely on purpose, I tell myself. Because this is just an act. And yet...

The gun reflected the light like it was metal, not the blue rubber I'd seen online. My breath hitches as I see it again in my head.

The website mentioned a safe word for the more violent kidnappings, but they'd never given me one. Since mine was a simple kidnapping there was no *need* for one. A door opens. Rough hands grab me by the waist and push me into a vehicle set high—an SUV or a pickup, I think. It dips slightly with my weight, the smell of an air freshener strong in my nostrils.

"Lie down," the man growls. When I hesitate—I just need to tell them they've got the wrong person—a hand smacks across my cheek hard, leaving my ears ringing. "Lie the fuck down," he snaps.

I do as I'm told.

Distant conversation.

A rush of thoughts—I'm not who they think I am. They shouldn't be taking me anywhere—they should be *letting me go*.

I rub my face against the back seat, catching the edge of the fabric blindfold on what must be the metal of a seatbelt. I drag it across the clip repeatedly, edging the fabric up until I can catch a glimpse of where I am. The back of a pickup, one with four doors.

The driver's-side door opens.

The truck settles as someone swings in and starts the engine. My heart thumps in my chest, heavy, and my limbs tingle. Adrenaline. Fear.

"Sorry." A man's voice, quiet, reserved. Different from whoever tossed me in the vehicle and hit me.

I mumble into the duct tape, hoping he gets it—I want to talk.

"No," he says. "None of that. I'll take it off when we get there."

The truck moves, and I listen for anything that will tell me more, but it's only the man and me in the truck, and it's well insulated enough I can't hear anything else. "I won't hurt you," he goes on. "I'm sure you're scared, but my job is just to hang on to you for a while."

That sounds more normal. Visions of stun guns and being held perilously out of a skyscraper-worthy building would have been my next concerns. Maybe it was a fake gun. Maybe they spray-painted them black, or used metallic paint, or—

Or, he's lying. Someone hit me. Hard. My cheek still burns, and I suspect if I were to look in the mirror, I'd find a handprint there. He's telling me what I want to hear so I cooperate.

No. The website specifically mentioned slapping. I just need to keep it together a little longer.

We drive for twenty minutes. The truck stops, the engine cuts off, and he gets out, slamming the door behind him. I listen intently, but there's nothing until the door at my feet opens. Hands grab my ankles, slide me down the seat like I weigh nothing, and before I can react, a hand is at the back of my neck, steering me.

"Step up," the man says. I still nearly trip over whatever's before me. My sense of the space around me changes, grows quieter. Light seeps in from one side, and where I've managed to get the blindfold up a smidge, I see brown carpet. We're inside somewhere.

"I'm going to take the tape off. Don't bother screaming or trying to run. We're in the middle of nowhere. No one to save you out here." His voice is curt, to the point, but not cruel. Matter of fact.

It's an act. It has to be. An actor who fakes a kidnapping, who plays out someone's twisted dreams or carries out a prank on someone's friend. No one in their right mind would pay to have a gun put to their head.

He unwinds the tape from my wrists first, then turns me to face him and peels back the tape from my mouth. I take a deep breath, my lungs expanding to their fullest. I can breathe again. The blindfold comes off last, and I can't help but stare.

Vivid green eyes meet mine. He has long dark hair, twisted into a ponytail. He's not just well built, but solidly muscled with wide shoulders and corded arms, tanned skin, a tattoo creeping from beneath the black leather jacket draped over his wide shoulders, crawling up his neck to his jaw. Tattoos cover his hands, too, one inked black, white skeletal fingers in relief. My stomach lurches. I try not to judge on appearance—at the hospital, I care for all sorts of people—but he's frightening based off his looks alone.

"You got a problem?" His words come out cold, tough guy. I step back.

"No. Sorry." I clear my throat. "But I think there *is* a problem." I take a quick glance around. It's a motel room, two beds covered in cheap plastic quilts, a nightstand, an old television, all in oranges and reds.

He grins, white teeth flashing. "That so?"

"I'm not who you think I am. You've got me confused with someone else."

"I can't help you with that." He points at the nearest bed. "Sit down."

He's playing tough. And he plays it well. But I'm the paying client, and I need to go, need to get away before Daniel catches up with me. Shoot, I still need to dispose of the phone he might be tracking at this very moment. If he can tell where I am, he'll come after me—I won't get the twenty-four hour lead time I've been planning on. I glance at the motel room door. How far behind me is he? An hour? Two? Would he have gone to his mother's for dinner without me?

"There's been a misunderstanding. I need to speak to your boss. Please."

The man closes the distance between us faster than someone his size should be able to, and I'm across the room against the wall in a flash. I stare at him with wide eyes, watching his movement for anything that looks like he's coming at me. I have no weapon, but I'll defend myself, fake kidnapping be damned.

He stops. Opens his mouth, hesitates as he flicks his eyes up and down me, then shuts it again.

"Wasn't going to hit you." He gives me a lingering look and points to the bed again. "Sit down." I'm not able to move, still staring at him waiting for his next move. "Please," he says, trying unsuccessfully to soften his voice.

If he's from Ultimate Kidnapping, he shouldn't be acting this way. He shouldn't apologize or tell me he's not going to hit me—because he *is* going to hit me, if that's what he thinks I'm paying for.

"What happens next?" I ask.

He shoots a look my way, then turns to peer out the curtains. "I'm on babysitting duty. Not my usual kind of job. My boss is gonna come get you so he can hand you off to"—a shrug—"whoever it is they're handing you off to. That's all I know."

That doesn't sound right. The words I heard before echo in my head. *Scare her a little.*

I go still, the pieces falling into place. The gun was real. They haven't asked for the money I owe them. They forgot to take the phone away and leave it in the apartment. He's going to *hand me off* to someone. Adrenaline rushes through me, and I wonder if the phone in my pocket might be a good thing.

Because that's it. I'm right. Ultimate Kidnapping won't be completing the job I hired them for. Someone else grabbed me first. My fake kidnapping has turned real. It's the only way it makes sense. But even that *doesn't* make sense. What are the odds? Nil. The rational nurse side of my brain can't force it to make sense.

But who would kidnap me, and why?

Daniel. Michael. Maybe someone who found out I'm investigating my aunt's death and wants to put a stop to it—but that brings me back to Daniel. Otherwise, I don't know anyone who would want to hurt me.

Except... I did have that patient die recently. The husband cried and filed a lawsuit and—no. I can't imagine him sending someone after the nurse who'd held his wife's hand as she passed away, even if he does blame me.

I come back to Daniel, who I've regained some level of independence from in the aftermath of the car accident.

My hand raises to my mouth, remembering the car nearly mowing me down mere days ago at Pike Place Market, right after that man bumped into me. What if...

My mind spins. Daniel could have arranged to have me followed. Could have arranged to have me hit by another car, which might mean he had me hit by the initial car months ago. Maybe this is some sick plan to keep me dependent on him. Needing him. *With* him, because surely he senses I've pulled away. And a second round of a car hitting me hadn't worked—I had avoided the car this time, hadn't I? Maybe this was his next attempt.

Which means I just have to relax. It means Daniel wants to play hero again. To come to my rescue. Except...

This isn't a game I want to play. One of these times, if it is Daniel behind all of this, success will mean the car hits me hard enough to cause permanent damage—or kill me. My mind buzzes, thinking of Sarah—of Justine—both gone in the wind, never heard from again.

Is this a twisted game Daniel plays with the women in his life?

The man twitches the curtain, watching for his associate, if he's to be believed; Daniel, if he's working for him.

I have to go. I have to get out. Daniel will not be my savior, because Daniel is almost certainly the dangerous one.

"Can I get some water?" I ask finally, keeping my voice quiet, tamping down the adrenaline spiking my nervous system.

He nods and points at the sink in the back, not one for words.

I slide off the bed and scurry to put distance between us, as if that will somehow clear my mind, let me think straight. The motel door is locked and chained, and I haven't heard another noise, save what must be the highway not too far off. I turn on the faucet, fill a plastic cup, and take a long drink. The water is grainy, almost sour, but I haven't had anything to drink in hours, and I refill it. I drink again, this time slower, letting my eyes wander into the dark bathroom. There's a window.

The phone in my back pocket vibrates. I grab at it, hit the volume down button, cutting the vibration short, but it's too late. He heard it.

"Give it to me. Now." He closes the space between us. He shucked his jacket when the heater kicked on, leaving him in a white T-shirt, the faint lines of tattoos beneath the fabric. He holds his hand out, and I shrink back. "Phone," he says in a commanding voice.

I swallow, pull it from my pocket, and he snatches it away.

"Who did you text?"

"No one, I—"

"Sit down." He points to the bed, and I go.

He strides back over, flashes the phone in my direction, getting access with facial ID. Then he's scrolling. After a moment he sits back on the bed opposite mine, much too close for comfort. I swallow, and it feels as though my heart is in my throat.

I haven't texted anyone, but what if he finds the spyware, just like I did? Will he blame me?

"What's up with this Daniel guy?" he asks, voice softer.

"Nothing."

"Really? Do you often get threatening messages and call it nothing?"

After a moment he tosses the phone down, opens his mouth to say something, hesitates, and then mutters, "What a dick." He goes back to the curtain.

I decide to try one more time. "Do you know who hired you? Or who hired your boss?"

He glances over his shoulder at me but doesn't respond. Not that I expected him to.

"What's your name?" I ask. Maybe if I can get him to answer one question, he'll answer another.

"Jack," he mutters. "And I don't know who hired me. I don't get to know stuff like that. My boss tells me what to do. I do it. Safer for everyone that way."

I bite my lip and wonder if he's lying. But it doesn't matter because I can't be here when Daniel arrives. If I'm somehow wrong, and Daniel *isn't* behind this, he'll blame me for getting kidnapped—of course, he will, and knowing what he's capable of, that he is dangerous too, I won't argue. A knot forms in my chest. He'll blame me, even though Jack is *not* the kidnapper I hired. I almost laugh at what my life has become—it would be a sad humorless laugh. And even worse is that it's entirely possible Daniel is behind this. Maybe he found out what I set in motion when I contacted Ultimate Kidnapping—maybe this is his revenge. Meaning, he'll blame me either way.

I eye Jack's truck keys, resting on the comforter of the second bed. Another glance at him, standing motionless at the window. I ease forward to the edge of the bed, reach across— and snatch them, as fast as I dare, as soundlessly as possible.

This is what matters: whether Daniel is behind this or not, I'm still gone. Still caught on camera being kidnapped from my home. My goal is still achieved. I just have to escape Jack now.

"Can I use the bathroom?" I ask in the smallest, most frightened voice I can manage.

He waves a hand at me.

I retreat into the bathroom, heart in my throat, and hope the window isn't sealed shut.

TWENTY-THREE

NOELLE

Two Months Ago

It's as though Justine doesn't exist. She didn't attend Daniel's high school, nor any of the neighboring ones, including the private schools. I even checked several years ahead and behind to account for Daniel dating someone younger or older. Furthermore, there are no women reported missing with the first name Justine, or anything similar. Daniel is not friends on Facebook with anyone named Justine. She doesn't exist in his mother's albums.

She is, effectively, a ghost.

I'm poring through an online missing person database, looking for anyone by the name Justine who would be the right age, when my phone rings.

"Hello?" I don't check the caller since I know it's not Daniel. He's busy on a case today, one that should take the next several hours. That's something else I do—memorize his schedule, giving me the ability to predict when I may hear from him, see him. I plan my life around these spurts of time when he can't touch me, even if he is recording my every movement.

"Noelle?" Kari's voice comes through the line.

"Hey! How's Bea doing?" Her surgery was this morning. I waited with Kari until it was over, when the surgeon came out and said she did great. She told us to go home, that it would be a few hours until she woke up. "I was going to come visit when—"

"She's dead." Kari's voice is short, somber. A weight to it I don't associate with Kari.

Her words penetrate.

"Dead?" I ask. "That's not—" I was going to say *that's not possible*. But it is. I see patients die regularly. Including patients who have routine coronary artery bypass. "The surgeon said—"

"She's dead, Noelle." Kari's breathing hitches, like she's holding back a sob. "I'm at the hospital. They're using all these medical terms, and I don't know what they mean, and—I need you."

Silence. I try to understand, to process how my aunt could possibly be dead. She was a good candidate for the surgery—a one percent chance of mortality, almost nothing in the world of medicine—the surgeon told me it went flawlessly. That she would spend twenty-four hours recovering in the ICU, then go to the step-down unit, where she'd recover until she could go home. At which point I would go to stay with her and Kari until—

My breath comes up short.

She's dead. *My aunt is dead.* And she shouldn't be.

Which means...

I'd warned Daniel he wouldn't see me for a couple weeks. That for several months, I'd be at my aunt's more than usual. But he saw through my thinly veiled attempt to get away from him. He petitioned me to find someone else to do it—volunteered to *pay* someone else to do it, but I had fought him on this one. I figured he'd come around to it—he liked my aunt, and he's a doctor, so surely, he could understand.

But, of course, that's not at all what Daniel thought, what he would allow for.

"I'll be there," I murmur to Kari. We hang up.

Not two seconds later, my phone rings again. Daniel.

"Hello?" I ask, my voice hollow, not quite able to fathom Kari's news.

"Noelle," Daniel says, and he uses a tone like he did when he mentioned things like *maternal mortality* and *higher risk of mortality for the child, too.* Except they weren't the ones at risk today. "How did your aunt's surgery go?" he continues, his voice too smooth, too knowing, and I realize, without a doubt, Daniel did something to her.

TWENTY-FOUR

DANIEL

Now

My Porsche can go from zero to sixty miles per hour in three seconds flat.

It's not why I bought it, but it's a nice detail, something people ask when they admire its sleek paint job, the streamlined body. It's useful now, as I race to the mountains for you. I saved you once—I suspect, Noelle, from your ex's attempt at revenge. Who else would mow down a young woman with a car? Pike Place Market is a pedestrian area. It had to be a targeted attack. You haven't connected the dots, but I have. I told you after that I would keep you safe. And I have. I can save you again, and it will be like last time—your undying gratitude. Your love. If there's any doubt in your mind who you belong to, it will be dispelled.

The mobile cSpy app is up on my phone, and you've yet to move a muscle. You're sleeping, likely, maybe in a car, or held in what is surely a seedy cheap hotel. I really do need you in my life, Noelle, and you need me. This is a great example of that.

Have they tied you up? Hurt you? Are you helpless to their desires? See? You think I'm bad, and I will admit, I have a temper at times, but I'm not like that. I, at least, keep you safe.

After such an experience, my home will no doubt be a slice of heaven you will crave and appreciate. I just have to get to you.

I'm not worried about whoever took you. I wrestled in high school, played football in undergrad, and spend several mornings a week in the gym to maintain a physique that impresses each and every female I pass, and some of the men, too. Plus, I can be quite persuasive.

I pull over for gas, foot tapping as the engine fills. There's only eighty-nine octane, not the usual ninety-three I use, and I cringe as I fill my tank with it. I should have filled up in the city instead of this backwoods piece-of-shit gas station in the middle of the night. Another sacrifice, Noelle. Do you appreciate me yet?

Aren't you glad I've been watching you, Noelle? Without the cameras, I wouldn't know you've been a victim of a crime.

You're welcome.

You practically owe me your life. No, you *do* owe me your life. The least you can do is be a good wife to me. I should have brought the ring. Propose to you the moment I pull you away from whoever has you. My mother's brows would knit, knowing what I'd done, taking off after criminals. She worries about me, as mothers do. But what a moment it would have been.

I picture you, sobbing, leaning on me, hugging me tight as though you'll never let go. I'd kiss you. Tell you no matter what they did to you, I still love you, don't blame you. I wouldn't prostrate myself at your feet, as so many men do, but I'd tell you what I wanted and ask if you want the same. Of course, you'd say yes. How can you say no to a man who has saved your life not once, but twice?

Maybe I'll ask you even without the ring.
Your knight in shining armor.
The Porsche does shine, you know.

TWENTY-FIVE

NOELLE

Now

Cold night air combined with adrenaline creates a fine tremble through my body as I peer around the edge of the motel, icy grass crunching beneath my feet. A pair of headlights sweeps over the parking lot, and I freeze, wait for them to disappear. But they only grow brighter.

I swallow back fear and try to summon the courage I found moments ago as I dropped through the bathroom window and sprinted around the building. I'm almost free—I need to keep hidden to stay that way.

Jack isn't at the front window, and when the headlights swing away from me as the car parks, I run across the lot to his truck. But there's no way to unlock it from the passenger's side without using the fob, and I can't risk it beeping.

I edge to the back of the truck, waiting for whoever has arrived to disappear into their motel room. But the car door opens, a figure emerges, and—

I stop breathing.

It's Daniel.

His face isn't visible, but after a year of monitoring his body language, I can tell it's him—the line of his shoulders, how he adjusts his overcoat, how his palm rests over the car as he steps away from it. His freaking *precious*.

For the briefest moment, I consider going to him and letting him play the hero again. To save me from this fiasco that I set in motion. But then I come to my senses and remember.

Sarah.

Justine.

Aunt Beatrice.

And now me.

The names pulse through me, all his victims, and my heart thuds faster as I realize that if he were coming to save me for real, he'd bring the police. There isn't a sound, much less a siren, for miles.

No, he did this. He arranged for my kidnapping.

When Daniel turns my way, I duck, frozen in place, the temporary courage that led me to snatch the keys, to climb out a window, to sprint to the truck, almost gone in the face of his presence.

He swaggers up to the motel door, tucks the phone into his coat, runs his hand through his Ken-doll hair like he's preparing for a date, not to save his girlfriend's life, and reaches out to knock.

The door swings wide.

Jack.

Daniel, who backs down to no one, takes a half step back, then straightens, as though realizing what he's done. Blood roars in my ears, and I'm unable to pull away. Daniel isn't acting like someone who's here to collect—from the way he pulls back, takes a beat to recover, I would say he's surprised by Jack, his presence, his stature.

With the two men distracted by one another, this is the best chance I'm going to get. If Jack hasn't realized I'm gone already, he'll know within seconds when Daniel demands he hand me over.

I can just make out their distant voices, echoing across the parking lot.

"I'm here for my girlfriend," Daniel says.

Jack grins and sweeps an arm toward the room and steps back, giving both Daniel and me a view inside the empty room. "Do you see your girlfriend?"

I take that moment to move around the truck, clasp the door handle, shove the key in, carefully open it the absolute minimum required for me to slide through.

Daniel growls something unintelligible, and just before I close the door, Jack sneers. "Let me guess. You're Daniel."

I close the door. Hit the lock button. Shove the key in the ignition—

I can't help but glance up one last time, wishing they'd step inside, that Jack realizes I'm taking too long in the bathroom, and maybe he could just go to check—but instead, he lets Daniel step past him—and looks right at me.

Right freaking at me.

He doesn't so much as blink.

I'm not about to wait around and see if he thinks he's hallucinating; if he's about to realize he's *not*, and that, yes, I am in fact in his truck.

I start the engine, slam down the clutch—thank god I can drive a manual—and pull away, shifting through second, third, fourth—through the parking lot, taking a right turn on the frontage road too fast, sliding on the ice.

In seconds, I'm on the highway, the motel, the men, fading into the past, right where I intend to keep them.

TWENTY-SIX

DANIEL

Now

White squares come into focus as I come to again, and I find myself counting them to the beat of a *ding, ding, ding*. It's a strangely familiar sound, though I can't quite place it. Footsteps, first slow, then fast, and someone touches my wrist.

"Mr. Ashcroft?" A woman's warm, soothing voice.

"Doctor," I echo her words. "Dr. Ashcroft."

I'm still counting the squares when a face comes into view. She's not much older than you, Noelle, and just as pretty. Her skin is dark, smooth, and her brown eyes peer at me with concern.

"I'm Zoey." She presses a hand to my shoulder. Her touch is gentle, her fingers warm, and I shut my eyes to bask in it. It's how my mother touched me when I was a boy. How you, a long time ago, cared for me when I had the flu. "I'm your nurse. Do you remember what happened?"

I remember you're gone, Noelle. That I failed to rescue you.

"No," I say and falter as I realize that's partially true. "But

I'm in pain. Ten out of ten. I'd like morphine. Or fentanyl. And something oral. What did the doctor write for?"

Zoey's eyes grow round, realizing I'm going to be *that* patient, but I don't back down. Being in control is who I am, even if I am nearly flat on my back, bandages over one arm, my side, and an IV in my arm. She promises to get the doctor, and I shut my eyes, let her go.

I lied to my nurse, Noelle. I remember a little. The most important part. That in the midst of trying to prove to you that I will do anything, *anything*, to make my plan for us work, I failed.

And now, you're gone.

That's not how things were supposed to go.

I remember a man, too. Tattoos. Long hair. Trouble. Are you with him now? Is he the one who—I try to sit up, but I can't, realize even pressing down with my hand hurts.

I raise my left hand—broken fingers, wrapped in gauze and tape. Blood has dried along the bandage. Something in my shoulder, too, and my abdomen feels like someone yanked out my intestines, then shoved them back in. I swallow. Ease back on the bed. Clench my eyes shut.

I thought this would be easy. I'd collect you. Pay off your kidnapper. We'd get back to normal, but a new normal—like before, when I saved you, and you realized how much you needed me. But now, I see my plan has gone awry.

What I want to know, Noelle, is what went wrong? Where did you go? Your phone was there, I remember seeing it on the bed, the weatherproof case I got for you recognizable anywhere, before I lose track of whatever happened in the aftermath— whatever left me in this state, begging a *nurse* for narcotics. But you were already gone.

A knock at the door and a white-coated physician strides in. She's short, blonde, and far too perky for my liking. How can I trust someone who's so damn perky when

I still don't have any morphine, and I've been beaten nearly to death?

"Dr. Ashcroft." She holds out a hand. "I'm Dr. Harrison. How are you feeling?"

She perches on the side of my bed. Doesn't she know that's against hospital regulation? Doesn't she know just wearing a white coat from one patient room to the next is a risk? I have *wounds*. When was the last time she laundered it? From the mustard stain on the collar, I'll bet at least a week.

"In pain." I repeat what I told the nurse, ending in asking about meds.

"Well, Dr. Ashcroft, I'm happy to give you pain medicine. You've certainly been through an ordeal. But before I do, the police are here to talk to you."

The police. Of course, they are. I, Dr. Daniel Ashcroft, was assaulted.

And they don't know that you're gone, Noelle. Is now the right time to tell them? I'd hoped to keep them out of this narrative all together. Though I know plenty of cops, have several willing to do me favors, they tend to complicate things.

The doctor disappears, and I try to get my thoughts in order —the biggest issue will be how I discovered you were missing, though cSpy is likely common in their world. And there's nothing illegal about it. Lots of spouses keep an eye on each other and another doctor I work with uses it with his kids. But the cameras, well, that's a different matter.

Two uniformed officers enter, but before they can so much as introduce themselves, Mother shoves in around them. Zoey is there, reaching to stop her, but she smacks her hand away.

"Daniel." Mother sounds relieved. "Are you all right?" She's at my bedside in a moment, the back of her hand to my forehead, my cheek, feeling for a fever despite the issue being that I got the shit kicked out of me. "I came as soon as they called. I've been trying to reach you all night—"

"Ma'am—" one of the officers begins.

"Get out," she snaps, whirling on them. "I know my son's rights. He has the right to a lawyer if you're going to question him."

"Mother, it's fine." I offer the cops a polite smile, as though I'm more than happy to assist them, but I know my mother won't be done until she's forced them out of the room, and that's fine by me. I need to find you, Noelle. The bureaucratic bullshit of working with the police will only slow that down.

"I'll call your attorney," she says, yanking up a folding chair and sitting primly on the edge. "The important thing is, you're alive. You're okay." She blinks through tears, then leans close, pressing one hand gently on my bandaged arm. "Oh, Daniel," she murmurs. "Who did this to you?"

The other officer opens his mouth to speak, but she shoots him a glare, and that's that. As it should be. My mother should be respected.

"We'll need a statement, Dr. Ashcroft," the officer finally manages. "But I can see you're busy right now." They take their leave with a prim nod from Mother.

I look over at her, still woozy from the pain, and force a smile. "What did you need, Mother? You said you tried to get a hold of me?" She touches my shoulder. I wince.

"Oh, darling." Mother pats my shoulder. Inhales through flared nostrils, eyes skimming the medical equipment around me, trying to hide her fear. It's nothing but another evening for me, except the fact *I'm* the one on the patient bed. But for her, surely this is intimidating. Maybe even a bit of a memory of the chemo she underwent at the cancer center. "You're okay. That's all the matters."

The nurse enters with what appears to be morphine. She offers Mother a smile. Scrubs the hub of my IV with alcohol. Slowly pushes the med and follows it up with saline. I was about to ask my mother, "What is it?" But I recline back, relaxing into the pillow as the morphine takes hold.

Mother gathers herself and looks at me the same way she did when I was a child, and irritation floats through the fading pain for a moment. But then adoration overrides it, and I reach out, grasp her hand. I have to find you, Noelle. Not just for me, for us, but for her, too. She's given me so much. It's the least I can do.

TWENTY-SEVEN

NOELLE

Now

The sun wakes me.

Yellow rays glare through the windshield, and I raise a hand to block them, blinking, swallowing the sticky pastiness that is my dry mouth. I wear a hoodie I found tucked into a black duffel bag in the backseat, and I yank the hood up, shove my hands into the front pocket, shiver as the engine warms and the heater clicks to life.

I can make out mountains on the horizon but they are not mountains I am familiar with—which means I drove pretty far last night. When the engine is warm, I find a gas station, grab a cheap coffee, a snack, and glance at the map nailed to the bulletin board inside.

I'm in Oregon, but not on the highway that's a straight shot from Seattle to California—somewhere along the way, in my panic to put distance between myself and Daniel, I turned off, and am now farther east than I realized. But that's not a bad thing. I-5 is the most obvious route to take. I just need to make it to California. To a place where I can pick out a new name for myself and be one more person who wanted to escape their so-called life.

My hand is on the stick shift, and I'm blinking from lack of sleep. The truck accelerates through the empty parking lot back toward the highway when a voice jolts me wide awake.

"Did you really think I'd let you take my truck?"

I stomp on the brake, forget the clutch, and the truck stalls out with a violent jerk. My hands, suddenly clammy, slide over the wheel, and my first thought is *Out! Get out of the truck!*

But a hand closes over my arm before I can. When I yank away, it tightens, and in a flash, too easily for someone his size, he maneuvers from the back seat to the front passenger's. I flinch, waiting for what's next—violence, whatever it is men like him do to the people they're paid to kidnap—and worse, the ones that get away.

But he doesn't do any of those things.

He releases my arm and sits back in the seat, palms up, relaxed. He stares straight ahead, out the windshield, right into that damn sunrise, which any other day I'd appreciate.

"How did you find me?" I manage after a moment. My voice doesn't even waver, and I clench my fists, feign confidence.

Jack taps the dash with one finger. "Got GPS tracking on it. Took your boyfriend's Porsche to follow you. Figured he wouldn't be driving it anytime soon." His hand lifts, in it, a key identical to the one I stole from him. "Got into the truck with my spare key back at the gas station."

I open my mouth to ask what *wouldn't be driving it anytime soon* means—visions of Daniel bloody, even dead, flash through my mind. No emotions follow, other than an awareness that if Jack has it in him to do that to Daniel, though Daniel certainly deserves it, he's not someone I am safe with.

I press my hands between my knees. They're cold, but also, they won't stop trembling. My whole body is trembling, in fact.

Jack knew where I was the whole time. Just like Daniel every moment of the past year. A hole of dread opens up in my stomach, threatening to swallow me. I have to get away. I can't live my life under the scrutiny of someone who's waiting for an opportunity to hurt me.

"What now?" I ask. I escaped Daniel. I won't let Jack be another man who tries to control me. Whatever it takes, I *will* escape him.

"Now?" He shrugs, sighs. "Some decent coffee would be nice. Instead of"—he waves a hand at the gas station cup—"whatever that is."

Jack directs me to a diner in the next town. Every mile we drive, I consider how I'll get away this time.

But he's weaving a tale, claiming I don't need to escape him.

"I lost someone I loved in a position not so different from your own. They had an abusive boyfriend." His lips press together. "That's why I beat the shit out of yours. Let him know what it feels like. Anyway. Your kidnapping, the whole babysitting-you thing? I don't need the job. Don't need the money. I *let you* get away last night. Now?" He turns back to me. "I'm offering my help."

"You're not working for Daniel?" I ask. This could be the next move in Daniel's game—let me escape, lure me into the illusion of safety, only to hunt me down again. It doesn't make sense, but *Daniel* doesn't make sense, so it doesn't stop me from considering the possibility.

He shrugs. "He might be who paid my boss for the job. I don't handle that part, like I said. My job is to carry it out—well, *was*. I quit."

I go still at his words. This complete stranger expects me to believe he's quit his job to help me, his would-be victim, escape. After spending all of half an hour in my presence.

"You tracked me down to offer me your help after you—" *Kidnapped me. Kept me trapped in a hotel room. All because he lost someone?* Whatever that meant. Then again, he *had* looked at me. *Right* at me—and done what? Kept Daniel's attention. Which let me leave. But it doesn't add up.

Even if he is a kindhearted criminal who's had a bad experience with someone he loves, people don't do this sort of thing—not unless there's something in it for them.

I eye him, wondering what that thing could be.

We arrive at the diner, a squat brick building with a row of windows facing the parking lot. Inside, we take the last booth in the row, sitting across from one another. Coffee is on the table in seconds, a waitress sliding menus in front of us.

Jack reaches for cream and pours it from a tiny carafe into his coffee.

I clutch my own mug in my hands, the heat seeping into me. Words are on the tip of my tongue, though it might be a mistake to confide in him. The waitress comes by again, we order, and I study him the whole time. I can't believe someone who would plan to hurt me would bring me to a diner where I could get help if I wanted to.

"I'm confused," I finally say. "And here is why." I outline my position—that I'd arranged to have myself kidnapped, that he arrived instead, then Daniel conveniently showed up. "I don't know who I can trust."

Jack stares at me a moment, eyes a little too wide. "You arranged to have yourself kidnapped?" Incredulity fills his voice, and maybe, a hint of admiration, too.

I hesitate. "I tried to. But I think you beat them to it."

He holds my gaze, then looks away fast, and I'm certain of it now—he's holding something back. But I don't think he's working for Daniel. At least, not knowingly.

"What were you supposed to do with me?" I ask again. That's what cops do in shows—ask the same question, over and over, waiting to get a different answer, to prove the person is lying.

Jack sips his coffee. "Wait for my boss to come get you."

"Not Daniel?"

A single shake of his head. "Nope. But that doesn't mean my boss wouldn't have had plans to turn you over to him."

"I don't want your help." My words come out strong, but I'm hiding hesitation. Something in me *does* want help, desperately, and that makes me question my own ability to make a rational decision. It makes me think I need to do the opposite of what I *want* to do, because probably, I'm wrong.

"Okay. But let me make sure you understand your situation." Jack steeples his hands. "You've got my boss after you, who gets paid a tidy sum of cash to deliver you to the client. You've got your boyfriend after you. Neither of them are good news, if you know what I mean." He raises one brow. "And you've got me, who let you *steal* my truck last night so you could get away. Now, I'm offering my assistance. I will help you escape. Help you disappear or whatever it is you planned to do. And you're saying no?"

"I don't need your help." My words come out weaker, and the upturn of his lips tells me I'm not the only one who knows I'm full of shit.

"Yeah, you do," he says, and there's a finality in his words that tells me he's not giving me a choice in the matter.

TWENTY-EIGHT

DANIEL

Now

The best part about having a girlfriend who is a nurse is that everyone loves you, Noelle. Even people who don't know you adore you. Nursing is the most trusted profession; did you know that?

Doctors come in at a lowly third place, though if they knew what's really said in the OR, or the conversations over drinks in med school and residency, I have no doubt we'd rank somewhere among used-car dealers.

A small crowd teeters on the edge of the police tape as I prep to do an interview with a local reporter in front of the police station. I've been patched up, given antibiotics, and taken pain medicine from my own stash. My car, which that Neanderthal *stole*, has been retrieved, processed by the police in record time, thanks to my friends in the department, and thoroughly cleaned. The Neanderthal kept my keys, so I'm using my spare set.

The physician urged me to stay another night at the hospital, but I have no time to lie around in a hospital bed. This is my sacrifice for you. One of many, to make sure we stay together no matter what. I will go to any length for you, Noelle, don't you see that?

I have work to do. This press conference, for example. Contacting my camera guy to remove all but a single camera from your apartment because that looks better for the police.

Being the concerned boyfriend I am, I explained, I installed a security camera aimed at your front door—per your request, of course. Same with cSpy—see, I even have it on *my* phone, so we can locate one another at a moment's notice. Just. In. Case. That's what I tell the police, and now, Megan, the blonde woman with bright red lipstick and a smile as big as her bullshit. I also had any other evidence of my keeping an eye on you removed—like your laptop, with its keystroke recorder—just before the police arrived.

No evidence left behind.

"Dr. Ashcroft, does Ms. Thomas have any enemies you are aware of?"

"Of course not, Megan. Noelle is well liked by everyone who knows her." I don't smile this time. I'm in pain, thanks to that Neanderthal, and besides, my mother reminded me grieving boyfriends don't smile. I am grieving, Noelle, I really am. I almost had you within my reach at that seedy motel before you slipped from my grasp. That's not how it was supposed to go.

I have to find you, even if my injuries will keep me here in Seattle. Which is exactly what I intend to do, just as soon as I escape my third interview of the day. Megan is talking again, asking basic questions, then giving me encouraging smiles not unlike those from the crowd watching the interview. Except one person, whose expression is more of a scowl.

Megan wishes me the best, I thank her, then I head for the Porsche, trying to hide my limp.

My phone vibrates, *Seattle General* pops up, and I decline

it. I've already canceled my shifts for the week to look for you, Noelle. There's no business that can't wait.

We're on a corner in downtown Seattle, the block split between the hospital and an espresso shop with outdoor seating. Another reporter calls my name as I go to leave, but she's shouldered out of the way by a young woman who doesn't have kind or thoughtful questions for me. Perhaps the only woman in Seattle I couldn't permanently acquire, should I want her— Kari, your oh-so-lovely cousin who never hesitates to make her opinion of me clear.

She swears what happened between us will never happen again—she was drunk and vulnerable, after all—incredibly convenient for me. But it was merely a means to an end. The challenge would almost be worth it, Noelle, but don't worry—I won't be tempted.

My phone vibrates again. I shut the screen off, ignoring the voicemail someone from the hospital has left me. Likely, they want to offer condolences that you are gone, perhaps assistance I don't need.

"Daniel!" Kari's voice rings out from behind me.

Your cousin is about to cause a scene.

"I have to find Noelle," I call, raising a hand to her. "Feel free to call—"

"Daniel!" Her voice is sharper this time, and there's something in the hard, furious set of her jaw that tells me not to ignore her.

I pause. "Get in," I say. "We can talk on the way."

Now she's the one who hesitates, likely remembering what happened the last time I welcomed her into my car, but a dozen people are watching, the camerawoman approaching, ready to record. The cold Seattle wind kicks up, bringing a chill from across the Puget Sound, and with it, the first sputtering of what looks like a downpour.

"Fine." She opens the opposite door.

The camerawoman is now filming, and I wonder if this will be used against me.

Then again, when they realize she is your cousin they will cast it in a different light. At least, for now. I am aware it's always the boyfriend, the husband, the guy who is the prime suspect. I'll just have to make sure they don't drag my name through the dirt for extra views on their website, which means I need to be more entertaining *looking* for you than being accused of being the reason you're missing.

Our doors shut, tinted windows limiting who can see us. I offer a perfunctory, grieving wave, and say through clenched teeth, "Look sad. Wave."

She does. I gas the engine, and we disappear around the next one-way street.

"What do you want?" I ask.

"What did you do to Noelle?"

I sigh. "Nothing, darling."

"Don't call me that."

"Why not?" I smile over at her. If looks could kill, I would be a bug on her shoe. "What should I call you? Baby Momma? You're taking your prenatal vitamins, yes?"

That's right, Noelle. I fucked your cousin. Right around the time you tried to die on me. It was the perfect revenge and grows more amusing every day. You have no idea. She was drunk, devastated you'd nearly died—of course your boyfriend would need to comfort her. Buy her a drink. Offer her drunk self a ride home. A hug turned into a kiss turned into... more. It was easy, too easy. Some part of her always wanted me—it was obvious—so I gave her what she wanted. And soon, she'll give me what I want. It's a good deal, don't you think?

What hasn't worked out so well is the part where she's waged war to get you to end things. But luckily, I've had the perfect line of defense for that—maternal morbidity being at an all-time high and all.

I have everything I need within my grasp. Except you.

"She's missing. You're in the spotlight," Kari says. "I think it's obvious what's wrong with this picture."

"I was nearly beaten to death trying to save her." I point to the bandages. "I shouldn't even be driving."

"Then why are you?" Kari, who isn't wearing her seatbelt, twists to look at me. Her belly bulges out, her shirt slides up, and I can see the bump that is the baby within. I reach out to touch it, but she yanks the shirt down and glares. She's feisty. Kind of like you used to be.

"I'm looking for Noelle," I say, drawing my hand back. She's fuming, her nostrils flaring—because of you? Because I tried to touch her stomach? Who knows with this one?

"By parading around Seattle doing interviews?" she asks.

"You really shouldn't get your blood pressure up like this," I tell her. "It's not good for the baby."

My words silence her for half a beat, her face going a darker shade of pink. Embarrassed? Angry? Guilty? I look away to hide my smile. I don't like Kari, but she does provide plenty of entertainment.

"Answer me. What did you do to her?" Her words are poison, so quiet I look away from the road for a half second to judge her mental state. Pregnant women tend to be unstable, a fact I regularly witness placing epidurals.

"Nothing." I pull to the side of the road and wave for her to get out. "I tried to save her. I *am* trying to save her. A man had her and he"—I motion a second time—"nearly killed me. I've contacted the police. I've offered a reward. And now, I intend to hire a private investigator to help me do all the things the police won't."

"Like what?" She still hasn't budged from her seat.

"Illegal things." I give her a look. "Things you shouldn't be involved in."

Her gaze softens almost imperceptibly, my charm working on her even now. No one can resist me.

"Don't fuck this up," she says and opens the door.

"Wait," I call as she starts to shut it. "Here." I hold out my hand as though I want to take hers, one of those in between handshakes/handholds men and women do when neither is quite sure if they should shake hands or not. Her eyes narrow, but she accepts my grip, and the five folded up hundred-dollar bills in my hand. It's the least I can do.

She is carrying my baby, after all.

TWENTY-NINE

NOELLE

Now

A motel appears in the distance, and Jack, who's taken over driving, pulls off. We left the Porsche where it could be found and drove several hours, Jack announcing we should stop for the night and pulling off the highway a mile or two back.

"Stay here, okay?" He turns the truck off and pockets the keys.

He disappears into a lobby with VACANCY blinking red, and I consider taking off on foot, trying to make it to the highway. But he's back out the door before I can even get out of the truck. Icy air fills the cab as he gets back in and drives us to the opposite end of the parking lot.

Another motel. Another room. The only difference is I'm not tied up and blindfolded this time.

"Let's go." He waves a hand for me to follow, and almost against my will, I do. There will be a time to escape. This is not it.

Inside are two full-size beds, flower-print comforters strewn over them. A tiny round table. A bathroom in the back.

Jack hasn't said a word, and when I look at him, his eyes are glued to my forearm. To an imprint Daniel left behind.

"Did I do that?" He sets his bag on the bed nearest the door.

"No." My face goes hot. Daniel rarely leaves physical evidence; he's too smart for that. And he's more of the gaslighting, controlling type, almost as though he considers physical violence to be for someone lesser than himself. But still, there are bruises sometimes. I've just never let someone else see them before, even Kari. I shove my sleeves down, deciding the discomfort of being too warm is better than having judgmental eyes on me.

"Daniel, then." It's not a question. He starts to ask something else, eyes softening, but his phone vibrates in his pocket, and he reaches in, shuts it off. I find my way to the opposite bed and perch on the edge, wondering if there's a bathroom window here and if Jack will be foolish enough to leave his keys easily accessible again. I hope so.

"Tell me more about Daniel," he says. "How long have you been together?"

I hesitate. I don't want to talk about it. About him. And yet, I've never been honest with anyone about Daniel before. No one before Jack has known who, *what*, Daniel really is. What's more, I don't think Jack really cares about my relationship with Daniel. He's asking to make conversation, to pass time.

"We've been together a little over a year," I say.

"How'd you meet?"

I look at him, his immediate follow-up question not so casual. "Why do you care?"

He shrugs. "Thought maybe it would be helpful for you to talk about."

He's being nice. Too nice. "You're being *helpful*?" I ask.

"That okay?" A partial smile, but it doesn't reach his eyes.

I press my lips together and look away. "We work at the same hospital. I'm a nurse."

"And he's a doctor." It's not a question. I turn back and eye him, suspicious. But he shrugs, grabs his bag. "Make yourself at home. Maybe order a pizza. I can pay cash when they bring it. I need a shower."

"Wait, can I use your phone?"

He comes up short. "What for?"

"I want to check the news for anything about what happened."

Jack pulls it from his pocket. Swipes through his passcode. Hands it to me with a smile I think he means to be kind, comforting, but given the situation, is anything but. He turns his back and disappears into the bathroom, and I'm left surprised he said yes so easily, that I have his phone in my hand. Maybe he does want to help me. The surge of hope that fills me leaves me disgusted with myself—that I want the help of a man. That I feel like, maybe, I need it.

But I don't have time to worry about societal pressures and who I should want help from.

I navigate to the phone's internet app, and *The Seattle Star*'s front-page details sports, a recent hiker gone missing, and hospital union negotiations. But it's the article below that I'm interested in.

Local physician beaten, girlfriend kidnapped. $50k reward.

My first thought is *Of course, he's using this for publicity.* And of course, he's offering a reward. Fifty-thousand dollars, if anything, makes him look innocent. I play the video above the article, and a nurse I work with pops up, a microphone shoved in her face by a reporter.

"She's so nice," she says, shaking her short bob of a haircut. "Patients adore her."

The next video is of Daniel, his face drawn, arm bandaged,

and he winces when the reporter places a comforting—too comforting—hand on his shoulder. It looks like it hurts.

Good.

The reporter apologizes then asks if there's anything else he'd like to say to the public about his missing girlfriend. With dramatic flair, the camera zooms in on his face, all high cheekbones and bright blue eyes. Enjoying the attention. But it's not his face I'm looking at. Beyond him, I swear there's a familiar form among the dozens of women with sympathetic expressions, but it fades into the crowd.

"We *will* find her," Daniel says, looking at the camera. It sounds more like a threat than a promise. The video has been shared over a thousand times.

I stare at Daniel's image, then realize his face is not the only one I recognize in the still video. Beyond him, the figure I thought I recognized is Kari, her curls tossed over one shoulder, her mouth drawn in a line.

The now familiar pang hits me hard. I miss her, the random, goofy texts, the sweet but snappy attitude that always made me laugh, even after Bea died. If all goes according to plan, I'll never see her again. And here she is, trying to support the search for me when I'm safer than I've been in a year. A sidelong glance at the bathroom. At least, I hope I am.

I redirect the browser to Instagram and type in her handle. No new photos, but I scroll through her old ones, finding myself in several of them. My favorite is us drinking at a wine bar, before my aunt's death, before Kari was pregnant, before I realized I had to escape.

My aunt's death. Her murder.

I hesitate, but it's worth the risk. I log in to my e-mail from a private browser window. Even if the police can somehow track this log-in, the account could have been hacked. I just want to check and see if the PI e-mailed me about my aunt's death, if—

I have a single new e-mail, besides the dozens of advertisements automatically filtered to another folder. It's from Kari: *Where are you!? Why aren't you answering your phone?* reads the preview. I swallow, play through opening and answering it— *I'm good. I'm safe. Well, safe-ish. I have a plan.* But of course, I don't.

I refresh the inbox once, just in case. It's Tuesday. Allison said she'd get back to me by tomorrow. I'll have to find a way to check it one more time, just to quench my own curiosity. I log out, close the private window, and go back to the local news.

A new article catches my eye.

The headline reads:

OUT WITH THE OLD, IN WITH THE NEW?

But it's the photo that makes my stomach flip—Daniel and Kari, walking side by side, away from the camera. She'd shown up for his interview, probably to ask what he'd done to me. And by the end of it, she'd walked beside him to his car. I stare at the photo, analyze the short distance between them. In the next photo, she's climbing into his car. I ignore the suggestive caption beneath the photo. Kari's concerned for me; she knows better than to trust him.

Through the wall, the spray of water hitting the bathtub echoes, telling me Jack is showering, and it's the moment I've been waiting for. I scramble for the wallet he left on the small table beside the front door.

I pull out the ID first—Jack O'Kelly. Colorado driver's license. Credit cards, all in the same name. A couple hundred dollars in cash. It's a wallet like every other man's wallet I've ever seen, brown leather with far more pockets to slide in cards than necessary, and his are mostly empty. I check every pocket anyway, until I shove a finger in the last fold, almost hidden behind the others, and feel thick paper. The edge of a photo— no, *photos.*

The thump of pipes through the wall—I stop breathing. Listen carefully. Did he really take that short of a shower? But then the spray of water resumes, and I breathe again. I watch the bathroom door for a full twenty seconds, frozen. What would this man do if he found me digging through his wallet?

The phone, which I mindlessly shoved in my pocket, vibrates, but I don't pull it out. Instead, I ease the top photo from beneath the layers of leather, careful to not tear it.

When I see who it is, I'm not surprised.

It's me.

The same employee photo of me the newspaper got ahold of, something accessible by anyone who worked at the hospital. Or anyone who had access to my apartment, because that photo is what graced one half of my employee ID, which I kept on my kitchen counter beside the front door between shifts.

If Jack had been told to kidnap me, it would make sense he had a photo. But then, who's the other one of?

I set my photo flat on the table and pull at the edge of the second one. This one is slightly crinkled, like maybe it's been in his wallet longer than mine.

I pull it out. Focus on it, a woman with blue eyes and mahogany hair. She's young. I recognize her immediately. My hand flies to my mouth as I suppress a gasp. A second later, the pipes thump again. This time, the shower definitely shuts off.

As I gaze down at the photo, I know I have to go. And now. Because I have no doubt Jack will help me disappear. Just like he helped the woman in this photo disappear—Daniel's ex, Sarah MacCleary.

THIRTY

DANIEL

Now

Calvin Phillips is three minutes late. Considering how much money I pay him on the occasions he works for me, he could at least be punctual. I pull away from the windows and pop another Percocet, washing it down with bourbon. Between the two, I'm almost myself. Almost.

When he finally calls to tell me he's arrived, I buzz him in and watch from a window as he steers his late-model BMW through a crowd of reporters on the edge of my property.

"My apologies." He offers a professional smile that does not look apologetic, but rather self-assured, as though he's used to people waiting for him. I wonder if this is how I look, and then try to decide if I appreciate that he and I are similar, or if it irritates me since he's not nearly as good at it as I am.

I decide to reserve judgment. After all, I need his help. With busted ribs, broken fingers, a previously dislocated shoulder, and a myriad of other injuries, just getting up the stairs into my own home was a task. Coming after you, dear Noelle, would be near impossible. Plus, it will look good that I've hired someone to help in the investigation—it will draw suspicion *away* from me, and after what happened with Sarah, I need that.

"Have a seat." I beckon to one of two chairs across from my own, larger one. The size and placement of the chairs are purposeful, to imply that I am in charge. Previously, I have gone to *him*, to his office, for small jobs. Background checks. Following an individual, before I discovered an app could do it for me. If Mr. Phillips understands I'm the boss from the get-go, we'll have a better working relationship.

Perhaps, Noelle, I should have tried this technique on you.

"Drink?" I beckon to an oak bar with crystal decanters and various glasses.

"No, thank you." He takes a seat and crosses one ankle over one knee—a position that implies he has no concerns, is calm and collected, even in another's quarters—and touches his fingers to a sparse reddish beard. A sign of nerves, I think triumphantly.

"Mr. Phillips, I have what is perhaps an uncommon request," I begin. "But I will first have to ask you to sign a nondisclosure agreement. This is all very"—I wave a hand—"confidential."

"As I said last time, please call me Calvin." He gives me another overly genuine smile, brown eyes crinkling. I feel my lip curl. "And while I believed I signed one the last time we worked together, I am happy to sign another."

"Good." I put a finger to the agreement I've had prepared, nudging it his way. "Sign here, then."

He does so as I eye him. He comes highly recommended as someone who will go to whatever length to serve his client—for a price. A price I am more than happy to pay in return for the strictest confidence.

"As you may be aware, my girlfriend was kidnapped."

Calvin nods, rests his chin on two fingers, and I realize he's mimicking my own body language, a manipulation technique to encourage me to like him. I decide to ignore it.

"I had heard about a missing nurse. That's her?"

"Yes. Noelle Thomas." I shift, and he moves too, chasing my movements. "I film her," I say, using awkward phrasing and a slight smile to communicate faux discomfort. "She's aware, of course."

"Oh? You *film* her?" An eyebrow hitches up, and his professional interest becomes curiosity. He forgets to mirror me.

"Yes." He wants to ask me if it's sexual, if you and I get off on the fact I can see you at all times. Perhaps he enjoys such things. Perhaps he will enjoy watching you. "I shared this with the detectives on the case, of course, but I only gave them a half-truth. I wouldn't want them to"—I tilt my head, try for a bashful smile—"get the wrong idea."

"No, of course not." Calvin sits forward. "So, how can I help?"

"The video I turned over to the police includes only the kidnappers coming and going from the front door, basic front door security camera setup. There are two other cameras that have more shots of the men, including a direct view of the one who grabbed her from her apartment. It's of his face, to be exact. The problem is he's wearing a mask. But certain features are very distinct, including his eyes."

"Oh." He nods.

"I would like you to figure out who he is."

Calvin's eyebrows climb at this. He sits back, rests one ankle on his opposite knee, and sighs. "That's expensive, and I can't make any promises. It will require me to access—"

"That's fine," I interrupt. "Whatever you need."

"And you don't want to turn this over to the police?"

"No. I'd like to deal with it myself." He is potentially the man who beat the shit out of me. I have plans for him the police wouldn't approve of.

"What did you say her name is?" Calvin asks.

I frown. Your name has been splashed across the media for the past twenty-four hours. Furthermore, he's a private investigator, and I've said your name once already.

"Noelle Thomas." I enunciate it in such a way there is no question how I feel about having to repeat it.

"Interesting," he murmurs.

"Is it?"

"I wouldn't usually share this, but you're a special client, and this is a special situation, what with her being missing and all. It's perhaps... *best* for her, what with her safety being compromised." Calvin pauses and his eyes gleam, and I know he's thinking of the money I'll pay him far more than your welfare. "My assistant is currently working a separate case for a woman of the exact same name."

THIRTY-ONE

NOELLE

Now

I take everything—the photos, the cash, the credit cards. I take his heavy leather jacket, and I take his keys. I steal his truck, again.

My heart pounds as I swing into the driver's seat. The leather is cold, the steering wheel frigid in my hands. But in seconds, he'll be out that door, probably spitting mad, because this is all an act. A way to get me to go along with him so he could make me disappear in the worst way.

Snow obscures my view, but it's light and fresh, and the wipers clear it instantly. I punch the button for four-wheel drive, hoping it's as easy as that, and it seems to be—the truck pulls out of the parking lot, snow crunching beneath the tires. The storm has settled down, no longer dumping white stuff from the sky, but rather scattering it in what any other time I'd perceive as beautiful.

But now, it's just one more thing trying to keep me captive.

I grew up in Idaho, which means I learned to drive in snow —but it's rare in Seattle, and even rarer I have to drive in a city where public transportation isn't great, but enough to get me around. Thankfully, the highway was plowed and salted at some point, so though it's not exactly clear, it looks manageable. The knot in my gut loosens, and I tap the brakes, stopping without so much as a slide as I reach said highway and realize there's a decision to be made.

Head north, back toward Washington, but also back toward Portland, a city where I could blend in. A city I'm familiar with. A city I can hide in. Or south, toward California, my destination. South also means at least one mountain pass that may be shut down with this snow, and it's also the vague destination I've shared with Jack.

A web of fear wraps around me as the magnitude of what is happening becomes a crushing weight—Daniel. Two of his previous girlfriends missing. And now me. And a criminal—Jack—somehow tied up in this.

I swallow the fear down. Shut my eyes and breathe. Clench the steering wheel. Take a left back toward Portland. I took Jack's phone, too. Which hopefully means he can't track the truck, at least for a while. Hopefully, he'll assume I continued south. I'll drive as far as I can. I'll find another vehicle, or maybe hitch a ride. I'll leave the truck for him to find.

I'll make myself disappear before he can.

THIRTY-TWO

DANIEL

Now

It's nine that night when my e-mail pings. I'm alone in my office, poring over medical records—your records, Noelle. I slam shut the manila folder with a shake of my head. Your accident really was unfortunate. It's a good thing I was there—to save you. And here I am, saving you again. Saving *us*.

I redirect my attention to the e-mail Calvin sent, which has two files attached.

The first file contains screenshots of e-mails directed from you to an Allison Montgomery, Calvin's assistant. Details are sparse—apparently, you know better than to put anything in writing you want to keep a secret. Perhaps we are even better matched than I have suspected. This means you contacted the PI via phone call or in person. Perhaps, during one of your damn runs. What use could you possibly have for a private investigator? Trying to catch me cheating? Do you know about Kari?

Unlikely.

It hasn't happened again, Kari made sure of that, and if she hadn't, I would have. I only had one need for her. Besides, even if you found out, I wouldn't let you leave me. You know that.

I open the other attachment, which contains the most recent e-mail Calvin's assistant sent.

Phrases like *Aunt's death, foul play, security cameras, hospital liaison,* and *visitors log* stare back at me.

I almost laugh, but the humor is cut short when I remember the earlier phone call from the hospital. It wasn't the first. It was the third, in fact, though I'd assumed it was merely the woman who does the scheduling, or perhaps one of the nursing managers, calling to offer condolences. I press my phone to my ear and listen.

"Dr. Ashcroft, this is Rebecca Stein. I work in human resources at Seattle General. There is a private investigator looking into a case that involved a patient death. They mentioned you specifically, though I don't believe you were part of the medical team. Please call me at your earliest—"

I delete the message without listening to the rest.

What the fuck is this, Noelle? Betrayal, that's what. Not appreciating all that I have done for you. What I'm doing for you right now.

The phone rings.

"Yes?" I bite out.

"It's Calvin. I sent the e-mails from my assistant's inbox. Listen, could we get access to Noelle's apartment? I'd like to make sure the police didn't miss anything. I have someone working on the facial recognition, though again, with the mask it will be difficult."

I take a deep breath. Release it slowly. This will be helpful. Will look good, too.

"Sure," I say. "Does tomorrow morning work for you? Nine a.m.?"

"Sure does."

"Great. I'll text you the address."

I sit at my desk, drumming my fingers over the firm leather that makes up the writing surface. Your photo sits right in front of me, one from our early days, on a date to the top of the Space Needle. You'd never been, so I took you. A small show of my affection, and you'd been overjoyed. I see it in your eyes, the way you so willingly wrapped your arms around me, kissed my cheek. Practically worshiped me.

I forgive you, Noelle, for whatever you suspect me of. It's better than you knowing the truth.

THIRTY-THREE

NOELLE

Now

Portland is different than I remember. Then again, I've never seen it covered in snow. Nor when I'm on the run, checking every face that passes in case anyone might have their eyes on me for too long or appear too interested.

I caught a few hours of sleep and left the truck near Hood River, a city dividing Oregon from Washington beside the Columbia River that runs all the way to the ocean. I parked it behind a building in a commercial area, the sort of place that might take a couple days to be noticed. A trucker stopped, offering me a lift into Portland, and though every true crime podcast I've ever listened to flashed through my mind, I knew I had to say yes—it was that or freeze. Or wait for Jack to come for his truck and ferry me off to wherever it was he'd hidden Sarah's body.

That must have been his plan—play the nice guy. The helpful one. Let me practically lead myself to my own death. Of course, Daniel had shown up at the motel. Maybe Daniel was going to be the one to do—whatever it was he had planned for me. Maybe they are working together and this is the twisted game they play.

Now, standing on the sidewalk near the last place I should be—Powell's Books, my favorite place in Portland—I realize for all the anxiety swirling through me, the actual reason it looks different is because it's been over a year since I've been here. Because once I became Daniel's girlfriend, he didn't want me traveling this far without him, and Portland wasn't the sort of city Daniel liked. It wasn't flashy or rich, instead favoring *local* and *authentic*.

The bookstore pulls at me—a longing to step inside, to browse the shelves. But if anyone suspects Portland is where I'd escape, they would also know I'd want to come here. So instead, I turn. Walk down an alley, past the road where Voodoo Doughnut has its usual line out the door, and don't stop until I find another cheap motel on the outskirts of downtown. I secure it with Jack's credit card but pay cash.

My room is on the second floor, up a set of rickety stairs. Inside has the requisite bed, a comforter that feels more plastic than fabric, furniture with sharp corners that moves a little if one applies too much weight. Through the wall, the murmur of another guest's television.

I toss what little I have on the sole chair in the corner of the room and go to take a hot shower. When I'm done, I crawl under the covers, pick up Jack's phone, and scavenge my way through it, looking for information that might help me—photos, texts, calls. I reverse lookup the phone numbers he has been in contact with, but there is nothing of use. Just a series of vague texts with whoever Jack's boss is. I stare at the number, wondering if it's Daniel on the other end. And then I pick up the room phone.

I press star sixty-seven first, then dial.

My hand clenches around the phone as it rings once, twice, three times. And then—

"Hello?"

I gulp. Hang up. Lay back on the bed, my heart pounding in my ears. It was a man's voice. But not Daniel's.

It doesn't make sense. There's no one in my life besides Daniel who would want me gone. I think back to my other suspicion—Michael. He swore if I ever left him, he'd find me, that we were meant to be. But I haven't heard so much as a word. I've googled Daniel before, so I don't bother doing that now—I know that without paying for special services, I won't find anything. Instead, I google Michael, and then the husband from the wrongful death suit, but there's nothing, save an old Facebook profile of Michael's I can't access without friending him. Next, I look for Jack O'Kelly—but he's as much of a ghost as Daniel's first girlfriend, Justine.

Another dead end.

I move on to the news only to find speculation on my whereabouts and who might have taken me. I navigate to my e-mail, type in my address and password, and suck in a breath—an e-mail from Allison Montgomery, PI.

Subject: Your Aunt's Death

Dear Ms. Thomas,

I followed up on everything I mentioned in my previous e-mail and wanted to update you.

As a nurse, I know you are aware that sometimes people simply die. We do not always get a satisfactory answer. Usually, in medical cases, the concern is malpractice. To cover this, I am going to go ahead and contact the cardiothoracic surgeon who consults on cases such as this one, which will help us determine if all appropriate measures were taken in your aunt's surgery.

I also spoke to the hospital liaison, who verified the secu-

rity footage was no longer available. However, the cardiovas-
cular unit is a locked unit, and therefore, the visitor log may
prove helpful. The hospital liaison has promised to get me the
visitor log by week's end. I will be in touch at that time. Please
feel free to contact me if you have any questions.

Sincerely,

Allison Montgomery
Private Investigator

I release the breath. My shoulders sag, grief weighing me down. A visitor log? A volunteer completes it, sometimes, if someone's available to work the desk. Contacting the cardiothoracic surgeon might show *something*, but it's a long shot, and besides... I bite my lip and squeeze my eyes shut. There's no going back. Why am I even looking at this? I'm no longer trying to prove Daniel's guilt. I'm simply running away.

I get to my feet and look out the thick curtain at the gray sky, wondering—no, hoping—more snow is to come. Anything to slow down the hunt for me, both those with nefarious goals, and those who hope to find me in one piece. People like Kari.

Speaking of Kari—I go to Kari's Instagram. What I see bottoms out my stomach.

The photo is of Kari's bump, and beyond that, her legs, perfectly manicured feet, and the edge of a hospital gown. The caption reads, *Almost thirty-four weeks pregnant. Not the baby bump photo I'd planned for. Hoping baby is okay. Lucky to have a doctor on speed dial.*

I zoom in, searching for details, breath caught in my throat. It's Seattle General, I can tell from the logo at the bottom of the hospital sheet.

Why is she in the hospital?
What doctor does she have on call?

Two tiny dots sit just beneath the photo, and I realize there's a second photo. I swipe. My whole body goes cold.

Daniel. The doctor she called is Daniel. It's a selfie of him perched next to her on the hospital bed, arm around her shoulders, them both smiling at the camera.

My mind races. I can't imagine a scenario where she would call him, but it's what is plainly in front of me. Something had to have happened—and she didn't have me to call for help. Or her mother, my aunt, who's months dead now. That left her with... nobody. Except Daniel. It's a gut punch, knowing it's my fault her family is gone—that she only had someone like Daniel to ask for help.

I go to Facebook and log in; hopefully Daniel isn't on, can't see the little green icon that indicates I'm online. I navigate to Kari's page and scroll for photos; she always shares more on Facebook, where only a select group of people can access it.

The same photos are there, plus two more. One, a selfie of her belly in the mirror of the hospital bathroom. The second, an ultrasound. The caption reads, "She's okay!"

Relief floods through me, and I take a slow deep breath.

Dozens of comments are below the photos, and I scroll through, reading each and every one.

Her cousin in Texas asks, *Who's the doc? ;-)*

She replies, *Friend's boyfriend* and leaves it at that.

The phone rings, jolting me from thoughts of Kari and Daniel. An unfamiliar number, *Oregon* flashing above it, identifying where the call is from. I know of only one person in Oregon.

Jack.

I hit Accept, adrenaline surging through me, anger in its wake.

"What's your plan?" I snap. "What were you going to do to me? What did you do to Sarah?"

Silence.

"Noelle, calm down. Just listen—" Jack starts.

"Oh, fuck off." I hit End. The last thing I need is another man trying to manage me, lie to me, telling me to *calm down*.

I shut the phone off because the battery is down to a mere twenty percent, and I need to preserve its life until I find a charger.

The clock on the bedside table reads 11:23 a.m. I set the alarm for 3 p.m., pull the curtains, and yank the covers up to my chin. I have to sleep. And when I wake, I'm determined to figure out who Justine is and what happened to her.

Maybe she's the key to staying alive.

THIRTY-FOUR

DANIEL

Now

Kari called me, Noelle.

When I looked down at my vibrating cell phone and saw her name, I tried to think of what exactly she might want.

Another demand to know what I'd done to you?

Asking for money? I doubted this. Kari doesn't like to ask for help, which you are aware of. You help her in gentle, round-about ways, and she pretends not to notice, but only for you. I'm mildly shocked she took the cash I offered, even if the child is mine. In fact, that's likely the only reason she took it. She probably thinks it's the least I can do.

"Hello?"

"I need help." Her words were more like gasps, pants over the phone. They became full blown sobs when I arrived at her shitty double-wide fifteen minutes later.

Blood. It stained her pajamas, and if I believed in God, I'd have thanked him for the insight to have the leather in my Porsche treated to withstand such substances. I fucking hate blood.

"Do you have a towel?" I inquired, and of course, she spat a curse at me.

I raced her to the hospital, because I don't want our child to die, either.

I made sure she was seen immediately, no waiting for the maternity unit to admit her from the emergency department—the OB-GYN came to her, instead.

My baby inside her is alive and well. Kari is alive and mostly well. And I get to feel like a hero. I rather enjoy this feeling, Noelle.

Kari thanked me profusely. Almost as shocking as her calling me in the first place. It's funny what being grateful can do for a person's attitude. You could take a lesson or two from her.

I sit here, waiting, thinking through what I know. Thinking of how I'll come out ahead in this situation, too, with you back to worshiping me the way you used to.

Kari shrieks.

"What?" I snap, nearly dropping my phone.

The nurse sprints into the room, and Kari flutters her hand at her, apologizing with tears in her eyes, explaining she is fine, the baby is fine.

"What is it?" I ask, ready to tell her she can walk home.

"Oh god, oh god." She bounces up and down, which takes effort at thirty-four weeks of pregnancy, and yet again, she cries. "She's alive, Daniel, she's alive."

My chest tightens. "Noelle?"

Kari turns her phone so I can see.

KIDNAPPED WOMAN SPOTTED IN OREGON? flashes across the screen, and then an announcer comes on, stern-faced, his *serious* expression for important matters such as this one. "An Oregon resident reported seeing a woman with a strong resemblance to missing Seattle resident, Noelle Thomas, at a diner in Madras, Oregon, this morning. Ms. Thomas was kidnapped from her residence in Seattle on Monday night, and security footage—"

I stop listening because there you are. You're in a dark hoodie, and though the announcer states it might simply be someone resembling you—the video is black and white and grainy—I *know* how you move, Noelle. I know it's you. But why are you in Oregon, of all places?

The muscles in my face go taut, a feeling similar to after I have Botox injected—I also know the man who hovers behind you, too close for him to merely be leaving the restaurant at the same time. He's *with* you. You're with him. As I watch, he touches you—lays a hand on your shoulder. *Directs* you to one side.

The man who didn't hand you over when I asked nicely. Who, instead, beat the shit out of me.

Beyond the fact he has what is mine—that would be you, Noelle, and don't you forget it—the rage boiling through my veins is visceral. Because this man is also the reason I ended up in the hospital. My Porsche ended up abandoned.

You pause, turn to look at him, your motions choppy, like you're not sure what to do, but he points beyond the camera's scope. You hesitate. Nod.

And then, you disappear.

But all that's okay, because this is good. This means you're alive, and I can work with that. We can still move forward with the plan.

It means I can still find you. I can still do exactly what I should have done months ago.

THIRTY-FIVE

DANIEL

Now

Calvin's late again, but I can't be bothered to care—a far more pressing matter is that there's a scratch down the passenger side of my car. No, not a scratch—an indentation. Someone *keyed* it.

"Goddammit." I crouch to get a better look, ignoring the pain shooting through my ribcage.

My phone rings.

"Hello?" I snap. I pin the phone to my ear using my shoulder and press a finger on my good hand to where the paint is destroyed. My mother's voice comes over the phone, and I grit my teeth and step away from the ruined side of my car, thinking of what *exactly* I'd like to do to whoever did this.

"Daniel, how are you feeling? I'm so concerned you left the hospital early, did you—"

"I'm fine, Mother." I inhale, and it hurts again, and thank god I'm an anesthesiologist with plenty of pain meds to spare. "Thank you for your concern, though."

A silence. "Noelle is missing," she says, and of course Noelle is missing, and it's not like her to state the obvious.

"I know. I'm working on it." I pinch my nose and walk into your apartment building. Screw Calvin. He can figure it out when he gets here.

"Maybe we should talk more, Daniel. I think—"

"I'm going to kill whoever did this." I'm not sure if I mean who took off with you, or who fucked up my car, and perhaps they are the same person, but either will work.

I wait for Mother to scold me for my turn of phrase, my cursing, but there's only silence.

"Mother? Are you all right?" I ask.

She clears her throat. "I'm concerned about her. Who could've done such a thing?"

"I know. Listen, about Noelle... She slipped through my fingers. This is my fault. But I'll fix it. I've talked to the police, and I hired a private investigator—"

"A private investigator? Like in the movies?"

"Yes, Mother." I unlock your apartment door with the key your landlord gave me. My eyes sweep the living room and kitchen—traces of fingerprint powder on every surface, items on your counter out of order from the police search. Your home, but you're gone from it. Nothing is quite right.

"Why?" Her voice goes quiet. "Do you think the police aren't doing a good job? Are you worried they won't find her?"

"No, but I want Noelle back. And soon." I take a breath and say in a calm easy voice, "The more people looking for her, the better."

"That's true." She's silent for a moment. "Listen, Daniel, we should be more involved in the search. She is basically your fiancée, after all. My future daughter-in-law. Come to dinner tonight and we'll talk more about this. I'll make your favorite and open a bottle of port."

A knock at the door draws my attention away from the phone call. "Sure, Mother, fine." I hang up and open the door for Calvin.

"Good morning." His smile is too big, too cheesy, but I don't care. As far as I can tell, he's doing a good enough job, other than consistently being late. He sidles in, surveys the space, and nods once. "I'll go from room to room looking for anything. Have you searched it?"

His question catches me off guard. Why would I search your apartment if I know what happened?

"No." I frown. "It didn't occur to me to do so." I think of the laptop computer I had removed from your apartment when I took all but one camera out. Perhaps I should search that. See what you've been up to. "Speaking of, is there any news on the man who took her?"

"Not yet. We're still running it through the facial recognition program." Calvin grins like he has a secret, and I try not to grind my teeth together.

"What?" I snap.

"Turns out facial recognition software has come quite far. When the pandemic hit, wearing a mask created big problems for security companies. The person I have working on it has access to the newest software, which apparently works even when the individual is wearing a mask. With any luck, I'll hear back within twenty-four hours."

"Good." One step closer to bringing you home.

"You haven't received any phone calls? E-mails? Letters?" Calvin strolls over to your kitchen and begins opening drawers, quickly sifting through them.

"Should I have?"

Calvin shrugs, his back to me. His shoulders aren't quite so wide as mine, but they are thick, and he obviously works out. Can he lift more than me? Squat more?

"No ransom requested, then." It's not a question. "Interesting." He hums to himself and squats down, pulling items from your cabinets—a blender, a stack of dish towels, items of no consequence.

"No." It's an intriguing thought, a way to spin this that hasn't occurred to me before. Would someone ever try to kidnap you for money? I am early on in my career—I have plenty of investments, but not the enormous wealth of many of the surgeons I work with. Would someone consider kidnapping you for revenge, then? A former classmate, maybe? I can't help that I was at the top of my class. That I make more than my medical school and residency peers.

"It's been thirty-six hours, give or take. I haven't gotten a text or a call or an e-mail. If it were sent via snail mail, it might not come until today or tomorrow." I play along.

"Let me know if you receive anything." Calvin finishes with the kitchen and moves from the laminate flooring to the gray carpet.

"I will." I fidget about the room for a minute or two. "Calvin, I've got a few errands to run. Are you okay here on your own?"

"Sure. Want me to lock up on my way out?"

"That would be great. Thanks."

I'm back in the Porsche in seconds.

No mail.

No e-mail.

Which is unfortunate. The police would be less likely to look at me if I *did* receive a ransom note of some sort.

Calvin texts: he's found nothing, which does not surprise me, but he will of course bill me for the three hours it took to go through your belongings regardless.

Speaking of—I open my own desk drawer and pull out your laptop. I can access your computer if I want to, there is remote desktop spyware for that. But you rarely use your computer, and it's not something I monitor frequently. Though after the e-mails Calvin sent me, perhaps I will be, moving forward, once I get you back.

Your password is your aunt's last name—the keystroke recorder picked that up the first day I installed it—and I'm into your computer within seconds. It's unremarkable, Noelle. You check your work e-mail when you have no shifts scheduled for several days. You look at photographs of the mountains and minimally use social media. You shop online for things like paper towels and toilet paper and shampoo.

I get up and pour myself a drink haphazardly—I use my teeth to pull the cork from my favorite bottle of bourbon, my broken fingers still pulsating with pain. It's too early for it, even for me, and I shouldn't with the narcotics, but what the hell. I'm in constant pain, there's a gash in the side of my Porsche, and my girlfriend has been kidnapped. You think I drink too much, but even you can appreciate the need to take the edge off a day like this one, right, Noelle?

I swallow the bourbon, pour two more fingers, and settle into my desk and your computer. Calvin searched every crevice of your apartment so thoroughly I almost felt he violated your privacy. This attention to detail must work for him, based off his reputation, and I will do the same with your computer.

I begin searching through your internet history, something I scroll through on rare occasions when I'm bored, or you're acting off. Which is more and more often. Maybe you *are* cheating on me, Noelle.

My phone dings—Calvin. *Would you like me to tell my assistant to terminate the investigation Ms. Thomas began?*

I smile. Why hadn't I thought of that? Maybe I like Calvin, after all. He certainly likes my money.

Please, I write back. One problem I can scratch off my list.

An official e-mail will be sent to her e-mail address with notification the investigation has been suspended, he writes back.

I navigate to your e-mail. Thousands of read and unread e-mails populate it, and I scroll down, far down, until I see my own name. It's an e-mail from last February.

I scroll back up, and there's a new e-mail from Calvin's agency. The text is bolded to indicate it's new, and that's when I realize—

The e-mail sent yesterday from the PI you hired has been read.

I don't move for a full minute, eyes shifting between the new, bolded e-mail, and the old, plain text one, trying to discern if I'm mistaken.

I'm not.

None of the other e-mails have been opened for four days. Only the one from Allison Montgomery titled *Your Aunt's Death*. I delete the new e-mail that confirms cancelation of the investigation, so you don't see it. As far as I can figure, this recently opened e-mail can mean only one thing.

Noelle, have you been checking your e-mail?

THIRTY-SIX

NOELLE

Now

I start by retracing my steps. Maybe I've missed something.

First, I buy a charger and supplies to conceal my identity at a corner store, and a cheap backpack to stuff it all in. I hesitate as I hold a box of hair dye—I've always loved my red hair. But escaping Daniel and Jack necessitates not being so easily recognizable, and red hair is uncommon enough that it has to go.

Then, disguised with a hat and makeup, I go to the best place for anonymous research I can think of—the public library. It's crowded with college students and senior citizens, a handful of homeless people warming up and accessing computers. Plenty of space to blend in.

I settle at an empty desk in a corner, where I can keep an eye on anyone who might approach me. It has a computer, and I plug in the phone to charge, then spend a moment trying to decide where to start. Justine. Daniel. What was their connection? I start with a web search, then move on to logging in to my Facebook account, a risk, but one I must take—it's the only way to see Daniel's account, which has its security set to "friends only."

But before I can navigate to his profile, a new photo of Kari pops up, over a hundred likes and loves and a dozen comments. A photo of the nursery, but this time, she's part of the photo. In her hands are tiny new outfits for her baby—and in the background, a hot pink camera is tacked to the wall, the fancy baby monitor we'd decided against. It was three times as much as the cheaper version, and we'd deemed it unnecessary. I lean closer to the computer monitor, as though that will somehow show me where she got the money for these things—these utterly unnecessary things that just a few days ago she'd rolled her eyes at.

A new boyfriend? But who gets a new boyfriend when they're mere weeks away from giving birth? Maybe an old boyfriend. Maybe the *father*, whoever he is, had reached out finally. But probably not, the way Kari refused to talk about him. I try to think back through the men and women she's dated over the past two years—is there anyone who would reconnect with her *now*?

I finally tear my eyes away and navigate to Daniel's profile. I can't exactly ask Kari these questions, and she seems happy enough. And that's all I wanted for her—happiness and safety.

I again scroll through Daniel's Facebook contacts, but no one has a name in any way resembling *Justine*. There are half a dozen Sarahs, but when I click on their profiles, none of them look like the blue-eyed brunette whose photo sits in my pocket. I sit back in what is a rather uncomfortable chair, cursing under my breath. Then again, I've done these things already—more than once. Did I really think an answer would magically appear before me?

How had Daniel met Sarah? I search the web for Sarah MacCleary, and of course get hundreds of results—from the early news articles detailing her disappearance, to crime podcasts that have featured her story.

The main facts are these:

- The police believe she was taken from her home in the early hours of the morning. Her front door was ajar, and all her belongings, including her keys and purse, remained inside. There was no evidence she was planning to take a trip and no activity on her credit cards. This is similar to what my case must look like.
- Sarah, too, had previously been in an abusive relationship and left her ex-husband.
- Her boyfriend, Daniel, was out of town at a work conference and had dozens of witnesses of his whereabouts. There was no evidence suggesting he had anything to do with her disappearance. Again, I can't help but notice the similarity—he was supposed to be with his mother the night I was kidnapped, providing an alibi for him.
- Daniel not only did everything he could to assist the investigation, he began a charity fund to help find other people who had disappeared, too. Just like he'd posted a reward for me.

I pause on this detail. It's not abnormal that a person of means affected by the tragedy of a disappearance would do this sort of thing, start a charity—it *is* abnormal he'd never mention it to me, though. That his *mother* would never mention it. Even if they still carried considerable grief from her disappearance. I do a quick search for said charity fund, and it looks legit—a businesslike website with testimonials from families who have received assistance from it. Other than mentioning Daniel began it, he otherwise does not seem heavily involved.

I go back to my web search, scrolling through one article after another, from time to time looking up as another library patron passes by, books stacked in their arms. Every face feels like a potential threat, which of course is ridiculous, but it doesn't feel ridiculous in the moment, considering what I'm up against.

The phone, which is plugged in and charging, rings silently, the touchscreen lighting up.

I answer, whispering, "Hello?" A man, who isn't Jack, gives a grunt and says, "This who I think it is?" and I rush to hit End and shut the damn thing off. *Holy crap.*

I force myself to take a slow settling breath and refocus on the computer. If it's Jack's boss calling me, he's calling because he doesn't know where I am.

I'm poring through every photo Daniel has ever posted on social media when I realize someone's watching me. I only notice because he wears a noticeable shirt—bright blue with some sort of sports logo on the front—and that bright flash of color comes into my periphery once, twice, three times. Photos are boldly on display on the monitor in front of me, but my attention is on the bookshelf he's just stepped behind, yet again. I can't look directly at him without making it clear I've noticed his attentions, but he's slight, that much I can tell. And he reminds me of someone—

Of the man who bumped into me at Pike Place Market, just before the car almost hit me. But I'm not sure. Maybe I'm misremembering. Maybe I'm paranoid.

To stay or to run, that is the question. He might be a concerned citizen who recognizes me from the news—or, he's the next Jack, sent by Jack's employer. Either way, I need to leave.

I delete my browser history, grab my stuff, and walk through the stacks. My chest is tight, my shoulders aching with tension. It's possible he's waiting for me around the next corner. He could have even called someone, called for backup—my throat constricts, and I realize I'm walking too fast, attracting looks from an elderly woman with a stack of books in front of her, a mother with two school-aged children poring over a book on animals.

I force myself to slow down. A women's restroom is at the end of this long beige hall, and maybe I can duck into it and hide out. But he might follow me—or wait outside. A better idea hits me, and I push the door open as I reach it, letting it begin a slow controlled swing shut. Meanwhile, I duck into a stairwell and take them two at a time upstairs.

Slender hardbound reference books line tall shelves, at least ten feet high, creating a literal maze within the library. A maze that could work to my advantage. I find a corner where three rows meet, giving me a way out regardless of where someone might come from, and I wait, heart pounding, practically holding my breath.

I stand stock-still for a full two minutes, listening as the heat gasps to life in the old building; as somewhere deep into the stacks, an old man coughs for a solid thirty seconds. Another two minutes of waiting. Then another.

I feel like an idiot.

And moreover, this isn't any better than when I was under the constant watch of Daniel and his cameras. At least then I knew who the enemy was.

By the time I reach the motel, dusk has settled in. I eat vending machine snacks and take another hot shower, jumping every time the pipes clank.

The local news pages have a deep dive and speculation into my life: I'm from Idaho. I have a mother, though a source close to me claims we are estranged. My father took off years ago. "Could it be her father who took her?" My aunt's death is mentioned. "Could it be someone wanting the inheritance? Who stands to benefit? Her mother?" But the "inheritance" was my armchair and a whole three thousand dollars, equally divided between Kari and me. The news cycle has turned it into its own mystery.

Only their third suspect gives me pause—"Michael Barnes in Idaho, who Ms. Thomas was reportedly engaged to some years ago." We weren't engaged. We were looking at rings, but not because *I* thought it was a good idea. Looking at rings was the moment I realized I had to leave him, and that's when I'd come to Seattle. According to the article, he'd refused to comment when the newspaper reached out to him. I bite my lip, wondering if I should take that as a sign he might be involved. He liked the limelight—I would have guessed he'd talk to a reporter all day if he got the chance.

But I keep coming back to Daniel.

I set the phone down and lie back on the bed. I consider what Daniel has to gain from doing all this. What if I *had* disappeared that night? What if Jack had turned me over to whoever he works for, and they'd passed me along to the person who ordered me kidnapped? Would Daniel be playing this exact same game with the media, but with the knowledge I was truly gone for good? Becoming Seattle's saddest bachelor, wanting nothing more than his girlfriend returned safely to him?

Isn't he too smart to make two of his girlfriends publicly disappear? Which makes me wonder, what if it wasn't Daniel?

A different idea occurs to me—what if it was Daniel, but he *hadn't* wanted me gone? What if he'd wanted to save me himself? But then, why hadn't Jack known to expect Daniel? Jack said he was to turn me over to his boss, who would then personally hand me over. Daniel coming to the hotel on his own doesn't fit that theory.

My head spins, trying to keep the threads straight. But I can't, because none of it makes sense, and Daniel is the only person I can think of with motive, even if that motive seems sociopathic.

I take my scratch paper from earlier, hoping I'll find similarities between Sarah and me to take note of, things that might lead me in Justine's direction, because if I can find her—if she's still alive, maybe that will mean Daniel isn't a killer. Maybe this is all a coincidence. Or maybe, she can tell me how she escaped him. And if I can't find her—if she's disappeared like Sarah did. Well, that means something, too, even if it proves nothing.

I start right where I left off in the library, pulling out my freshly charged phone, logging back in to social media, and scrolling through years of photos. Now, as an all-important anesthesiologist, he rarely posts anything beyond a new headshot or is tagged in photos from an event of some sort. But back in residency, and before that, medical school, he posted often. In fact, his life looks like it was almost *normal* back then, before the ridiculous salary, before Sarah.

The mindless scrolling leaves me tense, looking at photo after photo of Daniel. I pause when I see him dressed to the nines, decor strung up behind him, but not the haughty stylistic fashion of another gala—rather, almost cheaply done. Crepe paper. *Class of* and numbers blocked out behind other people in the photo. *Prom.* But not prom, because—I squint at the date. It's almost a decade after Daniel graduated from high school

And then it hits me. That was the year he graduated from *medical school.*

His mother hadn't meant high school prom when she'd mentioned the emerald dress and Justine to Daniel. She'd meant *medical school prom,* something I've heard medical students and residents talk about in passing at the hospital but never discussed with Daniel.

Exhilaration leaves me breathless, replacing anxiety, but as I tap through his photos, there are no more from the event—and when I go back, there's only Daniel and three other men. No woman in emerald. No Justine.

I bite my lip. Try not to let my heart sink.

Think.

Two of the three other men are tagged in the photo. I go to their profiles, and the last one has minimal privacy settings—meaning I can scroll through his photos. It takes another half hour of searching, but eventually I find what I'm looking for, buried deep in an album titled *Med School Friends*.

A group photo. Daniel. His arm around a woman who looks a lot like me, red hair and all. She's not tagged, but she is wearing green, and I'm pretty sure this is Justine.

THIRTY-SEVEN

NOELLE

Now

Subject: Visitor Log

Dear Ms. Thomas,

I am aware my boss sent an e-mail concluding this case at your request, but I can't in good conscience not send the information I found. Of course, what you choose to do with it is up to you. I understand you may wish to move on with your life and leave your aunt's death in the past.

The hospital liaison delivered via certified mail a copy of the visitor list for the date of your aunt's death. The following information is recorded:

Date: Sept 15 | Time: 3:05 pm | Visitor's last name: Ashcroft | ID type: Driver's license | Patient Visited: Beatrice Williams

Best of luck to you, and if you at any point wish to discuss this case further, please feel free to contact me.

Sincerely,

Allison Montgomery
Private Investigator

I'd completely forgotten Allison was supposed to e-mail me by today, but after going through social media, checking Kari's Instagram and Facebook, then Daniel's again, logging in to my e-mail was the automatic next thing to do.

Staring at the message, I almost wish I hadn't.

Not because I don't care about its contents. Quite the opposite—but the issue is *doing* something about it. I'm on the run, trying to disappear, which means I *can't* do anything about it. Which means if Daniel is guilty of something *and it sure looks like he is,* there will never be justice.

Daniel visited my aunt less than an hour before she died. Why? He wasn't the sort to check in on a girlfriend's relative. The only other Ashcroft I know is his mother, but she never even met my aunt, and furthermore, no longer drives as far as I know. I can't imagine she even has a driver's license.

I reread the e-mail, and my eyes catch on the part I'd been too wrapped up in to realize the meaning of before.

my boss sent an e-mail concluding this case at your request...

At my request? I never made a request.

The e-mail her boss sent. I never received an e-mail.

I check the spam folder, but there's nothing but advertisements for pizza, which sounds damn good after vending machine food. I search for Allison's company name, which shows only the e-mails I'm aware of. Then I go to Trash, the one folder I haven't checked, because I know the last e-mail I deleted.

And there it is. An e-mail someone—not me—deleted.

Confirmation of the closed case, pending a request from an unnamed party. It's sent from a Calvin Phillips, Owner. Allison's boss.

There's only one person I can think of who would arrange for my aunt's case to be closed—one person who might have access to my e-mail account.

Daniel.

THIRTY-EIGHT

DANIEL

Buying flowers in the rain is a poor decision, one I shouldn't have had to make, because you should be doing this, Noelle.

The flower stand has a line, of course, because everyone wants to buy flowers at five-thirty in the evening on a Wednesday. Maybe they're going to see their mothers, too. I stopped in at Pike Place Market on the way because it's where *you* go, and you swear it's the best. I'd hoped to somehow figure out which damn bouquet it is that you always bring that makes my mother's face light up and her leave the bouquet in a vase for longer than it has any right to be there. For the life of me, I can't remember what the damn flowers look like. Pink, maybe?

"Can I help you?" a woman asks.

"I need a bouquet for my mother," I say. "My girlfriend usually does this."

"Oh, okay." The woman looks over her shoulder at the arrangements. "She might enjoy this one?" She grabs a purple and yellow bouquet of tiny carnations, and I hand over a twenty with my good arm, clutching the bouquet in the elbow of my injured one. Anything to get out of the rain. My mother will have to deal with different flowers for once.

The bouquet is soaked by the time I set it in the passenger's seat, but the car needs to be cleaned, anyway—Kari sure as hell hadn't cleaned it up. Pike Place Market swarms with pedestrians, mostly returning from work, and for the briefest moment, I consider revving my engine, letting it loose. Smashing into a few dozen of them.

But I'm not a psychopath like the man who took you, Noelle, a man in the business of kidnapping young women. Not the man who mowed you down before. This is a perfectly normal thought—it's acting on it that would make me a psychopath.

The drive to my mother's is hazy, and suddenly I'm pulling up to her house and squeezing into her driveway beside a shiny black Audi I don't recognize.

Who is visiting my mother? Has she invited someone else to dinner?

Oh god, is she going to try to hook me up with another woman, so soon after your disappearance? I know she wants grandchildren, but surely, it's too soon for that.

I'm early to dinner, so I sit in the car, staring at the slightly less expensive German car beside me, turning over the facts in my head, coming to a conclusion that, quite frankly, pisses me off.

You suggested to the hospital I had some role in your aunt's death. You hired a private investigator to look into me. You've been e-mailing with her. I can tell from the e-mail history you met with her in person. What's the point, Noelle?

I can come to only one conclusion—you want to ruin me. Which makes me think your goal is to leave me. But why?

I mean, I know I can be overprotective. Overbearing, even, in my protectiveness and dedication to our relationship. But what we have is love. I have the perfect future in mind for you. Carefully sculpted and planned. I just need to find you, and then—then, we will be perfect. You'll remember how much you need me.

You're checking your e-mail. Does that mean your captor has taken a liking to you? Given you freedoms? It's a dangerous thing to do—give a woman an inch, she'll take a mile, and all that.

Also, you should be more careful. Maybe you've won him over with your womanly wiles. I've seen how people adore you—how you charm your patients, the man who sells flowers, the baristas who make you your ridiculously complicated coffee.

It's an actual diagnosis, Noelle, when you've been taken against your will—Stockholm syndrome. How long did it take you to convince him to give you these freedoms? Is he listening to you now, instead of doing his job? Have you promised him something in return? Are you sleeping with him? Did you know he kicked the shit out of me when I came for you? Was that part of *your* plan? Did you have him wrapped around your finger that fast?

So much for paying him off.

Anger burns through me. I've sacrificed so much for us, Noelle. Maybe you need to understand how much this hurts—the damage he did; the damage you did, wanting to leave me. Maybe you need a taste of fear and pain, too. How would you like that?

The media has suggested, based off a clip of you exiting the diner with him—Jesus, did you share a stack of pancakes? A goddamn milkshake?—that his name is Jack Flaherty.

I dial the private investigator.

"Calvin here."

"Have you seen the news?"

"I have."

"Then why haven't you called me?" I fight the urge to grind my teeth—they are veneers, after all.

Calvin pauses. "I'm waiting on the facial recognition of the man who took Noelle. It's not finished yet—"

"Jack Flaherty. The name is all over the news."

"Jack Flaherty *is* all over the news. However, Mr. Flaherty is not the man who took Noelle. At least, he's not the man whose photo the camera in her apartment got of her kidnapping. It was my first thought, and I had photos compared."

My chest unclenches a little. "He's not her kidnapper?"

"No. He's not the man in the video who took her. He could be the second man who came in, I don't know, your camera didn't get a shot of his face."

My thoughts muddle as I try to sort out the facts. Your kidnapper is not the man you're currently with. My mouth goes dry. How did you go from kidnapped to with *him*?

Can nothing go as planned?

Air hisses through my teeth as I exhale, seething. Of course not. It's you.

"Find out everything you can on Jack Flaherty," I tell him, and then I hang up and call the next number.

"Kari," I say, then clear my throat. "How are you?"

"Um, I'm okay."

"Listen, I have a gift for you. I'm having dinner at my mother's, but could I drop it off on the way home?"

"Sure, okay," Kari says, confused.

"Great, I'll be by in a couple hours." I hang up and cast a sidelong glance at the flowers. My mother will have to do without.

I'm still early, but it's my mother, she won't mind—so I step out of my car, ease the door closed, eying the Audi as I go. It's not the sort of car a young woman would drive—and indeed, when I get a glimpse through the front window of Mother's house, it's not a woman, at all.

It's a man. A physician. My mother's oncologist.

My blood turns to ice when I see what they're doing. My

mother is in his arms, pressed against the doorframe that leads from the living room to the kitchen. Dr. Steven Hannigan has his body—*shudder*—against hers, one hand raised to her chin as though they're *teenagers*. I almost stop. I almost turn right around and *leave*, and Mother can wonder why I haven't arrived for dinner.

This man, of all men, should not be kissing my mother. My teeth clench, my hands tighten into fists, and my breath all but halts in my chest. I won't lie—I bend the rules, go so far as to break them, when necessary. Rules are meant to be broken and all. But this is one rule I would never break. I look again—he strokes her cheek, and she gazes up at him with the disgusting enamor of a lovesick twit. He has a bushy white beard, and he smiles, and he looks like fucking *Santa Claus*, and I just might puke my guts out here and now, broken ribs be damned.

The door is unlocked, and I twist it carefully, letting it swing inward. Their hushed voices fill the air, the heat of Mother's house—the house I bought her—enveloping me. I close the door and stand there, listening.

"It will be all right, Eve, darling. We'll tell him soon, and things will be fine. He'll realize what we're doing is about love, he'll accept—"

I bite back a growl. I can't take it anymore.

"Mother?" I call. "You home? Door was unlocked."

Silence. My thoughts go from one to the next with furious speed—*Accept what? That they're lying to me? That my mother's goddamn oncologist is screwing his patient, going against all ethical and moral boundaries a physician can have?* And not only that, every *rule* Mother has ever made for me. "*Marriage, Daniel, will be the key to a happy life. And children. Lots of children.*"

My girlfriend is probably screwing another man, my mother is screwing *that* man. I've done everything in my goddamn power to follow her rules, her way of life, and she's *lying* to me, about *this* of all things—

"Daniel, I didn't expect you so soon." Mother swings around the corner, her eyes wide, hands clutched together. Steven is nowhere to be seen, and that's probably good for his health. "I have a guest!" Mother claps her hands together. Mother has *never* in my memory clapped her hands together, and I want to grab those hands, want to shake her. Jesus, what is wrong with you women, Noelle?

"Come in, come in. Wine, Daniel?" Mother's hands flutter, beckoning me into the kitchen. Half a bottle of wine sits open on the counter. Mother retrieves another glass, pours, hands it to me. She beckons to the attached dining room, and there he is—

"Dr. Ashcroft, what a pleasure." Dr. Hannigan stands. He claps me on the arm, as though we're old pals, and all I can manage is to stare at him, thinking, *You've fucked my mother.* I'll call Calvin as soon as I can. I'll find a way to get Steven Hannigan's license revoked. Get him tossed out of practice altogether. I'll show him the dangers of messing with me, with my family.

"Daniel?" Mother's voice is high, tight. "Steven—Dr. Hannigan—was just checking in on me. Isn't that sweet? Who says doctors don't do house calls, anymore?"

I summon a smile. Direct it at them both as they peer at me, guilty as teens caught in the backseat of a car. One teenage antic I never did, because Mother told me not to. My heart races. Mother watches me with watery bloodshot eyes, and it occurs to me she's drunk.

"Very kind of you," I say to Steven, but there's something in my voice, even I can hear it, that says otherwise.

"Well, Evelyn, I really must be going. I'm glad to see you're getting on so well. Your labs are—" Steven stops short, searches for the word. He grabs the wineglass, takes a drink, an excuse for his pause in speech. "Things are looking just fine." Another smile. A nod my way. "Great to see you, Dr. Ashcroft."

Then he's out the front door, and the house is silent once more. I almost round on her. Almost demand answers. Instead, I say, "Drinking on the job is a bad sign in a physician, Mother. Should I look into a new oncologist for you?"

I wait for her reaction. The dining area is a stark reminder of what I saw through the window—two place settings. Two glasses of wine. Another bottle, empty, sits between them. I contemplate how long it might have taken them to drink that bottle together. How long they have been carrying on together, in secret. How long Steven Hannigan has been taking advantage of my Mother, and how long she's been letting it happen.

"Everything is fine, Daniel. Could you please get me the spaghetti from the pantry?"

A pot clanks in the kitchen, a drawer opens—Mother, puttering around the kitchen, once again pretending everything is fine.

Noelle, you're not the only one with something up your sleeve.

I take a long swallow from the wineglass still held in my hand.

"Mother?" I say.

"Don't dawdle, Daniel, the spaghetti—" She's back to herself, but it's a show. An act. Or maybe it's an act with Steven. I don't know. Can a person really be two different people and truly be both of them? You can, Noelle. Maybe my mother can be, too. Maybe she's been carrying on this affair for months, or even since she started treatment.

"I know what you're doing." I turn a slow circle and step into the kitchen. Mother stops short, carrying a pot to the sink. She sets it down, eyes never leaving mine. Realization flashes in her eyes, then guilt, then shame—or maybe that's what I want to see.

"Oh, Daniel, you don't—" Mother blinks. A tear escapes. She wrings her hands. "Can you ever forgive me? I didn't mean to keep you in the dark this long, but—"

"I forgive you. I don't forgive him, though. It's against our code of ethics, a doctor dating his patient."

Mother studies me. Her mouth opens, closes. Finally, she says, "It just... happened. We've been working so closely, trying to cure the cancer, and it just happened. I should have told you."

Neither of us move. My appetite is gone, and besides, I have other things to concern myself with. Things that will benefit Mother, and hopefully fill this hole in her heart that has led her down this path to screwing her oncologist. She should have what she really wants—a grandchild. Me. You. Us, together, as a family.

In a way, maybe it's my fault, for not yet giving her the one thing she's asked me for. But I'll make good on that soon enough. Just as soon as I find you.

THIRTY-NINE

NOELLE

I can't imagine how Daniel figured out I hired a private investigator.

The itch at my neck changes, becomes a sensation best described as spiders crawling down my spine. He's watched me for half a year that I know of—cameras, spyware—but maybe it's worse than I thought.

My head throbs in time with my heartbeat. I press the heels of my hands into my eyes and wonder how the hell I got myself into this mess, how I'll ever escape.

Maybe there is no escape.

The words flit through my mind. I ignore them. Take a slow deep breath. Focus on what I *can* do, which is find contact information for Justine and more details on Sarah.

I pull up Daniel's medical school alumni website and search for Daniel's graduating year. A list of doctors pops up, including him. A quick scroll is all it takes.

Justine Peterson. Olympia Regional Cardiology. I gape at the screen, almost unable to believe I've finally found her. In fact, it's possible I've *spoken* to her, as Seattle General regularly takes patients from their hospital, which is smaller, unlicensed to do open-heart surgery.

What are the chances? I stare at her name, her contact information, and get up to brew a pot of weak motel coffee. I pace the room, then go to splash water on my face. I'm exhausted, but also keyed up—discovering Justine's name, that she's *alive*, that maybe, just maybe, I've found someone I can trust. If she knows what Daniel is like, if he did the same thing to her he's done to me, maybe she'll be able to help me.

I return to the bed and search social media for Justine, but she seems to not have a social media presence, at least not under her given name. Then I google her. Her cardiology practice makes up the top five hits, and I click on her professional profile to see a beautiful woman smiling with shiny white teeth, professional makeup, naturally red hair, a white lab coat. She looks almost exactly as she did in the photo that is now a decade old. The profile offers surface details—she lives with her family, including her husband and their adopted daughter, in Olympia, Washington. She plays racquetball and tennis, and travels to Seattle to see patients at the practice's other location twice a week. She volunteers with the local YWCA and is an active member of her church.

None of these details are helpful, and I lie back on the bed, holding the phone between my hands, swiping back until I return to the search. I switch to an image search, immediately finding photos of her that range from promotional photos for her cardiology practice to images of her in an underdeveloped nation, building a school, hugging a child, providing medical care to an elderly woman.

Still, not helpful. I scroll until I find a familiar face—a younger Daniel, his arm around her. They're at a wedding, I think, caught mid-laughter with other young people, the bride standing opposite of them. The group is gathered around a table, and is that—yes—Eve, in the background, and I can tell this photo is from some time ago—Eve's lost weight in the mean-time, probably from her battle with cancer. I click on the link associated with the photograph, and it takes me to a photogra-pher's website. But there's only one more that includes Justine, and it's only her red hair that lets me identify her—her back is turned, clutching Eve in a hug that tells me *they* had a better relationship than we do.

I'm about to swipe back, to pore through more image search photos, when it occurs to me I have everything I need. This proves that Justine is in fact *alive*. Alive and well, actually. Not disappeared. Not dead. Maybe there's not a pattern. Maybe Sarah really disappeared, and Daniel is innocent.

But no. *No.* My aunt. He killed my aunt. There's no way she's dead, Sarah's gone, and now someone's trying to have me kidnapped, and that's not tied to Daniel. It's simply not possible.

More than anything, I want to go on a run. Let this all fade away. Live in the moment, even just briefly. But I can't. Not only might someone recognize me in downtown Portland, but from a practical standpoint, I have only the clothes on my back, which do not include a sports bra, nor even vaguely breathable clothing.

I don't know what else to do, so I pull up Justine's clinic phone number. I dial star sixty-seven to make it anonymous, then the number. I shut my eyes and press the motel phone firmly against my ear. I feel like I'm calling a ghost. A person who somehow escaped him. A person who not only lived but continued *living*.

FORTY

DANIEL

Now

I get Calvin on the line before I even start the engine.

"What can I do for you, Dr. Ashcroft?"

"I need you to look into someone for me. A Dr. Steven Hannigan." I clench my teeth as I say his name, imagining a second time his paws all over my mother. "He's my mother's oncologist. I want to know everything—if he's married, if he ever has been. Where he got his medical degree from, how long he's been practicing. If he has any criminal record. Everything."

"I'll get you a full report by tomorrow."

"Great." I disconnect.

When I reach Kari's, she answers the door so fast it's as though she's waiting on the other side.

"Hello, Kari." I smile.

Kari's lips curl up and she nods a hello, but she's no longer the confident woman going after the man she believes to have hurt her cousin. She's the pregnant woman who asked a man she does not like for help when she had no one else. And after that video going up of you leaving the diner with Jack fucking

Flaherty, she must have decided I had nothing to do with it. For once, I'm not the bad guy in her book.

"For you." I hold out the bouquet and step past her, forcing her to step back.

"Th-thank you." She hesitates at the door—worried to close it? Worried to be alone with me?

I step from peeling brown laminate flooring to peeling, crusty brown carpet. The living room is small, poorly lit, stinking vaguely of cat piss, with a sagging futon its only furniture. Jesus Christ, how does anyone live like this? How does she expect to raise a child like this?

"I was thinking we could do a little publicity to keep interest in Noelle's case at the forefront of the media," I say as she shuffles into the room behind me. *And pull attention away from me.* The last thing I need is bad publicity. I have an image to uphold. So far the media is playing me as the concerned boyfriend—best to keep it that way. "Especially now that we know she's alive."

"Publicity?" Kari raises a defiant brow and crosses her arm. "To benefit you? Or Noelle?"

Ah, there's the Kari I know and tolerate. Not a flat refusal, but not readily desiring to help me, either. Her folded arms make her belly that much more prominent, and I smile again.

"How's the baby?" I ask. "You know, with Noelle coming home soon, we should discuss telling her."

Kari's eyes widen in alarm.

"We can't tell her." She hisses the words, her eyes skittering sideways as though she's afraid her roommate will overhear.

Even better.

"No?" I ask, raising my voice a notch. "You don't think Noelle would want to know?"

"Stop!" She steps toward me, whipping her finger over her lips. "Shhh. We can't tell her."

"You don't think she'll notice when the baby looks just like me? Blue eyes, blond—"

"The baby won't have blue eyes," she snaps. "Brown eyes are genetically dominant, I have brown eyes, the baby—"

"Oh, sweetheart, it's more complicated than that."

"Kari!" A woman's voice calls from somewhere deeper in the shithole that is her house. "Is something wrong?" Her roommate.

"Nothing. I'm fine!" she hollers back. When her gaze rests on me again, it's poisonous. So much for rushing her to the hospital and saving our baby's life. "What do you want me to do?" she hisses.

If your captor is letting you check your e-mail, what else is he letting you check, Noelle? You tried to screw with me—let me assure you, it's not fun being on the receiving end.

"Just pose for a few photos with me. Her cousin and her boyfriend, eagerly awaiting her return." Kari shifts closer, scowling. I switch my phone to selfie mode and wrap an arm around her. "Smile," I say. "We'll post them on your Instagram. Noelle will just *love* seeing these."

FORTY-ONE

NOELLE

Now

"Olympia Regional Cardiology Practice, this is an after-hours emergency-only line. How may I help you?"

I couldn't wait until morning to make this call, but I hadn't considered it would be after hours. I should have—I know offices usually close by six or seven, and a glance at the clock tells me it's just after nine. I take a deep breath and launch into the first story that comes to mind. "My husband is a patient of Dr. Peterson. I need to speak to her, immediately. *Please.*" I speak in a high, frightened voice.

"Ma'am, if your husband is in distress, I would recommend calling 911 or proceeding to the nearest emergency department."

Shit.

I think fast, remembering how many patients I've had who refuse to come in when they've started to show signs of a heart attack—how they wait and wait, until when they finally do go in, it's far worse than it would have been had they simply gone in when they first showed symptoms.

"He's refusing to until I talk to Dr. Peterson," I say. "Please."

A sigh. "Hold, please."

Anticipation burns through me. I stand up, pace. Check the window again. Force myself to sit down, to focus.

Justine comes on the line exactly two minutes later.

"This is Dr. Peterson. May I ask who's calling?"

My fist curls in the comforter. It's now or never.

"Don't hang up," I say. "I'm not a patient, but this is a matter of life or death." I cringe—Jesus, did I hear that in a movie?

"Um. This is an emergency cardiology line for—"

"I know," I say. "And you're Justine Peterson, right? You dated Daniel Ashcroft." My hands curl into fists, saying his name out loud.

A long pause.

"Listen," I continue, "I'm sorry to bother you, but I'm in trouble and—" And what? Daniel's chasing me? He hired a kidnapper, potentially a hitman to—I fidget, realizing how stupid this would sound; a hitman?—take care of me?

"You're Noelle." Her voice is soft, empathy oozing through the line. A desire to say *yes, yes, yes, help me, please,* fills me, leaves me clutching the phone, waiting for her to say something else.

But she stays silent.

"What happened when you were with Daniel?" I ask, hoping that empathy in her voice means she will answer my questions.

More silence. Has it been too long? Was he a different person back then? Does she not even know what I'm talking about?

"How did you get away?" I press when she still doesn't reply.

"I'm so sorry," she finally says. "I don't know what you mean. I think you have the wrong number."

"No, wait—" But the line clicks dead, and I'm left with the knowledge of two things: one, she knows who I am, and two, she's afraid to talk to me.

It's 10 p.m. when I leave the motel. I stride down the sidewalk, entering the hopscotched row of bars, interspersed with cafés and music shops and sex shops. Typical Portland, and with a newly purchased hoodie and hat, I look like any other twenty-something roaming the streets for a drink. The darkness offers me a protection the daylight doesn't, and I have to get out—I'm slowly going stir crazy, pacing my room. Wondering what the hell Justine meant, why she pretended to be someone else. What had Daniel done to her?

Justine is by all rights a strong successful woman, a physician, a mother and wife, someone who dedicated herself to helping others—and I'd heard that moment of empathy, when she realized who I was.

So *what* had happened to make her so afraid?

The light changes red at a crosswalk, and I pause next to a group of women, gossiping and gesturing and out for a night on the town. Just like Kari and I used to do.

But now, I'm alone. Wandering Portland, hoping no one looks at my face too long.

That's the moment I remember my hair—my auburn hair I failed to dye—and I tuck it into the sweatshirt, nestle the hood a little tighter over my head.

The world is collapsing in on me, like I'm in a medieval torture device, the sort where the executioner stacks one brick after another on the prisoner's body, slowly letting the pressure crush the person to death. Justine is one more brick. One more mystery that leads back to me not feeling safe, needing to get away, but being trapped instead.

In fact, the only person I *do* trust is Kari, but she's the one person I can't reach out to for help. I wander into a coffee shop behind the same group of women and order hot tea. It's dark in here, the sort of place that serves coffee, wine, sells used books, has comfy couches to lounge on during quiet conversation. It's warm, too, making me realize my fingertips have gone numb in the winter weather.

I find an empty loveseat in a corner and sit down to wait for my tea. Kari's still on my mind—we should have done a girls' trip to Portland—and I pick up the phone, navigate to Kari's Instagram, wanting just a moment of pretending things are how they used to be. But the first photo that pops up tells me that is not the case.

My hand flies to my mouth, stifling a gasp.

Kari. Daniel. In her home, on her futon, his arm wrapped tightly around her shoulders. She's smiling. He's tilting his head, almost touching hers. It's a selfie of the two of them.

The caption reads, *Best friends*.

I stare at the post, the photo, the word, lost in my own world for far too long—when I finally come to, the barista has rounded the corner of the bar, said my name at least a few times, from the look on his face, and is attempting to hand me a to-go cup, the little string from the teabag dangling out one side.

"Thank you." I take it, but he stands there a moment, a frown creasing his features.

"You okay?" he asks. "You look like you need something stronger."

I blink up at him, wondering what he would say if I explained it all—the controlling, abusive boyfriend; the fake kidnapping turned real; the fact I've escaped my kidnapper once, twice, but I have a sinking suspicion my boyfriend is behind all of this, and I'm only one of his many victims.

"Hey, do I know you from somewhere?" His frown turns into a smile. My heart goes rapid fire, and I feel myself stand up, tea sloshing over my hand. I ignore the burn. Hell, I embrace it, because it snaps me out of my reverie. I need to go. *Now.*

"I used to come here a lot in college," I say, the lie rolling easily off my tongue.

"Really? We just opened this past summer." He takes a half step forward, inspecting my face, like if he looks long enough, he'll recall where he knows me from.

Go. Now!

"Excuse me." I offer him a smile, slip around him, out the door and into a blast of cold wind. I speed-walk back the way I came, because screw being stir crazy, at least no one can recognize me in the privacy of my own motel room. I turn one corner, then another, then come up short.

Red lights. Blue lights. A flashing swirl reflecting off the chain-link fence of a nearby storage facility, the yellow paint of the motel. A police car. No, *two* police cars. And two police officers, standing out front of my motel room door.

Someone recognized me. Someone called the cops. I cannot go back.

The tea falls from my hand, splattering on the ground. I turn around. I walk away.

There is nowhere I am safe.

FORTY-TWO

NOELLE

It's 2 a.m. before I stop walking. The temperature has plummeted, and I take refuge in one of the twenty-four-hour bar-coffee shops near the University of Portland. They serve alcohol until 2:30 a.m., and I'm desperate enough to calm the anxiety clawing through me that when the bartender comes around for last call, I ask for a Manhattan. I usually stick to wine, or a beer on occasion, but a Manhattan was my aunt's drink of choice, and I'm feeling lonely, sorry for myself, with a healthy dose of fear sprinkled in. I find a dark corner to hide in, hat low over my face.

Kari has buddied up with Daniel. Justine is too scared to talk to me. Sarah is gone, probably dead. My aunt is dead. And I'm homeless, on the run, my options narrowing by the hour. I don't even have a place to sleep tonight. Just coming into this bar left me paranoid, but thankfully the two bartenders appear to be drinking as much as the customers, so it's unlikely they'll recognize me.

My drink arrives, and I put down half of it while staring at Kari's Instagram again. There's another photo beside the first one, which I'd been too shocked to notice before—a flower arrangement gracing her dining room table. Courtesy of Daniel.

The photo above it is the one of the new baby items—the ones Kari couldn't afford—and it hits me where they might have come from.

Daniel. But would he buy her flowers? *Baby* gifts?

It doesn't add up. He's buying her things. Taking *selfies* with her. He's somehow convinced her he's safe to be around after months of her actively disliking him. He closed the case I'd started against him, meaning he knew I'd hired a PI. He put up a huge reward for me and is likely paying somebody off to increase media coverage, judging by the amount of attention my disappearance has gotten in the news.

I sip the Manhattan. Savor the sting of the alcohol as it slides down my throat. Feel it fortify me in a way I'm not entirely comfortable with, and yet, sitting here alone at last call in a Portland bar, not a single person at my back, I also welcome.

The reality is I cannot escape Daniel. This knowledge settles inside me with certainty. He knows too many people. He has too much money, has his claws sunk too far, too deep for me to get away. Anyone who might be able to help me, like Justine, is terrified of him.

I don't want to be like Justine. I don't want to be a professional at the pinnacle of her career, terrified of an ex-boyfriend, unable to even take a phone call, for fear it might come back to haunt her.

Even if I make it out of Portland, get away from Daniel, I still have to deal with the police he's no doubt got in his back pocket, the media, the hundreds of thousands of people who have seen my photo and would love an extra fifty thousand dollars in their bank accounts—

What then?

I spend the rest of my life looking over my shoulder? This

cannot be my life. And it's clear that disappearing isn't in the cards. I need a new plan. A *better* plan.

Besides, I am tired of Daniel Ashcroft always winning.

I down the Manhattan. Catch the bartender's attention, request another, holding up an extra twenty so he'll bend the rules of last call.

I stare down at the phone. Consider my options.

I navigate to the news, hoping something will inspire me— that I'll magically figure a way out of my predicament. And there's my photo on the front page, and there's a photo of Jack O'Kelly, but—Jack O'Kelly is not the name listed.

Jack Flaherty is a person of interest... caught on security cameras with the missing Noelle Thomas... the two don't appear to have a relationship... Mr. Flaherty has been previously charged with several felonies... potentially armed, potentially dangerous, do not approach... may have been involved in Ms. Thomas' kidnapping...

I scramble to type in this new name, but mentions of him online are saturated with more of the same—news articles, mentions on the Twitter account Daniel has started to update the world on the search for me.

I chew my lip, then open every social media site I can think of, searching them one by one. It's not until the last tab, Facebook, where I get a hit for *Jack Flaherty*. But it's not his profile. Rather, someone mentioned this name, over and over in the comments of other photos. And as I squint at the tiny screen, finally zooming in on one, I see why: Jack, standing beside a young woman and several young men in what appears to be a series of family photos, half a dozen mostly grown children, arms tossed around one another, smiling, then a single photo of them goofing off—all dressed in jeans and black shirts and hairstyles that aren't quite in style anymore. The last photo is of two of them—Jack and the woman, and they appear to be maybe eighteen. The caption says, *Twins*, and then—

I stare at the names, blinking away my disbelief.

Jack. Sarah.

Jack Flaherty is Sarah MacCleary's twin brother.

I look back and forth between the photos of them, trying to understand, and that's when it hits me—*this is why Jack had a photo of Sarah*. Not because he made her go missing. His words echo in my ears, that he, too, had lost someone in a similar situation.

Jack lost Sarah to Daniel.

And Jack is here, somehow caught up in what's happening between Daniel and I. There's no way that's a coincidence.

I blow out a breath and make the last decision I ever thought I'd come to.

I scroll through my previous received calls and dial Jack Flaherty's motel room, on the off chance he's still there. I tap my fingers over the wood tabletop, half hoping he answers, half hoping he doesn't. My stomach aches with nerves—at talking to Jack. At what I'm thinking of doing.

"Hello?" A scratchy, sleep-rich voice.

"It's me," I say.

"Noelle?"

"Yeah." I pause. Sarah's picture in his wallet flashes through my mind. The moment he looked up when Daniel arrived at the motel, but he didn't make a move to stop me from stealing his truck. He told me he would help me.

But that doesn't mean I can trust him.

"You still there?" he asks.

"Tell me the truth. Tell me *everything*." My voice doesn't quake, and I'm proud for that.

Jack clears his throat. The creak of bedsprings, then he coughs and says, "Okay. Sure. I guess you saw—"

"Sarah is your sister."

Another silence.

"Was," he says. "She *was* my sister."

"So, she's dead?" My hand clenches around the Manhattan.

"I—" He hesitates. "I don't know that for sure. But, I think so. She never would have just taken off. She never would go years without contacting our family, without getting in touch with me. Even if it was a postcard, or an e-mail from an anonymous account, or—" His voice breaks off, his tone lowering with grief.

The same way I talk about my aunt. A wave of emotion hits me, and I hold my breath to keep from letting it take over. This is not the time. Not the place. Not the person to cry with.

"Why did you help with the kidnapping, then?" I manage. "What's in it for you?"

"It's a long story." He sighs. "To summarize? Sarah came out here for nursing school and met Daniel. I never trusted him. Some doctor suddenly wants to be with my sister? Don't get me wrong—my sister was a catch. But she had twenty bucks to her name, working paycheck to paycheck to get through nursing school. Always felt off to me."

"Then, she disappeared. She's my *sister*. My *twin* sister. So I had to come look for her. And I realized what I was actually doing was looking for *him*. Trying to figure out what part he'd played, because—" Jack pauses, his voice drifting. "I just had a feeling. Got a job in Seattle doing what I do—tough-guy stuff. And I heard from my boss there was a job to kidnap you—and I knew who you were, because I knew who Daniel was. I thought maybe... I'd learn something from you I didn't already know."

"From me?" I ask. "Why would you think that?"

"Maybe not you directly, but maybe you'd know something about Daniel that would help. I'd do anything to find her. To find out what happened. You know?"

I swallow. I do know. It's how I feel about my aunt.

"But then you were a real person. Not just a means to an

end. You were obviously terrified, and not just of me. Of *him*. I couldn't help Sarah, but..." The line goes quiet. "But I could help you. But by then I knew my story sounded crazy. Like I was a stalker. I thought I'd order a pizza, and we'd sit and eat, and maybe I'd figure out how to talk to you about it, but then you—"

"I snuck out a window."

"Yeah. And then Daniel showed up and it all went to hell."

The nervousness gives way to something akin to relief because I believe him. I actually believe him. It's too much for someone to have simply made up.

"That's why you let me take your truck."

"That's why I let you take my truck," he echoes, weariness in his voice.

"And now they're accusing you of my kidnapping."

A humorless laugh. "Yep. Just one more line on my rap sheet."

Silence stretches between us, and I finish my drink, search the room for the next one coming my way, because if ever there was a night for liquid courage, it's tonight.

"I have an idea," I say after I've processed it all. An idea that might mean I can stay. That I can help Kari, instead of leaving her in Daniel's clutches. An idea that could give me back my life.

The bartender sets down the new Manhattan, and I slide him the cash. He leaves, and I pause to sip the fresh drink. "He ruined my life. He ruined Sarah's. Now he's messing with yours, too, letting you take the fall for my kidnapping."

Jack makes a noise that sounds vaguely like agreement.

I take one more drink. Feel the heat spread through me. Let anger and fear consolidate into a fuel that drives my next words. "I'm going to tell you where I left your truck. And then I need you to come get me."

"What for?"

"We're turning the tables. He's been playing with other peoples' lives, so we're going to play with his. Let him see what it feels like. And we'll find out what he did to Sarah. We'll find proof of what he was going to do to me. We'll clear your name. We're going to end this. For good."

FORTY-THREE

DANIEL

Noelle, dearest.

I thought of you all night. You kept me up. Your auburn hair, a little curly, just enough it frustrates you. Your blue eyes, oceans of considerable depth I hope to someday understand. I thought of when I will see you again, what I will say, what I will do. The ring I will slide on your finger. You'll say yes after all that you've put me through.

First, you dare to accuse me of killing your aunt.

Second, you hire a PI to look into me when I could have saved you, brought us closer together than ever before.

Lastly, you take up with another man, One I can only assume you've been in contact with for quite some time now.

You're playing with fire, my love. Don't mind me while I turn up the heat.

FORTY-FOUR
NOELLE

The weather doesn't look good.

A fresh round of snowflakes flutters from the sky, turning downtown Portland into something picturesque, like a Hallmark movie. The fact I'm in a corner booth of the same bar I've been in since 2 a.m., plotting ways to screw with the boyfriend who's made my life a living hell, is a stark contrast. Between that and the two Manhattans, I'm numb.

I'm also watching the clock on the wall, waiting for Jack to arrive. It's just past 7 a.m., the world starting to wake up, college students and children alike delighted at said snow—but all I can think of is, *This will make it harder to get back to Seattle.* A plow creeps down the road, dumping salt in the pale light of the morning. My stolen phone beeps with a message from an unknown number—Jack.

New phone. Be there in ten.

He's made good time considering the Pacific Northwest doesn't often get this much snow, that the roads are surely icy.

I shiver, thinking of returning to Seattle.

"Coffee?"

I whip my head around to see the bartender who ignored last call for me. He has a to-go cup of steaming coffee in his hand, and he offers it with a smile.

"Thanks," I say.

He nods at the window. "Big storm coming. Supposed to get colder all day long. Make sure you drip your faucets." He hovers a beat, waiting for me to respond, to say something more. But I just smile, because I don't want to engage in conversation, don't want to say something that might tip him off as to who I really am.

Once he leaves, I pull up the weather on the phone and indeed, temperatures will drop to single digits throughout the day and into tonight, both here and in Seattle. Extreme weather for Western Washington, where proximity to the Puget Sound usually keeps it warmer. If I had a home, I'd agree with the bartender—faucets dripping, windows stuffed with towels to keep the draft out, maybe a couple days of food in the cupboard, just in case.

Something about that catches me. Makes me think, *I don't have a home I can return to anymore, but I know who does.* And wouldn't it be fitting for him to feel a little less comfortable in that home? Just like I had, knowing cameras were watching my every move.

Daniel's work schedule is posted online, and though a password is needed, it's a password I have; I used to request my shifts around his so we could maximize our time together. I sip the coffee, hot and strong, and just what I needed. The scheduling website loads. I scroll down to Daniel's name—but he's off the schedule entirely. I bite my lip, contemplating. Maybe because Jack beat him up or possibly because of the investigation into my aunt's death. Either way, satisfaction breaks through the numbness. I'd like to know his schedule—but I like even more knowing I've disrupted his life. Given him a taste of his own medicine.

Daniel will be busy, though. He'll have a meeting. He'll go to his mother's house. Maybe he'll go out to dinner. Maybe he'll fall asleep beneath his thousand-dollar down comforter and it'll keep him warm, and he won't notice the cold creeping in, especially if he has a few drinks first.

Maybe I can make his water pipes burst. It's petty—but I know it'll piss him off. Destroy at least one room in the house he's so proud of.

I download the app that connects to his thermostat, sign in again using Daniel's log-in, and adjust his home's thermostat settings—heat off. Temperatures will reach a low of ten degrees Fahrenheit tonight, according to the weather website, which doesn't happen often in Seattle. Maybe that's just cold enough for just long enough.

I hazard a smile at this small act of defiance. Chances are, he'll catch it and it won't work—but the *act* of it is something. Something that stirs a strength in me I thought I'd left behind.

"You're here."

I jolt, the coffee in my hand sloshing, that feeling of strength snapping taut as Jack Flaherty slides into the seat across the table. His gaze travels over me, and I size him up, too—still rough around the edges. A couple more days unshaven. Hair tied back. White T-shirt, with a zip-up black hoodie pulled around his arms. I clutch the coffee and force my face to a neutral expression—I invited him here. But he's still a criminal. I need him, but I don't totally trust him.

"How's the coffee?" he asks, tone mild, sinking low in the booth, and I swear he's trying to not look like the tough guy he is. I wonder if he's dealt with that his whole life—people afraid of him.

I straighten in my seat. Inhale. Press the coffee cup his way and decide *this is it*. If I'm going to go after Daniel, I can't be afraid anymore. Of him. Of Daniel. Easier said than done, but I have to try. I peer at Jack and remember the grief in his voice—remember he's as human as I am, and he's here for Sarah, because he loves her. I try for kindness.

"Decent. Want some?"

He accepts the cup and watches me as he takes a long sip. "Not bad."

"There's a storm coming." I nod at the street. "We should get on the road."

"We can do that." He takes another drink of the coffee and slides it back to me. "But before we do, I want to know your plan. And"—he raises a brow—"I'd like my photo of my sister back."

Of course he does. I paw through my bag of belongings, find it tucked between his credit cards, and I return those, too, as well as the cash I took. When my hand closes over the key, I look up.

"Is it safe to take the truck?"

"Yeah." Jack stretches an arm, his neck, gazes at the coffee shop goers, checks the people striding down the street. *Watching*, I realize. Looking for anyone who might have recognized us. This time it's me who sinks a little lower in the booth. Being recognized would be bad. Very bad.

"How can you be sure?"

Jack's gaze settles on me, and maybe I do see a bit of Sarah in him—the eyebrow ridges, the mouth.

"The truck isn't under my real name. The motel didn't have cameras. We're fine. You still haven't told me your plan?"

The reality is, I only have a vague idea of one. All I know is I can't run anymore. I can't be afraid, or let Daniel hurt Kari. I can't stand by as Daniel finds another woman like me and does this again. But what does that mean? What's the answer that solves these problems?

"You hungry?" I get to my feet and point at the counter,

where bakery goods now fill a glass case. I could eat, but mostly, I'm buying myself time.

"Sure," he says. "And a coffee, please."

I stride off, careful not to attract attention or meet anyone's eyes. The place emptied out after last call, but a trickle of early morning customers have come in for coffee or a muffin. I order and step off to one side to wait, stealing a glance back at the table.

Jack gazes out the window, his form folded in on itself, the picture of—what? A wanted man? Grief for his sister? Defeat? I take a muffin and a scone and a fresh coffee and go back to the table, setting everything between us.

"Help yourself," I say, then add, "Tell me about Sarah. And this guy you came to Seattle to work for."

He palms the muffin, slides the scone my way. "Why?"

"I need to know as much as I can. It might help." I don't know *how* it might help—more similarities? A better idea of what happened to Justine that has her so scared?

"Tell me more about Daniel," he replies. A challenge.

Our eyes meet, and I realize calling him was the right thing to do—we want the same thing, just different versions of it. Justice. Answers. And it might be nice to not be so alone in this.

"Daniel has had three girlfriends," I start. I detail everything I know about Justine, Sarah, and the events that have transpired since I arranged my kidnapping. "He works as an anesthesiologist. His father died—possibly by suicide—when he was young. He has a mother who lives in Seattle." I go on until Jack nods. He crumples the muffin wrapper in his hand and casts another glance at the room, which has filled up considerably.

"Let's go. I'll tell you about Sarah on the way. And you can tell me your grand plan."

By the time we reach the truck, he's shared a brief family history, the most important details being that he and Sarah were the babies of the family, with three older siblings, none of whom he's close with.

"Addiction. Criminal bullshit. Stuff like that," he says. "But Sarah, she was getting her life together. I always thought she came out here to get away from us." He pauses as we slide into the truck.

Jack cranks the engine, turns up the heat. He parked near Powell's Books, in underground parking, and we watch a stream of Priuses climb the circular parking garage in search of a spot.

"Anyway, Sarah didn't want to end up someone's pregnant girlfriend. She wanted to *do* something with her life. She came to Seattle, and—" A shrug. He rubs his hands together, looks anywhere but me, but his lips press together, as though he's holding back emotion. "That was it. We talked on the phone, but it was like she'd started a new life, and as long as we were doing the same dumb shit we did growing up, she didn't want to be a part of it. Then she met *Daniel*, said she was going to marry him..." His voice trails off.

I think he's said everything he has to say, but his jaw tenses and he continues. "Next thing I knew, a cop was at the door, interviewing me. Asking me if I'd heard from her. If I knew anything." He looks sideways at me. "Daniel supposedly was out of town when it happened. I talked to him once, on the phone. He was setting up some sort of charity in her name, and I couldn't believe he was calling it quits so soon—she'd only been gone six months. Anyway, like I told you, I came to see if I could find out what happened."

"Have you found anything?"

He snorts. "Nope. Nothing other than"—he waves a hand at me—"that you wanted out badly enough to try to have yourself kidnapped. Makes me wonder what Sarah was going through. Otherwise, Daniel's so sparkly clean, it's almost obvious there must be something else going on. But I don't know what."

I nod, familiar with what he means—Daniel's persona to the

public is perfection. The perfect, kind, caring doctor who plays by the rules. No one would guess what lies beneath all that.

"So, what's your plan?" Jack rubs his hands together for warmth and looks over at me.

I open my mouth. Close it. Think of the possibilities as Jack pulls from the garage, and we're hit with the white light that is sunshine reflecting on snow.

"I can't run anymore. Even if I could get away—and it's becoming more and more obvious it's only a matter of time before he finds me—I'd only be looking over my shoulder for the rest of my life. It pisses me off that he's done this *three* times and still parades around Seattle like he's a freaking king. No one knows who he really is. *What* he really is. He plays the part of philanthropist doctor, says please and thank you, smiles, and everyone assumes he's a good guy. They don't know what he's like in private. He's never suffered consequences for his actions." I pause. "I think he killed my aunt, too."

I tell him about her—about the PI. About Kari, the newest photos, her high-risk, threatened pregnancy. The more I say out loud, the more I realize how messed up it all is. Something I've known all along, but summarizing it for another person makes it that much worse—that much more terrifying. My heart beats louder, faster, as I rehash the last year of my life, and when I finish, I take a long, slow breath, trying to calm it.

"You sure it's him?" Jack asks after a beat. "He seems... smart. Like he'd know better than to have two girlfriends disappear back to back. You said you were hit by a car? Then almost hit again? Did you get a look at the driver?" I shake my head. "You ask the cops to look into your ex's whereabouts?"

"No, but—" I bite my lip, let my hands fidget with the seatbelt. "Even if it is someone else, Daniel wants me back and is actively trying to"—I wave a hand, thinking of the photos on Kari's Instagram—"get me back. Trap me, again. And, I have a hard time believing he can be associated with so many disappearances. And deaths," I add, thinking of my aunt. "What's that rule they always quote on TV? Occam's rule?"

"Occam's razor," Jack murmurs. "The simplest explanation is usually right."

I nod. "Yeah. That."

We sit in silence, and I realize I never answered his question. *What's the plan?*

I press a hand against the cool glass of the passenger's side window and stare out at the world whipping by—between Portland and Seattle sits plenty of lowland, farms and lakes and pine forests. People living perfectly normal lives. I'd like a perfectly normal life. *My* life, period.

"I want my life back," I finally say. "I need to be free of him. And if you will help me, we can at least prove you didn't kidnap me. Or"—I smile—"I can tell them that, anyway."

"But—"

"I'm not done." I swivel to face him. "That means Daniel has to be the one to disappear. Because while he's still around, neither of those things will happen."

A muscle feathers in Jack's jaw.

"Disappear? As in dead? Or prison?"

My breath catches in my throat. "Prison. Obviously."

Jack nods slowly, and I realize he would have been okay if my answer had been... not prison.

"The problem," I go on, "Is that nothing sticks to him. There's no proof. He's friends with cops. With the cops' bosses. He donates a ton of money to Seattle. He knows the mayor. He's connected, and he's well respected in the medical community."

"I've noticed." Jack hisses the words through his teeth. "Trying to get information on him has been hell."

"I want him to feel like I do. Like everything has been taken away from him." I pause, thinking of the thermostat—my attempt to make his home's pipes burst and destroy whatever room it happens in.

"How do we do that?" Jack asks.

"Little things," I say. First, the thermostat. The best I can do to take away the safety and security of his home, like he did mine. I relay this to Jack, and what I've done.

"Money," I say next. "I can't clear out his bank account, but maybe I can..." I shrug. "Cancel his credit cards. And—" I think of the job I left behind. The financial security. "Maybe I can put his job in jeopardy, too."

"How?" Jack steals a look my way as he turns the steering wheel.

"Anonymous complaints. I wouldn't even be lying." How many times did Daniel corner me at work, long after I'd stopped desiring his attentions? Or demand I join him on a date or at his mother's, while we both stood on hospital grounds, working as employees?

I'll make sure he can't buy his way through life.

"I'll think of more things to take away from him—to screw with him. In the end, we need to catch him in the act. Or find damning evidence. Or get him to admit to what he's done. But maybe if we put him off his game, it'll make him more likely to screw up. To lose control."

The answer zings through me.

"He has cameras in his house. They're tied to his computer; I've accessed them before. If we can get him alone, maybe I can get him to admit to it. To hurting me, to hurting Sarah and Justine. Killing my aunt. Especially if he's already on edge, because I've taken everything away from him. And if it's on camera, all we have to do is turn that in. Then it won't matter what kind of perfect reputation he has. No one will care in prison."

FORTY-FIVE

DANIEL

I've just undressed post-workout when my phone vibrates.

I ignore it.

Showering is an intimate moment, a brief repose in the day where one can stop, admire their hard work. I peel my bandages off, inspect the bruised and marred skin, imagine the scars they will leave behind. I'd declined plastics to consult on the wounds. Don't get me wrong—a perfect body is, well, perfection. And the rest of my body is exactly that—washboard abs, broad chiseled shoulders; I even make sure not to skip leg day, and my thighs and calves match the rest of me, instead of looking as though they belong to a goddamn bird like so many men's. Once upon a time, I'd have been angry over the scars. But Noelle, don't you think they unite us in a way? Battle wounds, from this little bump in what will surely be a very long road of our relationship? Besides, as the saying goes, chicks dig scars. And you apparently dig a criminal, so I'm betting a scar or two will light your fire.

The phone vibrates again, and this time, I answer, turning to admire the twin bulks of muscle that are my glutes—like I said, I never skip leg day.

"Calvin," I purr into the phone. "What have you got for me?"

"The man you got on camera who took Noelle has disappeared," he says. "It's believed he fled town."

The satisfaction of striking fear into the thug's heart gives me a hard-on, and I stroke it as I stare at myself in the mirror, focused on the line that cuts between my quads and hamstrings, where the muscles overlap and bulge. I've practically made myself into a Greek god.

"That's fine," I murmur. And it is—because I know you're not with him. You're with *Jack*. "Anything on"—my lip curls—"Jack Flaherty?"

"Plenty."

My hand squeezes around my cock. I meet my eyes in the mirror. *Blue steel*, as you used to tell me.

"Do tell," I murmur.

"Well, the less interesting part is he's a thug for hire, too. Whoever kidnapped Noelle hires people to do it for them. Puts a layer between themselves and the action. It's not uncommon— that way, if someone's caught, it doesn't come back to them. I believe Jack is this person." Calvin clears his throat. "But that's not the best part."

Irritation flickers through me. "What *is* the best part, Calvin?"

A pause, I suspect for fucking dramatic effect.

"Well, in my research, I found photos of you. With a young woman."

I go still. In the mirror, my eyes are wide. A fluttery feeling in my chest. I yank away, releasing my cock, turning my back on myself.

"Get to the fucking point, Calvin."

"A Ms. Sarah MacCleary."

Pain sears through me, hot, like when Jack stomped on my fingers, demanding answers I could not give him.

"What the fuck does Sarah have to do with Jack Flaherty?"

"Well, Dr. Ashcroft, quite a lot, it turns out. You see, he is her brother. Her *twin* brother. The only conclusion I could come to was that Sarah and Noelle were perhaps friends. Sarah *was* in nursing school, and—"

But I tune him out.

Jack Flaherty and Sarah are *twins*?

No wonder he wants to fuck me over after what happened. Maybe it wasn't from your past, Noelle—maybe it's someone from *my* past, in a roundabout way. Did you know Sarah? Did Jack reach out to you? Tell you what a shitty boyfriend I am? Did he convince you that you needed to escape me? He's using you to get to me, Noelle, and you, my dear, should have been smarter. Because I'll tell you one thing—it's not because he likes you. It's not because he gives a shit about you. It's because he blames me.

"One more thing," Calvin says before I can hang up.

"What?"

"The tip line setup has finally paid off."

More silence.

"Jesus, Calvin, spit it out."

He sighs, probably annoyed I refuse to play into his dramatics. "A young woman claims to have seen Noelle in the days prior to her kidnapping." Calvin's voice rises a notch as he talks, excitement in it.

"And?" I snap.

"According to her, Noelle was looking into an extreme kidnapping experience. It's apparently a sport of sorts. People have themselves kidnapped for fun."

My jaw ticks. My dick goes soft.

"What?"

"I have to wonder if she set this whole thing up, Dr. Ashcroft. Have you considered that? If she got in touch with this Jack Flaherty—"

But I stop listening, because I know the truth. I know it's the other way around. Jack got in touch with you. He somehow convinced you to turn on me. What was supposed to be me coming to your rescue has suddenly taken on an entirely different context.

"Nothing is going as fucking planned," I mutter.

"Pardon?" Calvin says.

I hang up.

Jack's out to get me and you're the pawn. He blames me. I blame him. If he hadn't been such a shitty brother, maybe things would have gone differently for Sarah. Regardless, you're still mine, Noelle, and you're still in the clutches of another man. Not at all what I thought I was dealing with when I watched the footage of you being taken. I'm going to find you and finish what I've started. I'm going to destroy him. And I'm going to thoroughly enjoy doing both.

FORTY-SIX

NOELLE

Seattle is a wonderland, the dark gray of the Puget Sound, snowflakes fluttering in the foreground. The pine trees lining streets and growing in thick clumps are covered in a dusting of it. The roads are salted, but still slick, and tiny cars slide down them, veering one way, then the other, trying to get home before they are unable to. Only the buses and those with four-wheel-drive vehicles move at a steady crawl.

I lean forward in the truck, taking in the city, a city I thought I'd never come back to. It's just after noon, and it's the first time I've seen so much snow here. I wish I could enjoy it. Find a sled and a hill and let the world fade away.

Instead, my eyes are peeled for Daniel's Porsche, which he's bragged more than once has no issue navigating snowy roads— *It's rear-wheel drive, but the engine is in the back, so the weight is distributed in such a way, and with snow tires.* I blink, clearing his voice from my head. I need to stop doing that. Stop letting him be with me, harassing me, even when he's not here.

"You okay?" Jack asks.

"I'm okay." I'm guarding my thoughts. I have to trust him enough to figure this out—and no further.

"We need to find a place to stay."

I nod, wondering when this is all done how long it will take Daniel to leave my thoughts all together. Months? Years? Will it help for him to be behind bars? I picture him behind steel, in an orange jumpsuit, no longer able—

Fuck. I'm doing it again, already.

"A place to stay." I force myself to the matter at hand. The flashing lights outside the motel echo in my head. *Not a motel.*

"What about a vacation rental?" I ask. "The people who rent their houses while they're away."

"Sure." Jack turns to climb a short hill, putting us high enough we can look over the city and see the water beyond. The Ferris wheel turns slowly at the waterfront, even in the snow. He parks and reaches into his pocket, then hands over one of his credit cards. "Use this one."

Another Jack O'Kelly credit card. I pull up the rental website and scroll until I find something on the outskirts of town.

"How about this place?" I pass it over, and Jack squints at the tiny screen.

"No," he says. "Looks like a condo. Too public. Too many people. If someone found us, it'd be hard to get out. A house would be better. Private."

I steel myself against the idea of being somewhere private with him.

"Okay." I take the phone back and keep scrolling. *If someone found us, it'd be hard to get out.* In other words, we need an easy escape. A shiver creeps up my spine as the seriousness of what we're doing hits home—back in Seattle. In *hiding.* "Have you done this before?" I ask.

"This?" He pulls his gaze away from the view and looks my way. "No. Not this. But—things."

Things. "What kind of things?" I ask. Then again, do I really want to know?

Jack avoids my gaze, instead looking out the front window, watching the snow fall. "Nothing awful, just... stuff. Intimidation."

"Did Sarah know?"

A humorless smile, a clenched jaw. "Yeah. She knew. She didn't like it. Probably why she moved out here in the first place. There was a perfectly good nursing school in Denver, but..." His words fade away.

I want to say something comforting like *it's not your fault*, but his body has gone rigid, muscles flexing as he grips the steering wheel and looks away. I feel my own body tense in response, the effect of spending too much time around men whose bodies and emotions I had to monitor to keep myself safe.

I refocus on the phone. "What about this one? It's on Lake Washington. It's a house."

Jack looks over, and I scroll through the photos—an entire house with three bedrooms, all decorated with lacy curtains and paintings of Seattle—the Space Needle, the Puget Sound, Pike Place Market. There's a backyard that leads to the lake itself, and a garage where we can park his truck.

Five minutes later, it's booked, and we're headed that way.

The house is filled with personal belongings—photos and knickknacks and clothes in the closet. Someone usually lives here. This isn't the typical home rental empty of personal effects—it's the rental of a couple who are out of the country temporarily, which is convenient for us. While space has been cleared for visitors, the house itself has everything we could need.

And I'm in dire need of a run, even if the ground is coated with snow and ice. I also need to warn Kari off Daniel—maybe not tell her everything, but enough she knows he can't be trusted.

"I'm going on a run tonight," I tell Jack. He's crouched, sorting through a cabinet full of canned goods in the kitchen.

"You can't be serious," Jack says. "It's still snowing."

"I'm serious." I put steel in my voice, to remind both of us he's not my boss. I have borrowed yoga tights, a long-sleeved shirt, a sports bra, and even a balaclava, which means I can step outside without being recognized. Not that there are many people out and about to recognize me. "There's men's stuff, too, if you want to go."

"I don't think so." He smiles, and the smile tells me that he thinks I'm crazy for running in this weather. And it is extreme, even for me. But I've been cooped up in a truck and a motel room for days now, and I need to move. Besides—

"I'm going to warn Kari," I say. "She's probably at work, and she walks there because it's easier than finding parking, so I can —" I try to imagine what I'll do. I'll have to wait until she clears the hospital area, where her office is. And then I'll... run up beside her? Whisper a message and sprint away?

Jack regards me as he piles tomato sauce and beans onto the counter. "I don't know. They looked pretty cozy in those photos. Maybe he won't do anything to her. You need to be careful—people are looking for you."

A tremor of fear runs through me at that, remembering Daniel's cop friends, what they might do if they did find me—mostly, return me to his waiting arms.

"I can't risk it," I say.

"Can you call her?"

"Not if he's found a way to listen in. I have to tell her, and he's probably tracking her phone, the same way he did mine." I frown as he sorts through more cans. "What are you doing?"

"We have to eat. Better to not go somewhere like a grocery store, in case—" A pause, like he's stopping short of saying his initial thought. "In case someone recognizes us," Jack finishes.

"Pot of chili will last awhile. Not fancy. But it gets the job done."

Jack turns his back to me and sorts through drawers. I eye him. He seems as harmless as a tough guy could—and yet, so had Daniel. I stretch, walk to the kitchen window, gaze out at Lake Washington, gray against the overcast sky. A smattering of trees stands between the house and the lake, plus a patio and a snow-covered fire pit. A beautiful place to live in summer, but winter in Washington, not so much. If it's not snow, it's rain. I imagine the couple that lives here does this every year— wandering the world when Seattle deep-dives into the dark skies and nonstop downpour it's known for. They escape some- where warm and sunny, together. It sounds like a nice life.

"What's next?" Jack's located a can opener and is in the process of opening cans and dumping them in a big pot.

I pull out my phone, and when he turns his back, tentatively snap a photo—he's wearing jeans and that white T-shirt, all wide shoulders and narrow hips, his hair pulled back in a pony- tail but coming loose. From the cut of his jeans, the way they fit him, the way he looks *good* in them, he must work out when he's not busy tracking down his sister's likely killer.

"What's that for?"

"Daniel." I zoom in and crop the photo to keep details out— the view out the kitchen window, a photo frame attached to the wall with the smiling couple who must own the house, who are likely galivanting around the world together.

"Daniel?" He searches the drawers until he finds a wooden spoon and gives the ingredients a stir. "Unless Daniel likes men —" Jack stops. Gives his ass a backward glance. "I'm not sure that's going to be much help."

I look down to hide my blush. "That's not the plan."

"Then what is?" He pops a lid on the pot, turns to lean his back against the countertop, folds his arms, and stares at me. I fidget, consider taking another photo, but what I really need is a photo of us together. And I'm not comfortable sidling up beside Jack for one alone in this house with him. I don't want to think about Jack like that. About *anyone* like that, not now. And I really don't want to give him the wrong idea.

"After I warn Kari, I'm going to send him photos."

"Of me?"

"Of us. *Pretending*." His eyes go wide.

"Us, pretending," he murmurs.

I nod.

Jack cocks his head. "You want to make him jealous?"

"Daniel won't just be jealous. He'll be pissed."

Understanding dawns in Jack's gaze. "I see," he says. "That's—" He searches for the word. "Smart."

"Thanks." I check my phone for the time, ready to leave the room, to put space between myself and him, but it's only two o'clock—too soon to catch Kari on her walk home. Which means I have a couple more hours to put our plan into play. I have a mental list of things to set in motion to piss off Daniel, to make his life inconvenient, to take away his freedom, one thing at a time. And I will slowly enact them, one by one.

Mirroring what he did to me.

"What can I do to help?"

Jack's question catches me off guard—I hadn't considered asking him for help with this. He seems more of the type to have standing by in case things go wrong, in case Daniel finds me. But there is something he can do.

"You said there's a tracker on your truck. I know Daniel's usernames and passwords, and I know he has a tracker on his Porsche. Could you figure it out?"

"Sure. Easy peasy." He smiles, that vague sad smile. I grow angry all over again that Daniel's taken someone from both of us. That he's effectively destroyed the lives we had. Jack claims to have dropped everything to come after Sarah. I'm living my own version of hell, on the run from him. Now, running after him.

"And what are you going to do?" Jack asks.

I give it some thought and consider waiting—but why? Why not pile on the frustration and anger? That's what he did to me.

"Daniel likes his money. So, I'm going to make sure he doesn't have any."

FORTY-SEVEN

NOELLE

Reporting Daniel's credit cards stolen is easier than it should be. Since he uses the same username and password for nearly everything, I easily log in to his bank account. From there, it's four clicks to report his debit card and two different credit cards stolen.

A notice pops up, asking me if I am sure I want to report them stolen—the numbers will be immediately deactivated, rendering his cards useless.

He'll be angry. And worse, embarrassed when they are declined. I lean back on the bed I've commandeered, hesitating with my finger over the tiny button on the phone screen that will confirm cancelation.

I'm going to warn Kari tonight, and I can't imagine he'll figure out what I've done before then. Even if he does, he has no reason to suspect it's me. Which means he won't retaliate against Kari.

I hit accept and exhale. A month ago, I never would have done this—even *thought* to do this—out of fear, mostly. But now, I'm far away from him. And I've committed two actions to give him a taste of his own medicine.

Maybe he'll notice the cards don't work today. Maybe tomorrow. Maybe he'll assume his card number was stolen, or that his bank shut it down for suspicious activity. It won't occur to him to consider me, because the Noelle he knows might scowl and look away, but she wouldn't dare act against him. There's something soothing in that—knowing that I'm finally *doing* something.

The page loads, giving me confirmation, and I take a screenshot—just in case it's the sort of thing I feel like sending Daniel later.

I navigate away to check in on Kari. She hasn't updated her Instagram since the last photo with Daniel. I frown at it, then hit the notification button, so the app alerts me when she posts.

I roll over, fluff a pillow under my elbows, and scroll through my recent phone calls. But before I can do anything else, my screen fills with an incoming call. I'm doused in panic, and my finger flies to cancel it without thinking.

Two seconds later, a text pops up.

Answer your phone, or you're a dead man.

I swallow—this was Jack's phone before I nabbed it and he replaced it. I run a quick search of the number, but there's no information on it—just that it's a mobile phone, that it's based in Seattle. Nothing I didn't already know or could guess. I'll have to tell Jack about it.

I swipe back to the missed calls and my original goal. Justine's work line is among the numbers listed. It's a weekday, midday, so it should go straight through to her office. Maybe she has answers, ideas—maybe she wants in on taking Daniel down.

I dial the number. It rings once—then goes straight to voicemail.

Strange.

Her website is still pulled up on a browser tab, and I navigate to that, double-check I'm dialing the correct number—I am. I dial again.

And again, straight to a recorded message.

I leave the room and step into the narrow hall that leads to the kitchen. The light from the windows has darkened a shade, typical Pacific Northwest afternoon, the sun already beginning its descent. The pot of chili simmers on the stove, its sharp aroma filling the kitchen, and a spoon covered in sauce sits neatly on a folded paper towel beside it. But no Jack.

"Jack?" I peek out the back door, but don't see his tall form, and the snow is smooth perfection, no footprint to give away he's gone out exploring. The living room, sparsely decorated with two couches and a coffee table, is empty of life.

I turn to go back to the bedroom, but there's movement behind me and a door slams and—

I jerk back, pulse going haywire. "You scared me."

Jack stands just inside the doorway to the garage, his phone in one hand, screen still lit up as though he just ended a call.

"Sorry." His forehead creases with concern. "You okay? I was in the garage—" He motions to the door. "Heard you call for me."

"Yeah, I—" My fingers tingle, the blast of adrenaline leaving my body. "What were you doing in the garage? It's freezing out there."

Jack's eyebrows shoot up. The word *caught* flits through my mind. But caught doing what? I take a half step back, putting space between us.

"Oh, just—" His gaze flicks behind me, and he darts for the stove, cursing under his breath. "Sorry, the chili is bubbling too much."

I step inside the kitchen, following him, relearning to breathe, and wait while he twists the stove's knob, pulls the lid off, stirs. The screen on his phone is still aglow, and the red notification bubble is still raised on one of his apps. A text? A call?

"Truck," he finally answers.

"What?"

"Had to get this out of the truck." He holds up the flask. "Empty, though."

I watch him a second, trying to decide if I believe him, or if he doesn't want to tell me the truth, whatever that might be—on the phone with someone, maybe. More questions fill my mind—on the phone with who? The same guy who sent the threatening text? Or trying to find out more about Sarah or Daniel, or—

"Someone tried to call you," I say, filling the silence as he raises his brow in question. "And then they texted. On this phone." I hold it up.

"Texted?" Jack spins, spoon covered in red sauce in hand. "Did you look at—"

"It popped up before I could clear it. I know this was your phone before, we can get me a different—"

"It's a burner, keep it. Already gave anyone who matters the new number." Jack sets the spoon down, wipes his hand on a towel, and steps toward me fast, sending my heart pounding. "Mind if I look at the text? Someone must have forgotten I have a new number, and I don't want to miss anything."

"Sure." My pulse thrums through me until I feel like I'm vibrating. I swipe to the message and turn it to show Jack. I don't take my eyes from his face as he reads the threat: *Answer your phone, or you're a dead man.*

His eyes crinkle. He lets out a bark of a laugh. "That's my brother. He's—" Jack shakes his head, smiles, turns away as if he couldn't care less. "Inside joke, that's all."

"I was a little worried," I say, but I don't take my eyes off him.

Didn't he say he isn't close with his family? And I'm certain his brother doesn't live in Seattle. He said so himself, that they're all in Colorado. But he seems truly unconcerned. And he's not my friend—he's only helping me with this situation with Daniel. The message seemed—*unusual*, but Kari and I sometimes texted like that: *Call me back, or else!*

"Can I use your phone?" I ask Jack. "I'm trying to call Justine, but it's not going through."

"Sure." Jack hands it over, no hesitation, and I breathe a little easier. Maybe I'm just paranoid.

But then I take it, and it's warm in my hand, like he's been on the phone for a while. I pretend not to notice and dial.

The call rings—once, twice, three times.

"Olympia Regional Cardiology Practice, how may I direct your call?"

I hang up and try the number again on my phone. One ring. Straight to voicemail.

Jack gives me the same look from earlier, when I said I was going running in the blizzard-like conditions. "What are you doing?"

"Justine blocked my number." I drum my fingers over the table. "Why would she block my number?"

Jack settles into the chair across from me. "Sounds to me like she's afraid. Someone from Daniel's past comes into her life? Sounds like she wants nothing to do with it."

"But—" I stop. Sigh. "She's a *physician*. It's been *years*. What could he have done to make her this afraid?"

Jack lifts his hands as if to say, *You know as much as I do.* "Exactly what he did to you?" he asks.

I bite my lip and nod. He's right. I want Justine to be this strong woman who conquered Daniel, but maybe she's not. Maybe she's just like me. In which case, if I can get her to listen, maybe she will want to help me.

"What I don't understand is why he would want to get rid

of both Sarah and me, but he would leave her. Especially if she's that afraid. We have to be missing something."

"We could track her down," Jack says. "Where is she? I could go talk to her."

"Olympia. But if she's afraid to talk to me, I can't imagine she'd talk to you."

"I can get people to talk. If we need her to talk to put Daniel away, I can make it happen." His words sound normal, but there's another meaning there. When I check his face for malice, there is none—simple statement of fact. And that alone, is concerning.

How far would Jack be willing to go to find out what happened to Sarah? I want Daniel to pay for what he's done— but I don't want to do something that could send me to prison, no matter how deserved it is. Then again, wouldn't I go pretty far to get justice for my aunt?

Looking at Jack, it occurs to me he would go however far was necessary.

And maybe that's what I should be doing, too. Maybe that's the only way to take Daniel down.

FORTY-EIGHT

NOELLE

Running in the cold means I run faster—fast enough to build up heat in my body, to keep me from getting chilled. It also means exhilaration, at least so long as my feet are relatively dry. My heart pumps, my lungs inhale cold crisp air, and for the first time in days, I remember what freedom is—feeling as though I could run like this forever, and no one and nothing can stop me. If I could maintain this feeling, I could be happy for the rest of my life.

It's with regret that I slow as I reach the edge of the hospital campus, a big blocky white building, the forested park beyond it.

Everything is frozen, and I practically ice-skate across the sidewalk, the street, and toward the park, where I let my shoes sink into the fresh snow of what usually is a grassy field at the park. The sun disappeared behind the Puget Sound and the mountains on my way here, and between darkness and the bala-clava, I'm relatively confident no one will recognize me, even if I am on my hospital's campus.

I pause on the sidewalk, catch my breath, get my bearings—and immediately see a poster nailed to a telephone pole with my photo. My name. A cash reward listed, a number to call with information.

Damn it. I pull the balaclava tighter over my face. *No one can recognize me.*

And yet, I feel exposed. I pace away from the poster, exhilaration doused, spin a slow circle, checking the world around me like Jack had in the bar—making sure no one has eyes on me. But I catch sight of a man in a black down jacket across the street. He's looking right at me. I am dressed in a hodge-podge of clothing, none of which is true winter running gear. That's probably all it is, right? I step farther into the field, letting the trees block his view of me.

Snow melts into my shoes, and I shiver. Without movement, the cold sets in immediately. A trail runs just another few feet away, salted in preparation for the snow and the number of hospital workers who walk home through this park; I step onto it, jog up and down the path a few times to keep moving.

In my head I rehearse how it will go. Kari will come down the sidewalk, on her regular walk home—she only lives a mile from the hospital, and parking is expensive in Seattle—and I'll call to her. I'll tell her not to freak out; that I'm safe; that she can't tell anyone she saw me, and that she needs to be careful. Not to trust Daniel. I'll hug my cousin, and tell her things will be better soon, and to go stay somewhere he can't find her. Then, I'll melt away back into the park after telling her to *go, just go,* to pretend she never saw me. I hope she listens. I hope she doesn't beg me to go with her because I can't.

My phone chirps. I pull it out, and I have an e-mail—an e-mail from Daniel.

My stomach bottoms out, and I can't do anything but stare at it, wondering why the hell he would send me an e-mail.

Dear Noelle,

I miss you. Do you miss me?

I've made recent discoveries that suggest things are not well for you. I remember you telling me in our early days of dating that your last relationship was—how did you word it?— manipulative. Abusive. You didn't realize how bad it was until you got out and could look back, see it for what it was.

I would suggest you pause and take a look around yourself, Noelle.

You've taken up with a criminal. Has it occurred to you he's using you to get to me?

To make me look like the guilty party?

I only want what's best for you, Noelle. I can give you a comfortable life, a family, everything your heart might ever desire.

Whatever you do, don't trust him.

I'll do whatever it takes to get you back, Noelle.

Literally anything.

I'm waiting for you with open arms, Noelle.

Yours forever,

Daniel

My eyes skim the page, heart jumping into my throat as I linger over the final promise that he'll do anything to get me back. But when I return to the top and read the bit about Michael—the part where Daniel is trying to get me to question my own ability to make decisions for myself, to see the situation clearly—the snowy cold fades away, and I'm hot, angry.

Daniel is still messing with me, even from afar. Still trying to twist things in his favor. Trying to get me to not trust myself, my own judgment. Well, fuck him.

I read it again, and that's when I notice the other detail that leaves anxiety climbing my insides—suggesting Jack is using me.

I stare at the words until they blur, trying to assimilate this suggestion with what I believe to be true—that Daniel is behind it. But how can Jack be using me if Daniel put all this in motion? If Daniel thinks Jack is responsible, and I think Daniel is responsible—*shit*.

No. He's gaslighting me. Again. Making me question my own knowledge, my own sanity. Suggesting *he* himself is not guilty, maybe to gain my trust, to get me to come back to him. Making himself the victim—Daniel, trying to make *Jack* look bad. And here I am, falling for it.

Unless he somehow found out I did try to arrange for my own kidnapping—and this is his way of getting revenge. Having me grabbed before Ultimate Kidnapping could.

Is it possible that's what happened? A man had come into Mira's co-working space right after me. Would Daniel have had me followed? Undoubtedly, yes. It irked him I'd go on runs alone. I wouldn't put it past him to pay someone to follow me when I left my apartment.

The door to a glass-front building opens, and I snap to, tucking my thoughts away for later. Kari will emerge any second. But it's a mother and child, and they bustle in the opposite direction. Another minute passes, then two. The same man as before now leans against the building, smoking a cigarette, now looking anywhere *but* me.

I fight paranoia—he's just a guy, standing there. I need to pay attention, to not miss Kari when she comes outside. Heat flushes through me again as I think of Daniel's e-mail. But I don't have time for anger—I need to stay focused. To *get even.* Even if he did find out I'd planned my own kidnapping, that doesn't change what I need to do.

Finally, at 5:11 p.m., the door opens again. This time, the person doesn't so much walk as waddle out the doorway, a lunch bag and purse over one shoulder, already huffing into her bare hands to keep them warm. My chest clenches seeing her, my only family. Relief washes through me, and I forget the icy wind cutting through my makeshift running clothes—I'll be able to warn her. To get her to leave. Get her to safety, and then—but she doesn't stride toward home, which would take her right past me. She just stands on the sidewalk, stamping her feet, blowing on her hands.

Her face is difficult to make out in the dark, but a streetlamp casts enough of a glow that when she approaches the road and looks first in my direction, then the opposite way—I can see she's searching. For who? A cab? Of course she would call a cab —she's *very* pregnant, and it's snowing. She wouldn't want to walk home in that.

Crap. I hadn't thought of this.

I step off the path and hurry to the trees to watch from the closer angle, hoping she'll set off down the sidewalk. But still, her gaze travels up the road.

I'm about to step out of the pine trees and onto the sidewalk, to call for her, but headlights flood the street, and the deep purr of an engine I'm far too familiar with makes me stop short. Forces me back, not just behind the trees, but *into* the trees, because if ever there was someone I couldn't let see me, it's him—

Daniel.

Kari doesn't get right in the Porsche. No, Daniel gets *out* of the Porsche with a wide grin. Hollers something I can't quite make out, and I can see the hesitation on her face. But another look at the snowy walkway, and she nods, steps toward him.

I force myself a step forward to make sure I'm seeing right, realize my mouth is hanging open and clamp it shut. My hands clench as he holds something up: *mittens.* Bright pink mittens.

And this time, I hear what he calls to her. "Thought you could use these."

Daniel breaks them apart, pulling the plastic tag off. He holds one open and steps close to her, within touching distance.

Jesus, Kari had *never* let him get so close to her on the rare occasion they ran into one another. My hand finds the trunk of a tree, and I dig my nails into the bark, holding on for dear life. Kari holds her hands up, uncertain, and Daniel opens a mitten wide, inviting her to slide a hand in. He repeats the action with the other mitten.

The man appears suddenly, strolling down the sidewalk as though it's part of his normal path from point A to point B, but this is *definitely* the same man, and he's already been outside for the better part of fifteen minutes. He casts a look my way.

Daniel waves at the Porsche and opens the door, yanking my attention back to the interaction he's having with Kari. He takes one hand as she and her belly ease into the passenger's seat. When she's safely inside, he strides around his car—a glint of something in his eye that I can't quite translate. Joy? Satisfaction? Happiness?

The man has disappeared again.

They drive away, the red beam of his Porsche's back end slowly fading into a flurry of snowflakes. And all I can think is *what just happened?*

FORTY-NINE

DANIEL

I've decided it's not your fault that you don't know how to dress, Noelle. I pull the Porsche from the hospital grounds, half a dozen nurses trooping by on the crosswalk ahead of me. You're a *nurse*—you're literally required to wear what are effectively pajamas to your place of work.

I eye Kari in her slacks and cowl-neck sweater; even she, a member of the lower-class—a data entry desk clerk, for Christ's sake—knows how to dress decently. When this is all over, when you've realized Jack Flaherty doesn't want you—he only wants to screw with me—I'll cut you some leniency with your *pajamas* until I make you quit, which will be sooner than later. And then I'll hire you a personal shopper and tell them what my requirements are. Maybe I'll have my mother help with that; she, too, has good taste.

"My house is—" Kari shifts in her seat, watching her street go by, then swings back to me. "I live down Everson Street."

"I'm aware." I offer a polite smile. "But it is dinner time, and you are carrying my child, and so I shall feed you. We can discuss my concerns at the restaurant, not—" I bite back my first thought, which involved something along the lines of *cat piss-smelling trailer-trash dump of a house*, and instead go with, "I would like privacy, and besides, we have to eat, right?" Another smile, and my immediate instinct is to go with *charming*, but of course Kari would see through that, so instead, I don't let it reach my eyes. I let it melt into a frown.

"You're worried," she says.

I nod once. "Very."

The Porsche fits nicely into its usual spot in front of our restaurant, though the gray snow sprays across the freshly cleaned wheels. I grimace and step out, avoiding it, lift my phone, and snap a photo of the restaurant, done up with snow and icicles, making it almost magical. Wouldn't want you to miss a moment like this, Noelle. The doorman is already at the other door, helping Kari from the car.

"Dr. Ashcroft." He nods at me, hurries back to his post.

I don't respond, because the help is there to *help*, not hold a conversation with (something you need to remember, Noelle), and I beckon Kari ahead of me.

She stops short and rounds on me. "Seriously?"

I frown. "What?"

"This restaurant? This is—*your* restaurant." She means *our* restaurant, Noelle. *Our*. And where are you? Not here. Not at my side. Not where you *belong*.

"It's also the only decent restaurant that has stayed open in the storm, so unless you'd like fries with that—"

Kari scowls and stomps inside, spraying snow everywhere, which is fine, because it's not *my* problem, it's the *doorman's* problem.

I wait until we are seated and have drinks in front of us to begin—bourbon for me, a sparkling water with a twist of lemon and cucumber for her.

"As I told you a few days ago, I've hired a private investigator to work the case. The police have been less than helpful."

Kari fusses with the mittens in her lap. I'd actually gotten a *smile* for those. The woman does like gifts, doesn't she? If only your love language were so easy to figure out.

"Something wrong, Kari?"

"I read—" She stops, looks up from the mittens, eyes me. "I read that your last girlfriend disappeared, too. That the police were considering you—"

My mouth goes dry. "Considering me, what?"

"Just that it's suspicious."

I eye her. Consider how much to tell her, and decide maybe with Kari, the whole story will work better.

"You are correct that Noelle is my second girlfriend to go missing. And I do think the disappearances are related. In fact, I think I've figured out who did it. And why. And I need your help getting Noelle back, because I'm pretty sure she's gone with him willingly."

"Willingly?" Kari's hands go still. Her eyes are locked on mine across the table.

I give a long sigh and sip my bourbon. "I'm afraid so. I have discovered she arranged for her own kidnapping—likely with the help of the man she is with. I believe he's manipulated her, to be frank with you. And I believe he's dangerous. He's using her to get to me. It's like in a cult—she can't see past him to the truth. Let me explain what's happened."

And explain, I do. How Sarah was my first true love. How she disappeared. How your kidnapper is Sarah's brother, and how he's using you to get to me. How he is in fact a *criminal*, and god knows what he'll do with you once he's achieved his goal.

Kari's food goes untouched. Her eyes grow wider and wider, her jaw slack. And by the end, all she can say is, "Tell me how I can help."

Kari doesn't like me, but she believes me. She believes I want you back safe and sound. After all, as the saying goes, better the devil you know than the devil you don't. Another bit of advice you should heed, Noelle.

FIFTY

NOELLE

The snow blinds me as it rushes down from the sky. But I can't stop. I have to know what Daniel is doing with Kari. Why she would willingly go with him. And I have to put distance between me and whoever that man was, even if he was just a random hospital worker out for a smoke break and a quick walk. The snow covers the sidewalk, and I slip, my feet losing purchase. I hit hard, the panting of my own breath loud in my ears in the otherwise quiet, dark world. I climb to my feet and ignore the ache of my hip where I hit icy concrete. I press to run harder, faster, my body pulsing with emotions I can't identify, can't catch hold of long enough to understand.

Fury.

Dread.

Anger.

Fear.

Kari is with Daniel. Daniel is with Kari. Their interaction wasn't right, wasn't normal, even given the circumstances, and something feels wrong, so wrong. Why was he there to pick her up? Why did she let him put mittens on her? Why did she drive off with him?

Is this what he meant when he said he'd do anything?

I stumble to a halt, yank out the phone, pull up her Instagram, inspect the photos one by one—the selfies, the flowers, the expensive baby crap. *Jesus*, is this what it looks like? His arm is wrapped around her. She's willingly accepting gifts and going with him. The photo where they held hands, the money *someone* has given her... No. No, it can't be. He's just giving her a ride home. It's *snowing*. Kari would know better than to get involved with Daniel.

Fine then, I'll run to her house. It's on the way back to the rental house, a short detour north, no problem at all. I huff breath out, tuck my phone away, press back the anxiety spiraling through me.

It's an uphill climb, and the temperature has dropped again, the roads have gone slick with ice, which means I have to trudge through the snow. My feet are frozen by the time I reach the top of the hill. I run anyway. I run, and I run, ignoring my aching legs, that I'm now shivering, that the snow has become ice pellets falling from the sky.

The phone in my sports bra vibrates, and I pull it out long enough to see it's a text from Jack:

You okay? You've been gone a long time. It's hailing here.

I don't answer, just keep running. A car approaches an intersection just ahead, and the driver is wearing a black coat and—

It's not him. It's not the man from the corner. It's just another person wearing a black coat. I need to keep it together.

I turn down Kari's street, stopping at the end of her driveway, staring at a house that is utterly dark. Like the power is out. Except every other house is lit up, and through windows I can see people moving around, sitting down at a table together for dinner.

Still, Kari's house is dark. Empty.

Which means she didn't get in his car for a quick ride home.

Another text from Jack.

Where are you? I'll come get you. The windchill is in the single digits.

Anguish fills the pit of my stomach, but I'm cold, too cold, and I can't sink to the ground, terrified at what this might mean. Maybe she needed to go to the grocery store and he agreed to take her. Maybe they had to go talk to the police, and she needed a ride, maybe—

No more maybes.

I just have to wait and try again. To hope Kari hasn't been snared in Daniel's web, too. To hope I'm not too late.

The wind blows harder, cutting through the fabric of my shirt, my pants. My fingers are numb. My toes lost feeling long ago. Jack's right—the windchill leaves me breathless.

My hands shake as I pull the phone back out, text him Kari's address, and press myself against a tree so the wind is partially blocked, so no one can see me from down the road, just in case I am being followed. I consider finding the spare key Kari hides beneath a yard gnome, but if she's as deep with Daniel as it seems, I have to assume there's a chance he's put cameras in her house, which means he might see me.

I press myself closer to the tree, squeezing my eyes shut against the flurry of snow speckled with bits of hard-packed ice. If she's *with* him, if he cares for her in the slightest, it means she's safe, that he won't hurt her.

But no, that can't be. That's what he does. He hurts the women he's with. And I'm pretty sure I've led her right into his trap.

FIFTY-ONE

DANIEL

"I'm sorry, sir, your card did not work."

The server is too close to my ear, whispering, as though Kari won't hear her words.

"Excuse me?" I look up. "Run it again. It works."

"I tried three times, sir." She's blonde, with deep brown eyes that blink with fear. I repress a shudder of pleasure at that. Summon a smile. Maintain the veneer that is necessary given the situation.

"Of course. Here." I dig another card out and offer it. She disappears behind the bar, and I return my attention to your cousin. "As I was saying, I think more than anything we need to remind her we care for her. That we are here for her. That we don't *judge* her for being duped by a criminal. After all, she's only human."

"What can I do?" Kari asks, dubious. She still doesn't trust me. I don't blame her.

"If she contacts you, tell her you need her. Tell her *we* need her. And let me know." I level a gaze at Kari. "I may be able to have the investigator track the phone calls. Then I can call the police, have them rescue her." I hold up my hand, taped against a splint. "I'm hardly in a condition to go after her myself, and besides, I worry that may trigger him to hurt her."

Kari nods, slowly, lips pressed together, looking a lot like one of my patients right before they throw up after anesthesia.

"Are you not well?" I ask.

Kari stares at her hands then meets my eyes across the table.

"Just—hard to believe. Noelle is smart. But I know... I know that's how it works. Even smart women get caught up in things like this. Get caught up with bad men. Like before, with her ex." She inspects me, as if trying to decide what to think about this. About you being kidnapped. About what I've told her.

I appreciate Kari's empathy, Noelle. It's nice someone in your life can be so damn understanding of the situation you've gotten us into.

"I'm sorry, sir, this one doesn't work, either." The blonde again. Nervous again.

I bite back a response. Force one of those damn Zen breaths. "I apologize. Here, I think I have cash."

Kari frowns. "I can pay," she says, but I wave her off and dig cash from my wallet.

"Probably just the storm has affected the bank," I say. But it's odd. I've used the same bank since college with no issue.

I tip the server in cash, ask her to snap one last photo of Kari and me, united in finding you—Kari stiffens, but doesn't argue—and we take our leave. I drop Kari at her house, pressing more hundred-dollar bills in her hand. "For the baby," I say, and once again, she hesitates, then accepts, wariness in her eyes that is slowly transitioning to trust as she watches me put every bit of myself into the search for you.

And now, I've ensured she'll help me. Because I have no doubt you'll contact her when you see the next round of photos I'm about to post.

FIFTY-TWO

NOELLE

Jack picks me up from where I'm huddled out front of Kari's, and we stop by the liquor store on the way back to the house. Jack emerges with two bottles—whiskey and wine.

The drive back is slow, despite it only being two miles, and I go straight for a hot shower the moment we pull into the garage.

I should have never left.

I should have told Kari the truth.

I should have—should have *done* something.

And here I am, screwing around canceling credit cards and turning off his goddamn thermostat and basically playing college-age pranks on a man who took away my relatively normal life. Who killed my aunt. Who probably killed Jack's sister. Who has homed in on Kari next, though I can't completely understand *why*, because he must know how odd it seems that he's had not one girlfriend go missing, but *two*, and now he's going after my cousin—

It doesn't make sense.

Once I've thawed out, I wrap myself in a towel and find pajamas in the bedroom dresser. I pull them on, no longer even blinking at wearing a stranger's clothes, no longer caring if when these people arrive back home, they realize their things have been used. I need comfort. Warmth.

More than anything, I need to pull myself together and *do something*.

I put together a mental list as I pace into the living room to find Jack, because he's part of the next step. A step that feels menial—much like my other taunts that Daniel has likely not noticed, but this one will cut closer to the bone.

I just have to work up the courage to do it.

"What's up?" Jack's in the kitchen, ladling chili into bowls. He nods at the bottles of amber and clear liquid on the counter. "Pick your poison. Wine, or I whip something up with the whiskey."

I search for a wine opener, because the idea of numbing myself feels right.

But I stop. I don't want to numb myself. I want to play hardball.

"Whiskey," I say. "Straight."

Jack's brows furrow, but he doesn't comment—just sets bowls on the kitchen table and goes about pouring bourbon. He sets the glasses down and settles across from me. We sit a moment, waiting, I think, for the other to say something.

"Someone was following me," I say.

"Following you?"

"There was a man. Black jacket." I shake my head, lift the glass of whiskey, hazard a sip. "I was there for fifteen minutes, and I saw him three different times."

"Were you wearing the balaclava?"

"Yes."

Jack tilts his head. "There's no way he could have known it was you, then. Did he do anything? Take a photo or act like he was going to call the police?"

"No, but—" I take another drink. "I don't mean like that.

Not a concerned citizen. Like he was *following* me." I look up, and Jack's lips quirk.

"Maybe you're just being paranoid. I would be, too." Jack gives me a look—not quite a smile—but full of empathy.

"Maybe," I say. He certainly hadn't hidden from me, and if he were actually watching me, wouldn't he have tried to go unnoticed?

"What now?" he asks. "Are you still going to warn her?"

I'm about to say *of course*, but my phone beeps, a sound I haven't heard before—the sound of Instagram alerting me Kari's posted a new photo.

My whole body clenches with dread.

Fuck. I think the word before I can so much as pick up the phone. And when I tap the notification and the photo pops up, I think it again and again. *Fuck, fuck, fuck.*

Because if I had any doubt, it's gone. Daniel has her under his spell.

They're at "our" restaurant, smiling. Together.

"I have to call her. I can't wait." I pull away from the table and dial her number by heart. It rings once, twice, three times. I hang up and dial again, because she never answers a call from an unknown number on the first try. It occurs to me I didn't dial star sixty-seven first, which means this won't be anonymous, but it's too late now.

"Hello?" Kari's voice fills the line.

"Kari, it's me. You have to get away from him. I know he's being nice to you. I know he's acting like the perfect gentleman. But it's bullshit. It's all part of his game."

A pause. "Noelle, listen to me." Her voice is full of the same worry mine is. "Daniel is not the enemy this time. The man you're with is dangerous. Daniel had a private investigator look into him and—"

"No, *you* listen to *me*." I hear my voice gain a pitch, my words tight with the need for her to understand. "He's dangerous. He's an anesthesiologist. He works at the hospital you're going to deliver at. He could *hurt* you and no one would even know!"

An intake of a breath over the line. I feel a presence at my back and turn to see Jack there, concern written over his features. He touches my shoulder, squeezes it gently, and I let him. Just the warmth of his hand there is enough to anchor me. Let me gain control over my own emotions long enough to speak.

"Kari, he's threatened—"

"He said you might say that," Kari says, her voice soft, understanding. "Noelle, listen. I know I haven't always liked Daniel. I know we've had our differences, but he wouldn't hurt me. He wouldn't—" Her voice drops off. Another deep breath. "He wouldn't hurt my baby. He *helped* me when I had to go to the hospital." But there's something in her voice, something *different*, and I can't quite make out what it is. And then her words echo through me. *He said you might say that.*

I'm too late. He's already gotten to her. Convinced her anything I might tell her is Jack manipulating me. When it's really the other way around. And the most messed up thing is, I don't blame her. It *does* look that way, doesn't it?

"Kari, he's lying. He's—twisting things."

"You need to get away from that man. He's only using you to get at Daniel. Listen, I love you like a sister, and I am telling you—"

"Kari—"

"He said you had yourself kidnapped, is that true? You had him kidnap you?"

I open my mouth. Shut it. Try to come up with the words to deny it, because *yes of course, I had*, but that's not what happened—

"*See?*" she continues. "That's not like you, Noelle. That's not *normal*."

"Kari, I had myself kidnapped to *protect you*. Daniel's the threat here, not Jack."

Kari sighs. "Noelle, listen to yourself. Protect me? From what?"

"From *Daniel*," I say.

But another sigh through the phone—she doesn't believe me. The world spins. Jack's hand tightens, and he steps closer.

"I have to go," I say into the phone. "Don't tell Daniel I called. And *don't* trust him. He is not your friend. I'll call you back when I can prove it."

I hang up. Look up at Jack, who's closer still, and feel the hot trails of tears down my cheeks.

"She doesn't believe me," I say. The rest, I only think in my head. *She thinks it's you. That you're behind it, using me to get to Daniel.* And I know that's not right, but I also don't trust Jack enough to say it out loud.

"This will all be okay," he says, giving me an awkward half hug, but nothing's okay. It's my fault Kari trusts *Daniel* of all people. I never told her the truth—the manipulation, the blackmailing, the gaslighting—because I knew she'd do something about it, and in doing so, put herself in the line of fire. But that was a mistake. I should have been honest from the beginning. And now, now he's got her. I have to fix it. To keep her safe. But I'm not just doing this for her or for me—as long as Daniel's out there, no woman in Seattle will be safe.

"What do you want to do?" Jack asks. He presses my glass into my hand. I take a slow drink, the taste of the alcohol too strong for my tastebuds, but the burn is good.

"We have to stop him. Before he hurts her. Before he can hurt anyone else." I gulp more whiskey and look at Jack, who stares back tentatively.

"What do you have in mind?"

"I have to keep him busy. Too busy to worry about Kari. Too

busy trying to find us to mess with her or target anyone else." I take another swallow and eye Jack and know what I have to do. "Come with me." I grab Jack's elbow and drag him to the nearest bedroom.

There's no time to be scared. No time to worry about myself. I have to reel Daniel in. I have to set him off. I have to get him to screw up. I have to fix this.

"Uh—" Jack stops abruptly just inside the door, his body filling it.

I flick on the bedside lamp in the darkness, creating a soft glow of light over the freshly made bed—fluffy white linen, too many pillows, curtains in the background, covering the windows, keeping our location safe from discovery.

"Shirt off," I say, yanking my own off, revealing the lacy lavender bralette I borrowed from the closet. I leave my pants where they are, crawl across the bed, and flop down on my back. "Jack, just do it." I pin him with a look, but he still stands in the doorway, blinking at me.

"What are we doing here?" He takes a half step in but doesn't move to take his shirt off.

"What does it look like?"

"Um..." He looks like he's holding back a grin.

I sigh. "Stop that. Take your shirt off. Get over here and take a sexy photo with me."

Jack rubs a hand over his mouth, shakes his head, and for all his hesitation, I'm certain he's not *upset* by this. "Okay, okay," he murmurs, holding his hands up. He grabs at the hem of the white undershirt, raises it overhead, revealing more tattoos—red and green and black, abstract art drawn in long lines and swirls, unlike tattoos I've seen elsewhere. But for all that they're impressive, he's even more impressive—and when he glances away at me watching, I realize he knows it and is maybe a little embarrassed, too.

But he's perfect for this. He's everything some part of

Daniel wishes he could be—taller, stronger, more *manly*, at least by Daniel's definition.

"Come on." I wave a hand at him, impatient.

"What do you want me to do?" He stops at the edge of the bed, keeping his eyes affixed firmly on my face.

"Seriously?" I roll off and point. "Fine, you lie down. I'll do the rest." I want him to hurry. To take the damn photo. To get this over with before I lose my nerve.

He follows the command, his biceps bunching and abs tensing as he maneuvers until he's on his back, arms outstretched.

I hand him the phone, selfie mode turned on. His gaze is locked on mine, still not straying from my face, and I appreciate this—I really do—but Jesus, this is not the time to be Mr. Nice Guy. This is the time to be Tough Guy, Sexy Guy, but not Nice Guy.

I crawl across the bed and then on top of him, straddling him, sitting upright.

"You ready?" I ask.

"For?" His brows shoot up.

I lean down, pressing the length of my body against him, the warmth of my stomach over his creating a heat that for the briefest moment makes me miss real intimacy, but *no*, that is not what we're doing.

"I'm going to kiss you. Grab my hair. Flex your muscles. Look passionate—" I raise my brows at him as if to say, *Can you handle that?*

His grin returns, and maybe he's not so shy, maybe he's not such a nice guy. Maybe he just enjoys *pretending* to be that guy.

Whatever. As long as he can play the part, that's what matters. We're not here to have sex. We're here to make Daniel *think* we're having sex. Because if anything will make him lose control, it's this.

I hand him the phone, selfie mode on. I lower down, focus

on his mouth, feel that bubble of anxiety that reminds me of the last time I was in bed with a man. Daniel. Threats hanging in the air. I hesitate, and Jack's gaze softens.

"Don't worry," he breathes. "This is just a game, right? Just pretend." He presses up, touches my hair, meets my eyes. "You're safe with me." And then his lips find mine, hand bunching my hair in a gentle grip. The anxiety melts away. I close my eyes, kiss him back, remember that once upon a time I *liked* kissing men—

Click. Click. Click.

The noise makes me stop. My eyes fly open, and our eyes meet, and there's a moment when neither of us moves, *what now?* written in our features. But it's over. The photos are taken. We can stop. I hesitate, our mouths so close his breath tickles over my lips.

"See? Not so bad." He winks, releases my hair, lets his head fall back against the pillow. I'm off him in the next instant, off the bed. I pull my shirt back on. Accept the phone he offers as he slowly gets dressed again.

The photos are perfect—clearly Jack, clearly me, looking hungrily at one another, him bare-chested, me in that bralette that isn't something I'd ever buy myself.

I return to the kitchen. Swallow a mouthful of whiskey. And start typing a message to Daniel, desperation in the speed at which my fingers fly over the screen.

I was nervous to shut off the thermostat. Scared to cancel his credit cards. Even with him far away, with Jack on my side, a part of me had trembled as I committed these small acts against him.

But those emotions have been replaced by anger, and I force myself to slow down my typing, to *breathe*, to think carefully about my words.

This time, when I hit Send, I don't hesitate.

FIFTY-THREE

DANIEL

Once Kari is safely home, I swing by Mother's to check that she still has electricity, that she has groceries, that she is making it through this winter storm just fine. But I don't bother parking. Don't bother going and knocking on the door.

The black Audi in the driveway tells me she's just fine.

I whip out my phone.

Calvin, where are we on the Steven Hannigan background check?

He messages back almost instantly.

I've got it, but there's been an issue with payment. I was just about to e-mail you.

Of course. The credit card.

Send it. You know I'm good for it. Having an issue with the bank. Will write you a check tomorrow.

A longer break between messages this time, and I check my e-mail, just in case the pause is due to him getting to a computer and sending it. Fucking bank. I should have known to switch to something national, somewhere that treats people like *me*, people who have a respectable income, in a manner they deserve.

Speaking of, an e-mail sits in my inbox *from* my bank.

I frown and open it. Maybe I spoke too soon. Maybe they are reaching out to assure me—

Ice runs through my veins. *Per your request, your account numbers ending in*—blah blah blah—*have been reported stolen and canceled. New cards will be issued but may take up to 72 hours to process. For expedited service, you may pay a $14.99 fee and*—

I dial the number at the bottom of the e-mail, but it's no help: "Our service hours are Monday through Friday between 8 a.m. and 7 p.m."

It must have been an error. Or maybe my account was hacked. Maybe the bank *had* to cancel my cards and it sent this automated message. *Fuck.* I have a few hundred dollars on me, but that won't be enough to get me through the rest of the week.

I sigh. I'll have to ask Mother for her card or go into the bank and pull out cash directly.

Still nothing from Calvin. I text him.

Hello?

The three dots appear, indicating he is typing.

It's sending now. Slow connection with the storm. You should have it in a few minutes.

I take one last look at the Audi and gun the engine—but of

course it's snowing, so I drive like a geriatric. It takes an hour to get home.

When I get inside, the kitchen is a goddamn freezer.

It takes me a minute to realize it, because I'm in the wool overcoat I most often wear with a suit. My hands tingle. The cold air nips at my face. I pause, halfway to the mahogany cabinet that serves as a bar.

Odd. But the electricity can't be out—the light in the hallway is still on. The cameras' green lights blink every so often, and though there's a battery backup, that color changes when there's no power. Maybe the thermostat isn't working, or maybe the maid turned it off to clean the heating vents. I find the little plastic box, find the heat is indeed off, and turn it back on, making a note in my phone to find someone new to scrub my damn toilets. I don't have time for this.

I continue to the liquor cabinet and pour myself a double. Take a long, slow sip, letting the burn of 120-proof bourbon calm the rapid-fire beating of my heart as the vision of Steven Hannigan with my mother pounds through my brain. I need to know what's in that file.

I refill the glass. Go into my office and navigate to my e-mail. The information on Steven waits there, a file attachment. I'm about to open it when I realize there's a *sound* coming from across the hallway, in my bedroom—

Drip. Drip. Drip.

Water is one of the few substances that expands when it gets cold. It expands by approximately nine percent, due to the structure of the water molecule. PVC pipes, on the other hand, do the opposite. They contract.

Which means my first-floor master bedroom is now a clusterfuck of water, sticky bits of ceiling plaster, and ruined bed linen.

I stand in the doorway, the Zen breaths not doing a damn thing, and stare at the mess. Water cascades over the edge of the broken ceiling, a river onto the down comforter, the state-of-the-art mattress, the carpet I brought in from overseas because I like the way it feels on my bare feet.

All ruined.

And I haven't the faintest idea what to do. But I do know who's responsible. The maid service.

"This is Dr. Daniel Ashcroft. Your maid turned the heat off just before the storm, and as a result, I came home to a freezing-cold house with busted pipes and water everywhere. You will need to cover these expenses. Please call me back."

My chest practically wheezes with the control I exert as I say these words without a growl, a snap—a perfectly reasonable human. That's me. I'll be firing them, but only after they've taken care of costs. No reason to keep me happy if they know they've lost my business.

Then I call a plumber.

"Plumbing Solutions, we are experiencing heavy call volume, please hold." Violins fill the line, shrill and not at all helpful as the water soaks through the rug and runs off the side —onto the hardwood floors I had imported from South America. Goddammit.

The water. I have to turn off the water. But where? How? Do I need to cut electricity, too? The breaker box is in the office, and I turn on my heel, still listening to the insistent whining of stringed instruments. It occurs to me more pipes could burst, more ceilings could fall from the weight of the water, more of my home destroyed—

I go to the computer instead. Google "what to do when pipes burst."

But the computer pings, and there's a new e-mail, and *I don't give a fuck about a new e-mail*, except...

Except I do.

Because it's from you.

Did you see the photos I posted of Kari and me at dinner? A thrill of excitement fills me, and screw the pipes. I can't wait to see your reaction. Can't wait for you to realize the error of your ways—yes, Noelle, I will forgive you. Yes, I'll still give you my mother's ring, and you'll accept my proposal.

Did you come to the realization that Jack Flaherty only wants you to fuck with me? Did you see me out with Kari and remember that it should have been you there with me? Are you ready to grovel at my feet and beg my forgiveness and realize just how lucky you are?

Oh, Noelle. I hope so. Everything is almost ready. Our life together will be perfect.

I can *feel* the grin on my face, feel it stretching my cheeks over my perfect teeth, anticipation thrumming through me as I click on your e-mail, and the computer takes a beat to load it, but there are your words and—

My smile disappears.

My body tenses.

Anger replaces anticipation.

Your bare freckled shoulder. His body, ruined with tattoos. Your mouth, pressed to his. His hand, buried in your hair, pulling you close to him. And the message. The message you sent along with it.

Dear Daniel,

I didn't realize how bad in bed you were until I fucked someone better. Thought you might like a photo of it...
    I know how you like to watch.

Xo,

Noelle

A fine tremble comes to my hand, my body. *You knew about the cameras. How? How did you know?*

I stare at the photo, trying to read it. If you want to be there, or if he's forcing you to be there. I can tell he took the photo, but I can't tell—

I can't breathe.

I shove away from the computer, spin in my chair, stand up, drive my fist through the wall, over and over. Fuck it, they'll come fix one room, might as well fix this one, too. And then something fills me that must be where the term *temporary insanity* comes from, because I howl like someone who has completely lost it. A roar, wrenching from my throat, my gut, because *you are mine*, Noelle. And I won't stop until I find you.

FIFTY-FOUR

NOELLE

I can't sleep.

Every time I close my eyes, I picture Daniel, pulling those damn mittens over Kari's hands; the two of them huddled close around a table at the restaurant; the knowledge that if I disappear, she's next. And what's worse, he's gotten her. Pulled her into his web. Soon, like the arachnid he is, he'll wrap her tight. Suffocate her.

The way he suffocated me.

I give myself a shake and toss back the covers, trying to force Daniel from my mind. I pad into the kitchen for a glass of water, sip it, decide sleep won't happen anytime soon. The living room has a reasonably comfortable couch, and I settle in, flip the television on, spend ten minutes trying to figure out the remote before I give up and instead stare out the window at the night sky, thick with flurries. But a pulsing *need* to do *something* pulls me away from the view—the peacefulness of it. I can't just sit here. I can't wait. Kari is in danger. My aunt is dead. Not to mention Sarah and whatever Daniel did to Justine.

Daniel discovering everything I've done to mess with him

flits through my mind. It's not enough. It doesn't come close to making up for what he took from me.

I pull out the phone and navigate to the hospital's website. There's an option at the bottom, *Anonymous Reporting*. I click on it.

I take a deep breath—and start detailing half a dozen events that have happened in the hospital, thanks to Daniel.

The time he backed me into a corner of the medicine room, even though I told him *no*.

When he demanded I join him in the otherwise empty physician's lounge.

Grabbing my ass when he came up behind me in a patient's room where the patient was unconscious.

Things that might have been normal in a consensual relationship, even if they were inappropriate in the workplace.

Once again, I hesitate before I hit Send. But not because I'm afraid to do it, afraid of his reaction. This is all too far gone for that. But because I'm not sure reporting this will matter, that I'll be believed, especially since it's anonymous. Daniel's popular. Liked. Respected. Will anyone care, much less believe me? The hospital *has* been trying to be more progressive, so there's a chance. I hit Submit.

I reload the page and start another report, this one on my aunt. But I stop short, because there's nothing *to* report—no evidence, save their visitor's log, and that's hardly damning evidence. I type in what few details I know, anyway, and include Allison's contact information because she has what little information there is. I'm under no illusions this will lead to justice for my aunt, not this specific report. But it might mean someone pulling Daniel aside; someone setting up an internal review board to examine him, because Allison was sniffing around before, and now someone else has filed a similar claim.

I take a second to consider what I could report about Sarah, if there's anything I know that could force the police to take another look at Daniel. But we know nothing new where Sarah is concerned. The key is getting to Daniel. Getting him to say it out loud.

It's a stretch. But it's *something*. And something feels like a lot right now.

FIFTY-FIVE

DANIEL

The plumber comes and goes. A repair company will be here by 8 a.m.

It's 3:43 a.m., and I'm in the spare bedroom, thinking that if I believed in God (which I don't, because science), I'd be thanking Him (yes, Him—obviously) for giving me the foresight to buy a decent mattress for the spare bedroom.

I would not, however, be thanking Him for your e-mail, Noelle.

You positively *wound* me. I'd have rather you stabbed me with my own goddamn kitchen knife than sent me this. I can't stop reading the words.

... until I fucked someone better...

... I know how you like to watch.

How long have you known? How did you find out? Is it my own fault? When I gave you the tour of my own home and showed you how cleverly I've hidden cameras? Or is this something else Jack helped you out with?

Fuck. Does this change everything?

My mouth tastes sour, despite having brushed my teeth

with my infrared toothbrush. A lump in my throat can't quite be swallowed down, even with another two fingers of bourbon. I can't sit still, and I can't sleep, and I'm not in my own goddamn bed, and my girlfriend isn't even here beside me.

I breathe in, out. Close your e-mail. Remember the information Calvin sent over and snatch my laptop from the office and open the e-mail on it, because there are too many pages to read on my phone. The full report pulls up on the bigger screen, and I skim it, heart rate climbing steadily as I read—I'd estimate eighty beats per minute, ninety, one hundred, one hundred ten—

Jesus Christ, what is wrong with you women?

You're with a criminal. And apparently, so is my mother. Steven Hannigan isn't an oncologist. He isn't, in fact, even a physician.

He's a con man.

The alarm blares at me at 7:30 a.m., and I'm up, going through the motions of making myself presentable, drinking coffee, taking ibuprofen for my raging stress headache (thanks for that, Noelle), and not letting myself open my e-mail. Not letting myself see your betrayal. I'm trying to understand, Noelle. Really, I am.

Mother, I text, *I'm coming over for breakfast. Shall I bring something?*

A knock at the door—the plumber first, and then from an even bigger van, big lumbering men with fans to dry out the carpet, get the bedroom back to normal, make sure there is no permanent damage. I wonder when I'll be able to turn the water back on, shower again. Fuck. Maybe I should do that at my mother's, too.

This is all very inconvenient timing. But at least I'll be at her house already, which will make borrowing a credit card easy enough. Maybe I should lead with that—with the news I have to tell her.

I'm in the Porsche, the engine running, the garage open, ready to go, when she replies.

Sorry, Daniel, this isn't a good time.

I've shifted from park to drive, but my foot remains on the brake; I can't tear my eyes away from her text. What does she mean, this isn't a good time? I'm her *son*. She's never refused me before, never told me—

A growl tears from my throat. I rev the gas, shift into reverse, and nearly hit a worker who's not watching where he's walking as I back up.

I know why it's *not a good time*. And his name is Steven Hannigan.

The melting snow and ice keep me from speeding, but only barely. I have to tell Mother what I found out. Her boyfriend, her oncologist, is a *fraud*. Has this all been a scheme from day one? Did he even treat her for cancer?

Mother has been sick for two years. She's in remission now, but with a high risk of relapse. She was diagnosed and went into treatment bravely, ducking into the cancer center when I'd drop her off, refusing to let me go with her.

"Please, Daniel, I'm not a child going off to kindergarten. I'm a grown woman. Go home," she'd said with a wave of her hand as she sauntered off as though it were just another hair appointment.

So, I'd let her go. I joined her for only one appointment, in her own home, her oncologist making a rare house call to meet her physician son and give a full report on the state of his mother's disease. It was the first time I'd seen a man in my mother's house since my father died.

"Your father abandoned us," Mother had said, even though

I'd witnessed the car accident, seen the final bloody seconds of his life. It didn't make sense at the time, but I never questioned Mother. She'd focused all her attention on making me the best man I could be. "A real man would never abandon a woman and her child," she'd chided me, when I showed casual interest in girls in high school. "You're not old enough to get married, so you shouldn't be dating. Dating is for one thing, Daniel. Marriage. And children."

And so, I waited. I met women who I could have loved, but for various reasons didn't work out. I waited for you, Noelle.

Dr. Steven Hannigan. His supposed credentials were impressive: graduate of Harvard. Medical school at Duke. In the whirlwind of my mother's diagnosis, just a couple years into my first position as a real physician, not a resident or a fellow, I'd never checked up on him. I'd failed her. Now I know he never attended either of those schools, or college at all, for that matter.

But if she's being treated for cancer—mostly follow-up appointments now, though for those first six months, appointments were far more often with chemo—Mother must know. She can't possibly have had fake treatment for six months at a cancer center and not recognized it. I frown, check the roads around me, accelerate through the red light. I must get to her, and fast. Something isn't right here.

Or is it possible she *was* treated, but by somebody else? Is Steven Hannigan simply someone she's dated this whole time, and she called him her oncologist to avoid telling me?

That makes the most sense.

But why lie to me? Because they didn't get married? I could have convinced Steven to do right by my mother. Why hadn't she come to me for help?

Noelle, if only you were here. You'd help me sort through the facts. As it is, I have to consider the very real possibility that my mother has been lying to me for quite some time about the man in her life. Which means the two most important people in my life have both been toying with me.

It's time I do something about it.

FIFTY-SIX

NOELLE

"Daniel is on the move." Jack's first words to me as I pour coffee through bleary eyes and try not to think about Kari.

"Huh?" I blink up at him.

"You asked me to track his car." Jack holds up his cell phone. "He left his house early. He's in West Seattle, has been for half an hour."

I gaze at the phone, then back at him.

"You love your truck, right?"

Jack's brows furrow. "It's just a truck, but... sure."

"What's the worst thing that could happen to it?"

Jack drinks his coffee, glances at the hallway, as if he could see the truck through the wall and shakes his head. "I don't know. Someone stealing it, maybe?" He gives me a pointed look.

I clench my teeth, smile. "Not sorry for that. But for real. Is that it?"

He shrugs. "I guess so. Stealing and crashing it."

I nod. "Okay. Let's do it."

Jack looks up from his coffee, eyes gleaming. "You want to steal his car?"

"And crash it. Tonight," I say. "Will you help me?"

He smiles, and it's genuine. "I'd love to."

Justine practices medicine in Seattle twice a week, a fact I know thanks to her website, which means she should be mere miles from me today.

"You sure you don't want company?" Jack asks, handing over the truck keys. I would usually walk those miles from the house to the hospital, as Seattle isn't known for easy parking, but given the snow and the fact half the city's on the lookout for me, it seems better to take Jack's truck.

"I'm okay, but thanks." Having Jack with me may cause trouble with Justine, especially given he looks more like a bodyguard than anything else. If she's already scared, his presence won't help. Besides, Jack's going to be busy researching Daniel's security system and trying to find a way to hack into his computer so we can get his camera feed and see what he's doing at every moment of the day.

Just like he did to me.

I leave the house, balaclava pulled halfway up, hair tucked into it. I find street parking easily enough, thanks to the weather, but the issue, of course, is that the hospital and its outlying buildings span a whole two blocks with hundreds of offices littered throughout the campus. If I can find Justine—and that's a big if, given the size of the campus, and the fact I don't know my way around this hospital the way I do my own—this conversation could change everything.

What if she'll talk to me this time?

What if she listens long enough for me to tell her she was the first of many women who Daniel targeted?

Or, what if I can't find her, and I'm risking being caught by Daniel, the police, whoever Daniel hired to kidnap me in the first place? I take a long look around me, throat tightening—but most of the people here are in scrubs, hospital employees. I head toward the building with Cardiac Care printed in bold letters along one side. I left the balaclava in the truck, but my hood is up, tight around my face—if I do find Justine, approaching her in a mask seems unwise. Besides, I want her to see me. To know I'm a real person. Not just another missing woman on a poster.

I pull up a map of the campus on my phone, double checking, wondering how I'll ever find her, but then I look up, and like fate has finally given me a freebie, I see a flash of red hair. I stuff the phone back in my pocket and take off after the tall, slender woman—with heeled boots on her feet despite the slick sidewalks—as she strides confidently toward the nearest building.

"Justine!" I call, because I'm not sure if it's her—

But she stops, turns, a professionally detached yet polite smile on her face—no doubt assuming it's a co-worker or maybe a patient. Then she sees me and that smile fades. The false charm in her eyes dissipates, and something else is left. Pity, I think. Her brows crease and her mouth opens, shuts. I jog to catch up to her, stopping a few feet from where she stands.

"Noelle," she says and scans me up and down. Anticipation burns through me—*this is it*. She's talking to me. Acknowledging me.

"You blocked my calls," I say.

"What do you want?" she asks.

"I just want to talk to you."

A huff of a sigh, and she nods. "I'm late. Walk with me. You have two minutes." She takes off, and despite her four-inch heels, I struggle to keep up.

"We both know what Daniel is," I say. "What he's done."

She doesn't answer.

"Justine—" She grips the door to a gray stone building, and I can't help but notice her perfect French-tip manicure, the kind Eve likes, the kind Daniel's mentioned I should get, more than once. "Listen, you don't want to talk to me, and I think it's because you're afraid of him. But I can help you."

A laugh. "I'm a cardiologist." She stops short at a stairwell, brushes perfectly straight and smooth auburn hair over one shoulder jacketed in a long black cloak. Her fingers loosen what looks like a cashmere scarf at her throat, and I realize that's who she reminds me of—*Eve*. Done up to perfection. No wonder Eve liked her. No wonder she was Daniel's girlfriend. She's the embodiment of who he wants me to be. "What could you possibly help me with? I make more money than I'll ever spend, I own half my practice, I have a wonderful husband and a child and—" She takes two steps up, then stops, turns to face me. "I don't need anything. I don't want to be a part of"—she waves a hand—"whatever it is you're doing."

"Really? He never squeezed your hand too hard? Never blackmailed you? Never *threatened* you or someone you loved?"

Her gaze meets mine.

"No, Daniel never did any of those things." She enunciates every word precisely, but something about her words feels off to me.

I try another way. "He killed my aunt. I think he killed Sarah MacCleary, the woman he dated after you. And he had me kidnapped. He's going to do it again and again."

Justine blinks, and I swear there's something there, something besides the stoic flat expression she gives back to me. But it's gone before I can understand it.

"Don't contact me again," she says. "I blocked your number for a reason."

"Why did you break up? How did you get away from him?" I call as she reaches the first landing and turns to go up the next set of stairs. "Did he hurt you?" My voice echoes, and she grabs the rail, glares down at me, clearly not wanting a scene. I don't want a scene, either, but maybe she doesn't want one more. I open my mouth to continue, and she skips down the stairs, impressively fast given her heels.

"We dated," she says, voice low, intense, her face inches from mine. "We broke up when we went our separate ways for residency. There was no"—she flits fingers at me, like I'm a bug she wants to disappear—"*getting away* from him." She inhales, glances down the hall, which is still empty. "Listen, I don't know what the deal is between you two but leave me out of it. Daniel was always a perfect gentleman to me." She glares. "Furthermore, have you even stopped to consider maybe he's not the one you need to worry about?"

My mouth opens, to reply, I think, but I'm left speechless.

Justine rolls her eyes, turns on her heel, stalks up the stairs, and is gone.

I stand there, one hand on the rail, staring after her. What did she mean by *that*?

She might mean Jack, who the media has portrayed as a dangerous criminal. Or she might mean someone else, though I can't fathom who. *Daniel's not the one I need to worry about?*

I stare after her, though she is long gone.

If not him, then who?

FIFTY-SEVEN

DANIEL

I'll be there in twenty minutes.

I'm texting Mother for her benefit, so she and Steven Hannigan can be decent by the time I get there. The last thing I need is to find them still in bed together. *Jesus*, how did she even meet someone like him?

I pause. How did you meet someone like Jack? Did you really know Sarah?

My usual coffee drive-thru is closed, so I settle for shitty coffee once again and go so far as to grab a prepackaged sugary "muffin" filled with god knows what. But I'm starving, and this isn't the sort of place to carry chia bowls or serve a smoothie made with real fruit, so sacrifices must be made.

The first bite of muffin and sip of coffee hit my stomach, and it's an instant burn, and of course I don't have antacids with me. I go to pay and tap my card and the clerk, who is college-aged with zits and wearing a hat that's too big for his head, looks at me and says, "Sir, your card didn't work."

Of course it didn't. I pull out cash.

My phone lights up on the way back to the Porsche; a work

number. Probably short-staffed and needing someone to cover a case, even though I'm supposedly on short-term disability for my hand and the fact my girlfriend is missing.

"Hello?"

"May I speak with Daniel Ashcroft, please?" A woman. I don't recognize her voice.

I frown, balance the phone between my shoulder and ear and open the car door with my good hand.

"This is Dr. Daniel Ashcroft," I say. I set the coffee in the cup holder, take another bite of the sugar- and fat-filled muffin, knowing full well my blood sugar will slam through the roof, but not caring this once, because I have bigger things to worry about. I slide into my car, and for a moment, the leather seat seems to hug me, and I almost feel like everything is going to be all right.

But then the woman says, "Dr. Ashcroft, this is Rebecca from HR. I'm calling to inform you that you've been put on administrative leave effective immediately."

My teeth clench. The Porsche is suddenly hot, claustropho-bic, despite the snow outside.

"What?" is all I can manage.

My heart rate climbs again, so fast and loud I can hear it in my ears.

"I'm sorry, sir, I cannot comment. My supervisor will be in contact to arrange a meeting with you pending an internal investigation."

"A what? Excuse me? An internal investigation of *what*?" My voice cracks, much to my annoyance. I inhale through my nose, exhale through my mouth. *Must maintain control.*

Another pause.

"I'm sorry, sir, I'm not at liberty to discuss this further. Have a nice day."

And *Rebecca* hangs up, just like that.

Administrative leave.

Internal investigation.

The only thing I can think of is Noelle's aunt, but that case was closed due to lack of evidence. Calvin assured me his assistant had found only vague circumstantial evidence that couldn't tie me to the death.

I drum my fingers over the steering wheel. My job. My *job* is at stake. I'm still hot, too hot, and I roll down the windows and breathe fresh air and just try to *think*. I can't lose my job. I'll have nothing. I already feel like I don't have a dime to my name thanks to my bank, and now I may *actually* lose my job?

No, that can't be right. I'm Dr. Daniel Ashcroft. I've done nothing wrong. So what is this about? I'm an anesthesiologist for god's sake, almost untouchable.

I redial the number Rebecca called from.

"This is Rebecca from HR, please leave a message."

"This is Dr. Daniel Ashcroft. If you could please have your manager call me as soon as they are available. I'd like to know what I've been put on leave for. I have a *right* to know. And as this may hurt my professional reputation, you should be aware I will have my attorney file a lawsuit as appropriate." I hang up, only minimally satisfied.

I dial my attorney next and leave a message with his administrative assistant apprising him of the situation. And then I take a deep breath, a Zen breath, and head toward my mother's.

"Steven is not who you think he is."

Mother stands in the doorway, her eyes fixed on me like I'm a misbehaving child.

"I know exactly who Steven is," she says. "I'm an adult, Daniel. I do not need you managing my life."

"He's not an oncologist," I say. "He's not even a physician. How did you really meet him?"

Her lips press into a line, her gaze shifts, her arms cross over her chest, and I don't know if she's in denial or simply doesn't believe me.

"I'm sorry, Daniel, I told you this wasn't a good time, and I meant it. I'm busy with important things."

But she's not. It's 9 a.m. on a weekday morning. She doesn't work, and Steven *isn't* here, probably because I gave them fair warning, and thank god, because after the morning I've had, I'd no doubt wrap my hands around his throat and *squeeze*. I would relish his eyes going big as he realized he couldn't breathe, feel the deepest satisfaction when he passed out and slumped over and—

I inhale. "Mother, listen to me. He's a con man. He's wanted for fraud and a dozen other things, he's been in *prison*, he—"

Mother holds up a hand. Her gaze softens. "I'm sorry, Daniel, but I don't want to hear it. Now, is there news on Noelle? She must be terrified. You said you were going to find her." She gives me a pointed look, and all I can think of is how I failed Sarah. How I promised Mother I wouldn't let the same thing happen with you. This is not how I imagined my plan going.

"I'm working on it, Mother. We're getting close. Now about Steven—"

"Has your PI found anything at all? Do we know where she is? Who's the man who has her? Jack somebody?"

My mouth opens, closes. Mother silencing me. Like a child. I try to understand her side of things, try to see what she must see—that I obviously didn't sleep last night. I'm sure I'm a mess compared to my usual handsome put-together self. My girlfriend is missing. The pipes in my house burst, and everything is going wrong—I probably sound as delirious and out of sorts as I look.

I need to get myself together. What the hell is wrong with me?

Fine, this is fine. I'll go home. I'll gather the evidence. I'll bring it to Mother, and then she won't be able to deny what is sitting right in front of her.

"Noelle is—" But what do I say, Noelle? That you willingly went to another man? That you're fucking him? Do I tell your future mother-in-law you've broken vows you haven't even taken yet? I don't blame you, Noelle. Yes, I'm upset, but I can understand how a woman like you could be tricked by a criminal like Jack. It will take some time, some work, but I'm sure we can heal from this.

"We believe she's with Jack Flaherty still," I say, and I leave it at that, but she peers at me, and she knows something's off. I've never been able to lie to Mother. I wish I could say the same of her.

"What aren't you telling me?"

"Nothing." I feel heat behind my eyes before I realize what that heat means—tears. Fucking *tears*.

I will not cry. Not here in front of Mother. Not ever. I will fix this. I will bring you home. I will prove to her I can keep one woman in line.

"I have to go," I say, and turn, but then I realize I need money. "Oh, I've had a problem with the bank. Could I borrow a card? Or some cash?"

Mother tilts her head, her hair swaying gently in the breeze, perfect even at this early hour. "You've never asked me for money before. Are you sure nothing's wrong?" Her eyes narrow, and I feel like a misbehaving little boy. Which isn't fair. *She's* the one lying to *me*.

"Jesus, Mother, everything's fine, there was just a problem at the bank and my card got canceled by accident and it'll take them a few days to get me another one." The words roll out of me faster than I can control, and I do not speak to Mother this way, and she gives me a look that says as much. "I-I'm sorry. I've just had a bit of a night. The pipes above my bedroom burst, so I didn't get any sleep and—" And *nothing*. The rest is not for her to know. The rest, I can fix before she ever finds out.

"Just a moment."

Mother disappears through the doorway, and I'm still standing on the front stoop, freezing. And that's when it hits me —she won't let me in because Steven *is* here. It's just his car that isn't. But before I can act, she's returned, passing me a black credit card, murmuring, "Love you dear," and closing the door, and all I can think is, *Really? Do you love me, Mother? Could have fooled me.*

FIFTY-EIGHT

NOELLE

Jack is in the bedroom when I get back. His voice is a low murmur through the wall, and though I don't want to interrupt him, I'm about to burst, wanting to tell him what Justine said.

I knock gently.

Jack goes silent. And then, "I've gotta go. I've got this under control," and a beat later he's opening the door, eyes darting around like he's not sure who it's going to be on the other side.

"You're back already," he says.

I peer at him. "Yes. Is that okay?"

"I just thought it would take longer." He edges around me, shoving his phone in his pocket, pouring himself a fresh cup of coffee, quick movements, and nervous energy.

I step back, making space, but wondering about the sudden shift in mood.

"Something wrong?" I ask.

Jack sips his coffee, folds his arms. "Nope. How'd it go with Justine?"

Before I left, I'd felt almost a connection with him—united toward our goal of stealing Daniel's car, pushing him to the edge, figuring out what happened to Sarah, what he has planned for me. But all of that evaporates as I can't help but think he's lying. If he is, he's bad at it, and I recommit myself to not letting my guard down, even if I do need his help.

I give him the rundown, ending with her saying maybe it's not Daniel I need to worry about.

He frowns. "That's vague."

"But what does it mean? Do you think she was referring to you? Since the media is saying you're my kidnapper?"

"I don't know. But it doesn't change what we need to do, right? What else did she say?"

"She said Daniel was a perfect gentleman. But I can't imagine she had this perfect relationship with him, at an age when men are usually *less* mature, less capable of managing their emotions, and now, well into his thirties, he's"—I wave a hand—"*Daniel*. Furthermore, if it was so great, why did she tell me I had the wrong number? Why did she *block* my number? I just—" I stop, my breath coming harder, realizing I feel like I'm about to explode with the tension climbing through me. "I feel like there's something she's not telling me."

"There probably is," he says. "But there's nothing we can do about it short of"—a shrug—"forcing it out of her."

"That would just make me like Daniel."

Jack opens his mouth to speak, but the phone in his pocket buzzes, halting all conversation. "Sorry. Gotta take this. We on for tonight? Crashing one anesthesiologist's car?"

I nod, force a smile, and watch him disappear back into his bedroom to talk to whoever is calling him.

I make my way to my own room. Hopefully, the plan is working. Hopefully, Daniel is getting madder with every inconvenience—his cards canceled, which surely he's realized; the complaint at work, which hopefully won't take long—the #MeToo movement should ensure the hospital deals with sexual harassment quickly. It will just be a matter of if they believe me when the complaint is against the beloved Dr. Daniel Ashcroft.

The pipes, which may or may not have burst; and lastly, seeing me with another man. Tonight, we'll destroy his car in a way that I'm certain will send a message.

The only question is, how do I pull this all together? How do I get him to the same place as me to demand answers, but without putting myself at risk, and how do I make sure he'll talk?

It's the most important part of the plan, and the one detail I'm clueless on.

FIFTY-NINE

DANIEL

The plumber is thankfully gone by the time I get home—a bill flutters on the door, and I yank it off, shove it in the mailbox for the maid to send to my accountant, and go inside. Fans still whir upstairs, their hum like a fucking mosquito circling me through my whole house. I stare at the damage—mostly to the ceiling, to my bed.

Mother. Doesn't. Believe me.

I'm not sure if I'm more pissed at her, at you, at Jack Flaherty, or Steven Hannigan. Jesus. Could life get anymore screwed up, Noelle?

I sigh. Find my way to my office. Pour *four* fingers of bourbon to save myself the trip back to the bar and sit down at my computer.

Kari picks that moment to call, and I answer, forcing my voice to sound *normal, put together, caring*—all the things I'd failed miserably at with my mother, evident in the way she'd looked at me, like *I'm* the one who's losing it.

"Kari, how are you?"

"Noelle called me."

I practically spit my bourbon out.

"When? What did she say? Tell me everything." I sit up, press the phone to my ear. "No, wait, what number did she call from?" I open a new e-mail and type a message one-handed:

Calvin,

I need everything on this number you've got, including GPS or at minimum triangulate the cell phone towers. I don't care how much it costs. Find someone who can do it. TODAY.

"Hold on," she says, and a second later, she's reading the number back to me. It's a local Seattle number—excellent. Maybe that will make it easier. Maybe it's registered to someone. Maybe I'll be able to *find you* and put a stop to *one* of the messes in my life.

"What did she say?"

"She—" Kari's breath catches, and maybe I should have done this in person. To comfort her. To take another photo of me being there for her when you're not, Noelle, to put it up for you to see. "She admitted she had herself kidnapped. Well, not exactly, but she didn't deny it, either. And she said she was *protecting me*, by *leaving*. She said..." Kari's voice fades off. "Everything you said. You were right. He's a psychopath, and he's got her." Kari's voice breaks off in a sob, and *pregnant women* are the psychopaths if you ask me.

"I'll come by tonight," I say. "I'll bring dinner." And my phone, to take more photos of us *bonding.* "Call me if you hear from her again."

We disconnect, but only moments later, my phone lights up again—a hospital number.

My stomach bottoms out, but I didn't do *anything* wrong, and *fuck* them, I'll sue them if this compromises my career.

"Hello?"

"Dr. Ashcroft, this is Helen from HR."

"Hello, Helen from HR." I try to put a smile in my voice, but the words come out through gritted teeth, and it sounds more like a growl. Well, too bad. I'm a doctor. She's *Helen* from *HR*. She probably has a bachelor's degree in art history and spends her nights with her cats, and that's why she has this job, so she can call people like me, who do something real for a living, who make *real* money, who—

"Dr. Ashcroft, my assistant spoke to you earlier about administrative leave."

I take a quick sip of the bourbon. "Yes." There, a word it's hard to fuck up. Jesus, what is wrong with me?

"I'm not at liberty to go into detail, though we will, of course, have a meeting to do so later this week. I can, however, tell you sexual harassment complaints have been made against you. You have the right to dispute these complaints and will be given the opportunity to do so once we investigate."

"My attorney—"

"Your attorney is welcome to contact me and to be present at said meetings. There is a protocol we must follow, Dr. Ashcroft, surely you can understand that. We take harassment very seriously, and we would treat it with the same importance if you were the one who filed a complaint."

"I have *never* harassed *anyone*," I say. "I demand to know who filed these complaints. People can be jealous, you know. Envious of my success. I can't help that."

"I'm sorry, Dr. Ashcroft, complaints of this sort are held in strict confidence to protect the victim."

The victim.

I want to say, *This is bullshit. Someone's screwing with me. There is no victim.* Instead, I summon the good-natured man I am at the hospital and answer, "I understand. I'll be in touch," and disconnect.

Who would report me for sexual harassment?

Sure, I flirt with nurses when no one else is around. But it's harmless. All the doctors do it. And the nurses *like* it—the attentions of a handsome rich anesthesiologist? I make their day. But when it's unwanted, I'm just as happy to ignore them and get down to business. After all, Noelle, I have *you*.

I put another call into my attorney to update him with details—again, the assistant takes notes and promises a call back as soon as possible. My e-mail sits empty, nothing back from Calvin yet, so I move on to the next most important thing. I must prove to my mother that Steven isn't the man she thinks he is. I must show her she's been duped.

I print the file Calvin sent, but I can't help going back to the photo you sent me. You and Jack. I inspect the background of the photo. Where are you? A motel? No, it looks less cookie-cutter than that. A neon-inspired painting of the Space Needle is pinned to the wall behind you. Curtains cover the window, so I can't see what's just outside of wherever it is you are, but I wonder—

Calvin, can you pull location from a photo? I'm attaching it.

I send it, drumming my fingers over the desk, staring at it, knowing I've seen that painting somewhere before—probably at Pike Place Market, probably on one of our dates, playing *tourist*. Probably thousands of these prints litter Seattle.

I'm letting myself get distracted. Yes, I need to prove to Mother that her boyfriend is not who he says he is, but I haven't lost her—I've lost *you*. This is not how any of this was supposed to go. And that pisses me off.

SIXTY

NOELLE

Daniel's car sits in front of Kari's house, and as we drive by, it's illuminated in the headlights. The scratch I left down the side is gone. Of course, it is—Daniel wouldn't let something ugly mar his everyday experience.

That same rush of adrenaline hits me, the knowledge of what we're about to do coursing through my veins, making my heart pound in my chest. His car won't look so pretty soon enough, and a quick patch-up at the shop won't fix it this time.

Jack pulls the truck to a stop two houses down. Night has fallen, and this street is without lamps, so we sit in darkness. I wonder if us going through with this means I can truly trust Jack, despite his suspicious behavior—that there's no way if he were somehow working for Daniel, he'd go through with it.

"GPS shows he's been here for almost forty-five minutes." He peers out the window, then glances at me, waiting for a response.

I lean forward, as though that will somehow let me see into Kari's house, let me see what they're doing. "That's strange," I say. "He hates any house that isn't..." I try to come up with the right word. Spacious? Museum-like in cleanliness? Perfection?

"Like his," I settle on. Kari's is the opposite—small, cramped, cluttered. But comfortable, too. We spent many nights on her couch, watching movies, chatting about who she was dating, drinking wine.

Jack shifts in his seat. "He's working to get and stay on her good side," he murmurs. "You sent him that photo of us?"

I nod, fighting a blush.

"He's playing you. Same way you're playing him. Like a game of chess. Don't fall for it, don't let him rattle you." Jack presses a hand to my forearm, squeezes it reassuringly, and I realize I really do *want* to trust him.

"Easier said than done," I say. "My cousin's life is on the line. Her baby's, too. I just wish she'd listen to me."

"Me, too," Jack says. He looks over, meets my eyes. "But we have a plan to fix this, regardless. You ready?"

I nod. It's time.

"You have the key?" I ask.

He holds it up, the key he took off Daniel when he "borrowed" the Porsche before. It hangs on a keyring I recognize as Daniel's—no house key needed, because he uses an electronic lock with a code.

Jack pulls on the balaclava, hiding his face. He opens the door, climbs out, and waits for me to slide over, taking his place at the steering wheel.

"I'll follow you," he says. "Text me when we're there. I'll make it happen, and then we'll go. I checked it out earlier—no cameras on the restaurant, but stay half a block away, just in case."

And then he closes the door, sprints across the road, and in seconds the Porsche growls to life. I slide the seat forward to account for our height difference, shift into gear, and drive down the street at exactly the speed limit—nothing to see here.

. . .

One thing I did not consider was the danger Jack would expose himself to in the process of crashing a car directly into *our* restaurant. So when he stops the Porsche facing the restaurant, grabs a sizable rock from the landscaping display, and puts it on the gas pedal, I breathe a sigh of relief. He won't get hurt. I won't lose my only ally. I won't be left to handle this by myself. The grumble of the engine becomes nearly a *whine*, but it's still in park, not moving.

Jack pulls back from the driver's seat. Turns to look at me, all broad shoulders and self-assured. Maybe he's done this before. He gives me a thumbs up, then reaches a long arm in just enough to hit the shifter into drive, leaping back with what looks like inches to spare.

The Porsche *goes*, and Jack doesn't wait to watch, turning and sprinting through the night toward me. Behind him, glass shatters, brick buckles, steel screeches, and the car alarm blares through the night.

I can't tear my eyes away. My heart vibrates in my chest as I watch the destruction of a place I suffered for so long.

The car. The restaurant. In some ways, it's anticlimactic— in the movies there would be an explosion. But in reality the car growls, the glass and brick cave in, and then... silence.

I exhale, force an inhale. Then Jack's there. I lean over, shove the passenger's side door open, and he swings in.

I smash down the gas, let the clutch out too fast, and we peel away. Thank god Daniel swapped his vintage Porsche for a 2019 a few years ago because he preferred the *color*, which better matched his complexion, according to him. The 2019 was a car that only came in an automatic when it was released, and I can't imagine how Jack would have managed, otherwise.

"Easy," Jack says. "Drive normally." He watches the wreckage in the side mirror; so far, no one has come, no vehicles have driven by—hopefully, that means we've gotten away. I slow down as I let my heartbeat return to normal.

I turn a corner, hop on the highway, putting distance between us and the crash. The next exit is ours, and in minutes, we're pulling into the garage, effectively hiding the truck and ourselves.

"So." Jack turns to me as I shut the car off, remove the keys, and the overhead light turns on. "Why that restaurant?"

I thought I'd feel elation at destroying Daniel's Porsche—at what we'd done. At the message this surely sends to Daniel. If anything will cause a rage, will throw him out of his careful control, it's his Porsche being destroyed. But instead, I'm numb.

"It's *our* restaurant," I say. I use air quotes, and Jack frowns.

"Our?"

"Every Friday he forced me to go on a date with him at that restaurant." A hint of a smile curls at my mouth. Maybe not numb, not entirely. Satisfaction flutters through me, knowing no matter how this ends, Daniel will never pick me up again in *that car* to go to *that restaurant.*

"Guess you sent him a message, then."

I meet Jack's gaze.

"Yes, I did. *We* did."

The knowledge of that tingles through me, leaves me feeling buzzed and anxious all at once, but mostly, satisfied.

Fuck you, Daniel.

SIXTY-ONE

DANIEL

One of my favorite things about spending time with your cousin, Noelle, is seeing that it's not *me* who is the problem in our relationship, it's *you*.

Kari is quite pliable—if I'd met her first, if my mother had fallen in love with *her,* maybe she'd have been a better choice than you. She's ready to believe everything I tell her, ready to grow closer to me if it helps us find you—and yes, we've established an *us*; specifically, *we* enjoy orange chicken and fried rice and wontons. But not to get off track, what I'm saying is that it's not me with the problem.

I've never had an issue making any woman understand her place until you came along. I thought maybe, just maybe, I'd lost my touch. I should have known better. Kari took a little convincing, but she's heeling nicely, now. If only you would follow suit.

"Do you think I should call her?" Kari asks, poking at a bit of rice. "She was *mad* when we spoke."

I rub my chin as if considering her question. With any luck, I won't need Kari to convince you to come back, after all. Calvin has assured me he should be able to find your location soon enough, between the phone number and the photo you sent.

Maybe a part of you *wants* to be found, Noelle—you're making it so easy for me.

"I wouldn't," I say. "Not yet. Let's see how the next twenty-four hours go."

Kari agrees, then uncomfortably asks, "So what did you do today?"

A perfectly normal question. A kind one, really. She doesn't like me, but she likes the silence between us less. It's more than you bother to inquire about me, these days. I open my mouth, but stop—what can I tell her? That I couldn't stop looking at the photo of you with another man? That I confronted my mother about her con man of a boyfriend, and she chose to believe him over me? That my house is a wreck, and will be for at least another day? That I may not have a job by this time next week? Or maybe that I still don't have credit cards in my own name, which got me a suspicious look today while purchasing fresh flowers for Kari?

I smile. "Oh, nothing much—"

My phone rings, and I frown down at it—not a hospital number. *Thank god.*

My teeth clench at the thought. The weakness it implies that I'm afraid to answer my own phone.

"Are you going to answer that?"

"Of course." I give her a tight smile. Swipe the green circle, press it to my ear, listen, and answer that I am indeed Dr. Daniel Ashcroft, and yes, I am the owner of a 2019 Porsche 911, and—

I can *feel* my veins constrict, my blood pressure notching higher, higher, as the police officer talks and talks and—

"What?" I snap.

"Do you know where your vehicle currently is?" the woman repeats.

"Of course," I snap. "Who is this?"

"This is Officer Hendricks. Could you please double-check your car is there?"

Fuck.

My chopsticks clatter to the table, and I'm at the front window in seconds, and—

It's gone. My Porsche is *gone*.

Kari pulls to a stop in front of our restaurant. Since my car was gone, she had to come with me, and I regret that. I regret she may see the rage pulsing through me in this moment. I get out, slowly, feeling as though I'm in a dream.

The front end of my Porsche is hidden beneath rubble—planks of wood and shattered glass and tile that's fallen from the decorative frame of the restaurant's windows. Most of the car is *inside* the building, driven straight through the plate-glass windows that let streetlight shine through at night, and that open outward during the day for an open-air lunch vibe.

My shoes are wet, as are the bottom of my pants, the icy water of melted snow seeping in, just like the dismay filling my body. I can't tear my eyes from the back bumper, the new wheels, from my fucking *Porsche*, my most prized possession after you, Noelle.

"Are you okay?" Kari asks, but I don't answer her, because no, of course I'm not okay.

"Mr. Ashcroft, when was the last time you saw your Porsche?"

My mouth opens, closes. No words come out.

"He got to my house around 7:30 p.m., so probably right then. We were inside eating dinner." Kari answers, but her voice is an apparition in the night, something I can *sense*, but is it real? Is anything real?

I can't take my eyes off my car.

Which is no longer in mint condition. It's probably not

totaled, because it's a Porsche, but Jesus, it might as well be. It will never be the same.

I clear my throat. "Doctor," I say.

"Sir? You need a doctor?" the officer asks.

"No, *I* am a doctor."

"He's—" Kari tries to fill the officer in as to who I am, and I hate that she's doing this, but I'm also grateful, because I can't quite form a coherent sentence. I'm thinking, and those thoughts shift from the Porsche to you.

The Porsche went far enough in to destroy my favorite table, the one along the back wall tucked around a corner. *Our* table. It's a coincidence, I know that, but is it a—

"Fuck."

"Sir, excuse me?"

I'm not an idiot. It may be a coincidence the Porsche took out the booth we've shared many dinners at, but it simply *cannot* be a coincidence that someone stole *my* Porsche and put it through *our* restaurant.

I let out a forceful breath and take a half step back, realization contracting the world around me. Kari reaches for my arm, but I flinch and move back again.

It's *not* a coincidence, is it, Noelle? Just like it's not a coincidence the last day of my life has been absolute hell. It was *you* who filed a complaint of sexual harassment. It was *you* who canceled my credit cards. No doubt you found a way to turn my heat off in the middle of the worst storm Seattle has seen in years. The only thing you can't possibly be responsible for is my mother's behavior.

I swallow, force myself to inhale, exhale.

Is this Jack's doing? Has he convinced you I'm a demon? Did he tell you to do these things? I have to shut this nonsense down, once and for all. I have to convince you to see him for what he is—a criminal. A criminal set on destroying us for reasons I cannot fathom.

I pull my phone from my pocket and search my e-mail for the message I sent to Calvin. I select the phone number I sent him.

I dial it.

I dial you.

SIXTY-TWO

NOELLE

The fireplace crackles, even though it's only gas, and flames lick at the top of the stone. I'm on a pillow inches from it, arms around my knees, both stunned and satisfied to take something so precious from Daniel as his Porsche.

When a phone rings, I assume it's Jack's—after all, he's the one who's been getting the calls. But he murmurs, "It's yours," and sets it down beside me. He sits a foot or so away, enjoying the warmth, too.

I gaze down at the phone. We left the lights off, poured wine and whiskey, and are sitting in quiet companionable contemplation. Something I haven't done with anyone in a long while. It's nice. And I'm putting off thinking too hard because I know it's almost time. Soon, I have to face Daniel. I'm out of ideas to throw him off balance outside of high school-like pranks, and besides, this is exhausting. I want it to be over.

My stomach flutters as I read the numbers from the caller.

"It's Daniel," I say.

"Maybe he found his Porsche," Jack says, a trace of something in his voice that tells me he's as happy as I am to make him miserable.

Maybe I really do have someone I can trust.

"You gonna answer? You want me to?" he asks.

Half of me doesn't want to—how had he gotten the number, anyway? Oh, of course—Kari. Kari, who thinks he's only trying to help me.

I pick up the phone, take a second to collect myself, to force myself to use my normal tone instead of the subdued version I usually talk to him with.

"Hello?"

"How *could* you?" Daniel hisses.

I wait a beat. My fingers tingle, hearing his voice, afraid of what he's going to say, but also hoping he's mad—hoping he's *livid.*

"How could I *what?*" I answer back. My voice barely trembles.

"You're destroying my life. After everything I've done for you. I'm bending over backward trying to *save* you, and you do this? We need to have a conversation, Noelle. Jack Flaherty is *dangerous.*"

I think through half a dozen ways to respond, but there's really only one thing to say.

"I'm taking everything from you, Daniel, the same way you took everything from me."

A pause. "What?" he asks. "I gave you everything. I kept you safe. I—"

He doesn't get it, so I clarify.

"Payback's a bitch."

A sound comes through the phone—a cry of rage? A wail of pain? I can't quite tell. And I don't care. I hang up the phone and lift my glass to Jack.

"Cheers."

SIXTY-THREE

DANIEL

Everything with the police takes too damn long, but I stand there, like a good concerned citizen, because I have an image to uphold. Besides, filling out their forms, answering dozens of questions that have nothing to do with anything important, it gives me time to plan.

And in the midst of all this, I get the message I've been waiting for.

Dr. Ashcroft—I was able to locate the phone. The address of its most recent location follows. Please let me know if there's anything else you need.

And just like that, I know where you are. Which means I can finally get my plan back on track.

SIXTY-FOUR

NOELLE

It's almost midnight, and we've had too much to drink. I got off the phone with Daniel, giddy with adrenaline and anger and a bit of fear, but victory, too.

It's working. We're *succeeding*. And no, I don't have the last piece of the puzzle yet, the part where we nail the lid on Daniel's figurative coffin, but we'll figure it out, Jack and I together. If we can steal a Porsche and get away with it, we can do just about anything, right?

Jack leaves long enough to grab food, and we sit at the kitchen table, sharing a bottle of wine, downing slice after slice of pizza, and all I can think is what I said to Daniel is absolutely true—I'm doing what he did to me.

The difference is, I'm doing it because I have to.

Taking away his freedom, his ability to live his life as he desires, one thing at a time. But I also know that we've reached the height of it all—that he's at his most frustrated, and that from here, we only have one way to go—straight for our goal. But tonight, as we eat and drink, and elation and alcohol leave us buzzed, we spend a moment enjoying ourselves—something I hadn't realized I needed so badly.

"The job as a bouncer was the absolute worst," he says. "Everyone was drunk—*everyone*—even the bartenders would drink. I think I was the only one who didn't." He screws up his face. "I got puked on more often at that job than—" He shakes his head. "It was awful. Money wasn't that great, either." He takes a swig of whiskey and lifts the bottle of wine. "More?"

I nod and he pours, and goes on, "Seattle is a nice change from Denver. Not as many mountains, but the Puget Sound makes up for it. Ever gone out on a boat?"

"I went to a wedding with Daniel on one, but it never left shore."

"A wedding on a boat that doesn't actually leave harbor? What's the point?" He goes on about that, tongue looser with the whiskey, and I find he's actually funny in moments—a far cry from the stoic man I've seen so far.

"The best way to see it is by kayak," he says. "Or paddleboard, but you can go faster on a kayak. Have you been?"

"Never." I lean forward, sip my wine, twirl the glass slowly. "I'd love to. I just... haven't." I haven't done a lot of things this past year. When this is all said and done, I resolve to do those things—to live again.

Jack's eyebrows shoot up, as though he can't believe this, and there's a moment where I think he's going to suggest we go kayaking together. But then we both remember the reason we're working together.

"Tell me more about Sarah," I say, to change topics.

He passes a hand over his mouth, and says, "She was amazing. The heart of our family. No one believed we were twins. She was beautiful. Me?" He shrugs, sheepish, and he must know he's good looking, even if it is in a rough sort of way.

"You're not so bad," I tell him and immediately wish I hadn't. He gives me a shy smile, and I look down. It's the wine. The adrenaline. The shared experience of doing something I would never have dreamed I'd do, of getting away with it.

Jack refills his whiskey. I tell him about growing up in Idaho —about vacations to the mountains. About how I used to explore the mountains here in Washington. For a moment, this night feels like something else—two friends, enjoying an evening together, almost. But it's not, and I know that, but I can pretend, just for a minute.

I know tomorrow we will have to get back to business.

We eventually find our way back to the fireplace, and this time Jack sits beside me, our shoulders brushing, and I feel the warmth from him, from the wine, the fire, and I realize I'm *comfortable,* just being here, with him. I have one friend I can count on through all this, even if it's likely we go our separate ways and never speak again once it's over. For the moment, it is enough.

I'm alone with coffee the next day. It's actually lunchtime, but we were up late, and I'm searching online for the usuals. Kari posted another photo with Daniel, but Jack's right—she's a pawn. I skim it for anything helpful, ignore the #Looking4-Noelle hashtag, and check the news. A photo of Daniel's Porsche is about halfway down the homepage of *The Seattle Star.*

My gut tightens, and I navigate away. A moment later, Jack wanders into the kitchen.

"Anything new?" His voice is thick, his eyelids still heavy with sleep. I smile at his appearance, at the easy companionship that's grown between us. I feel relaxed with Jack, safe. He grabs the coffee pot, refills mine, finds a mug for himself, settles across from me.

"More of the same." I log in to my e-mail last. I suspect what I will find in my inbox—the fact Daniel went so far as to call me last night is big. It means we're *close.* It means in a moment of weakness, he cracked and stopped being the grieving boyfriend

—he called, angry and hurt. *Shocked*, even, like he thinks there's a happy ending for us after all this. Like there was a happy ending to begin with.

But when I open my e-mail, there's nothing. Just a blank inbox, a handful of messages in my other folders advertising upcoming Valentine's Day sales.

I study the blank screen.

"What's wrong?" Jack asks, peering at me as he sips his coffee.

"Nothing." But there is *something*. It's strange Daniel *hadn't* e-mailed me, hadn't sent a thinly veiled threat after what Jack and I did. Of course, he had called, so maybe—

I shake my head. I'm paranoid. Reading into things. It's *good* I haven't heard from Daniel. And yet, I can't help but reload the page once more, because it does seem unlike Daniel to not do *something* to make himself feel better when he's on the losing end. And last night he lost big-time.

SIXTY-FIVE

DANIEL

I can't focus.

I'm getting phone calls constantly—my mother, work, the bank, Kari wanting to know if I've found anything, the drywall people.

All I want is to focus on you, Noelle. I silence my phone. Toss it onto the passenger's of the shitty rental car. Sure, it's a BMW, but it's not a Porsche. Not *my* Porsche.

I'll have to get a new one.

Once I get this bank and work stuff figured out.

I stare down the street, and I can see the house you're in. A vacation rental. How clever you and Jack are. Was that your idea or his? Are you enjoying playing house?

I'm not happy, but... I will say, the best part about knowing where you are, Noelle, is that I can now watch you again.

Sort of.

It's not my own personalized camera system, each camera angled for the best view, but I saw your shape through the blinds last night, as you moved around the living room, as smoke chugged from the chimney. I'm cataloging each indiscretion so we can talk about it when I get you back. Maybe you should come to therapy with me—what would you think of that? It's not your fault you're a woman, and that as a woman, you're susceptible to men like Jack Flaherty, who know how to twist and manipulate things until you have a different sense of reality.

The police will be here soon.

That's not ideal, either. It's not what I *wanted*. No, I wanted to corner Jack Flaherty and beat the shit out of him. Break his hands. Kick him with steel-toed boots sharp enough to leave bruises and break skin, just like he did to me.

But I'm still not up to my full strength, and I have no doubt he'd win.

And since the end goal here is to get you back, I will make this sacrifice. Besides, I have friends in the police department. Jack Flaherty is a kidnapper, and I have more than a little reason to suspect him of Sarah's disappearance, too. Hell, maybe he killed her himself. I may get my turn to go a round with him anyway, but with the help of the Seattle Police Department.

After all, money can buy you quite a bit, I've found.

Even if my money is inaccessible. I might lose my job. I have some cash in savings, in investments. It would be worth liquidating if it meant I got a shot at Jack.

But I digress.

I grab my phone, dial the number to the police captain who owes me a favor, and listen as it rings.

I'm coming for you, Noelle. Any second now.

SIXTY-SIX

NOELLE

"Someone's watching us."

Jack's words tear my attention away from my phone, which I have prepped to dial Justine one last time. I want to know if she knows anything about Sarah, and I want to ask what she meant by *maybe he's not who you need to worry about*. I figure I have nothing to lose. I found her cell phone on a medical school alumni online directory. Hopefully, she hasn't blocked me from this one, too. At worst, she'll hang up. At best, she'll crack.

"What do you mean?" I join Jack at the window. The blinds are drawn, but he's tall enough he can peek through a gap at the top and out onto the street. We've spent the last few hours recuperating after last night, trying to access Daniel's security system, and life has felt almost normal. At his words, I tense, that old anxiety creeping into my chest.

"Don't look. Go to the back room." Jack nods me toward the hall, and we traverse the length of the house to the smallest room. It holds a twin bed, like it's an afterthought, and is otherwise an office with a desk and a computer in one corner. I drop down and peer out through the side of the blinds. Sure enough, two cars are parked out front. The fading light of early evening makes it impossible to see who's inside, but there's someone.

"How long have they been there?"

"Noticed them half an hour ago. Figured it was nothing. But it's been too long. Especially with two cars."

He's right. I glance around the room, heart fluttering, as though looking for exits. We haven't gained access to Daniel's security system yet—Jack suspects he stores his data in his actual home, which would make sense as Daniel isn't just storing his own data, he's storing the camera feed from my apartment, too. And—it occurs to me with a jolt—possibly others', as well.

"Might be cops. Daniel is friends with"—I wave a hand—"people."

"Might be." Jack hesitates. "Maybe we should go. If it's cops, that's not good. If it's *not* cops—that's not good, either."

"Your old boss?" I ask.

He gives a little nod, eyes darting back and forth. "Yeah. Maybe. He still has a contract to fill. Still wants to deliver you to the client."

A buzzing fills my ears, and my stomach knots. Part of me hoped that had ended when Jack quit. When he agreed to help me. But two men had broken into my apartment and taken me. So of course, Jack abandoning ship wouldn't have brought everything to a halt. But if Daniel hired someone to do this, then why—*why*—was he still working so hard at it? Was he that desperate? Or is someone else behind it?

"We need to leave." I say the words and realize what it means—heading back out into the cold weather, looking over my shoulder constantly. The safety and security of being here with Jack was fleeting—an illusion.

I step from the room and do a quick sweep of the house—grab my coat, pull on my shoes, shove money and the phone in my pocket. Jack does the same. He drops a boot in the midst of pulling it on, and I flinch as it smacks the ground. My shoulders tighten. My pulse thrums faster and faster through my body, because at any moment, someone could come through the door.

"The truck?" I ask.

Jack stands in the kitchen, frozen, like a statue, eyes distant.

"What?" He blinks back to reality and focuses on me. "No, we need—" His voice fades off.

"What's wrong?"

"If it's the cops, they'll stop us. If it's my boss"—Jack shakes his head—"he'll stop us, too. Violently. We can't take the truck."

I grab for the counter, it's coolness under my fingertips grounding me. "Are you saying we're trapped?"

Jack shakes his head. "No. I mean, they may not even be here for us, but..."

The phone in my pocket beeps.

A text. One glance says it's a text from Daniel.

I don't have a chance to read it, because a *bam-bam-bam* echoes off the front door.

I jolt, and Jack's hand is under his jacket, and there's a gun in his hand—*a gun.* How has he hidden it from me this whole time? I take an unconscious step back, but Jack whips around, comes close, putting us eye to eye.

"You need to go," he says. "Out the back door. Run. Don't stop. I'll catch up with you."

"I'm not leaving you here. We're in this together."

Bam-bam-bam again. It feels like the whole house shakes with it.

Another buzz in my pocket. I ignore it.

"You have to go," Jack says, expression focused, serious, in a way I haven't seen since my kidnapping. "We can't get away together, not now. But I'll find you, and we'll end this. Okay?"

I open my mouth to object, but Jack's already spun me away, pushed me toward the back door. He steps around me, peers out the kitchen window into the backyard.

"Hurry. No one's out there yet, but if it's the cops, they'll cover all exits. *Go!*"

Another buzz in my pocket. Daniel hasn't texted me before—what if the timing is no coincidence? If I don't go, will he have me in his clutches in mere minutes?

I turn and give Jack a quick hug. "We'll find out what happened to Sarah," I promise. And then I'm out the door, running.

Until a lanky form rounds the corner of the house, putting me face to face with Daniel.

SIXTY-SEVEN

DANIEL

I almost can't believe it's you.

But it *is*.

Within arm's reach. I grab for you, and your eyes go wide, you backpedal, you *fall*.

"Noelle, it's me. You're safe now." I say the words and smile and crouch down like you're a scared dog. *Believe me. Trust me.*

I hold out my hand, let a warmth fill my eyes, which if I'm being honest, I don't really *feel*, but then again, you did wreck my car. I'm sure it'll come around, probably around the time you lock your mouth around my cock as you beg for forgiveness.

A shudder of pleasure runs through me at the thought, and I exhale, smile. The elation of victory surges through me. If it weren't so fucking cold out, I'd be hard.

I reach for you tenderly. You never know when cameras might be rolling.

"No," you say. "Don't touch me." Your face hardens, and my heart hurts for it.

"Noelle, you've been through something traumatic. I understand—"

You blink. Hesitate. Stop moving away. Your hair falls

forward, cloaking your face, and I see fear etched into your features, but something else, too.

Finally, finally you understand I'm only here to help you—

I step forward. Stoop to offer you a hand. You take it, and something flashes through your eyes, but you're *mine*, and after all this time, finally I have you. I can forgive it all, Noelle—and together, we can fix it. You can pull back your harassment complaint. I can get new credit cards. We will still have to deal with Kari, but I'll take care of that. Our relationship will be like my ceiling—smoothed over. Repainted. Fixed. Stronger for what we've been through. Ready for *the plan*. I'll show Mother I not only could save you, but we can be *happy*—

You yank me close, and I think you're going to embrace me, but—

Searing, suffocating pain. Your knee comes away from my crotch, and you kick the knee Jack nearly dislocated, and I fall to the ground, gasping.

"I said no," you whisper, and you take my hand still taped around a splint and yank it, and *more pain*, my nerves on fire, and your voice fades away, footsteps sloshing through snow, far, far away, and I'm on the ground, and *damn*, Noelle. I'm starting to think you may not be worth the trouble.

SIXTY-EIGHT

DANIEL

"I almost had her. But she—" I shut up, because this must be what it feels like to be a failure. How do people survive, feeling this way? How do they not off themselves?

Kari frowns and presses the cool washcloth to my face, as though that will somehow help my balls, my knee, my hand.

"What happened?" she asks. We're at my place. I couldn't deal with another moment in her claustrophobic clusterfuck of a house.

"She was there. Right *there*. She—" I take a breath, fight back the desire to tilt my head up to the sky and scream. "I need a drink."

"Okay." Kari nods. She crosses the room and pours me a bourbon at random. Brings it back. Obedient. Like you should be. Like you *aren't*.

"Maybe I should give up," I say, but the words are no more out of my mouth, and I cringe.

Me? Give up? I would laugh if it wouldn't hurt so damn bad.

I'm Dr. Daniel Ashcroft. I don't give up.

I get what I want. I win. Every time. Whatever it takes.

I tremble as I bring the glass to my lips. Kari stares at me with wide eyes, scared for you—for what you're doing to yourself, to us. And I know I can't just give up. I can't lose to you. Can't lose, period. And I can't disappoint my mother with another girlfriend slipping through my fingers.

The game is not over, Noelle.

SIXTY-NINE

NOELLE

Disappearing in Seattle isn't easy.

The fact I can't get out of my own head—flashing back through Jack seeing the cars, Jack insisting I go, *leaving him behind*, and then running into Daniel—that doesn't help.

I wander the waterfront, jacket clutched around me, hood up, turning away before anyone gets close enough to get a look at me. The gray waters of the Puget Sound lap against the sand-and-driftwood beach, and the breeze brings with it a humid salt-water smell.

I gaze out at the water, thinking, *What now?*

A seal pops its head out of the water and stares at me, and I stare back. I used to love watching the ocean wildlife—but the only reason I do it now is to avoid a pair of runners loping my way.

They pass, without so much as a backward glance, and I continue on, eventually stepping from the sand to the path as I approach the sculpture park. It's on the far end of Alaskan Way, maybe a quarter mile from Pike Place Market, an area I will avoid for how busy it is, how many cameras are there. But the park is mostly deserted—it's too cold and windy for most people to brave the weather. I buy coffee from a corner street vendor, keeping my head down, not showing my face or making eye contact. The reputation that Seattle has plenty of people who classify themselves as *weird* means no one questions this. I wander for another hour, up and down the waterfront, through the park trails, trying to decide what to do—and how to do it.

With Jack, the plan was to go after Daniel.

That feels much harder alone. Maybe I should leave Seattle. Leave this behind. But then I would be abandoning Jack. Letting him take the fall for my fake-turned-real kidnapping, and I'm doing what I decided *not* to do—running. Spending the rest of my life looking over my shoulder.

The phone in my pocket buzzes. I edge past a dock and drop down onto the beach again. I consider what else I could do to drive Daniel over the edge—to get revenge for this last bit—but haven't I done enough? Isn't it time for the games to end? I'm certainly not in the mood to play them anymore, and I've taken everything from Daniel I can. His money, the comfort of his home, his car—even his pride, when I didn't hesitate to fight back, taking advantage of his weaknesses, saving myself.

But it's not over, if the text messages filling my phone are any indication. An irregular barrage of texts coming in.

Come back. I forgive you.

I'll save you.

I'll hire my attorney to help you, and we'll put Jack away for good after what he's done to you.

Have you heard of Stockholm syndrome?

Noelle, I can help—

And somewhere in there, Kari texts, too—

Noelle, girl, I love you. Let us help you. That Jack guy tricked you, we know that.

I find a chunk of driftwood to tuck myself into, effectively blocking the wind, blocking the ability of anyone on the trail to see I'm there. I swipe the texts away and pull up the news.

SUSPECT CAUGHT IN KIDNAPPING OF REGISTERED NURSE

The article reads like Daniel wrote it—evidence piling up against Jack. A mention of his missing sister. Daniel quoted as wanting nothing more than me to come home safely. Another call to Seattle to assist in finding me. Guilt fills me—Jack's done nothing but try to help me, helping me escape the house—and in return for it all, he got arrested.

I stay hidden behind the driftwood, a sense of claustrophobia settling over me; even with the Puget Sound and beach all around me, I'm trapped. I can't come out. But I must. I have to figure out a way to save myself. To save Jack. To prove Daniel isn't the nice guy he pretends to be.

I'm half asleep when I hear the voices.

I go still. Feel every bit of air as I inhale, exhale, my chest tightening with the realization someone is *here*.

But of course they are. It's a public beach. But then why am I on high alert?

I hazard a backward glance.

Cops. Two of them. Palms held high on their foreheads, blocking the glare of the bright clouds, looking out over the walking path, the beach.

They murmur to one another. The wind makes their words unintelligible, other than, "Don't see her," and, "Wild goose chase," and thankfully, "Forget this."

I duck down, lie flat, tuck myself beneath the driftwood as much as possible, salt and sand scratching my skin raw where it gets between my skin and my clothes. I shut my eyes. Try to keep my breathing steady. Ignore that my hands are clenched into tight balls, and I feel as though I could scream.

I'm the reason Jack got caught.

Daniel has been tracking me, burner phone or no.

And I'm an idiot for not realizing it—hadn't he tracked me before? Doesn't he have my phone number now? Of course he could figure out a way to find me with that alone.

The cops leave. I stay hidden twenty minutes longer, and when the world around me dims, I brush off the sand. Shiver against the cooling waterfront of Seattle. I disappear into the fading light, a new plan in mind.

SEVENTY

DANIEL

"What do you mean, he might be released?" I bite out, the phone clenched in my hand.

"Exactly what I said. Bail has been posted. He's cooperating. He was at the house; Noelle was not. Nor any sign of her. This may make it harder to keep him here."

I didn't tell the police what happened, Noelle. Didn't want them to know you ran from me. I didn't think it would... look good. For you, the kidnapped. For me, the man you're supposed to trust.

"Listen, Daniel, I'm happy to help you with this. But—" Captain LeRoy continues his explanation as I grit my teeth and feel my blood pressure climb higher. "Flaherty insists he had nothing to do with her disappearance, and the only proof we have is that they walked out of a diner together. His attorney—"

"Motherfucker."

"Excuse me?"

I sigh. "Sorry, not you—I'm just—I want to find her. Get her home safely." Back to me, Mr. Nice Guy. *Dr.* Nice Guy.

"I understand. We want that, too. We're still working on the suspect, and I'll let you know if we find anything."

"One more favor." My eyes move to Kari, who's across the room on the couch, texting *you*, over and over. She's tried calling, too. Why won't you speak to your cousin, Noelle? She's your best friend. Don't you think it's a sign when a man cuts you off from the people you love, the way Jack Flaherty has?

"What is it?"

"Can I see him?"

"Flaherty?"

"Yes. I'd like to appeal to him personally. Maybe it will help. Maybe he knows where she is." I grimace as I get to my feet and limp over to the window with the view of the Puget Sound. I just want to see Jack Flaherty with my own eyes. Tell him how it is—that whether it's in prison or out in the world, he won't be safe from me, from what money can buy. You're *mine*. And if I can't remind him of that with my own fists, I'll find somebody who can.

"That's a stretch," Captain LeRoy says. "But I'll see if it's possible."

I thank him, tell him I owe him, which really means I'll continue to provide him pain medications without asking questions.

"Any luck?" Kari asks when I set the phone down.

"No." The word comes out brusque. She eyes me, and I know she still doesn't *like* me, and I suppose that's okay. Soon enough, it won't matter. But I do need her cooperation. So I smile. Say, "Sorry. I'm just worried." Her gaze softens. She's so easy to play, Noelle. You really should find more intelligent friends.

The phone buzzes, and I snap it back up, hoping it's Captain LeRoy already—but it's not. No, it's Mother, who I've been avoiding the past twenty-four hours.

"Hello, Mother."

"Daniel, can you come over?"

It's Saturday, late afternoon. She's not aware of the situation you've caused me at work, nor the re-injury you caused with your own hands. She might, however, have seen the news.

"I'm rather busy at the moment, Mother." And I am. Because as I said before, I can find out where you are. One phone call is all it takes.

"It's important." Her words are brittle. No room for argument or debate.

I sigh. "May I ask what this concerns?"

"Just get here," she says. "I have something important to discuss with you."

It can be only one thing. Mother has discovered who Steven really is. She's ready to believe me. Ready to ask forgiveness for brushing off my concerns. I don't have time for this. But she *is* Mother, and besides, it's not like you're running away, not when I have Kari on the hook.

"Sure, Mother. I'll be there soon."

We disconnect.

"I'll be back," I tell Kari. "You're welcome to—" I wave a hand. "Make yourself at home."

On the way to my car, I text Calvin.

Keep me updated on her location.

Calvin replies.

No problem.

I'll start by swinging by Mother's. And then, Noelle, I'm coming for you.

SEVENTY-ONE

NOELLE

I dial Justine. My last-ditch effort to have someone at my back—someone who's been there, too.

She answers on the third ring.

"Dr. Peterson." Her voice is quiet, thick with sleep. Maybe she pulled a night shift?

"I have an emergency," I say.

"I'm not on call," she mumbles.

"You're the only person who would pick up," I say.

"Hold on." The swish of sheets. The click of a door.

"Okay, who's the patient?" A pause. "Hello?" she asks. "Are you still there?"

"Me," I say. A particularly biting wind blows through the trees and echoes in the phone line. "Noelle."

"You—*fuck*. You *can't* call me." Her words come out in a panicked rush. And there it is—fear. She's hiding something. Something *bad*.

"Help me," I say.

"Help you *what*? I want nothing to do with this."

"I'm—" I'm what? I called her to ask for her help, not because I know *what* needs to be done. But... don't I?

"I'm going to confront him in his home," I say, though it's not really an answer. "I—" My voice fades off. Weak. Unsure.

Daniel won't stop until he has me. Until he wins. I don't even think it's about me anymore, so much as winning. Was it ever?

But that doesn't answer my question. *What do I do from here?*

Jack and I were going to go to Daniel's house. Jack was going to be there to keep me safe, to keep Daniel from doing whatever it is he has planned. He was going to help make sure I got to leave, and meanwhile, I was going to get Daniel to talk. Somehow.

I hoped the build-up of frustration, of anger, of losing bits and pieces of what mattered most to him would lead to him losing his temper when I was right in front of him. But I *was* right in front of him just hours ago, and that's not what happened—he was calm. Welcoming me back.

Of course, he was. We met on his terms. He'd been watching us. He knew where we were.

So I need to make this meeting *not* on his terms.

I pause.

Or maybe the opposite.

Daniel is the most conceited, self-absorbed man I've ever met. He's at his best—and therefore, his worst—when people cater to him. I need to make him think he's won. And he *will* believe it, because he thinks he's above losing.

This whole situation is him wanting to get to me—to control me, to keep me—maybe that makes *me* the best weapon against him.

"Hello?" Justine's voice through the line. I'd almost forgotten I was on the phone with her. "What do you want? What will it take for you to just leave me alone?"

I bite my lip, playing through the scene in my head. Justine being there won't help. If anything, having her there will make this more difficult. Why hadn't I figured this out before? It's so obvious. Daniel has to think he's won. That I'm going to him freely. That I want his forgiveness, that I want *him*.

The problem being, of course, if his goal is to make me disappear, this is the most dangerous thing I can do. And I'll be alone.

"Never mind," I say.

"What? Are you—are you crazy?"

"You're right," I murmur. "I shouldn't bother you. I'm sorry."

I hang up and send Daniel one last text.

Come and get me.

Then I toss the phone in the nearest trashcan and head to Daniel's.

SEVENTY-TWO

DANIEL

Seattle traffic is a fucking nightmare.

The bridge is shut down—again—meaning I have to get on the highway and drive south of Mother's house to then do a circular route several miles out of the way. Add the influx of people to Washington, as though it's a *destination*, and it takes forty minutes to drive the twelve miles to her house.

Ridiculous.

I come over the hill, and the sun has just set behind the Olympic Mountains to the west, a shade of blazing orange barely a line on the horizon. I bought Mother this house for the sunset view—one she rarely had when I was a child, when we lived in a rundown house on a bad street south of where she lives now.

My phone buzzes. I ignore it. Likely another reporter. Or Mother, wondering where I am. The highway exit is backed up, and I drum my fingers over the steering wheel, over and over, impatience making me grind my teeth, veneers be damned.

A call lights my phone up.

Calvin. "Got it. Sending you coordinates now. Looks like she's holed up somewhere near downtown."

"Thanks." I hang up and check the location—of course, back the way I came. Along the water, just ten minutes from my house. Oh, Noelle—are you hiding in plain sight?

The exit clears, and I take the right turn. Drive through the too narrow streets of West Seattle, and it must be nice to be one of these plebeians who have nothing better to do than sit on the waterfront with a camera and take *photos*. Why don't these people have a life?

One last turn, up a hill. A kid plays in the street, a basketball in hand, and he slows, waves at me, and I ignore him—he's playing in the *street*. Survival of the fittest is all I can say to that.

Mother's house at last.

I pull in. Step out of the rental carefully, regretting my choice to take one Percocet instead of two, and her car's not here. Odd. I can't recall the last time she drove herself anywhere. Maybe she called because Steven *stole* it. I frown and stride toward the door.

Knock once. Twice.

Nothing.

I unlock the door with my own key.

"Mother?" I call.

Silence.

My heart beats faster in my chest, heart rate climbing incrementally. Where is she? I spoke to her just minutes ago.

And then my heart spirals into my stomach, because Mother doesn't go anywhere. Which means Mother is missing. Just like you, Noelle. Did Jack get out of jail already? Did he snatch her to get back at me? I *just* spoke to her. I can track her phone, but only from my home computer. It occurs to me someone might have been here when she called me—and that's why she was so insistent. Wanting me to get here. To *save* her.

My phone is in my hand, and I dial Mother, because surely I'm overreacting, surely you would never let Jack do something like *this*. It rings—and rings—and rings.

I go to text you, because you and Jack clearly don't *hate* one another, and maybe you're in on it. You know where Mother hides the spare key, and you know your way around her house and—

You texted me, that's what the vibration was in the car.

Come and get me.

I hit Call because this is no time for games.

No answer.

My hands shake as I slide back into the rental. My ears pound, and the pain pulsing through my hand and knee has dulled—I have more important things to tend to. Where is my mother, Noelle? What have you done?

I put the address Calvin sent in my GPS, not because I don't know how to get there, but because I need the fastest route. Still, half an hour. I swerve through an illegal U-turn. Gas the engine, though of course it's not my Porsche, so it groans more than growls, but it does finally accelerate, and I'm racing toward you.

SEVENTY-THREE

NOELLE

What will it take for Daniel to believe me?

I contemplate this as I stride past the Space Needle, and into Queen Anne, the part of town most Seattleites enjoy wandering through, but could never afford to live in—which is likely exactly why Daniel bought there. The houses here are older, Craftsman and Victorian, all with fresh paint and bright trim, lawns full of flowering trees and well-groomed bushes, signs of people well enough off they hire someone to do their yardwork for them.

Daniel's house is only two blocks away. My step quickens, then slows—anxious to get there. Also anxious to get this over with.

I cut into an alley in case he's out driving. The sun is setting, shadows going long. It's still cold though, damp, and remnants of snow and ice edge the sidewalks and roads.

I can get into his house—the code for the garage hasn't changed in all the time I've known Daniel, and I can't imagine he'd change it now. I'll let myself in. Go to his office and make sure the cameras are on, that they are recording; maybe, I'll find a way to contact Kari, to try to convince her one last time of what's really happening. Or at least ask her to call the police tomorrow, to demand they check the security cameras, to tell them I've gone missing. Again.

Because that's what might happen. But it will be recorded, and at least then Daniel will be caught. He'll be questioned for me, for Sarah, maybe even for my aunt. I swallow, thinking through the *what if* of going missing for real. It's not in the plans, but it's a possibility. And hell, since no one else has seen me—though I did talk to Justine—blame would almost certainly fall on Jack.

I can't mess this up.

Daniel's house comes into view—glass and steel, a balcony he never uses on the back of the house facing the Puget Sound. The backyard is fenced, and the gate only opens from the inside, so I'll have to climb over, but that's easy enough. And it's dark, so no one will see me—no one but the cameras he has facing the backyard.

The rough wood of the fence bites into my hands as I grab on to it and pull myself upward. A nearby trash bin helps, and seconds later, I drop into his backyard.

A moment of "oh shit" adrenaline pulses through me, because I'm officially on enemy territory. But I can't run. I can't hide.

I have to face him, once and for all.

I stop long enough to peer in the windows of the garage—no car. But then, I did wreck his Porsche. Hopefully, he's not home. Hopefully, he took the bait, and he's downtown, tracking the phone I tossed away.

I flip the garage keypad open and dial in his mother's birthday. The door whirs to life, and though it's no louder than usual, I hurry to duck inside, to stop it from moving, to silence it, because tonight, breaking and entering, it feels like the loudest thing in the world.

The garage smells like all garages do—oil, grease, dampness.

It's dark inside, and I feel my way along the wall, not willing to risk flipping a light on. I find the door that leads to his basement, and I turn the knob gently. The door swings open without a sound.

I close it carefully and move into the basement, holding still, listening. But there's nothing other than the sound of my own breathing.

The staircase is carpeted, and I take one step at a time, slowly, because I can't remember if it creaks or not. Another door at the top—I take a deep breath, will my shoulders to relax, my hands to stop shaking.

There is no turning back, so I need to face him fearlessly—confidently. Play into his weaknesses, and when he's in a dopamine haze of winning, of getting what he wants, get him to say a little too much.

Am I crazy to think this will work? Or am I that desperate?

Maybe both.

The door at the top of the stairs opens easily. A single lamp illuminates the living room, casts shadows through the kitchen, and I peer through the dim light, searching for signs of life. I see none—but I know that's not entirely true. Daniel's cameras are hidden here, in a painting, in a potted plant, recording every moment.

As soon as I step through this doorway, I'll be on display, even if no one is watching.

Daniel's office is my goal. I want to make sure the cameras are recording. I want to find a way to give myself—and Kari—access to the videos. To make sure whatever happens tonight, it doesn't stay on Daniel's hard drive alone, inaccessible to the world. If I'm unable to do anything with it, Kari will watch it, and even if she thinks I've been brainwashed now, after tonight, she'll know the truth.

Another set of stairs. These are different, a floating stair-case, Daniel once told me, proudly detailing the renovations he'd had done before he moved in. I know they don't creak, because I've moved up and down them hundreds of times, first in the early days when I thought I'd found the man I would marry, when I thought this would someday be my home. And plenty of times since then, often sneaking out after he'd fallen asleep, leaving a note or a text as an excuse—*Couldn't sleep, went on a run* or *Kari called with an emergency.*

It's only been a couple weeks since I last spent the night here—ascended and descended these stairs, feeling like a pris-oner—but now, it feels like years have passed. A different time, with a different version of myself. How had I put up with him for so long? The answer comes to me easily—it wasn't a matter of putting up with him. It's not as though he had been a boyfriend with an annoying habit like chewing with his mouth open. No, this ran much deeper, and to simplify that is to ignore the fact I couldn't leave; for my safety; for Kari's.

I shove the thoughts aside. This isn't the time, this isn't the place, and the last thing I need is to remember feeling helpless. I have to be confident and strong and save myself, because if I've learned anything, it's that no one else is going to do it for me.

And Daniel won't give up. Not until he's won.

Or, until he's lost.

Daniel's office is through the first door at the top of the stair-case. I peer around the corner, checking where he usually is when I arrive at his home—at his desk, a wall of monitors before him. He typically has a patient chart pulled up on one monitor, a dosing calculator on another; something for entertainment pulled up on a third, and security footage of his own house on the fourth and fifth. I go still, staring across the room at them. Early on, he'd joked he could see me when I let myself in—but when I realized he could see me in my own home, I no longer thought it was funny or cute.

The room is much as it was the last time I stepped inside, with one main difference—it's not spotless. I might blame that on the mess I've made of his life in recent days, but even then, Daniel seems incapable of having anything but an immaculate desk, and the desk itself has three manilla folders stuffed thick with papers strewn across it—medical forms, I realize.

The tiny black typing on the overly bright paper. A patient's medical record. I frown, because most charts are easily accessible on the hospital's electronic medical record—the only time a record is printed is if a patient is being transferred from one hospital to another, and even then, mostly a rural to an urban one. Or, a patient or physician can specifically request a medical record be printed and sent to them, but I can't imagine why an anesthesiologist would need that.

A knot forms in my stomach as the only reason I can think of hits me hard—my aunt. Is this her medical record? Had he—

I fly across the room to look.

But it's not my aunt's medical record.

I can tell by the date of birth alone, which is—I frown, searching just above it for the patient name.

Noelle Thomas.

My finger rests on my own name, and I skim the pages laid over the desk haphazardly. Records of my accident. Of the three surgeries I underwent to save my life thanks to internal bleeding. But what I don't understand is why Daniel has them, and why they are *here*, on his desk, *now* of all times.

The door to the office slams shut, and I jump, spin around, eyes wide as I search for Daniel.

"Noelle. So nice of you to stop by."

It's not Daniel.

SEVENTY-FOUR

NOELLE

"Oh, Eve. You scared me." I offer a tentative smile, edging back a step, putting the desk between us.

Why is she here? Is Daniel here, too? I cast a quick glance through the doorway, behind her, but it's empty.

"I wasn't expecting to see you here." Her lips curve up, but I wouldn't call it a smile—there is no happiness, no joy—but there is *something*. Something that makes me want to bolt from the room. To put distance between the two of us, even if she is merely a judgmental old woman who's no doubt shocked to have stumbled across her son's missing girlfriend.

I open my mouth to explain, but Eve clasps her hands before her and asks, "Got free of Jack Flaherty, did you? Come to beg Daniel for forgiveness, now that you realize what you've done?"

A cold shiver of fear runs up my neck.

She knows. I don't know how much she knows, but suffice it to say, she knows *enough*.

"Yes." I nod. Maybe I can play her, too.

"I think maybe it would be better if you didn't do that." Eve steps forward. She wears dark slacks, a flowy silver top, and her ash-blonde hair is parted down the middle, a clasp of some sort holding it back from her face. Her makeup is perfect. Her manicure flawless. She carries a small purse over one shoulder, and she reaches inside it.

"What do you mean?" I try for an innocent, quizzical look. "Jack was arrested, and I ran, and—"

"Cut the crap, Noelle."

I go still—I've never heard that tone from her before.

What had she said? *Maybe it's better if you didn't do that.* Didn't beg Daniel for forgiveness.

What's the alternative? Leaving back out the front door and—

"Oh my god," I whisper. Because I know what the alternative is. *Disappearing* is the alternative. Which means it wasn't Daniel who had me kidnapped.

It was Eve.

SEVENTY-FIVE

DANIEL

The worst part of Seattle is that half the roads go only one way. *One fucking way*.

Who thought that was a good idea?

I drive down Second Avenue, where GPS says you should be, but you're not. A bus stop, full of punk-looking kids, an old lady with hair that better resembles a bird nest, an ensemble of twenty-somethings. Are you inside the building? It's half workout studio, half specialty tea shop, and the space next to it is for rent. I take a right and go through the process a second time—right turn, right turn, right turn—four right turns to look for you.

But you're not there.

I dial your number again.

And again, nothing.

Where are you, Noelle?

Another series of turns—but only three this time. Because this time, I'm going home. I'm going to find Mother, wherever she is. But don't worry, I haven't forgotten you. I'm coming for you next.

My phone beeps—a special beep, I hear only twice a week,

when the maid enters my house, uses the passcode to the front door I give out to anyone who's not me. My security company sends an instant alert to my phone, letting me know someone has used it to enter.

But I fired the maid service yesterday after an unsatisfactory response to the pipes bursting. In their defense, I've since realized it was *you*, but I don't tolerate insolence.

Only a few other people have this code.

One of them is Mother.

One of them is you.

I switch to the mobile app tied to my security cameras, and as it loads, switch lanes, darting through traffic, rushing to get home.

When I hazard a glance down, I realize it's not one of you. It's *both* of you.

SEVENTY-SIX

NOELLE

"I really thought you were the one." Eve frowns and steps forward. "Daniel loves you, you know. And you—well, you clearly don't deserve him."

I take another step back, and then another, because something is seriously *wrong* here.

"So, I will once again take matters into my own hands. Daniel's a good boy. He really is. But he's also blinded by infatuation. He struggles to see a woman for what she really is."

It was Eve. *Eve had me kidnapped.* I struggle to find a way this is possible, but if it is—that means she might be responsible for Sarah, too.

"Like with Daniel's last girlfriend? Sarah?" I ask.

My gaze darts to the computer monitors, and yes, they are rolling, recording every room except the basement, which means everything I can get Eve to say here will be recorded. I didn't have a chance to send a link to Kari or myself, but Eve's not the most formidable opponent; I would hate for it to come to a physical confrontation, but if that's what it takes, I can manage it.

Eve gives a dramatic sigh and pulls her phone from her bag.

She types out a message, tucks it back away, turns to me with a raised eyebrow. I stare at the bag, wondering who she'd text at a time like this. Certainly no one I want to meet.

"Sarah was nice enough. But she wasn't—*right*—didn't have the right sort of family, if you know what I mean. And Daniel wouldn't listen to me, so—" A wave of her hand, as if to say, *What was I supposed to do?*

"Did you kill her?"

Eve ignores the question, sets her purse down, and tsks to herself, eyes on the medical record.

"This is the other issue, Noelle." She presses a finger to a paper lying askew of the stack of medical records. I can't see which it is, what it says. "Lying to him. Lying to *me*. He figured it out, but of course he *loves* you by now, so he won't end it, like he should."

She's not making sense. If she were anyone else, if this were a different situation, I'd come close, look at whatever it is she's decided I lied about, but as it is, I've moved halfway across the room now. Eve already knows about the accident—about the surgeries.

Eve shoves her hand back in her purse—and pulls out a gun, a small silver revolver. I wish I'd sprinted from the room when I had the chance. The ground sways beneath me. A *gun*.

Daniel, I can handle. Daniel and his obsession and his narcissism and even Daniel and his manipulation and abuse. But a gun is something else.

Eve with a gun. It's almost an oxymoron. But sensical or not, it's deadly.

Deadly.

"Did you kill Sarah?" I repeat. "And what did you do to Justine? Why is she afraid?"

Eve's lips twist.

"Noelle, I hope you know I'm not the sort to go around *killing* people." Her watery blue eyes raise to me. The gun is in her hands, but she doesn't point it at me. No, she comes around the corner of the desk, she props herself on the desk itself, and waves the gun in my general direction. "Have a seat. Let's chat. Just us girls. I should have brought some port." Her eyes skate to the liquor Daniel keeps on a side table. "That'll do, I suppose. And it's not like I need to worry you're pregnant." Her lip curls as she curls the paper in her fist, crumpling it.

"I'm not—what?" What does that have to do with anything?

I don't take a seat. I stand frozen between the easy chairs and Eve, the door at an angle from here. My pulse thrums through me hard and fast enough I'm practically *vibrating*, and if it were anything but a gun, I'm sure I could escape.

Eve's face goes flat. "Please, Noelle. No more lies. *I know*. And since I do believe in honesty, I'll tell you I came here because a little birdie told me you'd be coming to give Daniel trouble. When Daniel wasn't here, I thought I'd take a look around. It's shocking what I found." Her eyes narrow, and she lifts the crumpled paper at me.

It still doesn't make sense. I have no idea what she's talking about, or why my records have anything to do with it.

"You had me kidnapped," I say. "You were going to have me killed, weren't you? Just like you did Sarah." I need her to agree. To say it out loud. To get it recorded, so maybe, just maybe, if I survive, I can prove it all.

"Of course not," Eve snaps. "Are you even listening? I *liked* you. I was trying to *save* you from yourself."

We're talking in circles, circles I don't understand.

"Noelle, I pulled out every stop trying to make things work between you and Daniel. Every last stop. And you somehow ruined it all, and good thing you did, considering you've been lying to us this whole time." She releases the paper and points the gun at me. My heart leaps into my throat, and time slows, and *I cannot die here, in Daniel's office*, but Eve doesn't pull the trigger. "Sit down. I don't want to have to tell you again."

I do as told, and she looks at her watch and back toward the door, and I realize she's waiting for someone. Whoever she texted, is my guess.

"What do you think I'm lying about?"

"There's no *think*," Eve says, a burst of anger punctuating her words. She spins a monitor and touches the mouse, and the photo I e-mailed Daniel pops up—Jack and I, in bed, and on a big screen, we truly do look as though we're in the throes of passion. "You hopped in bed with another man first chance you got. You *cheated* on Daniel. And you didn't have to worry about getting pregnant, because you *can't*, which is the sort of thing you should tell a man on a first date. Heck, *before* a first date. Don't you understand your role, Noelle? I know you at least understand what Daniel wants. What *I* expect."

My head buzzes.

I blink, trying to process. "You had me kidnapped because you think I can't have children?"

"No." Eve heaves a sigh. She collects herself and resumes her perch on the desk, and at another sideways glance, my heart rate picks up yet again. She's definitely waiting for someone. The masked man? Jack's boss? "I had you kidnapped so Daniel could save you again. To help him. To help *you*." She rolls her eyes skyward. "Some good that did."

"You—" My voice stops abruptly.

"It was your last chance, Noelle." She fixes me with a glare. "I know you were trying to leave him. I found out what you'd planned."

"What I planned?"

"Your own kidnapping," she murmurs. "You planned your own kidnapping."

How does she know that?

"My man was there, following you. You've been acting off for a while now." She shakes the gun at me as though it's a scolding finger. "I was livid," Eve says. "Absolutely livid. After all Daniel and I have done for you. But—we all make mistakes. And Daniel loved you. So instead of you being whisked away to wherever, I thought I'd show you how big and bad the world really can be. Your kidnappers would rough you up, and Daniel would rescue you, and—" That hand movement again. A flick of her wrist, indicating the obvious. "I know how heartbroken he was over Sarah. Justine, too."

I've stood up, and I'm trying to look thoughtful, like I'm pacing, but really, I'm edging around the room, slowly, so she won't notice. But the mention of Justine makes me go still. Eve said a little birdie told her I'd be here. Only Justine had known. And Justine *had* said *maybe he's not the one you need to worry about. She* knew. She knew all along—it wasn't Daniel. It was Eve.

Apparently, Eve and Justine are still on speaking terms. But speaking terms that include Justine being afraid to talk to me— afraid of *Eve.* Which tells me Eve has something on Justine— what, I don't know, but *something.*

And Eve claims I can't have children. Which doesn't make sense, but—

I frown. Justine's bio on her website said she had an adopted child. Was she unable to have children?

Is Eve somehow confusing us? Do I care? Eve is on her phone again, and I eye the door, wondering if I could make it. Wondering if I should try anyway, because whoever's coming will likely give me the same fate as Sarah, and there's only one way to truly make someone disappear.

Eve curses. She shoots a wary glance my way, then sets the gun on the desk, using both hands to peck away at her phone screen.

I wait for her to look down. I bolt for the door.

SEVENTY-SEVEN

DANIEL

Oh, Noelle. I am so sorry.

Mother had you kidnapped. I'm not *shocked*. But nor would I have expected it. I couldn't have, not really. Just as I couldn't have expected this. That she would discover our little issue.

I have a plan, Noelle, I swear it. Your problem is *our* problem, and we will fix it together. In fact, I blame myself now. If I'd been taking better care of you that day, this would have never happened.

I don't hear every word the two of you exchange through the camera feed on my phone—there's a dip in service as I circle the long way around. But I've heard enough.

I don't bother pulling into the garage when I arrive home. No, I skip up the stairs and key in my code, and I'm through the living room, halfway up the stairs—

And it hits me.

Mother had you *kidnapped*. To *help* me. Because she didn't trust me to woo you on my own. To get you to say yes on my own. She's *managing* me. Us.

And suddenly, I know why Justine insisted we end things

without so much as an explanation. A curt refusal to ever speak to me again.

I know why Sarah, who Mother disliked, disappeared.

I wasn't lying, Noelle—you're the first woman Mother has really loved. Until, that is, things started going south. And if your conversation with her is any indication, she knows what I know—that you've taken up with Jack. That your goal was to leave me. And, she found my copy of your medical records too, which means she knows our little problem. But I have a plan, a *good* plan, and I can explain it to her, show her I really *do* have this all figured out, prove to her once and for all I'm not a fuck-up.

But I hesitate, partway up the stairs, and if she didn't have a goddamn gun (women and guns do *not* mix), I'd step back into the living room, pour myself a drink, have a think about it while the two of you squabble in my office.

Justine broke up with me, I believe, because Mother forced her to—yes, I know I got Justine pregnant. I know she had a botched abortion. And if her choice to adopt a child is any indication, I would guess she is no longer able to have children. I'll bet Mother tried to get Sarah to break up with me, too, because according to Mother, Sarah was *trailer trash*. Not fit to be a doctor's wife.

But Sarah was stubborn. Sarah would have refused. Which means Mother likely—

A sob tears from my throat. No wonder Jack Flaherty hates my guts.

Sarah didn't disappear. Sarah was taken. Removed. Possibly murdered. By *my mother*.

But—*no*, this is Mother. *My* Mother. Who has done nothing but try to raise me to be a good man, a good father and husband someday, who has sacrificed everything—

Who has stopped at nothing to give me everything I want. *Everything.*

I sink to the stairs, my whole life unraveling before me. The private college preparatory school Mother couldn't afford that suddenly had a scholarship available. The waitlisted spot for UW Medical School, and how my number came up earlier than it should have. Have I accomplished anything for myself? Or was it all Mother, pulling strings in the background?

Am I a man? Or am I just a puppet for her to string along until she has everything she so desperately desires?

SEVENTY-EIGHT

DANIEL

I gather myself. Tell myself to *get my shit together, already*, even if my entire life has been one manufactured event after another since my father died and Mother became—well, *Mother*.

I reach the top of the stairs, piecing together the words in my head that I'll say to her. The questions I'll ask. I don't know if Mother and I can survive this, Noelle. I thought we had trust. I thought if anything, *I* was the one taking care of *her*.

But it seems that she has taken care of me, to the point it is, well, as my psychiatrist associates at the opposite end of the hospital might say, *problematic*.

I'm sorry, Noelle, but I'm thinking of another woman. Of Sarah, mostly, because where is she now? Did Mother offer her a sum of money and whisk her away to another part of the world? Or did she decide she needed to disappear for good? And where in god's name had Mother, of all people, found someone to help her with it? Fragile, recovering cancer patient Mother, I can't imagine her doing *any* of this, yet the evidence is clear as day as I clutch my phone and stare at her via the video feed.

She must know someone, someone with connections,

someone like—

A career criminal. Steven. Steven, who conveniently became her oncologist around the time Sarah disappeared. What, had she kept him around in case she needed my next girl-friend to disappear, too?

I almost laugh—yes. That must be it.

My office has gone silent. I raise my hand to knock, but it's my office, so I grab the doorknob, twist, open, and—

And you're right in front of me. Eyes wide, and your hand falls away from the doorknob. You backpedal, seeing it is me, but I grab you in my arms, pull you tight.

"I'm so sorry, Noelle."

And you don't stop resisting, and can I really blame you? But don't worry. I'll put this right.

"Mother," I say. You pull away, skittering back toward the giant windows overlooking the Puget Sound, and I stare across the room at Mother—whom I love—and very much hate right this moment.

"Daniel." Her voice is high, tight, almost a squeak. We regard one another, and her vulnerability shifts to a hardness I haven't seen in her since the day my father died. "I was just having a conversation with Noelle. Is there something you'd like to share with me?" She beckons to your chart strewn across my desk. The medical records I combed through for weeks, trying to understand if there was a way to fix it—to fix you.

But there wasn't.

You can't have children, Noelle. I'm so sorry. There was too much damage in the car accident, your internal organs smashed and torn and—you were lucky to be alive. At the time, it seemed like a small detail. The sort of thing that once you recovered, I'd share with you over a glass of wine. You'd cry. But we'd cope together, and we'd move forward, and we would be fine.

Mother didn't need to know.

And like I said, I had a plan.

"No," I say. "There's nothing I want to tell you, but I think there's plenty you need to share with me." I hold up my phone. I motion to where the cameras are hidden—to where we are pictured in a smaller version on a computer monitor. "I heard everything."

Mother's hand comes to her mouth, and she gasps.

I cross the room. I take the gun from her hand. I point her to a chair, and I raise one brow, and she goes, like a petulant child.

"What did she mean?" you ask me. "She said I can't have children."

I scrub a hand over my face. Stare at you and wish I hadn't fucked this up so badly. But it can still be fixed. We can still make this work, Noelle.

"The accident," I say. "I told your surgeon I'd break the news to you. But the time never seemed right, and—"

"Wait. It happened *while you were together*? How could you keep that from me?" Mother gasps. "You know all I ever wanted was more children, and when your father died, when I couldn't have more, I said I could settle for *grandchildren*. You could have easily taken up with any woman you wanted, yet over and over you found these women who weren't good enough for you, Daniel, and—"

"Mother," I snap. "Stop. Please." My chest tightens, and if I wasn't all but a professional athlete, I'd worry it was a heart attack, but I know it's just stress. Anxiety. Emotions I detest and generally blame on poor self-care, but this was unavoidable, wasn't it? How could I have known the depth of mother's actions?

"How could you keep that from me?" you snap, Noelle. And you're right, of course.

I try to smile encouragingly at you. Try to share that I understand how hard this must be, for you.

I take a step closer, hold out my hand, will you to come closer. "Don't worry, my love. I have a plan."

SEVENTY-NINE

NOELLE

"A plan?" I ask. "You have a plan for *lying* to me?"

I can't have children. I've never thought seriously about having them but being told I *can't* is a completely different thing. And that Daniel kept it from me—that the surgeon who saved my life let Daniel be the one to tell me (but of course, he did—everyone loved and trusted Daniel).

I feel like I need to grab the wall, or the edge of the nearest chair, for support—or hell, maybe I should just sink to the ground. But Eve mutters something, and reality snaps back, and I can't think about this right now. There's too much else that's important—that's life or death.

The hopefulness in Daniel's face sags as he watches me, weighing my response.

"Tell me everything," I say. "What's your plan?"

Daniel blinks, his mouth opening, closing. He looks sideways at his mother, as though for help, but hasn't she helped enough?

"Well—" he starts. "You couldn't have a baby. So I arranged for us to get one."

"To *get* one?" I ask.

"Kari looks a bit like you, and you're cousins, so I figured—"

Eve gasps. But all I can think is *Kari would never give up her baby*.

"Daniel, you know I want *your* grandchild, not—"

Daniel's eyes dart toward his mother. "I know, Mother. The baby *is* my child."

Which means something totally different—means...

"You slept with Kari?" I ask, proud when my voice comes out low, even.

Daniel blanches, and Eve looks like she might die of shock, and I feel the nasty rise of anger and betrayal, but again, this isn't the time. Isn't the place. There are a hundred ways it could have happened, including without her consent. It doesn't mean she did anything wrong other than keep it from me, but I'm getting a sense of how Daniel and his mother handle things they don't like—they threaten. Manipulate. Blackmail.

"And how were you going to acquire Kari's baby?" I ask.

The room goes silent. Which tells me everything I need to know. Daniel may not have been planning to kill me, but I have no doubt he'd have made sure the mother, *Kari, my cousin,* died in labor or shortly thereafter. *Maternal mortality is at an all-time high,* he'd said. Maybe it wasn't meant as a threat. Maybe he was preparing me for the possibility.

I count to ten in my head, trying to gain back my ability to breathe normally.

"You were going to kill her," I say. "Just like you killed my aunt."

Another beat of silence, but Daniel doesn't falter like I expect—doesn't admit to one more thing, as seems easy enough to do—he just shakes his head. "I had nothing to do with your aunt dying, Noelle."

But the visitor log had said *Ashcroft,* copied from the driver's license shown to get onto the unit.

It was right in front of me the whole time.

I look at Eve. Eve who I never suspected, because while she owns a car, I've never seen her drive it, never seen it so much as leave her garage. Because she's a little old lady. But I *had* seen her out in the days before my disappearance—I just assumed she'd had someone else drive her.

"How did you get here?" I ask her. "Bus? Taxi?"

She frowns. "I drove, of course. I'm quite capable."

A dull roar fills my ears. My heart palpates and squeezes in my chest painfully. I fight the urge to go after her. To choke the life from her eyes.

"You killed my aunt," I say, and one more piece falls into place. "And your pal Justine's a cardiologist. Did you get her to tell you how to do it?"

No wonder Justine wouldn't speak to me. Not only did she *know* who'd arranged for my kidnapping, she helped murder my aunt. She told Eve I'd be here today. Likely, because she had no other option. Which is no excuse.

"Well?" I say to Eve.

She pales, but doesn't speak, and it's all the answer I need.

I know who the real villain in the room is. And shockingly, it's not Daniel.

EIGHTY

NOELLE

"What did you do to Justine? Why is she helping you? Why is she terrified to help me?" My words are sharp, one question after another. Eve flinches.

Daniel's head snaps up, and for the first time in a year, we're united in something—the desire to know what she's done.

"Mother?" Daniel asks, his voice trembling. "What did you do?"

A single tear runs down Eve's face. "She killed your baby, Daniel. *Our* baby."

Their *what*? I'm breathless, one realization after another, glancing back and forth between them.

"Mother—it was an accident. We were *kids*. We weren't even out of medical school yet, and the baby was *killing* her. Literally."

Eve blinks back more tears and gazes at him with wide eyes. "What?"

"It was a medically indicated abortion. The pregnancy was going to kill her before she ever even had the baby." Daniel's face falters, and sorrow flits through his eyes, and if it were anyone but Daniel, I'd feel bad for him.

"Why is she so scared of you?" I ask.

Eve sighs. Daniel moves a step closer, the gun dangling in his hand, and I wonder if I can get to it. Hell, I wonder if I could make a break for the door, they're so distracted with one another. But I at least have to know what happened to Sarah so I can tell Jack.

"I blackmailed her," Eve finally says. "It goes against her religion to get an abortion, and her parents would have disowned her, her church would have kicked her out, and when she told me, because she thought I was her friend, I—I was *devastated.* She didn't tell me about the rest of it." Eve's chin trembles. "I'm sorry, Daniel. But I want grandchildren. *My* grandchildren. I was so upset with her that she'd killed—"

"How could you do that, Mother? I was an adult. She was my *girlfriend.* I loved her. We were both heartbroken when we lost the baby. That we had to make that choice."

"What do you mean, *we?*" Eve asks. "You condone what she did?"

"It was—" Daniel shakes his head. Crosses the room, picks up a glass like he's going to pour himself a drink. "Jesus Christ, Mother. Don't you get it? They *both* would have died. There was never going to be a baby." He huffs out a breath and rubs his eyes. When he looks back up at her, it's with tears streaming down his face. "What have you done, Mother? What the fuck have you done?"

"Sarah," I say. "What did you do to Sarah?" And I take the opportunity of Daniel moving to position myself so that I can leave. As soon as I know, so I can tell Jack, so I can have what Eve's done recorded, I'll take off. Daniel turns away from his mother and reaches for a bottle, his hands shaking, despite the flat expression on his face.

Daniel pours his drink, and turns back to her, one arm crossed beneath the other. The gun is still in his hand.

Eve starts to stand up, as though she's in court and needs to defend herself, one hand raised with a finger extended, but Daniel says, "No," and his voice is commanding, and she looks at him as though she barely knows him.

"Daniel, I love you. I've done all of this out of love. Justine killed our baby. Noelle was trying to escape you. Her aunt was taking all her time away from you. You told me Noelle was all but moving in with her. Can't you see this has all been for you? For *us?*"

"Sarah," he says. "What the fuck did you do with Sarah?"

A heavy pause. He really had nothing to do with Sarah. Or Justine. Could he really be the innocent in this?

"Steven disposed of her."

The silence goes on far longer than it has thus far. I never met Sarah, never spoke to her, but she was Jack's sister, and...

It's like a gut punch.

"*Disposed of her?*" Daniel's glass drops from his hand, shatters over the ground, and he falls to his knees. Eve rushes to his side and wraps her arms around him, but he shoves her away. I want to step from the room—want to escape—but it's like the train wreck you can't look away from.

What the fuck is wrong with these people?

"You killed Sarah," Daniel finally manages, and Eve shakes her head again.

"No, Daniel, I didn't. I hired Steven, and he arranged—"

Daniel straightens and grabs her and suddenly they're face to face, and I'm holding my breath, because while Daniel is cruel and manipulative, I've never seen him full-on strike anyone—but he looks like he could throttle Eve in this moment.

"Did you even have cancer?" he asks. "Or was that a lie, too?"

Eve looks like a fish—her mouth gaping open, smacking shut, trying to find words that aren't there. I stare at her, wondering what Daniel's talking about, but after a moment, she shakes her head no, and he lets her go. Melts backward. Slides down the wall to sit on the ground as though every bit of life has been stolen from him.

"Why, Mother? Why would you lie to me about that? How did you find someone like *Steven*, anyway? Since he's obviously not your oncologist."

"I was worried—I thought—Steven suggested—" But her voice fades away. "I wanted more children, Daniel. And your father didn't. You know I lost my own family growing up, and I wanted—I *needed* that. And your father refused to have more children, and then he died, and—I just hoped if you thought my time was limited that you would hurry up. I hired Steven to help with that. And then I—" She presses her lips together. "I took a liking to him. I figured it didn't hurt to have him nearby if I needed help again."

The news is stunning. Eve killed Sarah and my aunt. Had me kidnapped for real when she found out I'd arranged a fake kidnapping by having me followed. She pretended to have cancer, and apparently lied about her oncologist—what else has she done over the course of her life?

I blink, and they are still talking—Daniel demanding to know why they went wig shopping if it was all a lie, and Eve is saying something about having always worn a wig. And finally ignored by both of them, I move toward Daniel's desk. I read line by line what the surgeon's note says about being unable to have children. And I think, *This is awful* and *This is unfair*, but also, *It could be so much worse*.

I could be stuck with Daniel for the rest of my life. We could have Kari's baby, and she would be dead. It could be worse. So much worse.

Another glance up at the two of them, still arguing. I click through menus until I figure out how to save a section of the video file. I log in to my e-mail. I send it to the Seattle police along with their name and mine. I tell them Jack Flaherty had nothing to do with my kidnapping and was in fact trying to protect me.

And then I take Daniel's phone, which he left on his desk, and I call 911.

EIGHTY-ONE

DANIEL

Mother won't shut up, won't stop giving me excuses.

Telling me how much she loves me, and how everything she's done has been for me.

And all I can think is that *Sarah is dead* and *Justine* did *love me.* That in fact you, Noelle, are the only woman who wanted to be free of me. And I didn't understand why. But now, realizing the drama I've forced upon you trying to make my mother happy, I get it. I really do. And you know what, I'll let you go. There's no point in winning the game when you were cheating to begin with—well, Mother cheated, for me.

I think of how Sarah is cold in a grave somewhere. Like the baby I should have had with Justine. Like you almost were, but I was able to save you. Like my father has been for decades. My father, who is perhaps to blame for this mess. What if he'd just consented to giving Mother another child before he died? What if—

A cold question forms in my stomach, and I look at Mother, who's still talking.

"Mother," I say.

"Yes, sweetheart?" She tilts her head and her lip juts out,

and she's staring at me like she did when I was a child, except *she's* the child, isn't she? Twisting things. Manipulating to get what she wants. Lying to me, about *everything*.

"Father," I say.

And that's all I say.

The car accident she called a suicide.

When her lip trembles, I know—it wasn't a suicide. It was a murder. Because he wouldn't give her what she so desperately wanted.

I lift the gun in my hand.

I point it at Mother, who has utterly and completely destroyed my entire life. Manipulated me from day one. My past. My future.

That's not love.

I don't know what it is, but it's not love.

I steady the gun.

I pull the trigger.

EIGHTY-TWO

NOELLE

I can't so much as scream before he pulls the trigger.

A bang, so loud my hands are covering my ears before I realize what I've done.

I wait for Eve to collapse—for blood to spray, like the traumas I've seen coming in through the emergency department —but there is no blood. Just Eve letting out a high-pitched wail, the crackling of glass where the bullet landed, and Daniel collapses to his knees. The gun clatters to the ground. All I can think is *He missed*, and *Get the fuck out, now*.

I turn, but there's another person between me and the door.

Kari.

Her mouth hangs open, her eyes heavy with sleep, but quickly coming to.

Grief darts through me—that she's believed Daniel instead of me. That she's kept who the father of her baby is from me this whole time. And yet, there will be a time for that, once we're safe. She's still my family, my only family, and who knows what Daniel put her through to get her pregnant.

"Come on," I say. "We have to go. You have to trust me."

Kari blinks and stares beyond me at Daniel and his mother,

who are both on the ground, keening, and Daniel is full-on sobbing.

He's finally at his weakest. Finally had everything taken from him. Daniel finally knows what he did to me, but it wasn't me who turned the tables and took everything from him. It was his mother.

And I'm okay with that.

I grab Kari's hand and pull her from the room.

"Why are you here?" I ask her.

"I came to see Daniel, but he had to leave. He said to make myself at home." She turns down the hall and points at a guest bedroom. "I fell asleep. I'm always exhausted these days. But I heard yelling, and—"

Her eyes come to rest on me, dark brown, familiar, and oh-so wide. "What happened?"

"I'll tell you once we're out. Just trust me. No one tricked me, okay? Jack didn't"—I wave a hand—"manipulate me into anything. Daniel's been playing you."

Our eyes meet. Kari nods, and her lip trembles. "Noelle, I'm so sorry. I have to tell you—"

"I know." I glance down at her pregnant belly. "I know everything."

Her eyes widen. She opens her mouth to speak again, but we don't have time for that. Not here, not now. "We can talk later," I say. "We have to leave."

I help her down the stairs, through the living room. The world has gone dark outside, and I don't know how we'll get away, but maybe we can get down the block, then call a cab. Maybe the police will be here sooner than later. Maybe—

The outdoor motion sensor light flashes on.

Someone's here.

"Wait," I whisper. We are close. So close. Could we make a run for the basement and escape out the garage?

Kari comes to an abrupt stop, almost unsteady, and I think,

No, we cannot make a run for it. I can. But she can't. I peer through the frosted glass at the shape of a man out the window that runs the length of the front door. Eve had texted someone—someone who I think was supposed to come for me. This must be him.

"Come on." I pull her hand, and we race for the kitchen. "The pantry." Kari opens the door, crouches inside, but Daniel has a cart of bourbon in here, halving the space in what would otherwise be a spacious closet. With Kari's pregnant belly, there's only room for her. "Don't move," I tell her.

And I shut the door.

I move behind the kitchen island. I duck down. I hold my breath as the front door latch releases with an electronic *beep*, and the door swings open, a rush of air from the outside floating in. The scent of humidity and rain fill the kitchen.

And then footsteps—one after another—slow, controlled.

"This way," a man's voice says, all quiet and rough. A voice I'm sure I've heard before, over the phone. My throat constricts, and I try to breathe slow, steady. I'm balanced in a crouched position behind the counter but I'll have to move in a second, or he'll be able to see me as he ascends the stairs to the second floor.

But there must be a second person, because he's talking to someone.

And then, "I'm right behind you."

And I definitely recognize that voice.

Jack.

EIGHTY-THREE

NOELLE

There's not enough air in the room.

I clench my fists and squeeze my eyes shut, and try to take a slow, even breath, before I pass out. It doesn't make sense. So many things don't make sense today.

But somehow, Jack is out of jail already. Somehow, Jack is *here*, with *that guy*.

There are two possibilities.

Either Jack is here to help me. Or Jack let me escape because he didn't want the police to get me before his boss did. By sacrificing himself, he was showing the ultimate loyalty to his boss, his job—the one he supposedly quit.

Yet how many times had he snuck off on a phone call? How many times was I sure he was acting oddly, but hadn't asked him about it, because I assumed it wasn't my business?

If today has proved anything, it's that I can't take anyone at face value—can't believe them or trust them. Kari is the only one who has always acted in my best interest, but even she has been lying to me.

The footsteps circle the room. I press my hands to the slick tile floor and ease around the edge of the island, controlling my breath carefully. So long as I don't make a sound, this should be okay. Jack and his boss will go upstairs where they'll find Daniel and Eve squabbling or crying or whatever it is they're doing now.

I'll grab Kari, and we'll escape.

The police will be here any moment.

I just have to keep them from noticing us for the next ten or twenty seconds.

But then, "I'm going to check the rooms down here. I'll meet you upstairs," Jack says.

His boss mutters something that sounds like agreement.

The fading footsteps as his boss goes up the stairs.

Then silence.

Until boots come around the edge of the kitchen island, and Jack is right in front of me. I swallow, and there's no hiding anymore—he's right here, three feet away. I climb to my feet and take a half step back. Knives hang against a magnetic strip against the backsplash, just an arm's reach away.

My heart pounds as my eyes meet Jack's, that light green shade evident even in the dim illumination of the kitchen.

I wait for him to do something. To call to his boss. To pull out a gun and tell me it was all an act.

Instead, he presses a finger to his lips—*shhhh*. Points to the door. Beckons with a curl of his fingers to follow him out the door.

It could be a trap.

Or it could be my friend, helping me escape, again.

Our eyes meet. I decide to trust him.

EIGHTY-FOUR

NOELLE

We wait for the police half a block away in Jack's truck. The flashing lights appear soon enough, four squad cars and officers with guns drawn, crouched, surrounding the house. I'd told them there was a weapon—that two people were behaving irrationally, maybe dangerously. That the gun had been fired. A second later, as officers scale the front staircase, an ambulance appears around the corner.

I whisper a thank you to the universe we all got out safe.

Kari's tucked into the back seat, and we haven't talked about Daniel being her baby's father yet, but it's coming. A tension crackles between us, and I hate that, but we're both alive. We're both safe. And that's what matters. We'll figure out the rest.

"You really didn't know who hired you?" I ask Jack.

Jack's hands tighten over the steering wheel. He shifts in his seat to look me in the eye, utter sincerity in his expression. "No. My boss told me about the job to kidnap you and he set it up. When I was arrested, he sent someone to bail me out, then said I was going to help grab you again, so I came to make sure—" A pause. He swallows. "To make sure nothing bad happened."

He keeps talking, explaining he did lie about one thing—

Jack never actually quit working for his boss. He just told me he did. The phone calls and texts were him putting his boss off, because he knew his boss wouldn't let him go so easily. It was better, he explained, for him to pretend to be looking for me, than to go AWOL. It also kept his boss from looking for me himself.

On the drive to retrieve me, per Eve's request I be disposed of, he realized the guy who gave his boss the job wasn't a random criminal—he was Eve's boyfriend. On the car ride to Daniel's house, Eve's boyfriend—Jack says his name is Steven—told him everything, bragging about how he had me followed and realized I had arranged for my own kidnapping. Eve, who'd noticed I'd grown distant from her son, decided it was better to have someone else strike before the company I hired could. In a way, I set this whole chain of events into action. But I don't regret it, because Kari would have died if I hadn't.

When he finishes, I replay everything that happened in Daniel's office, leaving out the part about Sarah—which he immediately picks up on.

"What else? What about Sarah?" We watch as two more squad cars pull up, more police filtering into the house. This is almost over. Daniel and Eve will be arrested. Maybe Jack's boss, too, if he's still there. It will all be over, and I'll go back to some semblance of a normal life—though admittedly, it will be a new normal. I'm not the same person anymore.

"Noelle?" Jack repeats. "Did she say anything about Sarah?"

I reach across the car and take his hand. Jack's tattooed fingers curl around it and squeeze, and he looks over. Our gazes lock. And I tell him what Eve said—everything I know. Which admittedly isn't much, and I can't bring myself to use Eve's words—*disposed of*—but I'm honest.

When I finish, he nods. Exhales a long, grief-heavy sigh,

and looks away, out the window. I stretch over to hug him, feel his body heave with a wave of grief.

"Thank you. I just had to—needed to know. For sure."

I hug Jack tight, and wish I could make the pain go away, but I can't. And besides, he's not the only one grieving—my aunt's face floats through my mind. My aunt, who should be alive and well, but Eve offed her because her care after the bypass would take too much of my time and attention away from Daniel. It occurs to me Eve is very ill—that no one in their right mind would ever even dream of these actions.

I meet Kari's eyes over his shoulder, and she reaches out, pressing a hand to my shoulder, and though nothing is okay right now, the three of us have survived the worst of it.

We will be okay.

EIGHTY-FIVE
NOELLE

Six Months Later

Daniel isn't here. Behind me, a guard closes the door, and I sweep the room with my eyes again, searching the dozen prisoners scattered through octagonal tables, khaki uniforms combined with black slide-on shoes, not the bright orange jumpsuits so common on television. There's no tall man with broad shoulders, no piercing, confident blue eyes assessing and judging those around him. Just one prisoner after another, slouched over a table, card games between them, the others murmuring quietly to one another.

Sets of eyes turn my way, watch me. My skin crawls with their gazes, but I step forward, because I'm not backing down now. I said I'd come, and here I am.

I check faces and forms again, and this time, an angular cheekbone comes into view around another prisoner.

"Ashcroft," the guard beside me snaps. The cheekbone becomes a face, becomes a man, becomes—

He doesn't look like Daniel. There is no confidence in that gaze. No lithe swagger in the way he pulls to his feet and comes to heel before the guard like a well-trained puppy. No cruelness when he looks at me. Only surprise—elation—a real smile, like a distant memory of someone I used to know.

"Noelle," he says. "I'm so glad you came."

His voice is what finally makes me hesitate—makes me want to leave this place without laying eyes on him ever again. Sometimes, his voice is in my dreams, a cruel taunting, a promise to hurt me and Kari. To hurt *Ellie,* Kari's daughter, my niece, who's almost six months old now.

It's taken me this long to work up the courage to come here. To face him. He was charged with attempted murder, though he swore he aimed wide when he shot at his mother. He was also charged with bribing the police and stealing drugs from the hospital. He'll be in prison a minimum of ten years, and maybe longer.

"Did you get my letters?" he asks, motioning to a bench. He takes the one opposite, folding his hands on the plastic table between us, for once in his life looking harmless.

I swallow, remembering what I'd rehearsed with Jack over the phone this morning. Jack, who I've spoken to every day since he left Seattle to go back to Colorado to reconnect with his family. I brace myself. "You need to stop sending me letters, Daniel." Somehow, the words come out confident.

I wait for the scowl, the raised brow, the quirk of a lip that tells me Daniel has the upper hand, and he'll do as he pleases, but it doesn't come. There's only a blankness to his face that I think means he's hiding whatever emotion really lies there.

"I apologize," he says after a beat. "You're right, of course. It's inappropriate, after what I did to you."

After what I did to you.

A rush of anger—I want to say, "Which thing, which time?" But I let it go with a deep breath. He's required to go to therapy here—and I've been going, too. One of the reasons I came—

trying to confront the past and be at peace with it, allowing me to move forward.

"Is that what you came here to say?" he asks.

"No. Well—yes." I give a single nod. "My therapist thought it might be good for me."

Daniel accepts this information, stares down at the table. "Do you know how my mother is?" His voice is hopeful.

"No," I say shortly. The cameras got her admitting to everything—and she hadn't fought it in court. As far as I know, she'll likely spend the rest of her life in prison for playing a part in Sarah's death, in trying to arrange for mine. Only Steven got off scot-free, somehow escaping the house before the police could grab him.

"You look like you want to say something else," Daniel says. He raises his eyes to mine, and I can tell some part of him wants me to forgive him.

It'll never happen, but I do hesitate about this next part. I'm not sure which is crueler, to show him this or deny him, but he asked for it, and Kari said yes. "Here." I hand him the single photo I brought with me. The child who technically is made up of half of his DNA. "Her name is Ellie."

"Ellie?" he asks. "After you?"

"Yes."

Kari delivered without complications—her biggest concern after Ellie came safely into the world was that I wouldn't stick around to be a part of their family, considering who the father was. When I made it clear I absolutely would be there—would *always* be there—she'd asked if she could name her daughter after my childhood nickname. She also shared she hadn't just slept with Daniel—he'd shown up at the bar she was drunk at in the aftermath of my car accident. It was back when she thought he was a good caring guy, someone who would change my life for the better. She let him buy her a couple more rounds. Let him drive her home.

Let him comfort her. And when she woke up in the morning, she realized what she'd done. What *he'd* done—and hearing her story, I had no doubt he set it up. He realized I wouldn't be able to give him a child, so in his desperation to provide his mother with a grandchild, came up with a new plan, targeting Kari.

I exhale.

Daniel takes the photo, holds it in both palms as though it's something precious, and stares at it long enough I think maybe it was a kindness, though it might not be when he remembers he'll never meet her, something Kari and I decided when Ellie was only two days old.

It takes him a full minute to respond, and when he does, he only says, "Thank you."

I search for more words, but I have none. After what we've been through together, after what he put me through, after what he did to Kari, I have nothing left to say. But I've done this thing my therapist told me might help—faced him, told him to stop sending the letters with their thinly veiled attempts at reconciliation that left me nervous to check my own mail, to see his handwriting scrawled across cheap white envelopes.

"Noelle?" he says, maybe seeing I'm pulling away, preparing to go.

"Yes?" I look him in the eye. I don't soften my voice. I let him see I'm strong now.

"I'm sorry," he says. "For what I did to you. For what my mother did to you, to your aunt."

I nod. Realize there is no response, because he should be sorry. But he's paying the price, isn't he? He's in prison. He'll never work as a physician again. His life, as he knew it, is over.

I hold my hand out. I take the photo back. The thought of him staring at Ellie's brown eyes, her blonde curls, leaves me on edge.

"Goodbye, Daniel." I get to my feet and turn. I walk away. I leave him where he belongs, in the past. Five minutes later, I emerge from the prison and leave behind gray walls and tall fences. It's early summer in Washington, and it's still cool out, but the sun shines.

I text Kari and Jack.

I did it. I'm okay.

And I head back to Seattle, back to the life that is mine again.

A LETTER FROM JESSICA

Dear Reader,

When I was told I get to write a letter to *you*, I was both excited and nervous. Excited because—getting to speak directly to someone who chose to read my book? Awesome. Nervous because—what do I say?

First, thank you so much for reading *Make Me Disappear*. It is my debut novel and holds a special place in my heart. If *Make Me Disappear* had you on the edge of your seat, be sure to sign up for updates to be the first to know when my next dark and twisty thriller is out!

www.bookouture.com/jessica-payne

My personal newsletter is another great way to stay up to date with my book releases and more, and I'd love for you to join me:

https://jessicapayne.net/newsletter

My mother spent late nights at our dining room table, poring over a yellow legal pad, writing letters and poetry and bits of books. For me, it was the most natural thing to start scribbling away like her. I'd do it during class, at lunch, as I lay in bed before going to sleep each night. But it wasn't until my thirties, when I had a daughter of my own, that I realized, if I wanted to really do it—*to be a writer*, it was now or never. Life is short. And so, I started as most writers do—I began writing one day and never stopped.

Now I get to publish my words so readers can hold them in their hands. I can't believe *I'm an author*. I am so grateful.

The inspiration behind *Make Me Disappear* is complicated. I wanted to write about the young woman so many of us are in our twenties. Out in the world, trying to figure out our lives, our relationships, *ourselves*. In a world that often values men above women, abusive relationships are not rare. They are, I believe, incredibly common. I escaped one myself, and I wanted to write about it. To sort through the emotions and, in the end, give my character the happy ending that not all women get. I wanted Noelle to come out strong, free, and on top of the world, though I know it's not that simple in real life. This book was so important for me to write—to understand Noelle, and how someone who falls into a negative relationship isn't necessarily weak, just human.

Also, it was fun to write. Depicting the Pacific Northwest, which has become home to me. Twisting Daniel's character into someone you could almost understand—*almost*—much like our obsession with Dexter and Joe Goldberg. I also wanted to show true friendship, giving Noelle best friends in Kari and Jack. And perhaps most fun was imagining how one would arrange to have oneself kidnapped. (And yes, extreme kidnapping is a real thing!)

The thriller genre is meant to entertain, but I think it also carries important human truths like the desire to love and be loved. This book is for anyone who can identify with a relationship that seems good in the beginning and looks clean on the surface but evolves into something sinister. Sociopaths and narcissists walk among us, and they're harder to identify than most people realize.

It would mean the world to me if you would leave a review

on your platform of choice (Goodreads, B&N, Amazon, or even just recommend it to a friend) and help more readers like yourself find *Make Me Disappear*. My next book is out soon!

One last thing: I would love to hear from you. You can get in touch via my website, Facebook page, Twitter, Instagram, Goodreads, or TikTok.

I'm also a huge fan of book clubs! If you'd like me to join yours for an author chat/Q&A (and maybe a glass of wine!), I'd be delighted. Just contact me through my website, and we will set it up.

Thank you for joining me on this journey. Please know, you've played a role in this author fulfilling her lifelong dream.

Sincerely,

Jessica Payne

https://jessicapayne.net

facebook.com/authorjessicapayne

twitter.com/authorjesspayne

instagram.com/jessicapayne.writer

goodreads.com/authorjesspayne

tiktok.com/@authorjesspayne

ACKNOWLEDGMENTS

An author's journey involves many dedicated people who believe in her. I want to start by saying how grateful I am for my amazing agent, Kimberly Brower. You understood what I was trying to do with this book even before I did. Thank you for taking a chance on me. Also, thank you to Joy Kozu at Brower Literary. Your insight has been so helpful along the way.

Thank you to my editor Kelsie Marsden. Your keen eye for detail, enthusiasm, and dedication have taken this story the final crucial step—from a manuscript on my laptop to a book in the hands of readers. It is a privilege to work with you.

Thank you to Peta, Kim, Jess, Emily, Ian, John, Aimee, Lizzie, Alba, Alex, and Melanie, as well as the entire team at Bookouture—you've made the publishing process a dream. I hope every author has the chance to work with such a supportive and kind group of people.

Thank you to my husband, Virgil, who had no idea he was marrying an author. Life looks very different than how we envisioned it when we said, "I do," and by different, I mean better and happier than we could have imagined.

I am lucky to have my brother, Nick, the first person who supported my writing. Thank you for being in my corner, no matter what.

Thank you to Lilst Kitty, my writing cat, who never leaves my side, and is sure to wake me every morning at 4:30 a.m. on the dot so I can get my words in. You're the best writing companion I could ask for.

Thank you to my friend, Jess Scherer, who, when I broached the topic of writing my first book via NaNoWriMo in 2018, simply stated, "You should do it." And so, I did.

Carol, you have been a close friend and like a second mom. You were my very first reader and have always encouraged and loved me unconditionally. I don't know who I would be without you.

Thank you to Uncle David and Aunt Barbara, who showed me what unconditional love is. I miss you both.

Thank you to Jaime Lynn Hendricks, who I was lucky enough to befriend when I was still a baby writer, who mentored and wrote with me, and who I consider a dear friend. You said from day one that I would make it, and I'll never forget that.

Hugs to Sara Read, my author-wife and kindred spirit. I'm so glad we are on this wild ride together. Next time, we're drinking Manhattans.

To Evie Hughes, an entirely unexpected writing friend and critique partner—thank you for the early morning conversations, word count check-ins, and comma corrections! It's funny the roundabout way we found one another, and I'm so glad we did.

I'm grateful to Tobie Carter, who has always had an encouraging word and who has always been willing to listen and talk poolside (preferably with wine). Miss you.

To John Moore, who I consider an uncle and who, whether he meant to or not, has encouraged me to live a creative life.

Thank you to my critique group. Anu, Kathy, Paul, and Michael. I appreciate our community and the ways we help one another.

Thank you to the Tacoma, Washington, chapter of SCBWI, who adopted this adult thriller writer without blinking—my first taste of a writing community. Especially Mary, who has provided unconditional encouragement.

Thank you #MomsWritersClub—each and every one of you. It's been so incredible to be a part of such an extraordinary community of writers and moms. I'm lucky to call you all my friends.

To the Porch Crew—you adopted me when I was new in town and made a big fuss over my first book deal. Thank you for everything.

Printed in Great Britain
by Amazon

22836343R10209